Praise for Adrian Phoenix and The Maker's Song series

"The Maker's Song has a raw and complex storyline, incredible world building, and characters with multiple layers. Adrian Phoenix has developed Dante into someone who feels real, with flaws, faults and little quirks. . . . A must-read series for paranormal and urban fantasy fans."

—*Paranormal Romance Addict*

ETCHED IN BONE

"Edgy, fast paced and tantalizingly addictive, this is without a doubt the best novel in this amazingly enjoyable series to date."

—*Black Lagoon Reviews*

"There are not enough words to describe how much I love this series, or just how emotional this series truly is. Each book is better than the last."

—*VampChix*

"The intensity starts off with a bang and ends with the same sizzling impact! . . . This is one series that I will never miss a page of."

—*Fresh Fiction*

"Darkly haunting and impressively imaginative."

—*Night Owl Reviews*

BENEATH THE SKIN

"Adrian Phoenix has done it again! Complex, lyrical, and beautifully written . . . another unique and compulsive page-turner."

—Jenna Black, acclaimed author of *Dark Descendant*

"This violent, wrenching tale is something special."

—*Affaire de Coeur*

"Lush, sexy, and thrilling . . . darkly addictive."

—Jeaniene Frost, *New York Times* bestselling author

"This darkly dramatic tale is one wild ride in a series that only promises to get better."

—*RT Book Reviews*

"Another world comprised of both shimmering beauty and tactile violence. . . . Fusing and melding the worlds of angels, vampires, and mortals into a story where appearances hide greater truths ensures an engrossing and matchless reading experience."

—*Bitten by Books*

IN THE BLOOD

"Phoenix trips the dark fantastic in this wild, bloody sequel. . . . She keeps the plot thick and the tension high."

—*Publishers Weekly*

"Filled with twisting plots, shadowy government agencies, conspiracies, and betrayals . . . this dark urban fantasy is not only action-packed from beginning to end, but at its core, it is also a story of hope and love."

—*ParaNormal Romance*

"The atmosphere is dark, and treachery abounds, making this story white-knuckle reading in the extreme."

—*RT Book Reviews*

A RUSH OF WINGS

"Hard-charging action sequences, steamy sex scenes, and a surprising government conspiracy make this debut engrossingly fun."

—*Entertainment Weekly*

"Phoenix's lively debut has it all. . . . Phoenix alternates romantic homages to gothdom and steamy blood-drinking threesomes with enough terse, fast-paced thriller scenes to satisfy even the most jaded fan."

—*Publishers Weekly*

"Phoenix's gritty and original characters are instantly engaging, and the rapid pace keeps you glued to the pages."

—*RT Book Reviews*

"A thrilling tale of lust and murder that will keep you turning the pages to see what happens next."

—*Gothic Beauty*

"A complex, layered story filled with twists and turns . . . a dark, rich treat you won't soon forget."

—*Romance Reviews Today*

"This one pulled me in from the first page. Heather and Dante are among those rare characters readers so often look for and seldom find."

—Barb Hendee, *New York Times* bestselling author

"A fast-paced ride, its New Orleans setting appropriately rich and gothic, its characters both real and surprising."

— Kristine Kathryn Rusch, *New York Times* bestselling author

BOOKS BY ADRIAN PHOENIX

The Maker's Song Series

A Rush of Wings
In the Blood
Beneath the Skin
Etched in Bone
On Midnight Wings

The Hoodoo Series

Black Dust Mambo
Black Heart Loa

On Midnight Wings

Adrian Phoenix

POCKET BOOKS
New York London Toronto Sydney New Delhi

Pocket Books
A Division of Simon & Schuster, Inc.
1230 Avenue of the Americas
New York, NY 10020

This book is a work of fiction. Names, characters, places, and incidents either are products of the author's imagination or are used fictitiously. Any resemblance to actual events or locales or persons, living or dead, is entirely coincidental.

First Pocket Books paperback edition October 2013

POCKET and colophon are registered trademarks
of Simon & Schuster, Inc.

For information about special discounts for bulk purchases, please contact Simon & Schuster Special Sales at 1-866-506-1949 or business@simonandschuster.com.

The Simon & Schuster Speakers Bureau can bring authors to your live event. For more information or to book an event contact the Simon & Schuster Speakers Bureau at 1-866-248-3049 or visit our website at www.simonspeakers.com.

Manufactured in the United States of America

10 9 8 7 6 5 4 3 2 1

ISBN 978-1-4516-4534-7
ISBN 978-1-4516-4536-1 (ebook)

This one is dedicated to all the members of Club Hell and to each and every one of my fans for their endless patience and support, and to my editor, Adam Wilson, and my agent, Matt Bialer, for the same reasons. I can't thank you enough. Y'all are truly the best. Hellions RULE!

ACKNOWLEDGMENTS

AS ALWAYS, TO MY friends and family. I couldn't have done it without you.

GLOSSARY

TO MAKE THINGS AS simple as possible, I've listed not only words, but phrases used in the story. Please keep in mind that Cajun is different from Parisian French and the French generally spoken in Europe. Different grammatically and even, sometimes, in pronunciation and spelling.

The French that Guy Mauvais uses is traditional French as opposed to Dante's Cajun.

For the Irish and Welsh words—including the ones I've created—pronunciation is provided.

One final thing: Prejean is pronounced PRAY-zhawn.

aingeal (AIN-gyahl), angel. Fallen/Elohim word.
ami (m); **amie** (f), friend. **Mon ami**, my friend.
ange, angel; ma p'tite ange (f), my little angel.
Anhrefncathl (ann-HREVN-cathl), chaos song; the song of a Maker. Fallen/Elohim word.
apprenti (s), **apprentis** (pl), apprentices.
assolutamente (Italian), absolutely.
bastardo (Italian), bastard.
bâtard, bastard.
beaucoup, very, much, many, a great deal.
bien, well, very.
bon, good, nice, fine, kind.
bueno (Spanish), good.

buono (Italian), good.

ça fait pas rien, you're welcome. Also, **pas de quoi**.

ça fini pas, it never ends.

calon-cyfaill (KAW-lawn CUHV-aisle), bondmate, heartmate.

catin (f), doll, dear, sweetheart.

ça va bien, I'm fine, I'm good, okay.

Cercle de Druide, Circle of Druids, a sacred and select nightkind order.

c'est bon, that's good.

c'est vrai, that's true.

Chalkydri (chal-KOO-dree), winged serpentine demons of Sheol, subservient to the Elohim.

cher (m); **chère** (f), dear, beloved. **Mon cher, ma chère**, my dear or my beloved.

cher ami, mon (m); **chère amie, ma** (f), my dearest friend, my best friend; intimate, implying a special relationship.

chéri (m); **chérie** (f), dearest, darling, honey.

conjurer, also known as a hoodoo; a practitioner of hoodoo.

Conseil du Sang, le, the Council of Blood, nightkind lawgivers.

couche-couche, a dish made with a base of moist corn bread.

creawdwr (KRAY-OW-dooer), creator; Maker/Unmaker; an extremely rare branch of the Elohim believed to be extinct. Last known *creawdwr* was Yahweh.

creu tân (kray tahn), Maker's fire, a *creawdwr*'s power of creation.

cydymaith (kuh-DUH-mith), companion.

da (Russian), yes.

d'accord, okay.

dannazione (Italian), damn.

Elohim (s and pl), the Fallen; the beings mythologized as fallen angels.

faites-moi, make me.

Fallen, *see* Elohim.

fi' de garce, son of a bitch.

filidh, master Bards/warriors of the *llygaid*.

fils, son; **mon fils**, my son.

fille de sang (f), blood-daughter; "turned" female offspring of a vampire.

fils de sang (m), blood-son; "turned" male offspring of a vampire.

fratello (Italian), brother.

grazie (Italian), thank you; **molte grazie**, many thanks.

gris-gris, magic, spell, charm.

hoodoo, a system of folk magic; also means a practitioner of that system of magic.

houngan, an initiated priest in the religion of Vodou.

imposible (Spanish), impossible.

j'ai faim, I'm hungry.

jamais, never.

je connais, I know.

je sais pas, I don't know.

je t'aime, I love you.

je t'en prie, I beg you.

je te promets, I promise you.

je t'entends, I hear you; **je t'entends, catin**, I hear you, doll.

joli (m); **jolie** (f), pretty, cute; **mon joli**, my pretty boy.

j'su ici, I'm here.

j'su sûr, I'm sure.

llafnau, the special forces branch of the llygaid.

Llygad (THLOO-gad) (s), eye; a watcher; keeper of immortal history; story-shaper; **Llygaid** (THLOO-guide) (pl).

loa, spirits who serve as intermediaries between Bon Dieu and humanity.

ma belle femme, my beautiful woman, lady. Can mean wife or significant other.

Madre de Dios (Spanish), Mother of God.

mambo, an initiated priestess in the religion of Vodou.

ma mère, my mother.

ma naturalmente. Ti prego di perdonarmi (Italian), but of course. Please forgive me.

marmot (m), brat.

menteur (m); **menteuse** (f), liar.

merci, thank you; **merci beaucoup**, thanks a lot; **merci bien**, thanks very much.

merde, shit.

mère de sang (f), blood-mother; female vampire who has turned another and become their "parent."

mia bella assassina (f) (Italian), my beautiful assassin.

mi hija (Spanish), my daughter.

mio amico (m) (Italian), my friend.

Mon Dieu, my God.

m'selle (f), abbreviated spoken form of **mademoiselle**, Miss, young lady.

m'sieu (m), abbreviated spoken form of **monsieur**, Mr., sir, gentleman.

nephilim, the offspring resulting from Fallen and mortal unions.

Nightbringer, a name/title given to Lucien De Noir.

nightkind (s and pl), vampire; Dante's term for vampires.

nomad, name for the pagan, gypsy-style clans who ride across the land.

numéro un, number one.

oui, yes.

oui sûr, Yeah, sure; yeah, right.

padnat, partner, buddy, chum; close friend.

pardonne-moi, forgive me.

pas encore, not yet.

pas ici, not here.

pas possible, not possible.

père (m), father; **mon père**, my father.

père de sang (m), blood-father; male vampire who has turned another and become their "parent."

peut-être, maybe, perhaps.

peut-être que oui, peut-être que non, maybe, maybe not.

p'tit, mon (m); **p'tite, ma** (f), my little one (generally affectionate).

puttana (Italian), bitch.

quitte-moi tranquille, leave me alone.

shuvano, a nomad healer and shaman.

sì (Italian), yes.

tais-toi, shut up.

t'es sûr de sa? are you sure about that? **t'es sûr?** you sure?

toujours, always.

très, very.

True Blood, born vampire, rare and powerful.

tu sei un bastardo mentendo (Italian), you're a lying bastard.

vite-vite, fast, hurry, quickly, shoo.

wybrcathl (OOEEBR-cathl), sky-song. Fallen/Elohim word.

Caterina's lullaby (traditional Italian lullaby in an old dialect): *Fi la nana, e mi bel fiol/ Fi la nana, e mi bel fiol/ Fa si la nana/ Fa si la nana/ Dormi ben, e mi bel fiol/ Dormi ben, e mi bel fiol* . . .

Hush-a-bye, my lovely child/ Hush-a-bye, my lovely child/ Hush, hush and go to sleep/ Hush, hush and go to sleep/ Sleep well, my lovely child/ Sleep well, my lovely child . . .

1

DARK AND BITTER PEARLS

LUCIEN DE NOIR SAT beside the unconscious girl curled on the bed, box springs creaking beneath him. Midafternoon sunlight filtered through the golden, gauzy curtains covering the window, bathing the room in a tranquil glow. An illusion—no, worse, a lie—given the day's dark, violent, and unimaginable events.

My son has been shot and stolen and the mortal woman he loves, the woman who keeps his slipping sanity balanced, is missing.

Lucien's deltoid muscles flexed, restless, but he suppressed the urge to unfurl his wings and take to the sky in search of Dante and Heather; he feared that they had been spirited off in two very different directions. And he had no idea where to look, which path to follow, or even who was responsible.

Not yet, anyway.

Lucien focused his attention on Heather Wallace's drugged sister. A light sheen of sweat glistened on Annie's forehead. Tears wet the ends of her lashes. And her blood-speckled face looked light-years away from peaceful.

Guessing why wasn't difficult.

The blood freckling her face and throat was Dante's. Lucien knew by the scent alone—copper, a hint of adrenaline, a moonlight-silver tang—and had known from the moment he'd scooped her unconscious body up from the sidewalk in front of the club.

She must've been standing beside Dante when he'd been shot. Or damned close, anyway. A muscle flexed in Lucien's jaw. Shot repeatedly and without mercy. Dante's blood had saturated the Oriental carpet in front of the bedroom he shared with Heather.

So much blood when Dante should've healed. Too much blood. And the odd scent clinging to the shell casings Lucien had picked up from the hallway carpet had left him wondering. A troubling scent. Familiar.

Lucien studied Annie's pale face, pushed sweat-damp tendrils of her punk-style blue/purple/black hair back from her face. She shivered inside her fuzzy purple bathrobe as though it was woven from ice, instead of plush terry cloth.

With a soft chirp, Heather's orange tabby jumped up onto the bed and sniffed Annie for several moments before curling up beside her. Eerie blinked golden eyes at Lucien, then began licking the undersides of his paws, his tongue scraping delicately across the scorched pads.

Like the cat, Lucien also smelled the drugs on Annie's skin, in her sweat—a cold, chemical taint. He had no idea what drugs flowed through her veins, or how long she'd remain unconscious, but he had no intention of waiting for her to wake up. Not when answers rested like pearls in her mind. Not when he could play thief.

Too much time had passed already. Hours lost to the police

and their investigation of the shoot-out outside the club and the fire inside; a loss he'd finally cut short with a touch of a blue-sparked finger to the lead detective's forehead and a whispered suggestion: *You've already spoken to Dante. He saw nothing. Heard nothing. Knows nothing about the incident here or the fire that claimed his home four nights ago. You will write that down in your notebook.*

Blinking, the detective promptly put her pen to paper.

Lucien sighed. A temporary solution at best; the suggestion would eventually fade. But a problem for another time. Closing his eyes, he drew in a long, deep breath—in through his nose, out through his mouth—then another, as he worked on centering himself before delving into Annie's unshielded mind.

"How she doing?" a Cajun-spiced voice asked from the doorway. "Looks like she ain't moved an inch since I carried her in from the van."

Lucien's calming breath morphed into a low, frustrated exhalation. He opened his eyes. Glanced over his shoulder.

Dressed in jeans and a black T-shirt announcing LAFAYETTE MARQUIS, the interruption—better known as Black Bayou Jack Cheramie, Dante's band mate in Inferno—leaned one muscled, tribal-inked shoulder against the doorjamb, arms crossed over his chest, a bloodstained washcloth balled-up in one hand. The drummer's mane of cherry-red braids framed his face, his expression a tight-jawed mix of worried and angry.

"She hasn't," Lucien confirmed. He nodded at the washcloth in Jack's hand. "How are Von and Silver doing? Has the bleeding stopped? Are they healing?"

"*Oui*, it's stopped and they're healing, for true, them. But given that they're nightkind and all, it took longer than I expected. Thibodaux agrees with me," Jack added, with a tilt of his head toward the kitchen where the fugitive SB agent sat at the table cleaning his Colt .45. "Said his partner always heals up *beaucoup* fast. But he also admitted that she ain't never taken a bullet to the head before neither."

Lucien thought of the odd scent on the shell casings he'd found in the blood-spattered hall, wondering again just what they had contained. "I don't think normal rounds were used."

"Dunno, *padnat*. They sure as hell look like normal rounds to me. Course there ain't no telling what kind of load they-all contained." Jack uncrossed his arms and held out his hand, revealing two skull-dented and compressed bullets cupped in his callused palm. "They just kinda worked their way outta the wounds. Ain't never seen nightkind heal from bullets before. Weirdest goddamned sight."

"Let me have the bullets."

Jack stepped over to the bed and dumped them into Lucien's waiting palm. A faint tree-sap, amber-like odor wafted from the small bits of mangled brass. Whatever the substance had been, it seemed to be capable of slowing, perhaps even halting, a vampire's natural ability to heal. Even a True Blood's.

Remembering what he'd felt when he'd reached for Dante's mind back at the club—a psionic flatline that had sheeted Lucien's soul in black ice until he'd finally detected a low, ebbing life force absent of any healing spark—he once again felt the urgent desire to unsheathe his wings and vault into the sky.

He needed to find Dante before it was too late. Before destiny twisted in on itself and became fate.

"Tee-Tee? Heather?" Jack asked. "You think they were in the back of that van those assholes were trying to put Annie into?"

Tee-Tee. Jack and the other mortal members of Inferno had tagged their nightkind frontman with the affectionate nickname because, at five-nine, Dante was shorter than the rest of the band. *Petit.* Little one. *Tee-Tee.* And with Dante also the youngest, at nearly twenty-four, the name pulled double duty.

Young in years, perhaps, but not in hard and brutal experience. Dante was the last surviving member of a secret, decades-long project co-run by the FBI and the Shadow Branch—a government black ops division that answered to no one and didn't officially exist. Project Bad Seed had been devoted to the development and study of sociopaths. But in truth the goal had been to *create*, then control them.

And being the only nonhuman subject in the project, Dante had garnered special attention. Had been shoved with cool deliberation beyond boundaries no human subject would've survived. Just to see if he could.

Dante had been placed in the worst foster homes available, shuffled around constantly; everything and everyone he'd ever cared about or loved had been systematically stripped from him. Human monsters had fragmented and buried his memories, implanted deadly programming.

The muscle ticked in Lucien's jaw again. He'd flown away from New Orleans on a sultry July night unaware that he wouldn't return for eighteen years, unaware that Genevieve, his dark-haired *belle femme*, was pregnant, unaware that she would soon fall into cold and curious hands, or that their son—born vampire and Fallen—would be birthed into an experiment of unthinkable design.

Dante had escaped, his heart and mind scarred and damaged, haunted by things he couldn't even remember. Yet he led his household and Inferno with skill and focus, with quiet strength, fierce devotion, and stubborn will.

And I have failed at every turn to keep him safe.

"Lucien?" Jack's concerned voice scattered Lucien's dark thoughts, returning him to the bedroom and the unconscious girl he sat beside. "You okay, you?"

Lucien frowned. "Fine. Why do you ask?"

"No reason, really—other than the fact that you're getting blood all over the floor," Jack replied, tapping a finger against the back of his own hand, and pointedly arching one dark blond eyebrow.

Lucien's frown deepened when he looked down and saw drops of blood speckling the oak planks. He became aware of a distant, prickling pain. Exhaling in exasperation, he unclenched his hands, pulling his thick black talons free of his blood-slicked palms.

"Well. Perhaps *fine* isn't completely accurate," Lucien amended.

"King of the understatement. Here, you. Catch."

Glancing up, Lucien snagged the bloodstained washcloth Jack tossed at him, then busied himself wiping his palms and talons semiclean. The punctures were already healing, the pain nearly gone. His unbound waist-length hair brushed against his back and sides with the movement, soft as silk against his bare skin. He'd left his shirt behind on the club's roof when he'd taken to the sky—not caring in the slightest that it had still been daylight or that he might be seen.

Tossing the washcloth back to Jack, Lucien curved his lips into what he hoped was a reassuring smile, but when Jack's dubious expression remained stubbornly in place, he decided to shift the drummer's attention elsewhere. "You were asking if I thought Heather and Dante might've been inside the van, correct?"

Jack nodded.

"Heather might've been, yes," Lucien said, "but Dante . . . ?" He shook his head. "I saw a few things at the club that lead me to believe that whoever took him wrapped him up to protect him from the sun, then carried him out through the courtyard."

"Shit. You thinking two different vehicles heading off in two different directions?"

"That I am."

"Shit," Jack repeated. He skimmed a hand along the buzz-cut dark blond hair beneath his mane of braids, his hazel eyes fixed on his scuffed brown Durangos. "I shoulda been there," he said, voice bleak.

"And done what? Die?" Lucien's flat voice brought Jack's gaze up and lit a fire behind it. "If you *had* been at the club, you'd be dead now, a bullet buried deep in your brain—your mortal, unhealing brain."

"Me, I don't think you're giving me enough credit here," Jack replied, his Cajun accent thickening. "It mighta gone down a whole 'nother way, for true."

Lucien arched one dubious eyebrow. "Correct me if I'm wrong, but you're a drummer, one who learned to shoot growing up in the bayou, and not some trained-to-kill Navy SEAL who can turn even pocket lint into a lethal weapon. You're not a bodyguard, not a soldier, not even a rent-a-cop. Just a drummer with a gun." At Jack's less than enthusiastic grunt of agreement, he added, "And if you'd been inside the club, a *dead* drummer with a gun."

"No need to be an asshole, you," Jack growled. "But point taken. So what's next? Do we wait until sunset to see if Dante contacts you or Von"—he tapped a finger against his temple to indicate how he expected the contact to be made—"and see if he knows where he is? Or who took him?"

"I'd prefer not to wait that long," Lucien rumbled. He shifted his attention back to Annie. "With the help of Heather's sister, we might not have to. Perhaps she heard something—a destination, a name—that could put us on the right path."

"But Annie ain't awake yet."

"She doesn't need to be. Like most mortals, her mind is unshielded and open. All I need do is to go inside." As Jack's brows drew down in a worried V, Lucien added soothingly, "She won't feel a thing." Which was true, but even if it hadn't been, he still wouldn't have hesitated, not with Dante's life on the line.

No risk, no sacrifice would ever be too great.

Not just because Dante was his son—even though that was more than reason enough—but because Dante was also a *creawdwr*. The only one in existence and the first to walk the world since Yahweh's death more than two thousand years ago, not to mention his being the first mixed-blood Maker ever. Capable of creating—Making—places, beings, life itself. And equally capable of Unmaking it all, as well.

Untrained, unbound, except for his bond to Heather,

Dante strode the same edge of madness that each *creawdwr* before him had walked—a precipice crumbling beneath his boots—fighting the damage done to him by Bad Seed, fighting for his sanity, for the right to claim his life as his own, to piece together his shattered past.

If Dante fell into darkness and chaos, all worlds—mortal, vampire, and Fallen—would fall with him. And if Dante died . . .

Lucien shoved the thought aside, refusing it.

Centering himself with another deep breath, he rested his fingertips against Annie's temple, then closed his eyes. He slipped inside her mind. Absently, he shielded himself from the raw emotions swirling through her subconscious, a whirlpool of self-loathing, grief, guilt, and fury. He eased past her nonsensical narcotic dreams and delved into her memories. Looked through her eyes.

Images flashed and twirled, a mirror-bright disco ball of out-of-sequence fragments and splinters, a glittering puzzle-play of light, shadow, and betrayal.

Fragment: *Desperate relief pours through Annie. Dante is somehow awake. He leans drunkenly against the threshold to his and Heather's room, naked except for the bondage collar strapped around his throat, his pale hands clutching either side of the doorjamb for balance. It seems as though he's already slipping back into Sleep, but beneath his milk-white skin, his muscles are taut, corded, rippling . . .*

Splinter: *"It's not Dante I want. I've come for you, pumpkin."*

Fragment: *Two members of the black-uniformed posse carry Heather out from behind the bar on a stretcher. Flex-cuffs bind her wrists and tendrils of red hair trail across her face. Out cold. Tranked . . .*

Splinter: *"Shoot the others. Burn it down."*

Splinter: *"He won't be getting up again, not with those bullets inside of him."*

Fragment: *He presses the muzzle of his gun against Dante's blood-slicked chest, above his heart, and squeezes off two more rounds. Then he places the gun against Dante's temple.*

Once Lucien had prized each dark and bitter pearl of knowledge about that morning's events from Annie's mind—including a secret that made him glance at her robe-covered belly—he withdrew. A cold and furious anger thrummed through his veins. An acrid taste burned at the back of his throat. Words he'd once said to Dante came back to mock him.

The truth is never what you hope it will be.

Raking a hand through his hair, Lucien looked up and alarm flickered across Jack's face at whatever he saw in his eyes.

"What?" Jack asked, straightening out of his slouch, his voice knotted with dread.

"It was Heather and Annie's father—FBI agent James Wallace—and he didn't take Dante. He shot him"—Lucien's voice roughened as he visualized the trench-coated man standing over his son's motionless and bloodied form, gun in hand, an image acid etched into his mind—"then left him to burn with the others."

2

INTERRUPTED SLEEP

JACK STARED AT LUCIEN, his expression speed-shifting from stunned disbelief to bewilderment. "If not the FBI, then who the hell took him?"

Lucien had to force out each bitter word. "I don't know."

But one thing he was damned certain of—given what he'd witnessed in Annie's memories—the substance in those bullets had been designed to kill a True Blood. Dante in particular.

James Wallace had apparently done his research very, very well.

Having been a part of Dante's life only for the last five years, there was still so much Lucien didn't know about his own son. He could count on one hand—with a finger or two to spare—the born vampires he'd met during the nearly two dozen centuries since his escape to the mortal world from Gehenna.

Rare, brimming with power and magic and a riveting, nightbred beauty, they were solitary beings—an elemental, but dying, bloodline—who had eventually become little more than wistful myth for the global community of turned-nightkind.

But, myth or not, that hadn't stopped James Wallace from discovering the truth and learning exactly how to harm Dante.

He won't be getting up again, not with those bullets inside of him.

Lucien intended to make James Wallace profoundly regret

those words before he killed him. Rising to his feet, he headed for the doorway, the floor creaking beneath his shoes.

"Well, shit. So now what?" Jack asked, sucking himself up against the threshold in order to allow room for Lucien to step through. "Wait until twilight? See if Tee-Tee makes contact?"

"Dante's injured and I don't know how badly. He might not be capable of making contact."

But Heather . . . that was another story. If the temporary blood link between her and Von still held, the nomad should be able to find out where she'd been taken. *If* it still held. But given that most blood links lasted anywhere from twenty-four to seventy-two hours, and the one between Heather and Von wasn't quite forty hours old yet, the odds were slightly in their favor that it did.

Lucien strode down the hall. "I need to awaken Von."

"But . . . how?" Jack protested. "It's still daylight."

Lucien paused in the guest bedroom's darkened doorway, then glanced back at Jack. "I have a method for pulling night-kind up from Sleep. However, the results can vary, so it might be best if you waited with Thibodaux. This could get violent."

Jack looked unimpressed. "My mama says the same thing at every Cheramie family reunion."

"I'm serious."

"So's my mama." Jack blew out a breath, then nodded. "Okay. You do what you gotta do. I'll keep Thibodaux company, me. I'll just tell him to ignore anything he hears coming from the guest room—hissing, screaming, wing-flapping, girlish pleas for mercy." A smile twitched at the corners of his mouth. "Y'know. The usual."

"The only girlish pleas for mercy will be your own if you don't get moving," Lucien growled, pointing one taloned finger toward the kitchen. He appreciated Jack's attempt to ease the tension with a bit of dark humor, and it helped—for a moment.

"Another thing my mama says. Often."

"I can't imagine why," Lucien replied, voice dry.

Chuckling, Jack turned and headed down the hall. Just as he reached the dust-mote-flecked spill of sunlight emanating from the kitchen, he called, "We're gonna find them, for true. Tee-Tee and Heather both." His words and confident tone were as bracing as a tumbler of top-shelf scotch—for them both, Lucien suspected.

"Yes, we are," Lucien agreed.

There was nothing he wouldn't do to ensure that outcome. Nothing.

I would lay the world to waste for my son.

Foreboding trailed an icy finger down Lucien's spine, whispered arctic words in his ear: *What if you don't find him? And your son lays waste to the world in the meantime instead? Or tries to? What then?*

I will find him, Lucien thought numbly. *No other outcome is possible.*

Stepping into the room, he regarded Silver and Von, Sleeping side by side on the bed, a cheerful quilt covering them to the waist. Both pale faces were smooth and peaceful; another disquieting illusion, one revealed by the pillows with their dark stains, by the blood-matted hair pushed away from Sleep-cool foreheads.

Von McGuinn Slept on the side of the bed closest to the door, the ends of his nut-brown hair trailing over his bare shoulders. Even in the curtained gloom, Lucien could see the nomad clan tattoos blue-inked in graceful Celtic designs— dragons, antlered hunters, and ravens to name a few—swirling along Von's shoulders, down his arms, and across his pectoral muscles and abdomen and, beneath the quilt, even lower; each had been earned when he'd still been mortal.

But the crescent moon tattoo beneath Von's right eye, glimmering like star-silvered water, was unlike all the others. No mortal could wear it. It was the badge of his office—*llygad.* Keeper of history. Counselor. Warrior bard, one of many within the impartial, truth-seeking ranks of the *llygaid.* The guardians of nightkind history.

Lucien had no doubt that Von would know what James Wallace had loaded into the bullets, and how to counteract it.

Rolling his shoulders back to ease tension from taut muscles, he crossed to the bed, then knelt beside it, the floor creaking beneath his black-trousered knees. Underneath the odors of clotted blood and nostril-tingling antiseptic, he caught a faint, reassuring trace of Von's scent of frost and gun oil.

"I can't wait for twilight, *llygad,*" Lucien apologized. A bead of ruby blood welled up on the inside of his wrist as he pierced the skin with a talon. "We need to speak *now.*"

Lucien licked the blood from his wrist, then lowered his head over Von's pale face. Kissing the nomad's mustache-framed lips, he parted them with his blood-smeared tongue. Breathed energy and the pomegranate-and-copper taste of his own blood into Von, drew him up from Sleep.

And filled his waking mind with Annie's dark and bitter pearls.

When the nomad sucked in a sharp breath, Lucien ended the kiss and lifted his head to look into vivid green eyes wide with shock.

"Holy hell." Von's voice was a hoarse whisper. He struggled to rise, but, weakened by blood loss and the disorienting effects of interrupted Sleep, he fell back against the mattress, sweat beading his forehead. "We gotta find them."

"We will," Lucien promised. "Once we locate Heather through your link with her, her bond with Dante will lead us straight to him."

"Shit. My link. Their bond. Yeah."

"But right now I need you to regain your strength and clear your head." Lucien extended his arm to Von, offered his already healed wrist. "Feed, then we'll get to work."

Without another word, Von grabbed the proffered arm, tore hungrily into the taut flesh with his fangs, and drank deep.

3

ONE STUBBORN
MOTHERFUCKER

S NATCHING JEANS FROM THE small pile of clothing
Jack had left for him on top of the bureau, Von yanked
them on over his gray pin-striped boxers, zipping them up with
a furious jerk of his wrist. His pulse pounded in his temples as
he counted the many ways in which they'd been fucked over in
just a few short hours.

Heather drugged and nabbed by her own goddamned father.

Dante shot and left to burn, before some mysterious asshole
slipped into the building, bundled him up, then carted him out
into the blazing noontime sun. And disappeared.

Silver and himself shot. Annie, tranked. The club torched.

Oh, and don't forget the other little revelation Lucien had
plucked from Annie's mind: Heather's little sister was pregnant.
As for how far along she was, the identity of the baby-daddy,
and whether or not she even planned to keep the squatter in
her womb, that information was still tucked safe inside Annie's
head, hers to keep.

Von wondered if Heather even knew about her sister's pregnancy. A worry for another time, like *after* he'd found Heather, hauled her lovely ass out of the fire, then followed her psionic GPS of a bond straight to Dante.

Von had made his first attempt to contact Heather right after he'd fueled up on Lucien's blood—the Fallen/angelic stuff was like nitrous oxide to nightkind. A blast of furious energy had exploded through Von's every cell, lighting his mind up like a Las Vegas casino marquee, and thrumming like electricity through his veins. Despite that intoxicating rush, his attempt had been only partially successful. And, thus, a complete disappointment.

"Keep trying," Lucien commands in a voice of edged steel.

"No shit," Von growls. "I know you're worried sick, man, me too. But you're driving me nuts staring holes through me. Why don't you go raid Jack's liquor cabinet and give me some space?"

Lucien stares a few more holes through him with narrowed eyes before swiveling and stalking silently from the room.

Attempts two through ten had ended with the same frustrating results. And Von had decided to give it a rest, give the drugs in Heather's system a little bit of time to wear off. But he had also learned a few very important things.

One: his link with Heather was definitely still intact.

Two: Heather was drugged and unconscious, her mind wrapped up in a cotton ball of static and currently beyond his reach.

Three: he'd better keep his fingers crossed and wish with everything he had that whatever she'd been doped with would wear off *before* their blood link unraveled.

Grabbing the neatly folded olive-green T-shirt from the bureau, Von tugged it on, then went over to the bed to check on Silver before leaving to join the others. Dried blood darkened the right side of his midnight purple hair—thanks to goddamned James Wallace. Bastard would pay. And not just for Silver.

I've come for you, pumpkin.

He won't be getting up again, not with those bullets inside of him.

Hands clenched into white-knuckled fists, Von left the bedroom. When he stalked into the darkened kitchen with its blanket draped windows, AWOL Shadow Branch agent Emmett Thibodaux—long, lean, and looking like a young, ginger-haired Clint Eastwood—took one look at Von's chest, then quirked up an amused eyebrow.

"Sorry I missed that," Thibodaux drawled, folding his arms along the back of the chair he straddled. His assessing blue-iris gaze grew thoughtful. "*Real* damned sorry."

Frowning, Von looked down at the borrowed T-shirt, then groaned. It read GATOR FEST WET BOXERS CONTEST CHAMPION, each letter shaped out of tiny green and brown gators. He aimed a glare at an innocent-looking Jack. "Cajun smart-ass," he muttered. "Or maybe Cajun clairvoyant, given the title and all."

The drummer grinned. "More like Cajun delusional, given the title and all."

"I second that," Lucien put in. He leaned against the counter in front of the sink, expression neutral, pretending to be relaxed, despite the tension cording nearly every muscle on his six-eight frame.

"Sad how the truth can be too much for some people," Von offered with a long-suffering shake of his head.

Thibodaux made a sound that was halfway between a snort and a cough, then got up and went to the refrigerator for a beer. Von watched him closely as he returned to his chair, a frosty bottle of Dixie in hand. He caught a whiff of the man's scent— fresh ice and anise, sharp and cool—which mingled uneasily with the faint odor of smoke and acrid chemicals clinging to his clothes.

Fire extinguisher, I'm betting. Lucien said Thibodaux helped him put out the blaze at the club.

So throw confetti and pin a medal on the fucker. Didn't mean he could be trusted.

"We know James Wallace took Heather," Von said quietly, sauntering over to the table to stand opposite Thibodaux. He folded his arms over his gator-afflicted chest. "But who the hell grabbed Dante? I find it damned curious that all this shit went down right after you and your partner showed up bearing gifts for Dante."

Yeah, a Pandora's flash drive of a gift, one that should probably be left unopened—Dante's past from the moment he'd been born into Bad Seed.

Thibodaux set the condensation-dewed beer bottle down carefully on the Formica table, then met Von's gaze, his own wary. "Bad timing. Me and Merri had nothing to do with any of this."

"He's telling the truth," Lucien said. "I had the same concerns, so the first thing I did when I arrived here was scan his mind. Thoroughly. He's clean, *llygad*—no deception, no hidden agenda. That's not to say that the SB wasn't behind Dante's abduction—just that Thibodaux and his partner had nothing to do with it."

Thibodaux's expression tightened, chiseling his features into razor-sharp angles, hard planes, and narrowed blue eyes. "The bastards wiped my memory of everything I'd learned about Baptiste and Bad Seed for a reason. Could be they're planning to use him again, trigger his programming and have him waste another FBI agent like they did in Seattle."

"And want to keep him invisible," Von growled. "Out of sight, out of mind."

"*If* they took him," Lucien pointed out in a deep rumble.

"If," Thibodaux agreed. Lifting the beer bottle, he tipped it against his lips, took a long swallow.

"We'll sort out the who and why after we find him," Von said. He abandoned the table to join Lucien in front of the sink. "You got the bullets?"

Lucien answered him by unfolding his arms from his bare chest, extending one hand, and uncurling the taloned fingers. Cradled in his cupped palm were two bits of skull-mangled brass.

Picking up the bullets, Von took a quick sniff, even though he didn't need to. He'd caught and recognized the woody, amberish scent the moment Lucien had opened his hand. His stomach sank—hell, it cannonballed—into uncharted depths.

No True Blood can survive that . . .

Von closed his eyes, then tried to reach Dante through their link. His heart constricted painfully when he felt the low and erratic pulse of Dante's poisoned life force. At least he was still alive, but his continued survival was definitely in question.

<Little brother.>

But Von's sending hit a barrier surrounding Dante's mind— a barrier composed of poison, pain, and drug static—then bounced away, unheard. His breath hissed out in renewed frustration between his teeth. He opened his eyes.

"What did Wallace use?" Lucien demanded, dark brows slanted into a deep V. "What did he put in those bullets?"

"Something very few know about," Von replied. His hand knuckled shut around the bullets, squeezing them into his palm. "Resin from a dragon's blood tree."

"Tree resin?" Thibodaux questioned incredulously. "That's all it takes to put down a fucking powerful born vamp? *Sap?*"

"Sap," Von confirmed. "The resin from a dragon's blood tree is medicinal for mortals, but fatal to True Bloods. Nature's way of balancing shit out by giving born immortals an Achilles' heel, I guess." He scowled. "Goddamned nature."

Jack's breath caught. "Fatal?"

"Yeah, and with as many times as that bastard shot Dante, he should've been dead by now. The only reason he's still alive is because of you." Von nodded at Lucien, saw comprehension and relief flash in his eyes. "Because of his Fallen bloodline. But I don't know if or how long it's gonna keep him that way. This is uncharted territory."

"What does he need?" Lucien asked.

"That's the problem—I don't know what he needs. No one does." Raking a hand through his hair in frustration, Von fingered apart blood-matted locks, welcoming the distracting pull of pain at his scalp. "Any other True Blood would already be dead."

Gold light flared in Lucien's eyes, gleaming like stars in the gloom. "Good thing, then, that he's not any other True Blood."

"Doesn't hurt that he's also one tough, stubborn-ass sonuv-abitch," Von said. "That's another good thing. Damned good." He returned to the table, pulled out a chair, and sat down. He tossed the crumpled bits of brass onto the table. "We're gonna find him and his equally stubborn-ass woman, bring them both home."

"Yes, we will," Lucien rumbled. "And the sooner, the better. I trust you're ready to resume your attempts to contact Heather?"

Von shook his head. "No, I'm ready to *succeed* in contacting Heather, not *attempt* to succeed. But first . . ." Reaching across the table, he grabbed up Thibodaux's bottle of Dixie and, giving the man a quick *thanks-for-your-generous-donation* wink, poured the remainder of the cold, hopsy brew down his throat.

"Please, by all means, take mine," Thibodaux drawled, amusement glinting in his eyes. "It's a helluva long way to the fridge and back, after all. Would probably take at least four whole seconds. Maybe even five. Who's got that kind of time or energy?"

Von thumped the empty down onto the table, then belched. "Exactly. Y'know, I think I'm starting to like you."

Thibodaux lifted one ginger eyebrow. "As a person or as lunch?"

Von shrugged. "Don't wanna spoil the mystery. Thanks for the beer, man."

Shrugging, the former SB agent started reassembling his

just-cleaned gun, his long-fingered hands moving with a deft and practiced ease. "Eh. You're welcome."

Von closed his eyes, then reached out to Heather again.

<*C'mon, doll. Talk to me.*>

All he heard/felt was drug-thick static. But that didn't stop him. He could be one stubborn motherfucker too, especially when it came to family—and whether Heather knew it or not, she was definitely that.

So was Dante. Maybe they hadn't been born brothers, but they were brothers under the skin, their fates tied together. Von had known that inexplicable truth the moment he'd first seen Dante standing onstage with his band in a smoky N'awlins dive. And Von had made himself a promise that night.

Wherever his path takes him, he ain't gonna be walking it alone. I'll be right beside him. Each step of the way. I'll always have his back.

Really? Sure about that?

Right now Dante was very much alone, his back unguarded.

Jaw clenched so tight his teeth ached, Von leaned forward in his chair, elbows to knees, and rested his head in his hands. Drawing in a deep breath, he reached for Heather again.

<*C'mon, doll. I need you. And I mean that in a totally platonic way.*>

Only static.

Von kept at it.

When he felt Silver awaken through their link, felt his confusion at his unexpected whereabouts, he realized that the sun had slipped beneath the horizon. He shifted his focus from Heather to Dante, hoping against hope that his friend had awakened as well.

<*Little brother . . .*>

But once again, his sending bounced back from the barricade of resin, drugs, and pain that still surrounded Dante's mind, leaving him unable to determine if Dante was conscious or not. But gut instinct whispered, *He's out cold, poison racing through his veins, pulsing through his heart*; a whisper that left him cold.

Knowing he needed to get back to Heather before time ran out, Von reluctantly withdrew from his link with Dante, but not before arrowing a message at the barricade: <*We're coming for you, little brother. Just hold the hell on.*>

Drawing in another deep breath, Von caught a whiff of cinnamon and dried blood and knew that Silver had walked into the kitchen even before he heard his voice, low and tense, asking Lucien what the hell had happened. Heard Silver's breath catch rough in his throat as the fallen angel answered him mind to mind.

"Jesus Christ," Silver whispered.

"It's my fault." Annie's small and desolate voice disrupted Von's concentration. "I never should've fucking called Dad. I just wanted to rub his face in it . . . I wish I'd killed the bastard when I stabbed him in the throat with that goddamned dart."

So do I, Von thought, tuning everyone out and focusing every bit of attention on the fading link and the red-haired woman at the other end. As the hours unwound, he realized that Sleep might claim him before he could make contact with Heather. If that happened, the link would be well and truly gone by the time he woke up again.

He couldn't let that happen. He redoubled his efforts, feeling the cold prickle of sweat along his scalp. He didn't know how much time had passed when he caught a fragrant whiff of cloves and spice and rich tobacco. He felt a cool-fingered touch on his arm. Opening his eyes, Von looked up into long-lashed velvet brown eyes—a detective's penetrating gaze.

Thibodaux's nightkind partner, Merri Goodnight.

She wore black slacks and a white blouse beneath a black suede jacket and stood a slim but curvy five-foot-nothing. Apparently someone—Thibodaux and Jack, most likely—had left the house at some point to pick her up at the French Quarter hotel where the two former SB agents were staying.

"*Llygad.*" Merri Goodnight's face, espresso-dark and ageless and framed by sleek black hair, was respectful as she eyed him curiously, her gaze sliding over the tattoos on his arms. "Never met a nomad *llygad* before."

"Now you have," Von growled, not even bothering to keep the irritation from his voice. "So be sure to note the occasion in your diary with a smiley face and a kiss. I'm a little busy here, darlin'. What the hell do you want?"

Looking completely unfazed by his surliness, she replied, "To help you *keep* busy. It'll be dawn in a few hours, but I have a way to keep you from Sleeping." She offered him a small purple pill. "A stay-awake," she informed him. "Created for vamp agents in law enforcement divisions."

"How well does it work?" Von asked, studying the pill pinched between her thumb and forefinger.

"Perfectly. You'll be awake all day. But there're consequences."

"Ain't there always?" Von plucked the pill from her grasp, tossed it into his mouth, and washed it down with a warm swallow of a beer someone had kindly left idling on the table.

Merri folded her arms over her chest, then slung her weight onto one rounded hip. She arched an eyebrow. "Don't you even want to know what those consequences are?"

Von shrugged. "Not really. I'll take my chances. You've used them, right? And you're still upright and breathing. That's good enough for me, darlin'."

"I hope you remember that when you're twitching on the floor."

"If I don't, I trust you to remind me," Von drawled. Merri's quick smile told him that he'd pegged the situation right—she would rub his face in those repudiated consequences for all she was worth.

"Not to be rude, but . . ." Von closed his eyes again and

directed his attention inward. A moment later he heard the soft whisper of suede, the deliberate tap of boot heels against oak as Merri turned and walked away.

"By the way, Emmett isn't the only one who's sorry to have missed that wet boxers contest, Mr. Champion," she purred, her voice all silk and amusement, as she walked out of the kitchen.

"Holy hell," Von muttered.

Jack was going to eat the goddamned shirt, one tiny gator at a time.

With Merri's scent still spicing the air, Von returned his focus to Heather. <*C'mon, doll.*>

Minutes multiplied into hours. And, for the first time since he'd been turned, Von was awake to witness the sunrise he'd willingly sacrificed forty years ago. Or could've, if he'd opened his eyes, hauled his ass out of the chair, and twitched the curtain aside for a peek.

But he didn't.

Dawn came and went unlamented, then noon slipped past. The strength of his link to Heather was beginning to thin and weaken, when the static suddenly dissipated like smoke in the rain.

And Heather reached back.

4

POISONED APPLES

THEY DUMPED HER BLACK-HAIRED angel on the concrete floor, as if he were a piece of curbside junk, a banged-up gift for the donation truck. Dumped him right underneath the big metal hook hanging like a sharp and scary question mark from the ceiling of chalk-white squares.

Meat hook, the little voice in Violet's tummy had told her when the smiling orderlies in their white ice-cream-man uniforms had ushered her—black paper wings taped (after a bunch of pretty-*pretty*-pleases) to the back of her Winnie-the-Pooh sweater—into the empty room with its soft padded walls.

"Go ahead and color, sweetie. We'll be back in just a little bit."

Violet had stared at the hook, her fingers clenched around the box of crayons in her hand, her gaze fluttering like a hummingbird along the glittering curve of metal.

What's it for? she'd asked uneasily, her tummy suddenly full of fluttering moths.

But her little voice had become silent.

Violet was busy coloring the pictures she'd drawn on the

soft padded wall when the orderlies had come back, minus smiles and nice words this time as they dumped Dante onto the cold floor.

He hit the concrete with a soft thud, his long black hair fanning across his snow-white face, hiding his closed eyes and the faint blue smudges beneath them. He almost looked like he was sleeping. But Violet knew better. The metallic smell of pennies folded into the air as blood trickled from his nose. From his ears. Smeared his lips. Again.

Violet sucked in a breath. "I think he needs to go back to the doctor. He's still hurt. His owies are still bleeding." She couldn't believe she needed to point that out. They were grown-ups. Couldn't they see the blood glistening on his white skin?

Yes, the little voice in her tummy said. *They could and they do.*

Then why don't they help him?

They aren't supposed to. But someone else can.

"Me," Violet whispered. "That's why I'm wearing wings."

One of the orderlies kicked Dante from his side and onto his tummy, revealing the pale, pale hands twisted behind him at the small of his back. Metal gleamed around his wrists.

Bad-guy handcuffs. For her angel.

Violet felt the crayon she was holding—Fire Engine Red— snap in two against her palm. She let the crayon fall to the floor, the paper wrapper holding the broken halves together.

Bad-guy handcuffs for the angel who'd reeled her in like a lost kite from among the blazing stars when she'd floated away from her body.

Mommy turns on the TV in the motel in Oregon—the motel with the picture of a winking beaver chewing on a twig, outlined in glowing color—and is searching for the Cartoon Network when Violet hears firecrackers pop-pop-popping outside in the parking lot. Hears the sound of breaking glass. Then her mommy's scream, jagged and raw.

"My baby!"

Violet tries to tell Mommy that she's okay, but she can't. She just drifts up and away, leaving her body, with its wide, staring eyes and the new dark and bleeding hole above them; leaving behind her wailing mother, and wishing she could stay.

Then Dante catches her.

"Don't kick him!" Violet raced across the room, her paper wings rustling at her back. Crouching beside Dante, she glared up at the orderlies. "Stop being so mean! Mr. Purcell and the doctors promised that they'd make him happy, promised that they'd take care—"

"Hush, sweetie, don't you worry none," one orderly, a man with curly brown hair and a name tag reading *Joe*, said. "He's tough. He can take it, trust me."

"It's still mean," Violet insisted. "And he isn't even awake."

"Not yet, but he will be soon," the other orderly—blond ponytail and a name tag that read *Tyler*—said. His eyes darted toward the thick, heavy door like he wished he stood on the other side. "Almost sunset."

Violet nodded. "He's a nighttime angel."

She'd never actually seen his wings, but she knew deep down that they were there because she'd caught a glimpse of them—like black shadows outlined in Fire Engine Red at his back and arching above his head—when he'd lassoed her down from the sky and tucked her back into the body he'd held in his arms.

She'd known that it was her body, even though it was different now, her black hair, golden skin, and jade green eyes (a color her mommy always said she loved) angel-magicked into red hair, freckles, and blue eyes.

"Wake up, princess," Dante had whispered.

Blood had streaked the skin beneath his nose that night too. And his hands had glowed with pretty blue fire.

Joe and Tyler exchanged a look, one bristling with secrets— grown-up secrets—then Tyler swallowed hard and looked away. "Do it already and let's get out of here."

Kneeling on the concrete floor, Joe jabbed a needle full of red stuff into Dante's shoulder. He pushed the plungie thing until the needle was empty, then jumped to his feet. Sweat beaded his upper lip.

"Was that medicine?" Violet asked hopefully, her gaze still on her angel.

"Sure. Why not?" Joe's voice sounded like a shrug.

"Will it make him better?" She touched one of Dante's hands. His skin felt like ice beneath her fingers, nothing like the heat she remembered, his arms embracing her tight. Ice, when he should be fire. When he suddenly shivered as though he was lying in a snowbank without a coat or mittens instead of on a concrete floor, before going still again, she wasn't surprised. Unhappy, but not surprised. "He's cold. He needs a blanket."

"A stake through the heart more like," Joe muttered under his breath. "Shit. I didn't sign up for this—locking little girls into rooms with starving bloodsuckers. It isn't right."

Violet looked up, frowning, trying to puzzle out the meaning of Joe's words and the reason why he sounded so nervous. The orderly's gaze was on Dante. She remembered the flash of fangs she'd seen when her angel had smiled at her just the day before when she'd finally been allowed to see him. But only for a little bit since he was so sick.

Hungry, Dante'd whispered.

I didn't know angels had pointy teeth.

Ain't no angel, chère. *I'm nightkind*, he'd replied. Then, rubbing his forehead, face pained, he'd added, *I think*.

His low voice had made Violet think of sweet tea and *couche-couche* and the grizzled man in the baseball cap at the alligator tour place from the trip she and her mommy had gone on last year. *Cajun*, Mommy had said.

Do you bite? she'd asked Dante out of curiosity, touching a sharp fang tip.

Yup. All the time. A smile had slanted across his lips. *That I do know.*

Will you bite me?

His smile had vanished and his voice had turned fierce. *Never, princess. Jamais. I'd never bite you. That I know too.*

She'd believed him. But Violet had a feeling he might bite the orderlies.

The gleaming hook captured her gaze again and the moths in her tummy turned to pebbles. "Is that for him? In case he bites?" She forced herself to look away, to look at the orderlies instead, but their blank faces didn't make her feel any better. "But what if he promises not to bite? What if he promises to be good?"

Joe shook his head. "It's not right, leaving her in here with him."

"Shut the hell up," Tyler growled. He tossed a look at the camera poking out from a corner in the ceiling. "You trying to get us fired? Or worse?"

"Let me add another choice to those options, gentlemen," someone drawled. Violet looked over her shoulder to see Mr. Purcell standing in the threshold—the man who had brought her here while her mommy got better at the underground hospital.

So she can rest and get well and so you can spend time with your . . . angel . . . while she does. Pretty soon, you'll all go home.

His words had been smooth and slick and full of poisoned-apple smiles.

Just like now. A shiver creepy-crawled down Violet's spine.

He's a bad man, her little voice warned.

Bad enough to hurt angels?

Bad enough to kill angels.

"Tell me what you think," Mr. Purcell continued, "I leave *you* in the room to keep our little Violet company. You could even color while you wait for her angel"—his lips puckered as though the word *angel* tasted as sour as a pickle—"to awaken. I'm sure Violet would be happy to share her crayons. How does that option grab you?"

Shaking his head, Tyler hurried from the room and past Mr. Purcell without a backward glance. Mr. Purcell smiled.

"You don't need to be scared of Dante," Violet insisted, looking at Joe. "He's not mean. And I'll share my crayons if you want to stay and see."

Mr. Purcell chuckled. "Helluva offer. *Do* you want to stay and see, Joe?"

A muscle bunched in Joe's jaw, then he glanced away, his face looking like he had a tummyache. "Sorry, kid," he whispered, his shoulders slumping. "Keep as far away from him as you can. Keep yourself out of reach and—"

"Joe," Mr. Purcell said. Just the one word, and almost a whisper. A whisper once more full of poisoned apples and thick thorns. Then, just as quietly, "Give her the key."

The orderly's face turned white. The smell of sweat wafted into the air. He pulled a key from his pants pocket and handed it to Violet. Swallowing hard, he left the room without another word.

Violet studied the key the orderly had given her. Little and light, it looked like a toy key. She looked at the bad-guy handcuffs gleaming around Dante's wrists. "Is it for those?" she asked.

"I knew you'd figure it out," Mr. Purcell said. He reached for the big, thick door's metal latch and started to pull it shut. "He'll be awake soon, so you won't be lonely for long."

"Okay," Violet said, "but he needs a doctor." She brushed Dante's hair back from his pale cheek. Blood glistened beneath his nose, on his lips. "He's still hurt. See?"

"He'll be fine," Mr. Purcell said, his gaze flicking to the hook above. "Trust me. The only thing that'll happen will be history repeating itself."

The door swung shut with a heavy *thunk* before Violet could insist on the doctor again. Red lights lit up on the little panel beside the door. LOCKED.

Her angel shivered on the cold concrete floor for a

moment, then lay still again. She had a feeling the orderlies wouldn't be coming back with a blanket. Feeling the weight of the hook hanging above her, above her sleeping angel, Violet unlocked the handcuffs with the little silver key. Pulled them free from around his wrists and placed them on the floor. The skin of his wrists looked rubbed raw, bruised.

She thought about the lies—*just little white ones, sweetie*—Mr. Purcell had instructed her to tell Dante to make him happy. *Answer to the name Chloe. Call him Dante-angel and let him believe he gifted you with that Winnie-the-Pooh sweater.* Poisoned apples.

Why? Why are they hurting him? Why are they asking me to hurt him too? They promised to take care of him. Don't they know he saved me from Heaven?

Maybe that's what scares them, her little voice suggested.

"Then they're being stupid," Violet muttered, but not disagreeing, not really.

She grabbed Dante's shoulder and, grunting, pulled him over onto his back. He smelled of Halloween underneath all the blood and he was wearing clothes like the ones she'd first seen him in—leather rock-star pants, a black T-shirt, but without the sleeves with all the little holes this time, and boots with lots of buckles. And, just like before, a collar was strapped around his throat, a black collar with a steel hoop.

He looked like he belonged in the *Underworld* movies her mommy had Netflixed and Violet had watched in secret, hidden behind the couch, when she was supposed to be in bed. And those movies had been full of scary stuff, dark stuff, dangerous stuff.

The hook in the ceiling told Violet that Mr. Purcell's promises, every word from his mouth, were only juicy, red poisoned lies. Told her that scary, dark, and dangerous stuff was on its way, scampering on fast little spider legs. And her angel needed to be awake so he could face it. So he wouldn't have to take another kick in the ribs that he couldn't even roll away from.

Paper wings rustling behind her, Violet patted Dante's cold cheek and, calling his name, urged him up from his dreams. Relief spread through her tummy like hot cocoa when Dante drew in a deep breath.

Her nighttime angel was waking up.

5

TRUE NORTH

"YOU NEVER REALIZE THAT you're under the influence until you no longer are, but I'm finally thinking clearly— I mean crystal, y'know?—for the first time since I met . . . *him*." She shook her head. "I can't believe the difference."

Pacing the sand-colored carpet in her slippers, Heather Wallace was busy lying through her teeth, lying for all she was worth, an Oscar-caliber, rose bouquet–throwing, standing-ovation performance—or so she hoped, since she desperately wanted to remain free of sedatives and restraints—when an un-expected mental touch put an abrupt stop to her flow of words. Halted her in her tracks.

Llygad. Nightkind. Nomad. Friend.

Heather's breath caught in her throat as Von's image suddenly flooded her mind, saturating her senses with his masculine scent—old leather, frost, and gun oil—warm and reassuring. His sending, pearled with intense relief, threaded like silk through her mind.

<*Damn, woman. There you are. You okay, doll?*>

<*I sure as hell am now, road rider. But hold on, all right? I'm not alone.*>

<Ain't going nowhere.>

Boneless with relief of her own, Heather plopped down on the edge of the brown leather sofa, the cushions creaking beneath her. She exhaled, then carefully drew in another breath, in an attempt to calm her racing heart.

Von had caught her completely off-guard—but in one helluva good way.

Between the thick cotton fog of the drugs IV-fed into her veins and the ferocious tsunami of awakening emotions once the drugs had been stopped—a white-knuckled fury at the man she would never call her father again, and a deep, icy fear for Dante—Heather hadn't realized that her blood link with Von was still intact. Had believed it long gone.

"Heather? You seem very distant. Are you all right?"

Looking up, she met the gaze of the dark-haired therapist— *Allan Wade, but please call me Allan*—sitting across from her in a polished mahogany leather chair. Dressed casually in white shirt, sage-green tie, and khaki trousers, he studied her, head tilted slightly to one side.

"You look pale," he added, frowning. "Are you feeling ill?"

"A little nauseous," she said in a low, reluctant voice as though he were forcing the admission from her. She allowed her fingers to pluck at her hideous peach chenille bathrobe. "I think I'd like to go back to my room and lie down. This has all been so . . ." She paused as though searching for a word.

"Overwhelming?" Allan suggested.

"Exactly. *Overwhelming.*"

Allan rested his notepad and pen on the small end table beside his chair, then leaned forward, fingers steepled beneath his chin. "How do you feel about your father's decision to bring you here?" He regarded her with a penetrating walnut-brown gaze. Analyzing every word, every hesitation, every glance and gesture.

Heather wondered just how strong, how accurate, his bullshit meter ran.

"One problem at a time," she replied, meeting that gaze with steel of her own. "You're touching on an issue that goes way back."

"All right, then," Allan agreed easily. "We'll come back to that at another session. For now, let's get you back to your room so you can rest." He rose from his chair and Heather caught a strong citrusy whiff of his too liberally applied cologne. "Those sedatives can really take it out of a person."

Heather stood as well. "I don't think I need any more sedatives," she said. "I might not be happy with my dad, but I understand now that I need to be here."

"You *are* much calmer and more clear than you were last night. Less volatile. I think we can forgo them for now."

Relief surged through Heather, weakening her knees with its intensity. "Thanks," she said, then added a heartfelt lie. "You won't regret it."

"No, I won't," Allan said quietly. "But *you* will if you abuse my trust."

"Don't worry," Heather replied as he walked her across the room to the door. "I'll do whatever it takes to avoid restraints and drugs." Late afternoon sunlight slanted across the carpet from the two steel-meshed windows behind them, gleamed from the door's bronzed lever.

It hit her then. *Daylight.*

Daylight and Von should be Sleeping. De Noir must've pulled the nomad up from Sleep like he had with Dante the morning she'd served her search warrant—weeks ago.

A lifetime ago.

"Get some rest," Allan said, pulling open the door. "I'll see you tomorrow."

Not if I can help it. But Heather kept that thought to herself and gave Allan a quick smile instead, then stepped into the hall, where her assigned security escort, a trim blonde in a charcoal-gray suit with a name tag reading *Riggins*, waited for her.

Riggins started walking in a long-legged, easy stride and

Heather fell into step beside her, slippers soundless against the plush carpet, eager to get back to her room and resume her conversation with Von.

Riggins didn't pack a gun as far as Heather could tell; instead she carried a Taser in a slim black holder clipped to her belt underneath her suit jacket. Heather judged her to be in her mid-thirties, noted her air of athletic confidence, and wondered how hard it would be to take her down when the time came to make a break for it.

If I tried now, with the drugs still lingering in my system, she'd have me on the floor, arm twisted up behind my back and screaming Uncle! before I could even unholster her Taser.

But now that she had Von online . . .

"Here we go," Riggins said, stopping at an open doorway. "If you need anything, just use the call button."

"Will do."

Once Heather had stepped inside, she heard the click and buzz as the door was shut behind her and the locks activated.

Heather went to the bed and perched on the edge of the mattress. It was a hospital bed despite the resort flair to everything else in the place, from bathrobe to designer accessories in the bathroom to the minifridge stocked with high-end bottled water. A resort *minus* TVs, phones, and Internet in the guest rooms. But maybe the addition of restraints, burly orderlies, and forced sedatives made up for that lack, she mused darkly.

The air was conditioned and cool, and smelled faintly of ozone. And since it looked like the steel mesh–screened windows couldn't be opened—at least not from the inside—the air-conditioning was a good thing.

She reached out for Von. Felt him respond, brushing like a cat against her awareness.

<Right here, doll. Tell me where you are so we can come get you.>

<That's the problem. I don't know. It's a mental health facility of some kind—a rehab apparently for the brainwashed victims

of religious cults, deep-cover operations, and apparently, in my case, nightkind.>

<Brainwashed? Shee-it. You? Your old man really doesn't know you at all, does he, doll?>

<No. No he doesn't. I know I was told the name of the place last night, but I don't remember. My goddamned memory's been drug-bombed. I haven't seen anything naming the place. Not on stationery, or on the walls, on uniforms—nothing.>

<Relax, and it'll come back to you. Keep looking. Maybe you'll spot something.>

<Dante—what did my father do to him? The things I felt . . .>

Last night, before the honey-talking nurse had released a flood of sedatives into her IV with a single button push, Heather had been convinced Dante was dying, that she was losing him.

In anticipation of her session with Wade, the drugs had been stopped in the morning, and once the fog had cleared from her mind, Heather had reached for Dante through their bond. Their bond still held, the flame that was Dante's presence burning deep within her, reassuring her that he was still alive. Last night that flame had been guttering, now it was steady again, but subdued—a candle beneath a dark mirror.

She'd tried to connect with him, to fill his dreams—or, much more likely, his nightmares—with white silence and calm, to let him know that he wasn't alone, that she was with him even in the darkness.

But he'd been beyond her reach, swallowed whole by pain and whispers and the acrid bite of drugs. She'd kept trying though, again and again, until her security escort in the form of Riggins had come to walk her to Wade's office.

Dante's silence scared her—without question. But Von's sudden silence was scaring the holy loving hell out of her.

<Von? Nothing you can say will be worse than the things I've imagined.>

But Von proved her dead wrong on that point.

He answered her with a controlled stream of images—images gleaned from her sister's memory. Heather had never imagined any of *this*. Dante shot in cold blood with bullets designed to kill a True Blood. Von and Silver gunned down in their sleep as well. The club torched. Her pregnant sister tranked and slung like a deer carcass over their father's shoulder—*no, dammit, he would only be James Wallace from now on, nothing more.*

But the worst of all—the one thing she hadn't imagined: Dante missing. Stolen from the burning club by parties unknown, for reasons unknown, destination unknown.

Heather swallowed hard, feeling hollow and sick.

All because James Wallace didn't approve of her relationship choice or career decisions. No. It was even simpler than that. Control. It was all about control. He'd felt like he'd lost control over his daughters and he'd decided to rectify the situation.

Jesus Christ. Bitter acid burned at the back of Heather's throat.

<I hate breaking it to you like that, doll. I'm truly sorry.> Regret curled thick through Von's sending, as did a brass-knuckled resolve. *<But we can find Dante—through your bond. You're like a living, breathing GPS where Dante is concerned. We'll find him. We just need to find you first. So keep working that memory.>*

<I am,> Heather assured him. *<Annie? Is she okay?>*

<She's worried sick about you . . . but, yeah, she's safe.>

<Safe is good. But is she okay?>

Apprehension sank an anchor into Heather's belly as she realized she no longer felt the thrum of the nomad's energy through their link.

<Von?>

Empty silence.

Heather's hands clenched into fists on her chenille-covered thighs. If the link had finally given up the ghost before she could even give him a hint, some clue as to her whereabouts—

<Heather. Hey, the damn link is starting to go.> Von confirmed her fear. *<And I have a feeling it ain't gonna last much longer. If you can remember anything that might help me find you, now would be the time, woman. But know this>*—a deep and deadly determination composed his sending, a promise mind-to-mind—*<whether you remember anything or not before this goddamned link falls apart, I will find you. You and Dante. No matter what it takes.>*

A smile stole across Heather's lips. *<I know.>*

<Good. Now get to work, woman.>

Closing her eyes, Heather did exactly that. She shoved her way past sedative-thickened dreams and shock-hazed memories to the previous night, in search of the words that had spilled so damned cheerfully from James Wallace's lips.

A ceiling dotted with soft, recessed lights; a fuzzy where-am-I? feeling that quickly morphs into an icy ribbon of fear as she realizes she doesn't know; the pull of restraints at her wrists and ankles as she tries to sit up.

"Pumpkin."

James Wallace stands in the doorway, his eyes hidden behind the reflections glimmering on the lenses of his glasses.

"What have you done to Dante?" she asks, her voice tight, simmering with bitter fury despite the drugs cocooning her mind.

"You need to focus on your own life, Heather. You need to reclaim it. And once we've freed you of that damned bloodsucker's influence, once we've scrubbed the taint of his touch off you, you'll be my daughter again, the brilliant FBI agent."

Heather's eyes opened. James Wallace didn't realize he no longer had a daughter. Not yet. But what else had the bastard said? She rubbed her forehead as though she could summon the memory like a genie from a lamp.

A nurse in blue scrubs pads into the room carrying an IV bag, which she starts to connect to the IV stand positioned beside the bed. "You'll feel much better once the drugs start to work," the nurse assures Heather. "It'll make the therapy easier, as well."

And there they were—the magic words.

Welcome to the Strickland Deprogramming Institute.

Heather quickly sent the memory to Von with its priceless nugget of information, then realized with a hollow feeling that he was gone once again. Hoping against hope that it was just a brief glitch like last time, she continued to send the memory to him on a repeating loop.

<*Von. Come in, Von . . .*>

Heather opened her eyes, then rose to her feet. Maybe she could gather a little more intel for him—provided it wasn't too late. Hurrying to the window across the room, her slippers whispering across polished tile, she looked out through glass and steel mesh into a parking lot surrounded by forested green and a high fence. Several dozen cars, SUVs, and pickups populated the blacktop, bumpers glinting in the sunshine. She narrowed her eyes trying to make out a license plate. Was that Texas?

<*Doll . . .*>

Heather exhaled in relief. The link was still working—for the moment, anyway. <*Did you get it?*>

Frustration sliced through the nomad's sending. <*Only bits and pieces . . . full of holes . . . again . . .*>

Gripping the smooth wood of the windowsill, Heather poured everything she had into sending the memory one more time, knowing it might be her last chance. Focused on the most important part: *Welcome to the Strickland Deprogramming Institute* and *Texas.*

<*Did you get it this time?*>

But once again, Von's energy had disappeared, leaving only silence behind. Heather had a sinking feeling that the link had finally unraveled. Sighing, she rested her head against the sun-warmed glass and wearily closed her eyes. She had no way of knowing if the information had reached Von or not. While she hoped it had, she needed to plan as if it hadn't.

She needed to steal a Taser and a phone. A tight smile curved her lips. Hell, a nail file had saved her ass in the past, maybe she'd get lucky again. She also needed to find a way out of Strickland, a path past all the security escorts and door guards, past the alarms she knew had to be rigged into every entrance and exit.

She'd bet anything the fence outside was electric—not a lethal charge, but one strong enough to stun. And even though she hadn't seen it from the vantage provided by her window, she had no doubt that there would be security personnel patrolling the grounds and guarding the front gate.

Stealing a car would be difficult—unless she could find an older, pre-computerized model. Possibilities streamed through her mind. Maybe a hostage. Maybe a fire. She could attempt to slip away during the confusion that was sure to happen when the facility was evacuated.

Heather felt an urgent tug to the east through the bond connecting her to Dante, a restless drive to *go now*, and knew—down to the bone, heart-deep, and gut-sure—that if she followed that intuitive eastward pull, she'd find Dante at the end of it.

Living, breathing GPS, Von had called her. Maybe, but Heather sensed only a general direction, nothing specific like 'left turn in two point five miles.' She had a feeling another analogy was more accurate—she was a compass and Dante true north.

All she needed to do was start walking.

But the cold prickling along Heather's spine warned her that she needed to hurry. A timer set to an unknown hour was ticking away the minutes. A deadline with an unspecified but looming date was breathing down her neck.

Words Dante had said only two nights ago returned to her. Stark, whispered words she was determined to prove wrong— a lie.

I feel like I'm running out of time, catin.

No, cher, no. I refuse to lose you.

But if she remained sitting on her butt in Strickland gambling that Von had received her last transmission, that was *exactly* what would happen, she would lose Dante. Lose the man—nightkind/Fallen/*creawdwr*—she'd chosen to stand beside, come Gehenna, Molotov cocktails, government assassins, or even her own damn father.

I feel like I'm running out of time, catin.

<Stay with me, Baptiste,> Heather sent to him. <Stay here-and-now. Show me just how pigheaded you truly are.>

This time her sending vanished instead of bouncing back unheard, but Heather had no idea whether that meant Dante had actually received it or if his pain and nightmares had simply devoured it.

It didn't matter. She would keep trying. Just like he had in the club. As she'd seen through her sister's eyes in the images Von had poured into her mind.

Dante half slides, half falls to his knees on the Oriental carpet in front of their room, his black-painted nails scraping furrows along the threshold on his way down. "J'su ici, catin," he whispers, his words Sleep-slurred. "Je t'entends."

I'm here. I hear you.

Heather had believed it impossible to reach Dante while Sleep embraced him, but when James Wallace had sauntered into the club she'd hammered a warning against his shields anyway. And he'd heard her. He'd fought his way free from Sleep's talons for her. Stubborn will. Quiet strength. Fierce.

She would do no less for him.

Prying her fingers loose from the windowsill, Heather turned away from the tempered glass and the lowering sun and shadowed grounds beyond it, and headed back to the bed. Hours and hours of forced sedatives and emotional stress had taken their toll. She wouldn't be any good to anyone, let alone herself and Dante, if she keeled over from exhaustion.

Heather kicked off her slippers and slipped beneath the bed's flowered comforter. She'd rest for a little bit, then eat. Despite having no appetite, she needed to refuel, to build up her strength. She had no idea how far "east" might turn out to be.

As she draped an arm over her eyes, a dark and terrifying scenario popped into her mind. Crackled ice through her veins. Suppose Shadow Branch operatives had been watching the club and, witnessing James Wallace's little snatch, murder, and burn routine, had decided to take advantage of what must have seemed like the perfect opportunity.

A black ops version of a Powerball win.

And what if the SB discovered that Dante was much more than a True Blood? Discovered he was also a *creawdwr*? That he could not only Make and Unmake anyone and anything, but open gates to other worlds as well?

With just one whispered word, the SB could trigger Dante's programming and twist him, force him, into becoming—

An image flickered to life in the darkness behind Heather's eyes, an image infused with Dante's scent of burning leaves and November frost; a recurring vision of a possible future, of a destiny embraced.

Tendrils of Dante's black hair lift into the air as though breeze-caught. Gold light stars out from his kohl-rimmed eyes. He looks up as song—not his own—rings through the air. The night burns, the sky on fire from horizon to horizon.

—the Great Destroyer.

Heather still didn't know which path her vision revealed— Dante as never-ending Road fighting to save the mortal world and everyone in it or as Great Destroyer leading the Fallen to war—but it wouldn't matter if Dante didn't survive what James Wallace had done to him. And Dante's survival was all that mattered. The rest could wait.

<Stay with me, Baptiste.>

But that sending also vanished, a single rain drop into a vast, black lake. Despite the cold fear knotted around her heart, exhaustion could no longer be denied. Sleep swept over Heather in a relentless tide, claiming her as she sent to Dante one more time.

<Stay, cher. *Please.*>

6

ONCE ONLY

L UCIEN, DECKED OUT IN a black Prada suit and a scarlet silk tie, offered the receptionist a warm smile before swiveling and short-circuiting the security camera with a tiny arc of electric blue fire flicked from his fingertip, the movement too swift for human eyes. The sharp scent of ozone cut into the air.

"May I help you, sir?" the receptionist asked cheerfully.

"Yes, you certainly may."

Crossing to her desk, Lucien leaned over it and, before she had time to do more than widen her brown eyes in alarm, he touched two fingers to the center of her forehead. Blue light glowed cool against her skin.

"Sleep," Lucien commanded in a low voice.

The receptionist's eyes fluttered shut. She slumped into her chair, head lolling against her shoulder. A soft sigh escaped her lips. Lucien removed his fingers from her forehead, then straightened, his gaze on the door that she and her desk had guarded.

Etched in delicate gold letters on its frosted upper panel: *Special Agent-in-Charge Oscar Heyne*. James Wallace's direct supervisor, the person who had needed to approve his leave of absence, and the person most likely to know exactly where to find Wallace and the daughter he'd drugged and kidnapped.

And the very man Lucien sought.

After Annie's attempts to call her father had ended in voice-mail messages, Lucien had gently interrogated the guilt- and bourbon-numbed young mortal about her father, his habits, and his role in the FBI. Then Lucien had taken to the sky, winging for Portland.

As Lucien grasped the door handle, a conversation he'd had with Heather not even a week ago played through his memory.

I'm not with the Bureau anymore. According to the FBI, I'm a much-valued agent, but one now lost to paranoid delusions, due to a hereditary mental illness, and in desperate need of treatment.

Are you expected to survive said treatment?

I'm sure it'll end in a tragic suicide.

And Dante?

Snipped as the final loose end linking the Bureau to Bad Seed.

Perhaps Wallace had been doing the Bureau's dirty work when he'd shot Dante.

With a flip of the handle, Lucien opened the door and stepped inside. Heyne's office was modest, full of clean lines and masculine leather furniture and framed forest scenes. The desk was neat, the chair behind it unoccupied. On the west wall hung a six-by-six foot painting of forested hills wreathed in ragged mist.

Oscar Heyne stood in front of that primal and lonely scene, gun in hand.

As he studied the silent FBI agent, Lucien skimmed one hand along the back of a leather chair parked in front of Heyne's desk. The buttery aroma of sunblock filled the room. Beneath that, he detected another familiar, but surprising, scent.

SAC Heyne wasn't mortal. He was nightkind.

And using stay-awake pills like those Merri Goodnight had given Von.

Slim and of average height, Heyne's skin was a shade lighter than his dark coffee eyes, his short-cropped hair flecked with gray. Given the lack of lines in Heyne's face, Lucien suspected the gray came courtesy of Clairol in an attempt to mimic the passage of time.

"I admit, I didn't expect a vampire," Lucien commented. "I must applaud the FBI's efforts at diversity."

"Who are you?" Heyne looked Lucien over, speculative gaze drinking in and weighing details. "Suit's too expensive, too fine for government wear, so I think I can safely eliminate you from the SB rank and file." His nostrils flared. "*What* are you? You're not mortal, not vampire—"

"No, I'm not," Lucien agreed, unknotting and removing his tie. He draped it over the back of the chair. "Who I am doesn't matter. As for what, perhaps it'd be best if I demonstrated. Save us a little time in pooh-poohing, denials, and demands for proof."

Heyne arched one eyebrow. "Color me intrigued," he said in a dry baritone, keeping the gun—what looked like a standard-issue Glock—aimed at heart level.

"You might as well put that away, it won't do a bit of good."

"I think I'll keep it."

Lucien shrugged. "Suit yourself."

"If this is a stripper-gram, supernatural or otherwise," Heyne said as Lucien continued to undress, "I'm all out of cash."

"It's not. And keep your wallet in your pants."

Once his suit jacket and shirt had joined the tie on the back of the chair, he flexed his shoulders and unfurled his wings, fanning the smoky incense scent of wing musk and deep, dark earth into the air.

Heyne's gun dropped from his hand to thud against the carpet. His eyes widened in mingled disbelief and fascination. "Fallen," he whispered.

Blue flames arced around Lucien's body, electrifying the air, and glowing as reflections from picture frames, the polished leather, and in Heyne's eyes. Lucien's hair, tied back in a pony-tail, snaked into the air on the currents of Fallen power.

"What do you want?" Heyne asked with surprising calm.

"Information," Lucien said. "And I'll ask each question once and once only."

"And if I refuse to answer?"

"You have a choice: pain free or not. To be honest, I hope you choose *not*. It's been a long time since I've delivered a bit of Old Testament–style wrath."

Heyne's face turned the color of ashes. "Ask, then. If I know, I'll tell you."

"Does James Wallace know that he was the Bureau's Trojan horse?"

Heyne scooped up the Glock, but by the time he fired a split second later, Lucien was already on him, wrenching the gun from his fingers and enfolding the vampire within his smooth black wings.

Lucien smiled. "Old Testament it is, then."

7

BENEATH A CURVED SHADOW

"DANTE? DANTE-ANGEL? YOU NEED to wake up before they come back."

A child's voice—*Chloe?*—patted against Dante's consciousness just like the fingers against his face. Her words sounded worried, a frowning downward turn of tone that suggested she was dealing with something she didn't quite understand.

He tasted blood at the back of his throat—his own. Smelled it, thick and copper bright. Pain throbbed at his temples, prickled deep in his chest. Hunger scraped through him with razor-edged claws, leaving him hollowed, empty.

A woman's voice whispered through his memory, the words as casual as a shrug, *You won't save her, you know. You'll fail.*

And from deeper within: *Again.*

Dante's eyes flew open. Black specks pinpricked his vision. The brilliant overheads spiked jagged shards of light through his pupils and into his brain and, wincing, he lifted a hand to shield his eyes.

"Goody! You're awake!"

He blinked until the specks vanished and Chloe's freckled face, framed by long tendrils of red hair, swam into focus above him. Given his perspective, Dante realized that he had to be lying on the floor, the eight-year old kneeling beside him.

"What's wrong, princess? You okay?" Dante asked. His words sounded slurred—even to himself, as fuzzy as the thoughts shuffling through his aching head. And he didn't feel like he was waking up at twilight, hungry and alert; he felt more like he did at dawn, just before Sleep rushed over him in a cool, dark wave and yanked him under.

Worse, he felt shaky and weak, like he'd hadn't fed in days.

Another voice whispered: *This is all wrong. You need to wake your ass up.*

"I'm okay, but you're bleeding again, Dante-angel," Chloe announced, touching her nose, then her ears to demonstrate from where. "I don't think the doctor fixed your owies right."

Fixed my owies? Dante rubbed a hand gingerly along his chest and felt an aching tenderness under his T-shirt on the left side, near the pec. Right at heart level. A bullet, maybe, or—an image wavered behind Dante's eyes like a raindrop-dimpled pond.

A blond man in a tan trench coat aims a big-ass gun, his finger already squeezing the trigger. Behind his glasses, his glittering eyes are cold and implacable, a guillotine's falling blade. . . . Pain smoothed the pond, erasing the image, and leaving him wondering what the hell he'd just been thinking about.

Dante coughed, tasted blood. *That's right.* Something bad had happened. He just fucking didn't know what. He sucked in a breath of air and felt it drown in the wet, heavy depths of his lungs. A completely new and messed-up sensation.

"Awesome," he muttered, pushing himself up into a sitting position, then onto his knees. The room gave a couple of lazy twirls around him, then pirouetted to a slow stop. That, he reflected, could only be a good thing. Unlike how he felt.

Waking up from Sleep with his head aching as though an elephant had used it as a trampoline—heavy emphasis on the tramp—wasn't all that unusual, unfortunately, but drowning in his own blood most definitely was.

Whether he'd been shot, stabbed, staked, or skewered with a cocktail umbrella, he should've healed. The disturbing fact that he hadn't, that he couldn't even remember how he'd gotten hurt in the first place, let alone where he was, coiled like a rattlesnake in his mind—waiting with venomous fangs.

"Doctor? *T'es sûr*, princess? I don't remember a doctor," Dante said, another blood-kissed cough punctuating his words. Behind the blood, he tasted something else at the back of his throat—amber-thick, woody, and ice-cold—something he couldn't name. But whatever it was, it left him feeling uneasy. "Hell, I don't even remember yesterday. Is this a hospital or—"

His words jammed up in his throat as he stared at the steel hook bolted into the white-tiled ceiling. Light slid like hot grease along its wicked curve. Not a hospital, no.

Dante felt the floor shift beneath him. Cold dread twisted through his gut.

You can do this hard or easy, kid.

Welcome back, S. We've missed you.

His vision blurred once again while memories flipped back and forth as though someone in his head couldn't choose between two favorite channels.

Flip: *Himself as a punk-ass kid in a Muse tee, jeans, and duct-taped sneakers bolting from Papa Prejean's ramshackle foster home of fucked-up delights, Chloe tucked tight against his side and squeaking with surprise . . .*

Flip: *Himself as a smart-ass adult in leather and buckle-strapped mesh fighting beside a tall man with a crescent moon tattoo beneath his right eye and a red-haired woman with twilight eyes, who smells of sage and rain-fresh lilacs, a woman of heart and steel, a woman who tells him,* Stay with me, Baptiste. Stay here-and-now—

Flip: *The newborn evening races past punk-ass kid Dante in a cool, rain-wet blur as he moves, his fingers practically welded around Chloe's wrist, determined that she'll never have to pay a visit to Papa and Mama Prejean's shadow-eaten basement/pimp crib. Never have to learn the things he has in its depths . . .*

Flip: *Hands, warm and callused, grasp smart-ass adult Dante's shoulders and steady him. A calm male voice, one achingly familiar, says,* Gotcha, little brother—

Flip: *Punk-ass kid Dante pulls a small ninja-type metal star from his throat, its points blood-slicked. It tumbles from his fingers. Chloe yells at him to run, tugs on his arm. He tries, but his feet refuse to move. His thoughts ice over as well. The night whirls around him, a streak of pale clouds and glimmering stars and skeletal branches . . .*

Hadn't he awakened in a room just like this one? Or was *this* the first time?

Pain wheeled through Dante's mind, stole his breath. Shivved his heart.

Wrong. This is all wrong. Wake the fuck up.

Bad news: he was pretty damned sure he *was* wide awake. Dante tried to grab hold of the broken memories and the voices that had followed, but everything faded, disappearing back into the aching ball of cotton that was currently his brain. Gone. He felt the warm ooze of blood from his nose, felt it pool in his ears.

"Fuck." He blinked. Rubbed at his temples. What had he been thinking about?

Feeding.

Hunger scraped. Clawed. Shook him like a baby in the remorseless hands of a jonesing tweaker. Blood pulsed hot and berry-sweet right next to him. He smelled it beneath Chloe's skin. Heard it—a fast-paced *shush-shush,* rhythmic and primal and seductive. Sweat sprang up along his hairline.

You can't save her.

Yeah? Fucking watch me.

Dante kicked and stomped his hunger back into the hollowed-out depths within, funneling every bit of strength he still held into the effort. And prayed like hell it would stay there until he could get Chloe out of—wherever the hell they were.

"Dante-angel?"

"Chloe." He swallowed hard before continuing. A cold sweat slicked his skin. "Where are we?" Lifting the hem of his T-shirt, he wiped at his face. Smearing the blood, more than cleaning it, he suspected. "Did Papa take us someplace? Did that fucking asshole hurt you?"

Chloe sucked in a sharp breath. "My mommy says never to use bad words even if they might be the best words for the situation." Her carrot-colored brows knitted together, perplexed, as she admitted, "But I don't know what that means. Not exactly."

Dante frowned. "Your mommy? Since when, princess? You never knew her . . ."

Chloe pressed a finger against her lips, then shook her head, her hair swinging against her back. *Someone's listening.* Moving in front of him, she looped her arms around his neck. Dante looked past her to the camera tucked into a corner near the ceiling.

Motherfuckers wanna watch, huh?

Dante pulled Chloe closer, slipping his arms around her as he held his left hand up behind her back for prime camera view. Extended the middle finger and turned it slowly so it could be admired from every angle—a not-so-still life masterpiece of fuck-youitude.

"What are you doing?" Chloe whispered.

"Perking up someone's boring day."

Dante hugged her tight, his arms crinkling the black paper wings—those were new, yeah?—taped to the back of the Winnie-the-Pooh sweater he'd swiped for her from Walgreens. She radiated a banked-coal heat and smelled of strawberries and baby shampoo and waxy crayons. He shivered as his chilled body drank in her warmth.

Why am I so goddamned cold? I've always burned hot—hotter than other nightkind.

Wait. Nightkind? *What the hell?*

Dante felt Chloe's fingers tuck a lock of his hair behind his ear, then her breath warmed the ear's icy shell as she whispered into it. "I got a secret to tell you . . . again. My name isn't Chloe, it's Violet, remember? You were pretty sick when I told you yesterday after you came back from the operating room."

Operating room?

Dante pulled back just enough so he could look at her, his heart drumming a drunken Motorhead solo against his ribs. "No. I *don't* remember. Where's Orem, *p'tite?*" he asked, scanning the concrete for her plushie orca, and ignoring the desperate edge to his voice. "Did you drop him?"

"I never had an Orem," she said, voice a solemn, but patient whisper. "I'm not Chloe. I'm Violet. You saved me when I died and floated away from my mommy. You changed me with blue fire—made me look like this."

Electricity prickles through him. Crackles along his fingers. His song sweeps up from his heart, a dark and intricate aria, dancing in time to the blue flames flickering around his hands . . .

The memory fragment vanished, winking out like a match beneath a pair of pursed lips. Dante blinked. What the hell had he been thinking? Remembering?

"My name is Violet."

A deep unease uncoiled within Dante. He searched her eyes for any sign of a prank in their blue depths, but saw only truth. He also noticed what he *didn't* see, hadn't heard—Chloe's bright smile, her giggles when he swore. And that scared the holy loving shit out of him. Tore a hole through the middle of him. A hole that threatened to swallow him whole.

You won't save her, you know. You'll fail.

"Bullshit," Dante whispered, and wasn't entirely sure if he was answering the voice in his head or the little girl in his arms.

He swallowed back the blood rising in his throat, stealing his oxygen, then coughed. If she wasn't Chloe, then where was—

She lies on the concrete floor, staring up at the hook, her blue eyes as wide and empty as a doll's. The blood from her slashed throat stains her hair a deep red.

As her life, already cooling, soaks in through the knees of his jeans, Dante stares at his blood-sticky hands, his fingers, his sharp, sharp nails. He struggles to breathe.

A woman laughs, the sound low and throaty and pleased: That's my boy.

"No." One simple blood-soaked word, repeated over and over in a strained voice, a voice thick with guilt and grief and denial, and only the raw ache in Dante's throat told him that the voice belonged to him.

The copper and tart-berry smell of her blood still hung heavy in the air, saturated his every breath. Glistened on his nails. Hunger glided like a gator to the surface. Ravenous. His heart slammed against his ribs. "No. No. No."

"Are you okay, Dante-angel?"

He didn't know how to answer that, didn't know if he even could. But he knew what he had to do. He let go of Chl— Violet, gently pulling her arms free from around his neck, then shoving her away.

Her blood spills hot and fragrant and crimson over his fingers . . .

"Are you mad at me?" Violet asked in a small voice. "I know I can't be your princess, but I made wings so I could be your angel."

Dante started to reach for her, to hug her tight, but stopped himself at the last second. His hands knotted into fists at his sides, sharp nails biting into his palms. "No, *p'tite*, no. That ain't it, not at all. This ain't your fault. But you gotta keep the fuck away from me," he said, his voice low and husky and more than a little desperate—even to his own ears. "You gotta keep yourself out of reach."

"But why?" Violet stood under the hook and Dante wanted to yank her from beneath its curved shadow. But he couldn't trust himself to let go again.

"Cuz you ain't safe with me, *p'tite*. Now get away." Dante scowled as he flapped his hands in a dismissive, move-your-ass-already motion. "*Vite-vite.*"

But despite the hurt darkening her blue gaze, hurt that Dante regretted, no matter how necessary, Violet refused to move, the stubborn tilt of her jaw declaring loud and clear: *You're being a butthead, so I'll be a butthead right back. So there.*

Fine. So he'd move instead.

Coughing, the sound harsh and liquid, Dante staggered up to his feet. He managed—just—to keep his balance as the room did one dizzying Tilt-A-Whirl spin and dip, before steadying beneath his boots. But before he could take step *numéro un*, his vision suddenly fractured like ice beneath too much weight and split into jagged halves. His breath caught rough in his throat.

He saw both Chloes at the same time: Chloe dead on the floor, snow-angeled in a thickening pool of her own blood. Chloe standing several feet away from him, still regarding him with complete trust, despite the confusion darkening her eyes.

The room took another Tilt-A-Whirl spin and Dante stumbled. He closed his eyes, jaw tight. His head felt full of broken glass, his heart full of ash. Images of Chloe dipped and fluttered through his mind like fast-winging night birds.

—*Chloe happily brushes his long black hair, then pulls it into a ponytail while she teaches him—the boy who can't go out into the daylight—how to read and write.*

—*He awakens at twilight to find Chloe curled up and napping against his side, Orem tucked between them. And for that moment, they are just a boy and the chosen little sister he protects, instead of a monster cuffed to his bed to keep him from murdering his child-pimping foster parents in their sleep, and a little girl who doesn't know any better.*

—*He stands in front of Chloe, hissing, as the door swings*

open. Three men in black suits—bad fucking men like Papa Prejean, like all the groping assholes who walk down the basement steps—spread out in the white padded room.

When Dante opened his eyes again, he saw only Chloe standing in front of him with her paper wings colored black; the other Chloe had vanished from the concrete floor. A wary hope unfolded within him. Maybe it hadn't happened yet. Maybe he could make sure it never did. Could make sure he kept his promises.

I won't let anyone hurt you, princess.

Himself included.

Dragging in another wet breath of air, Dante snatched up the discarded handcuffs from the floor and ratcheted one steel bracelet shut around his right wrist, leaving the other cuff open and dangling. He wiped automatically at the blood trickling hot from his nose, smearing dark color across his pale skin.

He was aware of Vi— *Chloe's* gaze, her watchful silence, as he prowled the padded room, searching for something solid to latch the other cuff around. He was running out of time. Black spots pixilated the air. His vision was graying at the edges.

But his hunger remained, all razor teeth, unhinged jaws, and endless gullet.

And Chloe's fast and steady heart was a pulsing dinner bell, one that reverberated through all the spaces hunger had hollowed out within him. A hunger that even unconsciousness might not stop. Dante couldn't—*wouldn't*—pass out until he'd made goddamned sure she was beyond his reach.

Of course, the motherfuckers who had locked him in here with Chloe had intended otherwise. Bastards. Dante regarded the camera spying on them, a pale spider motionless in the corner. He tilted his head, wondering.

What would happen if the camera no longer worked? If they could no longer see?

Let's fucking find out.

Dante peeled off his Mad Edgar tee, handcuffs clanking

together as he pulled them through the armhole. Then he tossed the black cotton blindfold over the camera. The movement cost him, stabbing splinters of frost and fire deep into his lungs. He coughed, deep and harsh, blood bubbling up in his throat. Pain throbbed at his temples, behind his eyes.

"Won't that make them mad?" Chloe asked.

Dante nodded, then touched a finger to his lips, then to one ear, tilted his head toward the now-blind eye and mouthed, *Let 'em wonder*. Chewing her lower lip, Chloe glanced at the T-shirt draped camera before returning her attention to him. She mouthed, *Okay*.

Vision wavering, Dante stumbled, but managed—barely—to keep his balance. Paper wings rustled. Sneakers scraped against concrete, and he knew that Chloe was hurrying over to help him. He threw out his arm, palm extended, and shot her a dark scowl.

Chloe stopped short with a frustrated sigh that sounded decades older than the both of them put together. Dante flapped another *vite-vite* hand at her. Not waiting on her, he turned around, steadying himself with a hand to the wall, and made his careful way to the thick gotta-keep-the-monsters-inside door—and the steel handle welded to its surface.

He hoped it would be strong enough.

Even though Chloe turned and went to the opposite side of the room, the hypnotic rush of the blood through her veins plucked at Dante, as did her scent—strawberries and soap—and the flush of her freckled skin.

Her blood spills hot and fragrant and crimson over his fingers . . .

Throat tight, eyes burning, Dante refused the image and kept moving.

Hunger kept insisting that he was going the wrong way, that he needed to turn his ass around and follow his nose to the appetizer now sitting glumly in the far corner with her arms wrapped around her purple corduroy–clad legs.

Fuck you, fuck you, fuck you. Ain't listening. And we ain't feasting until some curious asshole opens that door and saunters inside.

Laughter, dark and knowing, sounded from the depths below. Jaw tight, Dante blocked it out, stubbornly adhering to his *ain't listening* declaration.

Just as Dante reached the door, the room took a gleeful, stomach-dropping plunge, before spinning around him again with wild Tilt-A-Whirl abandon. Stumbling, he slammed against the door shoulder-first, before falling to his knees on the concrete. A high-pitched humming filled his ears. Darkness oozed like oil across his sight.

"*Pas encore,*" he said, his voice a barely audible growl, "*pas fucking encore.*"

Fumbling the open cuff around the door's steel handle, he snapped it shut with a shaking hand. The cuff *tunk*ed as he sat back on his heels. Then he sagged against the door, his captive right arm bent at the elbow and stretched up alongside him. Dante shivered, the door's steel like ice against the bare skin of his shoulder and side.

"Dante-angel?" A worry-thick whisper.

Dante's vision was tunneling down, swallowed by deepening shadows, as he focused on Chloe. He held a finger against his lips, reminding her. She mirrored his motion, a finger to her own lips, freckles and dismay stark upon her face. He tried to offer her a reassuring smile, but given her unaltered expression, he had a feeling he hadn't pulled it off.

Behind her, he saw the cheerful red balloon she'd drawn on the padded wall. A small stick figure with black wings held the balloon's string.

You saved me when I died and floated away from my mommy. Creawdwr . . .

The word and its meaning itched at the back of his mind; hidden beneath miles of cotton, an itch he couldn't reach. Dante dragged in another gurgling breath of air, then coughed, lungs spasming. Choking. A heavy weight crushed down on him as though the sky had fallen on his chest, bringing the moon with it. He couldn't breathe.

But he *could* drown. *Could* suffocate on his own blood. Even sitting up. Sinking into cold and darkness and high-pitched humming, Dante fought to suck in one more breath.

And failed.

8

FULL OF SURPRISES

RICHARD PURCELL'S GAZE SKIPPED along the patient room monitors set into the wall above the observation booth's control panel until it came to rest once more on the only monitor that interested him, the only monitor that also happened to be blank—blindfolded by a goddamned T-shirt.

Smug little bloodsucking bastard.

No visual, but the audio worked just fine, and at the moment Purcell was listening to wet choking sounds as someone quietly drowned in their own blood. Sweet music—damned sweet—given it was S doing all that quiet drowning.

A little less sweet were Violet's frantic cries for help, her words punctuated by fists banging against the steel door, but hey, you couldn't have everything. Such as a working camera feed when it mattered most. Such as watching a certain smug little bloodsucking bastard go down for the count. Even if it was only temporary.

"We need a doctor! Please, Mr. Purcell! Please, please, please! Open the door!"

The wet choking sounds slowed, then stopped.

For a second, nothing but silence crackled through the speakers. A slight pause, just long enough for someone to suck in a shocked breath, then Violet intensified both her fist assault against the door and the decibel level of her shouts.

"Mr. Purcell, please, pretty please, open the door! Tyler! Joe! Help!"

With a grimace of annoyance, Purcell lowered the volume, reducing Violet's distraught cries to faint background noise. "Christ."

"I knew this wouldn't work. We need the Wallace woman," Teodoro Díon said, a faint European accent giving his words a sophisticated flow that almost hid the accusation beneath them—you *fucked up and wasted* my *time.*

A quiet fury curdled in Purcell's belly and he tasted bile, bitter and hot, at the back of his throat. In an effort to keep his anger in check, he stared at the green telltales winking and glowing on the control panel.

No one could've predicted that James Wallace would show up at the club—and on the same goddamned day, no less— with hired assault-rifle wielding thugs to snatch his daughter before Purcell could grab her. He'd been given no choice but to make the best of a bad situation, which had meant improvising.

And that's exactly what he'd done.

Purcell had snatched an unconscious S—already pumped full of bullets and bleeding like a motherfucker—from the burning club, instead of doing as Díon had insisted and chasing after the van carrying Heather Wallace, a van burning rubber all the way to the interstate. No. Instead, he'd brought S here. Where he belonged.

Much to Teodoro Díon's displeasure.

Fuck Teodoro Díon.

This unofficial and unsanctioned little mission had originally been Special Operations Director Celeste Underwood's baby, a mission she'd entrusted to Purcell alone, a mission he'd accepted without hesitation, even though he knew it would mean the end of their careers—hell, the end of their lives—if discovered.

Both he and SOD Underwood viewed themselves as loyal SB agents, even though they hadn't always agreed with certain policies—such as allowing a dangerous killer like S to roam free. Both agreed the world would be a better, safer place with S turned to ash.

The plan had been for Purcell to quietly see it done.

But then SOD Underwood's socialite daughter-in-law had been acquitted of the murder-for-hire death of Underwood's only son, Stephen. Not unusual when the bastard charged with the actual killing conveniently hangs himself in his jail cell (with shoelaces he wasn't supposed to have), leaving an equally convenient note behind proclaiming he'd acted alone and the death was the result of a robbery gone wrong, that no one had hired him to murder Stephen Underwood, let alone his wife, Valerie.

So the plan had changed slightly. Underwood decided to employ S one last time, a fanged vehicle for much-delayed justice. Purcell's job had been to travel to New Orleans, activate S's programming, and sic him on the daughter-in-law.

Then permanently retire S afterward.

It was the least Purcell could do for the woman who'd mentored his career from the very beginning and who'd always entrusted him with her secrets.

But all that had changed four days ago when Díon called him in New Orleans to inform him of SOD Underwood's sudden and unexpected death by stroke.

So how come you're breaking the news?

So we could discuss mutual concerns.

Those being . . . ?

Terminating Prejean and fulfilling Underwood's last request. She told me about the gift for her daughter-in-law you were set to deliver.

Prejean—the name given to S by his final set of foster parents. He'd thanked them by making sure they were deader than doornails before torching their house.

Dante Baptiste—S's true full name, according to Díon.

S—the Bad Seed designation that Purcell preferred, a

reminder of what the bloodsucker truly was, a programmed True Blood sociopath that had been allowed to slip his leash.

Keep talking.

We're not going to kill S, we're going to break *him.*

Díon believed Heather Wallace to be an intrinsic component of that goal and had built his plan around her. A simple plan, really. Since he was already in New Orleans on Underwood's behalf, Purcell was supposed to grab the redhead at the first opportunity, transport her to the SB-operated sanitarium/study lab—S's old training grounds as a kid—and then make sure the bloodsucking psycho knew right where to find her.

So he could watch her die. Hard and ugly.

But then James Wallace and his ill-timed paternal outrage had showed up . . .

Purcell nodded at the T-shirt-blanked monitor. "Heather Wallace, my ass. Maybe if the bastard could've focused on his hunger instead of his next goddamned breath, he might've drained the kid like he was supposed to."

"The resin keeps him from healing," Díon explained patiently. "Slows him down, and the continued blood loss keeps his hunger sharp. Hopefully it short-circuits his telepathy as well. Perhaps even his other gifts."

Purcell frowned. "Other gifts?" He swiveled his chair around so he could see Díon. "What other gifts?"

The SB interrogator regarded Purcell with amused purple eyes from where he leaned against the wall, hands tucked into the pockets of his trousers. Toffee-colored hair and short, stylish sideburns framed his face, making him look younger than the forty-two or forty-three Purcell pegged him at, as did his tall, athletic build.

"He's a True Blood and it varies, but you can bet he's full of surprises," Díon said, shrugging one shoulder.

"Surprises like what?"

"Flying. Fire. Shape-shifting. Telekinesis."

"How about making little girls look like someone else?"

Another very European shrug—from a man Purcell suspected wasn't even completely human. "With True Bloods, you never know."

Whatever Díon was, it wasn't vamp. Not with his tanned olive skin and regular daytime hours. But given his ability to alter and wipe memories, to extract information from even the most reluctant mind with a soft word and a deft touch, he couldn't be human either.

"But *you* seem to be in the know," Purcell pointed out. "Sounds like you stumbled across a copy of *True Blood Psychos for Dummies* in the bargain bin at Barnes & Noble. Care to share?"

"Psycho," Díon rolled the word slowly as though tasting it. "Given that the whole purpose behind Bad Seed was to create sociopaths, I'd think that you'd be proud of S. But it sounds like you resent him for being what he was conditioned to be. Did you feel the same contempt for the human members of Bad Seed—before they were permanently retired?"

Folding his arms over his chest, Purcell shook his head. "See . . . I always thought Bad Seed was one huge fucking mistake—not that my input was sought, needed, or welcomed. Creating sociopaths to study them? What bullshit. That was *never* the plan."

"But creating them to use and control was?"

"Bingo. The day that I transferred out of the project to become Underwood's assistant was a good day. But I never forgot S. Never forgot what he was capable of. Or what he was programmed to do. Fucking little psycho."

Díon shrugged. "I'm not convinced that term applies to Baptiste. He did everything he could to keep away from Violet, despite his hunger and blood loss. Hardly the actions of a psycho."

"That's what he wants you to think. S is just playing games with us. You don't know him the way I do. Let your guard down and I promise you, that fucking psycho you're so busy defending will tear your heart out and eat it."

"Hence the resin," Díon pointed out. "I have no intention

of letting my guard down. And I'm not defending, merely trying to understand. Know thy enemy, yes?"

"Definitely," Purcell agreed, holding the interrogator's gaze. "Always wise." But S wasn't the enemy as far as Purcell was concerned, only an evil in need of eradication. Díon, on the other hand, was another story entirely—especially since Purcell had an ever-deepening suspicion that Díon had somehow caused Underwood's fatal stroke.

She never would've told Díon about our plans. Never would've included anyone else. Not when our lives depended on no one ever finding out we were behind it.

"Looks like we're going to have to try something else where Baptiste is concerned," Díon said. "This bit with 'Chloe' didn't work."

Purcell glanced sourly at the blank monitor. "Even if the bastard *had* killed the kid, I never thought it would break him. He survived Chloe's loss the first time he murdered her."

"Which is why I wanted Heather Wallace," Díon said. "For now, let's get Violet out of that room, then send a medic to clear Baptiste's lungs."

Activating the com set hooked around his ear with a touch, Purcell issued the orders, making certain his men understood that restraining S was their first order of business. "Don't hesitate to put another bullet in his skull, if necessary. And get that goddamned T-shirt off the camera."

Purcell caught a whiff of Díon's cologne—a hint of vanilla spice and dandelions—when the interrogator moved from the wall to rest one hip against the edge of the control panel. "Have you heard anything yet from your Bureau contacts about where James Wallace might've taken his daughter?" he asked.

"The Bureau's official line is that Special Agent James Wallace is on leave while he tends to personal matters," Purcell replied. "Wallace didn't say where he was going or what he was doing, and his SAC probably didn't ask, but whether it was by GPS tag or a tail, you can bet your well-tailored ass he knows."

"No doubt."

"But the only way we're going to find out where Wallace went is for you to fly to the Portland field office and extract the information directly from the SAC's mind." Purcell shook his head. "Forget Heather Wallace."

"No, she's key to breaking Baptiste."

"You're wrong," Purcell stated matter-of-factly. "I doubt Heather Wallace is anything more than a piece of ass to S. Just a way of literally fucking authority."

Díon folded his arms over his chest. "No, she's more than that to him. I have reason to believe he loves her. His hold on reality is slipping and Heather Wallace balances him, anchors him. If he loses her, he loses everything."

Purcell regarded the interrogator skeptically. "Loves her? Anchors him? How the hell do you know any of that? Sounds like bullshit to me."

"A reliable source, one close to Baptiste."

Meaning Díon plucked the information from someone's mind, someone in the know where S was concerned. But that didn't make it true. Didn't make it stink any less of bullshit. S could've easily fooled the unintentional informant into believing that he actually gave a rat's ass about Heather Wallace.

But, devil's advocate and all, what if it was true?

"Why the hell is it so important to break him, anyway? I don't understand what your goal is here. If you succeed, then what? What's in it for you?"

All expression vanished from Díon's face. His gaze turned inward. "I get to fulfill a promise I made a very long time ago."

Purcell frowned. "Not good enough. Not this time. I need you to be a little less cryptic for a change. What promise? To who?"

"I could tell you, but then I'd have to erase it from your memory after I did. Are you sure you want those answers?"

A chill rippled down Purcell's spine. Despite Díon's teasing smile, he suspected the interrogator meant every word. Díon *would* tell him, and then he'd take the knowledge away again. "Think I'll pass," he managed to say through a mouth gone dry. "Thanks, anyway."

Díon shrugged as if he didn't care either way. Bastard probably didn't either. Purcell twitched upright in his chair when a voice buzzed into his ear over the com set. Holding up a wait-a-moment finger, he listened as Bronson reported in, then repeated the information being relayed to Díon.

"They're in. And you were right—S cuffed himself to the door handle. The kid is quiet at the moment, coloring on the wall." Purcell directed his gaze to the empty monitor and increased the volume on the audio. "Camera should be working in—ah, there it is."

Images sprang to life on the monitor as a black-suited man with a blond buzz-cut—FA Bronson—tossed S's T-shirt onto the concrete floor. Behind him, S was sprawled on his side on the floor, one arm stretched up above him, wrist cuffed to the door handle. A small puddle of bright blood encircled his pale face, stained his lips, like water forced from the lungs of a drowning victim.

Bronson's partner, a tall and rangy black man named Holland, was bent over the handle, trying to unlock the cuff. Across the room, Violet watched silently with red-rimmed eyes, her box of crayons clutched in her hands.

Bronson stepped away from the camera, touching a finger to the com set hooked around one ear. "You receiving the feed now?" he asked, the monitor's audio echoing the words Purcell heard directly in his ear.

"Yes, and you need to secure—" A sudden movement near the door caught Purcell's eye and stopped his words cold. It hit him then—*like water forced from the lungs of a drowning victim.* His heart leapt into his throat.

It was already too late.

S *moved.* Twisting up from the concrete floor with deadly grace and speed, his fangs slashed into Holland's throat with all the unerring accuracy of a preternatural predator—a true, natural-born killer.

Blood sprayed the air in a glistening crimson arc as S ripped his fangs free of Holland's throat, then shoved him away. Eyes wide, mouth a stretched and silent O, Holland was still crumpling to the floor, one hand futilely clutching his ruined throat, when S curled his cuffed arm, hard biceps bunching, and yanked.

With a screech of metal, the steel handle wrenched free of the door to dangle like a charm from the cuff still encircling the bloodsucker's wrist.

The handcuffs were vampire-proof. The door handle, not so much.

S was on his feet. He blurred up behind Bronson in a streak of leather and blood-smeared white skin, just as the agent, a frown pinching the skin between his eyes, was starting to whirl around, his hand reaching inside his jacket for his gun.

"J'ai faim."

S buried his fangs in the man's throat.

Bronson never even had the chance to fire a single shot.

"Madre de Dios," Díon breathed, stunned. "Even with the resin . . ."

"No, he's slower than usual. You were right about that, anyway."

"That's slower?"

Purcell didn't waste time on words like *I told you so*. Not now. Instead, he sounded the alarm and tersely issued kill orders through his com set while he watched S turn a human being into a meal. Again.

"No more attempts to break the psychotic little bastard," Purcell snapped when Díon started to protest. "Those were my men he killed. S dies. He's too goddamned dangerous."

"I'm sorry, truly," Díon said quietly.

Before Purcell could decide if the interrogator was referring to the idiocy of his plan or apologizing for the men who'd just died needlessly because of it, he felt warm fingers brush against his temple. Panic surged through him, only to vanish as his mind blanked like a T-shirt-blocked monitor. A request, quiet and reasonable, and made in a faintly European-accented voice, dominated his awareness.

"You need to rescind that order."

9

BENEATH PAIN AND BROKEN GLASS

"THEY'RE COMING. WE NEED to *hurry*."

The voice, small and tremulous but insistent, tugged at Dante, drew him up from his unfinished feast, from the coppery, adrenaline-peppered taste of the blood flooding into his mouth and pouring strength and energy into his veins. The cold icing him from the inside melted away. The liquid weight eased from his lungs—not gone, no, but less.

Pulling his fangs free of the warm, whisker-stubbled flesh beneath, Dante lifted his head. He swiveled around on his knees, wiping his mouth with the back of his hand, then—*her blood spills hot and fragrant and crimson over his fingers . . .*

—reality shifted and a cold hand squeezed around his heart.

She lies on the concrete floor, staring up at the hook, her blue eyes as wide and empty as a doll's. The blood from her slashed throat stains her hair a deep red.

Dante sucked in a sharp, painful breath and squeezed his eyes shut. Pressing his fingers against his temples, he desperately scrubbed the image from his mind.

"They're coming," the dead girl repeated. "What do we do?"

His answer came without hesitation, a rough whisper. "Make 'em pay."

"Or run. We could try running. I think that'd be better."

"Yeah?"

Dante opened his eyes. Relief flooded through him at what he saw, knocked him back on his heels. *Not dead.* Chloe stood a few feet away, freckles stark on her pale face, her blue eyes huge, red-rimmed as though she'd been crying. She hugged the box of crayons tightly against her chest instead of Orem.

"Dante-angel? You . . . um . . . okay?"

"*Oui. Ça va bien.* Now. But where's—" Dante looked down for the plushie orca and his words jammed up in his throat. A man in a blood-soaked black suit lay sprawled on the floor, throat savaged, a cooling and unfinished not-so-happy meal. "Shit."

He remembered taking the asshole down as he reached for his gun, remembered tearing into his throat with ravenous relish. Remembered the panicked, fire hose intensity of the blood pulsing between his lips.

All while Chloe watched.

"Shit," Dante repeated, shifting his gaze to Chloe. "Did you close your eyes?" he asked, hoping against hope.

"I did," she confessed in a tiny voice. "But I could still hear . . ."

Dante sighed. "*Merde.* Sorry, princess."

"That's why you cuffed yourself to the door, huh?" Chloe said. "Why you told me to keep away from you. So you wouldn't"—she looked at the dead man sprawled on the concrete, then swallowed hard before returning her gaze to Dante—"do *that*."

Dante rose to his feet. Pain jabbed his skull, dizzying him for one brief moment. Even though he felt better after the gulped infusion of hot and heady blood, he definitely wasn't at one hundred percent. Not even close. But it would have to be enough.

Survival for both of them depended on it.

"*Oui, chère*. That's why," he replied.

Out in the hall, Dante heard the thunder of multiple pairs of running feet. Still a fair distance away, but getting closer with each passing second. He glanced at Chloe. Wondered if she was safe with him or not. Although his hunger was currently under control, it was far from sated, leaving his control unreliable at best.

But one quick look at the hook hanging from the ceiling, at the merciless slice of curving metal, told him that Chloe was safer *with* him than without. Besides, safe or not, he could never leave her behind. Never leave her alone. He'd made a promise: You and me, princess. Forever and ever.

Dante shifted his gaze back to Chloe. "They're coming like you said, princess, so we need to haul ass." He reached for her, but she took a hesitant step away from his blood-smeared hand. The fear in her eyes was an ice pick to his heart.

"You said to keep away."

"I did, yeah. Because I couldn't control my hunger. I've got a grip on it now, thanks to him"—Dante nodded at the black-suited body cooling on the floor—"but before that, with all the blood loss and the—"

"And the owies," Chloe finished, the fear fading from her eyes. "They made you even hungrier, huh?"

"Yup. And I'm damned fucking sure that's why they put me in here with you in the first place. They wanted me to . . ." Dante shook his head, unwilling to finish the sentence.

But Chloe finished it for him. "Drink me all up. Monsters and fairy tales and poisoned apples."

"'Fraid so, *p'tite*."

Footsteps pounded ever closer. Dante heard the humming-bird-pulse of mortal hearts. Heard the slide of rounds being chambered. "We need to go, princess. Now. Even if you say no, I'm taking you with me. I ain't leaving you for them."

Chloe nodded, her tangled red tresses dancing against her purple Winnie-the-Pooh sweater. "Okay," she said, "here"—she extended her hand, the fingers uncurling to reveal the key resting on her palm—"I kept it."

Dante accepted the key with a quick smile and unlocked the cuff with its dangling door handle charm from around his wrist. Cuffs, key, and door handle hit the concrete, the room's padded walls swallowing the musical clang.

Chloe's paper wings rustled and her sweet strawberry-and-soap scent washed over Dante as he snugged her securely against his side. She looped an arm around his waist, instinctively tucking her fingers through his belt. Anchoring herself.

He frowned, wondering when he'd grown so much taller than her and, taking in the leather pants and boots he wore, he also wondered where his jeans and duct-taped Converse sneakers had vanished to. Not that he was complaining, but . . .

Wrong. This is still all wrong. Wake the fuck up.

Dante shoved the troubling thought aside. It would have to wait.

"Hold on tight, *chère*," he warned, snugging her even closer.

"'Kay."

After aiming a dark and savage fuck-you smile at the camera, Dante *moved*. He sped out into the hall, streaking past rows of closed steel doors and security/medical monitoring stations, and bewildered faces as he blurred past, a cool and unexpected gust of wind—one most likely smelling of fresh blood, death, and strawberries.

"It feels like we're flying," Chloe said happily. "Even without your wings."

Dante was about to remind her that he wasn't an angel and therefore lacked wings in the first place, when he heard determined shouts behind them, followed by muted *thwips* as bullets or trank darts breezed past. Whatever they were—bullets or darts—one breezed through his hair. Then pain burned across the top of his shoulder as another grazed his flesh. Blood trickled hot down his back.

"No bullets!" someone shouted, voice tight and furious. "You might hit the girl."

Surprised that anyone gave a damn, but still not risking a glance over his shoulder to see who, Dante tightened his grip on Chloe and kept moving.

He'd survive a bullet. Chloe wouldn't.

He surged forward, pushing for more speed, and hung a left at the next corridor T. More doors and surprised/puzzled faces blurred past. The shouts and sounds of pursuit faded, then vanished.

A glowing red EXIT–STAIRS sign appeared on the right and instinct insisted he take the stairs even while a more rational part of his mind warned him he'd have nowhere to go but down—the hard way—if he did.

Grabbing the handle, Dante yanked the door open and followed his instincts. An alarm blared and he winced as the steady shriek pierced his eardrums and his aching head. By the time the steel door thunked shut behind them, thankfully muffling the alarm, he'd already vaulted up the first flight of stairs.

He'd just rounded the fourth flight of concrete stairs when he heard the door bang open again below.

"Baptiste!"

The same determined voice from before. How was the fucker keeping up? Frowning, Dante mulled over the name said fucker had used—not Prejean, not goddamned S, but Baptiste. . . .

"There's no way out, Baptiste. You're boxing yourself in." Closer, the voice.

Ignoring it, Dante kept going until he hit the final door, wrenched it open, and raced onto the roof and into a night smelling of old tar and damp blacktop and, faintly, of dewed grass. A sudden pain spiked behind his eyes.

<Baptiste.>

A star, cool and white, burned at his mind's core. A bond. A familiar and constant presence buried beneath pain and broken glass and barbed wire. The sending carried with it the scent of rain and lilacs and sage, a scent he knew intimately.

<Baptiste. *I'm here*, cher. *Right here in the here-and-now. Find me.*>

He saw her then—waves of red hair. Twilight blue eyes, that brightened to moonlit cornflower when she laughed. Lovely, heart-shaped face. Deadly aim with a gun. A woman of heart and steel.

Heather.

10

CARNIVAL BARKER

THE WORLD TREMORED VIOLENTLY beneath Dante's feet, cracked open. The past receded. And the here-and-now poured in like storm-frothed water through a breached levee.

Lucien soaring through a star-jeweled sky—

Von feeding his blood to Heather—

Guy Mauvais and Lake Pontchartrain—

Trey transformed beneath his hands in blue fire—

Annie slapping his face, telling him, *Heather's in trouble*—

A cold-eyed man in a tan trench coat, pulling a trigger—

Dante's breath caught rough in his throat. *Heather's in trouble.* A dark and chilling possibility unfolded within his mind; maybe he wasn't here alone. Maybe Heather, Von, Silver—hell, even Annie—were locked in their own padded cells and were busy eyeing hooks curving sharp and deadly from the ceilings. One way to find out.

<Catin.>

Dante's sending boomeranged, slamming into his aching mind. His vision grayed. He tasted blood at the back of his throat as blood oozed from his nose. Puddled hot in his ears.

Dante stumbled to a halt near the roof's edge, and his heart constricted as he looked at the little girl he held so tight, so close. He couldn't breathe, but it wasn't blood that stole the air from his lungs this time.

"Chloe," he whispered.

Her blood spills hot and fragrant and crimson over his fingers . . .

She lies on the concrete floor, staring up at the hook, her blue eyes as wide and empty as a doll's. The blood from her slashed throat stains her hair a deep red.

She shook her head. "I'm Violet, remember?"

You saved me when I died and floated away from my mommy. You changed me with blue fire—made me look like this.

Creawdwr. Fallen. Nightkind.

Not a punk-ass twelve- or thirteen-year old fighting to protect his princess, but a grown-ass monster who'd killed her instead.

The truth is never what you hope it will be.

Yeah, and it usually carries a motherfucking shiv.

And at the moment, truth and the here-and-now were busy cutting the heart right out of him. It didn't matter one fucking bit that he hadn't *meant* to kill Chloe. It only mattered that he had.

Dante struggled for air, for balance, finding neither—until the rooftop door creaked open behind him. Survival instinct and the need to keep his promise—*I won't let them hurt you*—lent him all the balance he needed. Shoving Violet behind him, Dante swiveled, hissing, to face their pursuer. His warning, razor-sharp and primal, cut through the still air.

It was a warning their pursuer, tall and tawny-haired and wearing the prerequisite black suit, seemed to take to heart. The stranger came to an abrupt halt in front of the door. A com set was hooked around one of his ears.

Awesome. No doubt the bastard's already spread the word.

Dante couldn't catch said bastard's scent beneath the thick smell of his own blood. But he didn't need the bastard's scent to know that he wasn't human; the slow pendulum swing of an immortal heart and the pale green sheen of lambent eyes gave that much away.

"There's nowhere to go—unless you're planning on jumping," their pursuer said matter-of-factly. His voice carried a faint accent, one that reminded Dante of Quarter-slumming European tourists. "You'd survive, of course, but Violet might not, if your grip should slip or you landed wrong or even passed out on the way down—not unless you choose to remake her yet again"—he inclined his head respectfully—"*Creawdwr.*"

So the motherfucker knew. Even about Violet. Not good.

"You must be the trouble that showed up at the club," Dante said, voice low and tight. "You take Heather too? My friends?"

"That's Mr. Díon," Violet volunteered, peeking out from behind Dante, one hand gripping his leather-clad hip. "He's been taking care of my mommy and he gave me my crayons and he sent me here so I could see you again. It was my second time on an airplane."

"Yeah? Second time, huh?" Dante questioned, keeping his gaze on crayon-gifting Mr. Díon. Molten anger bubbled in his chest, chasing away the chill that was starting to creep back into his bones.

Bastard had intended for Violet to die beneath his fangs.

Had put her on an airplane for that reason alone.

And if he truly held Heather, his intentions for her would be equally fucked.

"As far as I know, your friends are still in New Orleans. But Heather"—Díon's lips quirked up at the corners, a tiny smile of regret—"died defending you."

Dante tensed at the cold, brass-knuckled words, then flexed them away. He felt Heather's presence at the back of his mind, a blue-white star—but distant now, galaxies away. Incommunicado. Whether it was due to drugs, pain, or whatever was preventing him from healing completely, or a mixture of all three, he didn't know.

But she was alive. That he *did* know.

Díon's little lie was a stalling tactic, yeah, a carnival barker's sideshow lure, but it also suggested that he didn't have Heather, otherwise the prick would've just said so, would've dangled her in front of Dante like the ultimate carnival prize—*hand yourself over and WIN!*

"*Menteur*," Dante said, offering a smile of his own—one dark and full of fangs and tasting of blood. "And you just told me everything I need to know."

The mocking amusement leaked from Díon's face. His expression became still, thoughtful. "And that would be?"

"You don't have Heather."

"You're wrong. She might not be dead—yet. But that can always change."

Just more lies. More carnival barker lure. More stalling bullshit.

Or so Dante desperately hoped. There was one way to be sure, to be absolutely positive, but he couldn't risk trying to send to Heather again, not if he hoped to remain conscious enough to get Violet out of there before more assholes—with guns, this time—joined the party.

A muscle ticked in Dante's jaw as he decided to ignore Díon's threatening words, choosing not to play his game—*if he truly has her, he'd offer me proof*—and lifted Violet, her paper wings crinkling, into his arms and onto his hip. She tucked her box of crayons inside her Winnie-the-Pooh sweater, then looped her arms around his neck, interlacing her fingers beneath his hair. As Dante locked an arm around her waist, he heard footsteps pounding up the stairs beyond the door.

Time to go.

Dante flexed his shoulders. His deltoid muscles rippled, then he felt the slide of velvet across his bare skin as his wings emerged, arching above his head. They unfolded behind him with a soft, leathery rustle.

"*There* they are," Violet said with quiet satisfaction.

Díon sucked in a shocked breath. The pendulum rhythm of his heart tocked a little faster "But . . . you're only a half-blood. You can't have wings . . . it isn't—"

Dante turned and leapt up onto the roof's three-foot-high concrete border. Violet tucked her head into the hollow between his neck and shoulder and snuggled in tight. His wings flared, sweeping through the air. He rose into the night, his boots lifting off the concrete.

"Hold tight," he murmured.

"'Kay," was Violet's happy response. "This is my first angel flight."

"Well, you're my first passenger, *p'tite*."

Díon's voice cut through the air. "Heather *is* here. She's hanging on a hook of her own, bleeding out, and waiting for you to come for her."

The night spun. The stars disappeared beneath the rolling wheel of the past. A memory only weeks old, still fresh, still fanged, circled into place; the loss of his *cher ami* literally at the hands of a manipulative nightkind crime journalist, who'd learned about Bad Seed and thought it time Dante learned too—the hard way.

Mon ami. *I knew you'd come for me.*

A figure hangs by the ankles from a metal hook, wrapped and hoisted in dull chains, strapped into the white cocoon of a straitjacket. Blond hair sweeps against the floor.

"Wake up, S." Ronin's finger slips across Jay's throat. Blood sprays across the grimy floor and spatters Ronin's face, the white straitjacket. Jay chokes.

"*I knew you'd come for me.*"

Jay's last words. He wouldn't let them be Heather's as well.

"It's not too late," Díon urged. "You can still save her—"

Díon's words disappeared beneath the deep droning of angry wasps. White light flickered at the edges of Dante's vision. Pain pulsed at his temples. Shivved his lungs. He swallowed back blood.

He focused on the sounds behind him—the door slamming open, the heavy thud of footsteps as more suits raced on to the roof, the sharp intake of shocked breath. Focused on *Jesus*

Christ and *holy shit*. Focused on multiple *cha-chunk*s as gun slides were pulled back.

"Hold your fire!" Díon yelled.

Wings slashing through the air in powerful strokes, Dante swung around to face the tall immortal in his black suit. He regarded Dante with wary eyes, sweat glistening at his hairline. Six suits—male and female—formed a semicircle around Díon, guns held in white-knuckled, shaking grips, faces drained of all color. A hard sweep of air from Dante's wings plastered their clothes to their bodies, gusted through their hair.

"Surrender and you can still save—"

Dante's song sprang to life, bristling with dark fury. Violet squeaked in surprise as power crackled to life along the fingers of his right hand in pale blue flames. Ghost flames, thin and wavering, barely there, but power enough to cram down Díon's lying throat. Díon's eyes suddenly widened. Panic flitted across his face. He took a careful step back toward the door.

Not now, not fucking now, that prick ain't escaping, Dante thought in mingled frustration and fury as a lightning bolt surged through his skull, torching his mind. The seizure bit into him with electric teeth. The flames surrounding his hands flickered, then vanished as though doused with water, and his song spilled away in a jumble of harsh and jagged notes.

The stars returned in brilliant and broken and endless prickles of light behind Dante's eyes. His body arched. His fangs pierced his lower lip as his jaw locked. He tasted blood, smelled it.

"He's going to drop that kid or break her damned ribs," someone warned.

"Let him," Díon replied. "Either is fine."

Just as Dante's vision whited out, he caught a quicksilver flash of movement, then felt Chloe—*no*, Violet, ma p'tite ange—yanked from his arms. Heard her scream his name. Heard Díon cursing in furious Spanish at whoever had disobeyed him.

The world whirled and Dante went with it, a torn kite tumbling from the sky. The ground rushed up at light speed, eager to meet him. He had no idea if he'd plummeted eight stories to the Dumpster-strewn blacktop below or just to the roof. Eight stories or ten feet, he hit hard. The air exploded from his lungs. Retching, he tried to suck more in, but his shock-paralyzed lungs refused to work.

"Give me your trank gun," Díon demanded from somewhere above him.

But breathing seemed like a small thing, really, maybe even an unnecessary thing, as the seizure devoured Dante with a voracious white-hot appetite. Tore him apart, joint by joint, tendon by tendon. Torqued each muscle and limb and wing without mercy.

Send it below or fucking use it.

But *below* seized the opportunity to fucking use *him* instead when the dart pierced his throat and threaded ice through his veins.

Below yanked Dante under.

Shoved him down.

Kicked his convulsing ass into the shattered, wasp-droning depths.

11

DARK PROPHECY

S HE SEES DANTE, DESPITE the fact that he's blurring up
endless flights of concrete stairs, a red-haired little girl tucked
against his side. Sees a determined scowl on his beautiful pale
face and crimson striping the deep brown of his irises. Sees blood
smeared on the skin above his heart, staining his lips, the skin
beneath his nose. His black hair trails behind him, a silken slice
of starless night.

For a moment, she thinks she has somehow stumbled into
Dante's memories since he's carrying Chloe in her Winnie-the-
Pooh sweater and purple cords tight against him. Thinks he's
caught in an old and heartbreaking loop—himself and Chloe
at the sanitarium—but then she realizes he's not the thirteen-
year-old version of himself in jeans, T-shirt, and sneakers, but the
lean-muscled adult in boots, leather pants, and bondage collar.

Not the past. Not haunted memories.

Then she notices that black paper wings are taped to the
back of Chloe's sweater. Black paper wings. No plushie orca.

The little girl isn't Chloe at all.

She's Violet. The head-shot child Dante had transformed
in the motel parking lot in Oregon. And she remembers all the

SB agents that had been there. Remembers the sweating, grim-faced agent who ordered the resurrected and newly freckled Violet and her mother away from Dante and—no doubt—into their custody.

And she knows, bone deep—no dream. Not memories. Reality.

Her pulse races. She's found him at last. Then fear knots cold in her belly. She's found him, yes—in a desperate run for survival.

A voice with a mild European twist echoes up the stairwell, calling Dante's name, but he never slows. Yanking open a door, he streaks out onto a rooftop.

She's right behind him, close enough to touch. She feels the cool night air against her face, smells old tar, coppery blood, and Dante's scent of frost and burning leaves. But when she tries to grasp his arm, to pull him against her and to safety, her fingertips brush a smooth, invisible barrier—like a one-way observation mirror in an interrogation room.

So she reaches for him through their bond instead, to let him know that he's not alone and that she's okay, to guide him back, to anchor him in the present.

<Baptiste.>

He stumbles. Nearly falls to his knees. Blood trickles from his nose. His face blanks and his shocked gaze turns inward—and seeing that, she knows he was mentally locked into the past, her psionic touch triggering an avalanche of now inside him.

<Baptiste. I'm here, *cher*. Right here in the here-and-now. Find me.>

She hears Dante's breath catch in his throat as an expression of stunned revelation washes over his face, sweeping the blankness away. Then he looks around, his expression sharp and aware and troubled, a dreamer awakening to find himself on the floor beside a bed he doesn't recognize.

She has a feeling Dante reaches back—or tries to—but scalding pain blasts through the bond and he disappears from *her sight as the mirror ripples, then shatters into thousands of glittering pieces.*

HEATHER AWAKENED, HEART THUDDING hard against her ribs, temples throbbing as the lights overhead pierced her eyes.

"Found you," she whispered. Closing her eyes again, she draped an arm across them to seal in the darkness and to prevent any last needles of light from sliding in. Her headache dimmed.

Found Dante, yes, but where? An institutional building of some kind, judging by the stairwell and the big air-conditioning units on the roof. Heather realized that the urgent, insistent tug she felt to the east was now defined as *southeast.*

It she truly was in Texas, then maybe, just maybe, Dante was still in Louisiana.

And what had happened, anyway? What had she just experienced?

Not a dream—or not *just* a dream.

Or maybe it was a vision like the ones she had of her murdered mother's last walk. But while those were glimpses into a twenty-year-old past, Heather felt in her gut, that what she'd just seen—vision, dream, farsight, whatever the hell you wanted to call it—was actually happening as she watched.

Heather was pretty damned sure that she'd been connected to Dante, that for a moment, the drugs and/or resin in his system had receded enough for her to reach him. But not enough for him to reach back, to send to her.

And attempting to had cost him—a lot.

Heather's throat tightened as she replayed the details she'd seen. Partially healed bullet wounds on Dante's chest. Blood smeared on his face, the bare skin of his chest. Bluish shadows bruising the skin beneath his eyes. Dilated pupils. A sense of wrongness, his frost and burning leaves scent tainted with a bitter undertone.

She attributed the sense of wrongness she detected to the dragon's blood tree resin and whatever drugs were being pumped into his veins, to his injuries and the muffling of their bond, to his worry for her and the others. To his goddamned captivity.

At least she tried to, anyway. But Von's warning looped through her memory, a grim whisper: *I think he's had all he can take, doll. Heart and mind . . .*

Throat tight, Heather silently agreed.

Rubber soles squeaking against tile brought Heather's arm down from her eyes. As she cautiously opened them, she discovered that her headache was gone and the light no longer bothered her.

A nurse with short, dark hair and wearing blue scrubs met Heather's regard with a quick smile. Her name tag read RN *Sue Bieri.*

"I'm sorry," the nurse chirped without a hint of regret. "I hope I didn't wake you. But there's someone here to see you, and I thought, since it's coming up on dinnertime, that it might be nice if you could share a meal with your visitor."

"Visitor?"

Frowning, Heather sat up and pushed her hair back from her face. She glanced toward the window. Night glimmered like a dark jewel beyond the glass. "Wait. What time is it?"

What if her visitor was a certain *llygad,* a green-eyed nomad?

"Seven thirty. Dinner's at eight."

"Kind of late for dinner, isn't it?"

"Not in Europe," Sue replied, then smiling, she rolled her eyes. "I know, I know—this isn't exactly Europe. But there's a very good reason why our dinners happen to be served at such an hour—it's the meds. Most of our clients sleep late because of their treatments." She shrugged. "So we adjust."

"Very civilized," Heather murmured dryly.

Seven thirty. Jesus Christ. She'd slept nearly three hours.

Even if Von *had* received her last message—something she was far from sure of—she doubted that enough time had elapsed for the nomad to a) figure out where in Texas the Strickland Institute was located, since she was pretty damned sure the place was off the grid, and b) arrive. Besides, he sure as hell wouldn't stand around waiting politely for her invitation to what would surely be a yummy institutional dinner—bathrobe optional.

Not Von, then. Heather sighed, knowing who her visitor had to be—the last person she wanted to see. But if she refused dinner with her father, it might be viewed by the Strickland powers-that-be as a setback in her therapy and cost her all the drug-free ground she'd gained.

Heather shook her head. "I'm too drained, Sue," she said, truthfully. "Another time, maybe."

"You sure, sugar? I thought you might like to have a nice meal together since it's your last night here."

Hope fluttered within Heather, a fragile butterfly. Maybe Von *had* found her, after all, and was playing it by the book. Maybe belated paternal instincts had awakened within James Wallace's cold, cold heart and he'd realized the mistake he'd made.

"My last night? Why? When did this happen?" But even as the questions bounced past her lips, another more likely possibility suddenly unfolded in Heather's mind, pricking cold along her spine.

The Bureau had found her.

Worse—what if they'd been behind everything—from James Wallace's kidnapping, arson, and attempted murder spree to Dante's disappearance—sharing the Bad Seed wealth with the SB?

Sue shrugged, a glimmer of sympathy in her eyes. "The FBI has decided to pick up the cost of your treatment, apparently, but they've chosen a different facility."

Heather sucked in a breath, belly knotting, her fear realized. But she was grateful that she'd been forewarned. "What if I don't want to go?" she asked. "I'm just getting settled here."

"I know, and it's a shame. But I'm afraid you have no say in the matter." Sue tsked and shook her head. "Just know that everyone has your best interests at heart."

Heather knew better, but kept that knowledge to herself. "Do you know where I'm being transferred?"

"No, I don't," Sue replied. "But I'm sure it'll be fine—wherever it is."

Heather doubted that with every fiber of her being. The FBI planned to fulfill their dark prophecy—mental illness and a tragic suicide. One less loose end.

She couldn't wait for Von to find her. She needed to escape before morning.

Before the FBI made her vanish. Permanently.

"So how about it? Dinner with your father? Might be your last chance for a while."

"Does he know about the move?"

"I don't believe he does. Yet. The news just came down."

Heather's pulse raced as an idea, a wild and dangerous gamble, took shape in her mind. "Y'know, I think you might be right about that last chance stuff. Please tell my"—she forced the word out through clenched teeth—"father that I'd love to have dinner with him."

Sue's smile returned full force, a whitened laser beam of cheer. "That's wonderful, sugar. I'll let him know."

Heather smiled as well, but the cheer offered up by her lips was cold and hollow. "You do that," she said.

12

NOTHING PERSONAL

TEODORO DÍON PULLED A chair up beside the steel examination table and sat, elbows to knees, chin to steepled fingers, and studied Purcell's handiwork.

The white, leather-strapped straitjacket fit as snugly as though it'd been tailored specifically for Dante, which, Teodoro had no doubt, it had been, its thick leather straps pulled painfully tight.

Straitjackets worked just as well on vampires as they did on mortals. Of course, straitjackets for vampires were woven of more durable stuff than those manufactured for mortals. Still, the simple fact remained—if you couldn't move your arms or use your hands, you couldn't tear free—even with preternatural strength.

But Purcell hadn't stopped at the straitjacket.

Double loops of steel gleamed at Dante Baptiste's socked ankles, a pair of handcuffs on each. Each cuff's twin and linking chain had been pulled down through a slot in the table and pulled taut from underneath, before being looped back over the table's edge to snap the second cuff shut around the same wrist or ankle.

Handcuffs double-looped. Slots that couldn't be wrenched free like welded-on door handles, since they were part of the table. Metal bands across Dante's chest and thighs.

All made of reinforced vampire-proof steel.

But *creawdwr*-proof was another matter entirely, Teodoro knew.

When Purcell had called yesterday to tell him that Dante wasn't healing from the bullet wounds, that he was, in fact, bleeding out, Teodoro had instantly known what James Wallace had put in his bullets, because he'd once used sap from the dragon's blood tree himself for a very similar purpose centuries ago.

Fatal to True Bloods, yes, but Dante's Fallen heritage had saved his life—barely. And because of that, Teodoro had believed—no, be honest, had *hoped*—that the resin, in combination with the damage James Wallace had wreaked with his oh-so-well-placed bullets, would short-circuit Dante's use of the *creu tân*.

And it had. Until Dante had managed to make a snack out of Bronson.

Until that awful moment on the rooftop.

On midnight wings, Dante rises from the sanitarium's roof.

Fury shadows his pale, blood-streaked face. His eyes blaze with gold light. Blue flames flicker to life around his fingers as his anhrefncathl *slashes a dark and savage melody into the night.*

Teodoro stares, dread and awe pulsing through his veins in equal measure. He's never seen a creawdwr in action before, never seen a living creawdwr—*until now. And he has a gut-knotting suspicion that it might be the last thing he ever sees.*

But a split second later, Dante's eyes roll back into his head. The seizure's sucker punch breaks his song, snuffs the flames, and slams him back down to the roof.

While the seizure had been a welcome surprise, the wings had been both unexpected and problematic. Teodoro had never imagined that Dante would have wings. No half-blood did. At least not those born of Fallen and mortal unions. Perhaps it was different with vampire-Fallen offspring, although he didn't know of any. More likely the reason rested in who and what Dante was—*creawdwr*.

In any case, Teodoro had carefully erased the memory of Dante's wings from the minds of each agent on the roof. No one else needed to know what Dante was.

Not yet.

Not even Purcell. Although Teodoro could just imagine the man's reaction.

You're telling me that this bloodsucking son of a bitch not only has wings and a fallen angel daddy, but he's also a fucking god? What goddamned bullshit.

A fucking god, yes. Bullshit, no.

"So do I get your stamp of approval?" Purcell asked from the foot of the table.

Back in the moment once more, Teodoro nodded, then murmured, "Nice work. This should actually hold him."

"Personally, I think shooting him full of resin and hoisting him onto the hook would hold him even better," Purcell grumbled. "But, yeah, this'll work. Lucky for you he had that seizure. Why the hell couldn't he have had the damned thing *before* he slaughtered two of my men?"

"Their error," Teodoro pointed out with a shrug. "You *did* tell them to make sure Baptiste was secured before doing anything else and they failed to do so."

Purcell blew out an exasperated breath in agreement.

"His file doesn't mention seizures," Teodoro commented, slanting a glance at Purcell. "I take it that's something new?"

Purcell raked a hand through his gray-flecked sandy hair, then nodded. "Definitely. And he had one yesterday following surgery, but I have no idea what's causing them and—to be honest—I really don't give a rat's ass. For all I know maybe it's an indication that his sanity is about to take that plunge you've got such a hard-on for."

"Perhaps," Teodoro agreed, straightening in his chair. He thought of the elaborate scar on the *creawdwr*'s left pectoral, near his heart. A sigil. One Teodoro had recognized—as any nephilim would. His jaw tightened.

"And the mark on his chest?" He jerked his chin at Dante. "Is that new too?"

"He didn't have it the last time we picked him up and brought him in," Purcell said. "But that was six, almost seven, years ago. S usually keeps his shirt on when he's onstage with his band, so there's no telling when he got it. What does it matter? It's just one of those neoprimitive cuttings or whatever."

Teodoro shrugged. "Simply curious."

"So what now? You still plan on breaking him even after all this?"

"Definitely. But I think I'll take a look inside this time"— Teodoro air-tapped a finger next to his own temple—"and see if I can find the best way to accomplish that goal."

"Christ." Purcell sighed. "Talk about a waste of time, but fine. You do that. I'll go check on the kid, tell her that her goddamned angel is all right and blah, blah, blah. Any other instructions before I go?"

Teodoro frowned, considering. Bright blood welled up from the half-healed bullet wounds above Dante's heart, soaking through the canvas straitjacket in a small dark circle. It also trickled dark along his temple and pooled in his ear.

"Yes," Teodoro replied. "Have a medic waiting on standby."

"If you want the bastard to heal, then you should quit giving him the resin."

Teodoro lifted his gaze to Purcell, met his unreadable olive green eyes. "I don't want him to *heal*. I want him *weak*."

"Weak is good," Purcell said. "Dead is better."

"Be patient and we'll both get what we want."

"Bronson and Holland are dead. How's that for patient?" Turning, Purcell kicked Dante's discarded boots from his path and strode from the room.

Teodoro wondered if he'd made a mistake in taking only temporary control of the prickly agent's mind—a brief visit, one just long enough to make Purcell rescind his shoot-the-little-fucking-psycho order and erase the memory of having ever given that order in the first place.

If so, it was a mistake that could be corrected, if necessary.

Once Purcell had exited the room, Teodoro scooted his chair closer to the table and gave his attention to the sigil above the drugged and dreaming *creawdwr*'s heart.

He'd lied when he'd told Purcell the scar didn't matter. In truth, it mattered a great deal because it was the Morningstar's mark and a blood pledge. Which begged the very troubling question: How had Dante managed to remain free in the mortal world, given that the Fallen—or at least the Morningstar—apparently knew of his existence?

Teodoro touched the blood-soaked spot on the straitjacket, his finger tracing the sigil's design from memory upon the material—an upside-down pyramid with a smaller reversed triangle hooked to its base with graceful curlicues.

"Foolish child," he whispered. "What bargain did you make with the Devil?"

Dante's head was turned toward Teodoro, his pale, pale face half hidden beneath a fall of night-black hair. Blood glistened beneath his nose, smeared his cupid's-bow lips, its coppery odor mingling with the autumn sharp scent of frost and burning leaves. Teodoro moved his hand up from Dante's chest and trailed a finger along his smooth jawline. Brushed the pad of his thumb across that full kiss-me-bite-me lower lip.

Breathtaking.

Even bloodied and unconscious, the *creawdwr*'s beauty scorched. Hinted at tangled sheets and hungry moans. Moonlight and fire seemed to pulse white-hot through his veins, smoldering beneath his alabaster skin, skimming the length of his lean-muscled body—intoxicating and deadly.

Tempting.

A unique creature—even in beauty and power and blood-line.

And the only *creawdwr* in existence.

Teodoro felt a sharp, unexpected pang of regret. He planned to shatter a *creawdwr*'s fragile sanity and reshape him into the Great Destroyer, leaving the Fallen no choice but to kill the Maker they'd spent thousands of years yearning and searching for before he unmade the mortal world and their own.

But no matter how beautiful Dante was, or how brutally he'd been used by others, no matter how innocent of long-ago Elohim crimes, Teodoro refused to let his sudden sympathy sway him from his course.

He'd waited too long. Committed too many crimes to simply shrug and walk away. Not after subverting minds and ending lives to reach this very moment.

A moment the Fallen had brought down upon themselves when they'd sentenced his daughter to death by poison simply for speaking out for change, for a better place in Elohim society.

His Felicia had also been beautiful, and ill-used, and innocent. No sudden sympathy had spared her life. As she'd died in his arms while the Fallen had idly watched, Teodoro had given her a promise: *I will take everything from them,* mi hija, *just as they have taken everything from us.*

No, Dante's beauty and power and unique bloodline would end with him.

It was nothing personal. Just a knife into the cold, dark heart of the Fallen.

Wheels. Circles. Cycles. The Elohim's long-overdue Second Fall lay strapped to a steel table, fate incarnate in leather pants and ringed collar.

Teodoro slid his fingers up to Dante's temple. He bowed his head, closed his eyes, then inhaled deeply. He slipped through the *creawdwr*'s drug-thinned shields, pushing into his mind with ease, and entered—

—Hell. Searing heat engulfs Teodoro in a fiery maelstrom of nightmarish images, of angry droning and mocking whispers and molten pain, scorching his thoughts, his senses—

Metallic wasps burrow beneath milk-white skin . . .

I'll make sure you regret every breath you've ever drawn . . .

An anarchy symbol cut into a pale torso . . .

A fire-blackened and broken window stretches across an endless horizon . . .

No escape for you, sweetie . . .

A face composed of blue neon ones and zeros flickers between glowing hands . . .

We ain't done, you and me . . .

Wearing shades and a wide, cheerful grin, the Perv lifts a blood-smeared knife into the air, then slashes it back down . . .

That's my Bad Seed bro . . .

Holy, holy, holy . . .

Teodoro retreated—no, *fled*—snapping back into his own body with a jolt that left his heart pounding and his mouth dry. ¡*Madre de Dios*! He felt Dante stir beneath his fingers, his blood-smeared face troubled, and Teodoro fought against the instinctive urge to snatch his hand away.

Any regret he still felt withered and died. Dante had been doomed even before Teodoro had found him. All he had done was speed up the process.

Whether it was because of the implanted programming, the memory fragmentation, the countless cruelties he'd endured, or all of the above, Dante's mind was irreparably damaged and he already walked the path to madness. Stood near the mouth of the abyss, in fact, his walls and defenses beginning to crumble around him.

All Dante needed was one more good shove.

Teodoro had no idea—absolutely none—how Dante managed to remain on his feet and functioning, let alone coherent. His ability to do so hinted at a stubborn strength that Teodoro respected—even as it left him feeling just a tad uneasy.

Just how hard would that shove need to be?

Fumbling his handkerchief from his trouser pocket, Teodoro wiped the sweat from his brow as he imagined the sigil scarring Dante's chest. He still hadn't learned what pledge had been made between Dante and the Morningstar.

Unlike Purcell, who didn't give a rat's ass about certain details—the identity of Dante's father, the reason for his seizures, to name a couple—Teodoro preferred to be armed with every bit of information available. That way, some missing piece of knowledge wouldn't sneak up behind him and bite him on the ass later.

No choice—Teodoro would have to go back inside. Tucking his handkerchief back into his pocket, he drew in a deep breath, carefully shielded his mind, then took the plunge back into Dante Baptiste's mind.

The second time wasn't any easier—the raging chaos still hit like a brass-knuckled fist. But this time Teodoro noticed a cool, blue-white light radiating calm and quiet and stillness at the firestorm's furious heart.

A bond. Someone had bonded the *creawdwr*.

Teodoro's stomach sank. *What do you want to bet that someone is the Morningstar? No wonder Dante wears his mark.*

Teodoro negotiated his way past waves of never-ending whispers and swarms of droning wasps, their metallic wings ablaze and trailing drops of molten steel; skirted around memories rippling from past to present and back like a deck of cards in a magician's sleight-of-hand flourish—first the faces, now only the backs—presto, chango.

When Teodoro reached the steady, but muted—the resin and/or drugs?—flame of the bond, he made an exciting discovery. The bond belonged to Heather, not the Morningstar.

Something else never before seen: a *creawdwr* taking a mortal as bondmate—Dante had claimed a *human* as *calon-cyfaill.*

It made him vulnerable.

All Teodoro needed to do was forge a temporary link to the

bond; then, even outside Dante's mind, he could tap into it and follow the ethereal tether straight to the former FBI agent—like a Heather-centric dowsing rod.

And the beautiful redhead would become that last good, hard shove.

Just as Teodoro reached for the bond's cool light, he heard laughter, low and dark and amused from the ember-lit depths below. Smelled frost and burning leaves and cold, cold rage. He froze.

"Hey, motherfucker." From right beside him. "I don't remember inviting you."

Teodoro caught a glimpse of a pale, hard-knuckled fist, orange flames glinting from silver rings on the fingers and thumb, then an explosion of electricity shocked through his skull and whited out his mind.

TEODORO BLINKED. THE SQUARE white ceiling tiles swam into focus. He was no longer in his chair, but flat on his back on the hard, concrete floor. He sucked in a mouthful of ozone-flavored air, trying to calm his triple-timing heart.

Had he just been *sucker punched* by an unconscious subject? Tossed out of a doped and damaged mind and onto his ass?

An icy finger trailed the length of Teodoro's still-tingling spine. *Imposible.* He sat up, then eased to his feet, holding on to the back of the chair for support like an old man, an unbalanced man, a *weak* man, in need of a walker. He fisted his other hand at his side to destroy any illusion that it was shaking. He stared at Dante.

Dante hadn't moved. Was still out cold. Still cuffed to the table. Head still turned toward Teodoro, breathtaking face still partially veiled by tendrils of black hair. Fresh blood trickled from one nostril.

Nothing about him had changed from a moment ago.

Everything had changed.

Despite being ice-cold, sweat plastered Teodoro's shirt to his back, beaded his forehead. As he scrutinized the unconscious *creawdwr*, he realized that he needed to get back on the horse, so to speak, before his shock and dread deteriorated into belly-knotting fear. He needed to link to that bond, to follow it to Heather.

But first, he'd shoot Dante full of more resin and tranquilizers. No more dark laughter or blurring fists, then. Never mind the fact that there shouldn't have been this time either. Maybe the drugs were wearing off—

Teodoro's cell phone buzzed, interrupting his speeding train of denial. He pulled it from a trouser pocket and frowned when the ID showed Webster's number. Why would his supervisor be calling? Sinking into the chair, he thumbed the Talk button.

"Díon."

"Sorry to interrupt your vacation," Webster said, sounding—to his credit—vaguely apologetic, "but a situation has come up that requires your special expertise."

Teodoro sighed, rubbed the bridge of his nose. Leave it to the SB to ruin even pretend vacation plans. "Can't you put whoever it is on ice for a few more days? I'm leaving for Barcelona tomorrow. If I miss the flight, I'll be out the money."

"Afraid not. This one comes directly from the Oversight Committee. And"—Webster lowered his voice—"I hear it involves the director."

Teodoro sat up straight, suddenly more interested in the conversation. It sounded like the file he had left on the table following his meeting with the very-soon-to-be-dead-facedown-in-her-pancakes Underwood had been found. And studied.

Just as he'd intended—but the timing was unfortunate.

Given that the file revealed that SB Director William Britto had sold his soul, not to mention the SB's integrity, to the powerful Renata Alessa Cortini, high priestess of the vampire

Cercle de Druide, in exchange for new dusk-to-dawn life for his terminally ill son, Teodoro imagined it had made for fascinating reading.

And it wouldn't take much deductive skills for the members of the Oversight Committee to realize that the only thing the Cercle would be interested in would be intel about a True Blood known as S. And where to find him.

"You're expected at HQ by midnight," Webster informed Teodoro.

"And my vacation?"

"Reinstated the moment you've finished with the interrogation."

"Well, then. I guess I'll see you at midnight."

"Not me, you won't. I hope to be in bed asleep by then. Too damn old for vampire hours," Webster grumbled. "I'll let the OC know you're on the way."

Conversation finished, Teodoro stood and slipped the cell phone back into his pocket. When he returned from HQ, he'd tap into the bond between Dante and Heather, follow it back to the FBI agent. Then sever it. He stepped over to the table, his strength and balance restored—no longer a tottering old man—and gently brushed the strands of black hair away from Dante's face.

"Beautiful," he whispered.

A dark satisfaction curled through him. Soon. Very soon. With a severed bond and a *creawdwr*'s deep sea dive into madness, the Second Fall would begin—and then the air would fill with weeping and wailing and gnashing of Elohim teeth.

Turning, Teodoro strode from the room.

13

THE FIRST BREATH
OF WINTER

THE FALLEN ANGEL WAS gone.

Guy Mauvais stood in the doorway of the riverboat's workroom, his fingers clenched around the crystal goblet of stove-warmed blood he held—never microwaved, since the damned contraption destroyed what little flavor and nutritional value bagged blood possessed—as he stared in disbelief at the wooden table.

Empty—save for bits of white stone scattered across its surface and the melted stubs of candles left by the hoodoo woman, hardened tendrils of wax hanging like pale icicles from the table's edge.

The smoky aroma of incense and wax mingled with the fading scent of the hoodoo woman's hex-removal potion—mint and wintergreen, salt, and the lavender-clove-citrus spice of Florida Water.

"*Mon Dieu*," Mauvais breathed. "It actually worked." Excitement tingled electric along his spine. He entered the room, powdered stone gritting beneath the soles of his dress shoes as he hurried over to the table. "It actually worked," he repeated.

It'd been nearly three nights since Mauvais had chiseled the stone from the fallen angel's nude body, revealing black leathery wings, waist-length red hair, and taloned fingers and toes. Celtic designs—concentric circles, triskelions, delicate loops—were silver-inked along the motionless figure's right side from torc-collared throat to hand.

Freed of stone, then, but not the spell that had trapped him within it, the fallen angel's mouth had remained frozen in a silent scream, the moss-green eyes unseeing, the tight-muscled body locked in a crouch.

So, last night, refusing to give up or admit defeat, but lacking any magic useful to the situation, Mauvais had ordered the riverboat's return to New Orleans. Once the *Winter Rose* had docked at the Esplanade Avenue wharf, he'd sent his mortal servants into the Quarter and out into the bayous to find someone—be it hoodoo conjurer, Vodou *mambo*, or nomad *shuvano*—possessing the necessary magical skills to shatter the thrice-damned spell.

Mauvais's servants had returned first with a Vodou *houngan* who'd taken one look at the *Winter Rose*, then declared it and its master cursed. Refusing to step on board for any amount of money, the *houngan* had shouted his sincere condolences up to Mauvais, then turned and walked away without another word.

From where he stood against the wood railing, Mauvais regarded his chagrined servants with thin-lipped displeasure as they scurried away to resume their search.

They returned a few hours later with Clémentine, a slender hoodoo dressed in chocolate brown cords and a mustard-yellow sweater. In her mid-thirties with a wild mass of auburn curls and sky-blue eyes, she seemed to have no qualms about working for a man rumored to be a vampire or about breaking a hex on what appeared to be a fallen angel.

She'd studied Mauvais for a long moment, her blue gaze taking in the wheat-blond hair tied back at the nape of his neck with a black satin ribbon, the aristocratic features, his elegant, if old-fashioned suit, the pale skin and lambent eyes.

"Well, madame?" he'd finally inquired. "Do you also believe I am cursed?"

"Oh, without a doubt, *M'sieu* Mauvais. You got an angry *loa* on dis here boat, one I want nuthin' to do wit', but I'll take the job."

Mauvais had arched a skeptical eyebrow. "Even with an angry *loa* on board?"

"Got a mortgage, me," Clémentine had replied with a philosophical shrug of her shoulder.

Mauvais had chuckled. "I appreciate your forthright and practical nature."

Clémentine's lips had curled into a smile. She'd extended her hand, palm up. "And I appreciate cash, *m'sieu*."

Once she'd been paid, and paid well, she'd immediately gone to work with her potions and powders and gris-gris, her juju bags and holy water and oil-anointed candles, promising Mauvais that his fallen angel would rise once again.

But when the conjurer had finally left shortly before dawn after murmuring one last Psalm over the angel's utterly unchanged form, Mauvais had been disappointed, and believed himself duped perhaps.

The empty table was proof that he'd been wrong.

Which begged the question—where had the angel gone?

Mauvais drained his cooling breakfast, grimacing at the blood's flat, lifeless taste, then set the goblet down on the table as he glanced around the room. Faint glimmers of light from the wharf filtered in through the porthole—more than enough to see that he was alone in the room. The taste of blood turned bitter on his tongue.

He picked up the chisel. Particles of pale stone still dusted its end. If, after everything, the damned angel had simply flown away without even a word. . . .

Mauvais hurled the chisel across the room. It struck the wood paneling at the far wall, driving in deep, handle quivering.

From the corner of his eye, Mauvais caught a flicker of blue light and spun to face it. He saw only the stone-littered table, the goblet glinting with ruby light from the porthole, and shadowed shelves filled with boxes and coils of rope and tools.

No blue flickers. No ghostly movement. Nothing.

He was merely jumping at shadows—or, more accurately, blue light. Again.

Ever since they'd docked in New Orleans last night, he'd been catching odd glimpses of blue light in his peripheral vision, along with disturbing whiffs of ozone and heated metal. On a couple of occasions, his skin had prickled as though lightning crackled in the air right above him, filling him with an odd and inexplicable dread.

You got an angry loa *on dis here boat . . .*

"*Non,*" Mauvais refused with a shake of his head. "*Pas ici. Pas possible.*"

He marched over to the light switch and slapped it on. Nothing. He uselessly hit the switch a few more times, as if that would make a difference. Annoyed with himself, he dropped his hand and blew out a long, frustrated breath.

Yet another thing that had happened ever since they'd docked at the Esplanade Avenue wharf—lights blew out, equipment short-circuited, and computers—navigational and otherwise—glitched.

And now the fallen angel, the one he'd rescued from being a good-luck charm for tourists, drunks, and the desperate visiting St. Louis Cemetery No. 3, the one whose mere presence (grateful, of course) at his side could've elevated Mauvais in status far beyond Lord of New Orleans, was just . . . gone.

This riverboat and its master are cursed. My sincere apologies . . .

No damned curse—not unless the *houngan* or conjurer

had hexed him in hopes of making more money, which seemed unlikely, since the problems had begun *before* either one had arrived. And no angry *loa*. Just a run of mechanical problems and bad luck.

Closing his eyes, Mauvais rubbed his temples, forcing his body to relax, coaxing the tension from knotted muscles. Like it or not, the angel was gone, and there was nothing he could do about it.

He needed a good stiff drink of fine bourbon, then he would go into the Quarter and dine. Perhaps a naïve tourist as an appetizer, followed by a full-course meal, in the form of the hunt, chasing down a more canny New Orleans native, and feasting on their fear and adrenaline-simmered blood.

Feeling the tension drain from his muscles as he pondered his meal options, Mauvais gave his temples one final circular rub before ending the massage. Eyes open once more, he left the workroom and climbed the stairs to the deck, his shoes soundless against the iron. He breathed in the river's cool, muddy scent.

Perhaps Laurent and Rafe would finally track down that betraying *bâtard* Vincent, and bring him home as a flesh-and-blood gift, one offering superior tension-releasing opportunities. Perhaps Vincent could even be the dessert capping a night of fine dining. Mauvais smiled at the thought.

Lanterns hung from hooks spaced evenly along the riverboat's length, casting wavering pools of pale yellow light across the teak deck and infusing the air with the pungent aroma of kerosene. Even though it meant the generators still weren't working, Mauvais felt nostalgic at the sight of the lanterns, the sound of their steady hiss, remembering a time when there were no such things as electricity or GPS or computers.

Once we relied on only the moon and stars to guide us.

On our instincts. Our hunger. Our blood.

We've become lazy. Complacent. Stagnant.

An image flashed through his mind, one nearly four nights

old: Dante Baptiste on his knees, held in place by Mauvais's vampires, his pale face defiant, a smirk on his bloodied lips as he jerks his chin free of Mauvais's grasp and meets his gaze.

Dante, Dante, Dante . . . You refuse to recognize my authority.

Authority over what? Wharf rats? Ass kissers?

You're disrespectful. Defiant, and rude. You even break our laws.

Fuck your laws.

Another smile curled across Mauvais's lips. *Well,* he amended, as he remembered the intoxicating taste of Dante's blood—copper and pomegranates, heady adrenaline and sun-warmed grapes—and the power that had surged through his veins, courtesy of the True Blood's unwilling donation. *Perhaps not all of us have forgotten our instincts.* His smile deepened. *Nor our hunger.*

As Mauvais strode toward the wheelhouse, he heard the familiar tread of his majordomo hurrying behind him. An acrid tang—concern, unease, perhaps—smudged the man's scent of cedar and Irish moss.

"What is it, Edmond?" Mauvais called lazily, not bothering to slow his pace for the mortal. "I am not in the mood for any more problems."

"Not a problem, *m'sieu,*" Edmond said in hushed, if somewhat breathless, tones as he drew up alongside Mauvais. Tall, lean, and in his early forties, he was impeccably dressed in his usual uniform of black morning coat and vest, sharply creased black trousers, and shoes polished to a mirror-bright gleam. "Well, not exactly, I should say."

"Then what is it exactly? Spit it out."

"*M'sieu,* it's the tailor—"

"The *tailor*? Why are you bothering me with the tailor? Has he run off to design his own fashion line? Everyone seems to be doing so these days."

"No, he has not. But it's not the tailor, per se, *m'sieu,* it's—" Edmond's words stopped cold at a warning shout from one of the guards at the riverboat's gangplank, a warning answered with a contemptuous string of fluid and very imaginative Italian.

Giovanni Toscanini.

Mauvais sighed. Whether he was in the mood for it or not, another problem had just arrived in the form of Renata Alessa Cortini's emissary, her *fils de sang*; a guest Mauvais had, admittedly, lied to and deceived and had hoped to avoid for a while longer.

Perhaps he was cursed after all, he mused ruefully. Well, nothing for it, but . . .

<*Please allow* Signor *Toscanini onboard*,> Mauvais sent to his guards. <*And do not insult him with an escort—he is still my guest.*>

"M'sieu, the tailor," Edmond persisted quietly, "he—"

Mauvais flapped a dismissive hand. "Can wait."

Edmond shot a glance toward the stairs leading belowdecks, then gave a nearly imperceptible shrug. "As you wish, m'sieu. I shall fetch brandy for you and your guest." Turning, the majordomo left in a brisk stride.

Mauvais crossed to the railing and leaned against it, elbows resting on the gleaming wood, the night-blackened waters of the Mississippi at his back. Giovanni blurred to a stop in front of him a mere moment later, fragrant with the scent of the sea—salt, sand, and deep waters.

Dressed in a black, silver-buttoned short-sleeved shirt, and tight designer jeans, Giovanni folded his arms over his chest, biceps defined against the black material. He looked down his proud Roman nose at Mauvais, his hazel eyes no longer warm or full of playful mischief, but narrowed into an icy glare.

"*Tu sei un bastardo mentendo*," he said, voice tight.

Mauvais arched an eyebrow. "And a good evening to you, as well."

Giovanni snorted. "I don't want to play the innocence and denials game. I haven't the patience."

"Actually, neither do I," Mauvais said, somewhat relieved. He usually looked forward to the verbal chess playing and mental sparring between vampires, but tonight—between the ungrateful and missing fallen angel, the bizarre electrical mishaps, and claims of curses and angry *loas*—he just didn't have it in him.

"You knew I wanted to be notified the moment Dante Baptiste returned to New Orleans," Giovanni said, dark brows slanting down in a scowl. "Yet you sent me off to the French Quarter like a drunk tourist, knowing that Baptiste was not only in town, but right here"—he stamped one boot against the deck—"right under my feet. And against his will, no less."

"A necessary deception," Mauvais replied, "for which I apologize."

"Playing me for a fool was a necessary deception?"

"Unfortunately. Again, my apologies. I truly had no choice."

Giovanni laughed, darkly amused. "No choice? How is that possible? You're the Lord of New Orleans."

"Indeed I am." Mauvais held Giovanni's gaze. "And part of my responsibilities as lord is to discipline vampires who flout our laws. Dante happens to be one of those."

"Even though I told you that, as a True Blood, he is to be treated with the utmost respect?" Giovanni's voice slivered ice into the air. "Even though I told you that his crimes would be taken before the Cercle de Druide for proper consideration?"

"*Oui*. I'm afraid that wasn't good enough for my *fille de sang*. She'd lost so much at Dante's hands." Tension crept back into Mauvais's muscles, his spine, at the thought of Justine. Twin blades of loss and betrayal sank deep into his heart—just before he hardened it once more.

Foolish girl, ungrateful child. I gave you your justice when I ordered Dante's home burned to the ground. Why couldn't you let it be enough? "And where *is* the lovely Justine?" Giovanni asked, lowering his arms to his sides. A breeze from off the river ruffled through his razor-cut burgundy locks. "I haven't seen her."

"And you won't," Mauvais said coolly, "as she is no longer a member of this household." Refusing the question in the Italian's eyes, he pushed away from the railing, and glanced aft. "Ah, here comes Edmond with our drinks."

And, oddly, not alone. A tall figure walked beside the majordomo, his stride confident and relaxed. The height and waist-length hair along with the glowing golden eyes made Mauvais think of Lucien De Noir. His heart stuttered against his ribs.

Not De Noir, no. *His* fallen angel had returned.

"Who is that?" Giovanni asked, his tone a verbal frown.

"One of the Elohim," Mauvais replied with a deliberate nonchalance that suggested he played host to fallen angels all the time and, really, it was becoming a bit of a bore.

"Truly?" Wonder skipped like a child in that single word. "Which is he?"

Mauvais shrugged. "We haven't yet had an opportunity to speak—not even an exchange of names. But I think that is about to change," he mused as the pair drew to a halt in front of him.

The angel's scent—fallow earth and cold stone and thin, crackling ice, the first breath of winter—chilled the air. Tendrils of his red hair lifted on the breeze and moonlight glinted from the torc curving around his throat. He wore a white linen shirt and charcoal-gray trousers, a matching suit jacket draped over one arm.

A wry smile tugged at Mauvais's lips. *So that's what Edmond was trying to tell me—that my former statue was up and about and getting a fitting from my tailor.*

"M'sieu Guy Mauvais, Lord of New Orleans," Edmond smoothly informed the immortal at his side, "and his guest, *Signor* Giovanni Toscanini of the Cercle de Druide, arrived from Rome."

"Welcome aboard the *Winter Rose*," Mauvais said, studiously ignoring the *I-tried-to-tell-you* twitch of the majordomo's eyebrow. "I'm pleased that my tailor has managed to accommodate you in such fine fashion, *m'sieu* . . ." He trailed off, giving the angel an opportunity to gracefully supply his name.

An opportunity the fallen angel ignored. Instead he smoothed a hand down the front of his pristine shirt and replied in a deep, musical voice, "Your tailor is quite skilled, yes, and seemed to enjoy the challenge."

Chuckling, Mauvais accepted a half-filled brandy snifter from the tray Edmond extended with white-gloved hands. "I'm sure he did."

"Ah, refreshments," the fallen angel said, golden eyes brightening. Ignoring the snifters arrayed upon Edmond's tray, he instead plucked the white rose from the pocket of the majordomo's morning coat and popped one snowy petal into his mouth.

Edmond neither blinked nor frowned, simply inclined his head, as though to say, *Excellent choice*, m'sieu, then offered his tray to Giovanni. At Mauvais's nodded dismissal, he quietly withdrew.

Mauvais slid a companionable arm around Giovanni's shoulders and murmured, "I need to have a private chat with my winged guest. It shouldn't take long. If you wait for me in the casino belowdecks, perhaps play a few rounds of roulette, we shall resume our conversation once I'm finished here."

While Mauvais felt a deep satisfaction—not to mention a bit of triumph—in knowing that Giovanni would immediately contact Renata and the rest of the Cercle and inform them that Guy Mauvais had found favor among the Fallen, he did not want the details of his upcoming conversation with the angel to be included in the handsome Italian's report.

A vampire needed secrets, after all.

Giovanni's muscles tensed beneath Mauvais's arm. "This had better not be another trick to get rid of me," he warned in a low voice.

"I'm merely asking you to wait, not leave."

With a soft, frustrated sigh, Giovanni looked past Mauvais to the fallen angel, then lifted his snifter of brandy to his lips and tossed back its dark amber contents. "Fine, then," he muttered, resting the empty glass on the railing. "I'll wait. But don't make me wait long."

"Of course not," Mauvais replied with a warm smile. He gave Giovanni's shoulder a companionable squeeze before releasing him. "You have my word."

With a derisive snort—one Mauvais chose to ignore—Giovanni strode away, following after Edmond. Once they were alone and the only sounds Mauvais heard were the hissing kerosene lanterns, the creak of the wood beneath his feet, and the Mississippi's wet kisses against the riverboat, he gave his attention to the immortal standing silently beside him.

"For a guest, he seems somewhat cranky and demanding," the fallen angel commented. "Although, given that he's a vampire, I suppose that's to be expected."

Mauvais pursed his lips, considering, then admitted, "True."

The angel laughed, the sound of it like the joyous pealing of wedding bells. "I understand that I have you to thank for my freedom," he said, once his mirth had passed. He drew in a deep breath of air, seeming to savor the simple action of breathing. "I truly appreciate it."

"I'm glad I could help," Mauvais replied with an elegant half-shrug, knowing the gesture would suggest a careless modesty and an altruistic nature that he didn't possess. "We're fortunate that my people stumbled across you while chasing down a rude *marmot* in desperate need of a lesson in manners. How *did* you end up as a stone statue guarding a tomb, anyway?"

"The usual way. Treachery. Betrayal by a brother." A smile—dark and somehow eager—curved the fallen angel's lips, revealing sharp white teeth. "But I intend to pay back in kind."

"I am willing to help in any way possible," Mauvais said, then took a sip of the brandy, savoring its smooth oak- and- rose flavor.

"Wonderful." The angel pulled several more petals from the rose and ate them, chewing thoughtfully. Swallowing, he said, "Perhaps you can help me find the guilty party since I believe he resides in the area—or did, before he tricked me with lies and a blood spell."

"Of course. What's his name?"

"He's known as the Nightbringer, but it's his son I'm most interested in."

"Son?" Mauvais stared at the fallen angel, startled. "Lucien De Noir—the Nightbringer—doesn't have a son. At least, not that I'm aware of."

But even as the words left his mouth, a dark suspicion snaked through Mauvais's mind as he remembered how De Noir had always guarded Dante Baptiste, remembered how he used to wonder why one of the Fallen had chosen to stand beside the beautiful and dangerous True Blood—or any vampire for that matter. He'd often wondered if Dante had pulled a thorn from the lion's paw.

Mon Dieu. Is it possible?

"Oh, but he does," the fallen angel said. "A very special child, he called this son. Unique. And one I'm most eager to meet." His smile darkened even more, became an abyss. "I have plans for the boy."

Apprehension iced Mauvais's blood. He had a feeling neither Lucien De Noir nor his son would enjoy that meeting very much. But he reminded himself that he owed nothing to either De Noir or—if his suspicion proved correct—Dante. Their fates were their own. Still. . . .

"As I said," Mauvais murmured. "I know nothing about a son, but I can tell you where to find De Noir."

"Lucien De Noir," the fallen angel mused, shaking his head. "Where *does* he come up with these names?"

"And *your* name, *m'sieu?*" Mauvais prodded gently. "What shall I call you?"

"Loki," the immortal replied. "Call me Loki."

Mauvais drained his brandy in one swallow.

14

FUCK MURPHY AND HIS STUPID GODDAMNED LAW

VON STOOD OFF TO one side of the club's kicked-in door, Silver's coiled presence right behind him, and listened to the chaotic and brutal sounds issuing from the darkened and grafittied entrance hall—shouts, the fleshy thud of fists against flesh, pained grunts, the spatter of blood hitting the floor—a free-for-all battle.

"The fuck?" Silver muttered under his breath. "What *now?*"

Von heartily agreed. The fuck, indeed. It sounded as though a posse of idiots—*nightkind* idiots, given the lack of mortal heartbeats—had broken in, drunk all the booze, then decided the fire-scorched club was the perfect place for a UFC bout.

But he was pretty damned sure that something else very different was going on.

Someone was fighting for his or her life.

Von slipped a hand inside his leather jacket for one of his holstered Brownings—a gesture as natural and automatic as breathing—and felt a cold shock when his fingers brushed against only the jacket's soft lining.

No guns. No holster.

Hell, it wasn't even his jacket, but a brown bomber borrowed from Jack—one smelling of stale beer and spearmint gum and thankfully missing any pithy declarations or tiny gators.

Standing across from him on the other side of the boot-battered door, her Glock held in both hands, Merri Goodnight arched one eyebrow, her expression asking: *Missing something or just feeling your bad self up?*

With a let's-keep-her-guessing wink, Von pulled his hand free of the jacket. Maybe his Brownings were inside, upstairs in his sprinkler-drenched room along with his double shoulder holster, leather jacket, and non-gator-infested clothing, but he sure as hell wasn't weaponless. Neither was Silver.

But he couldn't say the same for Thibodaux, despite the gun in the man's hand. Merri's partner towered behind her, his attention focused on the darkness beyond the battered doors, his Colt held down at his side in a one-handed grip.

A nightkind rumble was no place for a mortal. No matter how good a shot.

Von suddenly regretted his decision to bring the former SB agents along in the hope that their investigative skills might turn up a clue as to who had snatched Dante. And where he might've been taken.

"On three?" Merri whispered.

Von nodded, then glanced over his shoulder at Silver. Clothed in more of Jack's generous donations—a black Voodoo Fest tee, jeans, and classic Converse high-tops, all suspiciously gator-free—his purple hair smudged nearly black in the moonlight, Silver met his regard with gleaming eyes.

<Ready?>

Silver flashed fangs for reply.

"One," Von said, low.

"Two," Merri picked up.

"Three," from Silver.

Von *moved*, Merri and Silver right on his sneakered heels—
sneakers, for chrissakes—the entrance hall blurring past in a
smoke-reeking streak of black walls, fluorescent paint, and red
flickering light.

BURNBURNBURNBURN

Even as he sped into the club, Von heard only a few low,
pained moans—the hard-knuckled combat had ended. As he
came to an abrupt halt in the center of the soot-streaked dance
floor, he also realized that only one vampire remained standing.

One he recognized. Murphy and his stupid law had struck
again.

Holly Miková pushed silky tendrils of hair the color of
honey butter back from her face. Red light from the buzzing
neon BURN sign jittered along the crescent moon tattoo beneath her right eye.

"Ah, there you are, McGuinn," she said, a faint Russian accent flavoring her words. She wore a curve-hugging rose-red lace
mini over black tights and wedge-heeled black boots, looking for
all the world like a pop diva during a video shoot break instead
of what she was—deadly. "Just the man I was looking for."

"Well, you found me, darlin'," Von drawled, despite the
tight knot forming in his belly.

Holly's return to New Orleans so soon after her last visit
could only mean bad news given the summons she'd delivered
less than a week ago—and a lifetime of shit had passed since
then—and the promise he'd made in response.

You are to report to the filidh *in Memphis in one night's time to
explain why they've learned of a True Blood through outside sources
and not from the* llygad *serving this alleged True Blood's household.*

*Why'd they send you? Because they thought you'd enjoy
breaking the news?*

*No, they thought you'd listen to me—because of what we
once had. Is Dante Baptiste a True Blood?*

Ain't my place to say. You need to ask him.

Of course it's your place! It's your duty to observe, compose, and report. This is information vital to vampire society and you've kept mum. Abandoned your duty, your impartiality. Oh, Vonushka. You've got a lot to answer for.

Tell the filidh I'll be there. And have a safe trip back, darlin'.

A promise made to buy time. But a promise he'd intended to keep—*after* he'd kept his promise to Dante, a promise never voiced, but held deep in his heart: *I will see you free and whole and walking the path* you *choose.*

And in Holly's deep blue eyes, Von read the truth.

That time you bought with a few easy words? All used up, man. Every last second.

Von nodded at the half dozen nightkind sprawled or crumpled on the floor, like plucked and discarded petals from an unwanted rose. A couple had even tucked themselves into fetal balls of pain. One unlucky bastard who happened to be more mobile than his buddies was busy trying to crawl away. He dragged himself across the floor, blood glistening in his wake like a snail's moist trail.

Von shook his head. "Still making friends, I see. Didn't your mama ever teach you to play nice?"

"*Da*, she did. But only if they played nice first."

Von chuckled. "Woman after my own heart. Sure you ain't nomad?"

"Absolutely positive. Good thing I stopped by to take out the trash for you, yes?"

"Well, that remains to be seen, darlin'."

Frowning, Holly stepped forward, bent, then twisted the unlucky bastard's head to the left. His neck broke with a sharp snap. He went limp, down for the count until his body healed.

Silver, now standing at Von's left, whistled, low and impressed. "Can all *llygaid* kick ass like she does?"

"Aside from me, you mean?" Von said, dryly. Folding his arms over his chest, he added, "Miková there used to be *llafnau* before she came to her senses and joined the *llygaid* ranks."

Silver whistled low again. "No shit?"

"No shit, indeed."

Von caught a peripheral flash of movement from his right and looked in time to see Merri push her partner's gun hand down. He felt a sudden pang, missing Heather and her quiet confidence, her inner strength.

You hold tight, woman. We're coming for you too.

"See the crescent moon?" Merri murmured to her partner.

"Yeah, okay. Got it. But what the fuck is . . . lav-nigh?" Thibodaux asked, brow furrowed.

"*Llafnau* are the nightkind version of Navy SEALs," Merri replied, sparing Von the necessity. "The special forces branch of the *llygaid*."

"Roger that." The wariness in Thibodaux's sharp blue eyes throttled down a notch, but he didn't holster his gun. He kept the Colt ready at his side and glanced at Von. "I also get that this is vampire business. Think I'll go upstairs and take a look around. Make sure our Navy SEAL there didn't miss someone."

Crossing the floor in a long-legged stride, the former SB agent headed for the staircase.

Von watched him go, amused. *Double-checking our hearing and our noses. Man doesn't take anything for granted—including supersonic nightkind senses. Gotta admit, I like that.*

The reek of smoke, scorched wood, and freshly spilled blood hung thick in Von's nostrils, at the back of his throat, as he got his first good look at the damage to the club, courtesy of James Wallace.

The fire-blackened bars of the Cage, the fetishes nothing but ash.

The flame-gutted stairs leading up to Dante's cheesetacular bat-winged throne. Or the twisted and fused thing that used to be his cheesetacular bat-winged throne, anyway.

Water damage.

Fire extinguisher foam—thick and petrified and reeking of chemicals—on walls and floors and furniture.

The stink of scorched wood and plastic and metal.

It hit Von again—the cold, furious feeling that had struck him like a brass-knuckled fist to the gut when he'd learned from Lucien what had happened while he'd Slept. His jaw tightened, pulse throbbing at his temples.

An image stolen from Annie's memory flashed behind his eyes.

Dante half slides, half falls to his knees in the bedroom doorway, his black-painted nails scraping furrows along the threshold on his way down. Head bowed, black hair veiling his face, he whispers, "J'su ici, catin. Je t'entends."

I'm here, doll. I hear you.

Those words alone told Von that Heather had managed to summon Dante up from Sleep—through their bond, no doubt—and most likely saved his life in the process.

J'su ici.

But that was the problem. He wasn't here.

Worse, they still had no idea where to find him.

Everything could be repaired, rebuilt, bought anew. Tougher security installed. Guards hired. But without Dante, none of it mattered.

"I don't know who they are," Holly was saying. "But I followed them in."

"Thanks for that, Miková," Von said.

Holly shrugged. "I needed the workout. Sadly"—she glanced down in disdain at the nearest unconscious idiot— "they didn't give me much of one."

Von tilted his head, studied the groaning nightkind on the floor. "Might've seen a few of these bastards aboard the *Winter Rose*."

"Figures," Silver growled. *<We should stake them and send their ashes back to Mauvais. For Simone.>*

Von met and held Silver's seething gaze. *<Mauvais needs to pay for Simone, no one else. And once we have Dante and Heather home again, trust me—the motherfucker will pay.>*

Silver nodded, then looked away, a muscle flexing in his jaw.

Shifting his attention back to Holly, Von said, "Did anyone happen to say why the fuck they were in here?"

"*Da*. They mentioned looking for some poor bastard named Vincent. Seems they wish to tear him a new one."

"Well, they can stand at the back of the line." Von looked at Silver, perplexed. "Wanting to tear Vincent a new one I get. But why look for him here?"

Silver shook his head. "Beats the hell outta me."

"Who's Vincent?" Merri asked.

"Magazine Street lord," Von replied. "British. Seventies glam. Looks like Ewan McGregor in that movie *Velvet Goldmine*. Full of himself. Annoying. Generally harmless. Until recently."

"And what happened recently?"

"None of your business," Von said, looking at Merri pointedly from beneath his lashes.

Comprehension glimmered in her eyes. To her credit, she didn't even look in Holly's direction. "Fine. Be that way."

Holly said softly, "We need to talk, McGuinn."

Von nodded. "I figured as much."

"Alone," Holly suggested.

"Okay. But before we talk, I wanna haul the rest of this trash out to the curb."

"Fine. Haul away." Holly sauntered across the nightkind-littered floor to the bar, stepping on anyone in her path and leaving a renewed trail of pained grunts and groans in her wake. "There's a restaurant across the street. Meet me there when you've finished."

"I'll do that," Von said.

For a split second, as she passed him, Von caught a whiff of her homey, warm-kitchen-in-a-snowstorm scent—honeyed black tea and vanilla—before it was swallowed up by the stink of charred wood and melted plastic.

"Still like your style, darlin'."

Heading for the exit, Holly shrugged. "I know."

15

LIKE DISTANT
THUNDER

BARRY LANG STEERED HIS Prius into his slot in the
condo parking lot, switched off the engine, and barely re-
sisted the urge to thump his head repeatedly against the steering
wheel. Instead, he leaned back in his seat, the vinyl squeaking
beneath him, and rubbed a hand over his face.

The news from Portland was bad.

No, worse than bad, unbelievable.

As if the mess dumped into his lap following Monica Rutgers's abrupt resignation hadn't been enough, the murder of
an FBI agent at the satellite forensics lab—inside his own goddamned office, no less—was definitely the tasty cherry on top
of the steaming shit sundae Barry's life had become since he'd
taken over Rutgers's position as ADIC.

Sighing, Barry lowered his hand to his seat belt, his gaze
focused on the night-draped greenery beyond his windshield.
Normally, a soothing sight—the neat landscaping, the tranquil

design of flower beds and trimmed hedges and blossoming cherry trees. But now he only saw darkness and shadows pooled beyond the sidewalk.

Someone had sauntered into the Portland lab, disabled the security cameras and audio equipment, then killed SAC Oscar Heyne. A *vampire*, for chrissakes. No one had seen anything, remembered anyone unusual. Heyne's assistant couldn't account for close to an hour of her time prior to the discovery of his body—or the various scattered parts of it, anyway. Simply drew a blank. Of course, after the discovery, she'd fainted dead away. A sample of her blood was currently being tested to see if she'd been drugged.

As for the manner of Heyne's death, it had netted Barry a call from Deputy Director Phil Beckett himself.

"Heyne was torn limb from limb," Beckett says, voice grim, *"and his head was found perched in his outbox."*

"Christ. The killer couldn't have been human, then. Another vamp?"

"Maybe, but that's not all. When his heart was found, it had been turned to stone."

"Stone? How the hell is that possible, sir?"

"I don't know. It's a new one on me."

"Do vampires even have that kind of . . . of . . . power or magic or whatever you want to call it?"

"According to folks in the know, a True Blood vamp might."

"Not does, but might?"

"The only other option I was offered by those same folks in the know was fallen angels."

"Sir, I . . . no disrespect, but given the options, I think we can assume that Dante Prejean is still slaughtering FBI agents. And that the SB is allowing it. Maybe even sanctioning it."

"So it seems. We need to talk. Somewhere private."

And talk they had.

Barry powered the driver's-side window down a quarter of the way, letting in cool air and the smells of cherry blossoms, bark mulch, and grass wet with dew.

He wouldn't get out of the car and head for his condo until he'd filed away the day's events—clearing his mental palate—so that when he walked through the front door, he was only Barry Lang, husband and father and golden retriever owner, and not Barry Lang, FBI ADIC.

The meeting with the deputy director had taken longer than Barry had expected, running well past the dinner hour, but DD Beckett had ordered food in—turkey, bacon, and avocado sandwiches and chips—from Subway.

Either the deputy director's expense account had been slashed during the latest round of budget cuts, Barry had mused, or he was a frugal man—or he just liked Subway.

Barry ticked down the list of topics that had been discussed over Lay's potato chips, Subway subs, and iced tea.

1. James and Heather Wallace.
2. The SB, Bad Seed, and S—Dante Prejean.
3. The murder of Oscar Heyne and other FBI agents.
4. The mysterious events at Damascus, Oregon, and the SB's subsequent cover-up.
5. How to give the SB a good, old-fashioned, prison yard–style shanking.

Before Monica Rutgers's resignation from the Bureau five days before, she'd created a firestorm between the FBI and the SB when she'd defied joint orders and put a tail on Prejean, resulting in a bit of death and destruction in Damascus. But given the intensity of the SB's reaction—severing all Bureau ties to project Bad Seed and Prejean, further straining already tenuous cooperation between the two agencies—Barry had suspected that Rutgers had done a helluva lot more than put a simple tail on Prejean.

She'd sent an assassin. One who'd missed. Unfortunately.

However it had gone down, the result was the same: the SB had claimed Prejean as theirs only, absolving the Bureau of any responsibility for the murdering bastard.

And now, with Heyne's death the latest in a recent string, it seemed Prejean's new fave habit was slaughtering FBI agents. One couldn't help but wonder if he killed with the SB's blessing.

Not that it mattered.

Barry and Beckett intended to end Prejean's new habit. Permanently. Unofficially. And over a long discussion/argument over how—humans had failed before and vampire agents couldn't be trusted to execute a True Blood, no matter how psychotic—they'd finally realized the answer was sitting in a room at the Strickland Deprogramming Institute, most likely looking for an escape route, unaware that it was too late. They were already coming for her.

Heather Wallace.

A second epiphany, this one on Barry's part, was to use a new, powerful explosive that was now a deadly favorite of terrorists—N21. A few drops could level a house, a few more a city block. It could be transported inside the human body, implanted under the skin in a tiny disk of plastic much like a GPS tracker, and triggered by a remote.

It had been used on more than one occasion on airplanes with devastating results.

Instead of "helping" Heather Wallace into that tragic suicide the Bureau had planned for her, she would be transformed into a suicide bomber—albeit an unknowing one.

"Christ," Beckett says, "that just might work."

"We'll just dope her up, implant the explosives and a GPS tracker. Once she's recovered from the sedatives, we'll do an intensive interrogation just as she'd expect, but—"

"Make sure she finds a way to escape afterward."

Barry nods. "So she can run straight to Prejean."

"A touch of a button and BOOM. Prejean, Wallace, and anyone near them won't be coming back. Ever. And the SB won't be able to do one damned thing about it."

"Only sit and spin, sir. Sit and spin."

"Good. Let's see how they like it for a change."

A team would fetch Heather Wallace from the institute in Dallas in the morning, spinning the first part of their plan into place. Nothing more to be done until tomorrow.

Barry drew in a deep breath and caught a whiff of green leaves and deep dark earth, a summer smell in the chilly beginnings of spring. Powering up the window, he grabbed his keys and briefcase and got out of the Prius.

As he stepped onto the sidewalk, Barry caught a shower of blue sparks from the corner of his eye. A glimpse quickly followed by an electric crackle and the thunderstorm scent of ozone.

All the parking lot lights went out.

The tide of darkness and shadows lapping at the edge of the sidewalk spilled over into the parking lot.

Barry's pulse jumped in his throat. His fingers clenched around the handle of his briefcase. What the hell? Had to be some kind of massive surge or power failure or maybe a late-night squirrel having a fatal encounter with a transformer or . . .

From the heart of darkness flooding the yard and swirling around the Prius, Barry heard a soft, leathery rustle, as of wings. Big ones. Twin golden stars pricked the blackness, the gleam of glowing eyes. He froze, heart kicking against his chest, primal instincts whispering, *Drop and curl up and maybe it will pass you by.*

But Barry had a feeling it was much too late for that.

The darkness spoke in a deep rumble, like distant thunder, "I have a question for you, one I shall ask only once: Where is Heather Wallace?"

Barry's legs gave out and he dropped to his knees.

16

CAPTURED IN
CHARCOAL

V ON TOSSED THE LAST bruised and battered intruder—
a dude with GQ cheekbones wearing a sleek European
suit—onto the pile of black garbage bags heaped up in the
gutter in front of the pizza place next door. One of which split
open, its decaying contents spilling out in a stinking sludge of
garlic, spoiled sausage, coffee grounds, and rotting lettuce.

Gasping for air, Cheekbones staggered up to his feet and
began brushing frantically at his suit.

"Haul ass," Von suggested in a low growl.

Cheekbones looked around and, realizing he was alone, set
off in a stumbling run down the narrow street. Something white
fell from his pocket, floating to the street, a pale leaf.

"What's that?" Merri asked.

"Dunno."

Von stepped off the curb, walked out into the street, and
picked up a folded sheet of paper—thick paper, like an artist

would use. A sketch, maybe. A dark, vanilla-spiced tobacco odor permeated the paper, an odor that reminded him of the cigarettes that Vincent seemed to chain-smoke. Although he didn't see the Magazine Street lord often, every time they had crossed paths, Vincent had been puffing away on one of the Pink Elephants he favored.

And Vincent was an artist.

Straightening, Von unfolded the paper. And realized with a sharp pang as he stared at the oh-so-familiar face it revealed, that the Magazine Street lord was not only an artist, but a damned good one.

The sketch also revealed why Mauvais's crew had broken into the club—they believed Dante and Vincent friendly enough to play artist and model.

Dante in charcoal—his eyes closed, jaw tight, caught in the act of wiping a dark trickle of blood from his nose with a hoodie sleeve, moonlight glinting from the ring in his collar.

A simple drawing, not yet completed, or so it looked to Von, but somehow Vincent had managed to capture not only Dante's beauty, tension, and pain in bold strokes of gray and black, but had symbolized in that casual swipe of a hoodie sleeve the quiet will that kept Dante on his feet, kept him moving, kept him fighting.

At the bottom of the sketch, printed in charcoal letters: *Secrets.*

Von reached for Dante. <*Keep fighting and stay stubborn, you sonuvabitch, or I'll kick your ass when I find you. Kick your ass into tomorrow.*>

But all Von received was more silence prickling with barbed-wire pain.

"Is that Dante?" Merri asked as she joined him out in the street, her scent electric with interest. She'd only seen Dante in photos, Von realized, had never met him.

"Yup," Von replied, his voice rough. He quickly folded up the sketch, then slipped it into his jacket pocket. "Vincent's work."

"You never mentioned he was an artist."

"Never mentioned a lot of things."

"True," Merri said without rancor. "The sketch—is that normal? I mean, does Dante often get nosebleeds during what I'm guessing to be a killer headache?"

Von hesitated for a moment, then said, "Normal for Dante, yeah."

"Christ. Sorry to hear that."

Returning to the sidewalk, Merri paused in front of the club's battered green shutter-style doors and lit up one of her clove cigarettes. They were alone. Silver was inside, salvaging what he could from his room and keeping an eye on Thibodaux.

"So spill, nomad. Let's hear what you didn't want to say inside about your artist friend."

Lucien's old-school Chevy van with its blacked-out side and back windows was parked at the curb, so Von rested his back against it. He folded his arms over his chest, bomber jacket creaking. "Vincent ain't my friend."

"I'm hearing history . . ."

"Just the usual. Two cocky bastards. One town. Yada, yada. Not to mention that Vincent was playing two sides—namely, Dante and goddamned Guy Mauvais—against the middle."

"The Lord of New Orleans?" Merri questioned, frowning. "He's the mofo who ordered the house you all lived in torched, killing your friend in the fire, right?"

"Simone, her name was Simone," Von said, voice harsher than he'd intended. "And, yeah, Mauvais was the one. He also had Dante grabbed and held long enough to ensure he couldn't do a damned thing about it." He shook his head, throat too tight for words.

But we felt her burn. Felt the fire devour her. Heard her screams.

"Shit," Merri said. "Then what happened?"

"Lake Pontchartrain."

"Tell me," she said softly.

"Is your nosiness natural or something the SB trained into you?"

Merri snorted. "I'm a born snoop, nomad. Get used to it."

"Nosy *and* full of sass," Von observed, grinning. "I like that in a woman."

Merri laughed, shook her head. "Shee-it. Look, no need to play the old flirtation distraction game with me. If you don't want to tell me about what happened at Lake Pontchartrain, no problem."

"Ooo. Minus points for being touchy. But"—Von unfolded his arms and held up a *just-be-patient* hand when she scowled, brows knitting over her velvet-brown eyes—"I don't mind telling you what went down."

Von drew in a deep breath, one laced with smoke fragrant with spice and cloves and tobacco, then released it and started talking. Some things he kept to himself, like Dante's *creawdwr* abilities and how he turned a ticking time bomb of a yacht into a living, breathing leviathan—or mostly, anyway.

And what he did to Trey.

Dante holds Trey's face—a face that now flickers and shifts, a face that seems composed of blue neon ones and zeros—between his blue-flamed hands. Trey's dreads, transformed into gleaming and twisted bundles of wire, snake into the burning air . . .

But he told Merri the rest in a low, flat voice—Vincent informing Dante that Mauvais would be meeting the arsonists responsible for the fire and Simone's death at a wharf on Lake Pontchartrain and picking them up; Dante's determination to avenge Simone, to give her brother Trey a reason to keep breathing; the nearly empty yacht, minus Mauvais, a decoy; the explosion.

"After all the shit that went down on Lake Pontchartrain," Von concluded, sweeping his gaze along the busy street, "Vincent probably figured someone—Mauvais or Dante—would be coming to rip him and his entire household new ones for being treacherous SOBs, so I'd bet my left rim he went into hiding."

"So was he?" Merri asked, dark eyes glinting. "A treacherous SOB?"

"Well, now, that depends on who you ask," Von replied, smoothing his thumb and index finger along his mustache. "Vincent was definitely betraying Mauvais when he gave us the info he did; but since the info was false and it led to a trap, he screwed us as well—even if it was an unintentional screwing."

"If Vincent was the guy whose web-runner you planned to borrow, then that unintentional screwing isn't over yet," Merri said softly.

"The screwing that just keeps on giving and giving," Von agreed. He trailed a hand through his unbound hair; Jack seemed to be lacking in hair ties, but not gator print shirts, go figure. "I think my search plan just got flushed down the toilet."

So far they had only one piece of the puzzle leading to Heather's whereabouts and that had come from Heather herself: Strickland. Lucien had questioned a fed in Portland and learned that James Wallace had been unaware that the Bureau had been using him as a means to Heather.

Unfortunately, that had been all that particular fed had known. He'd been left out of the loop as far as any details of FBI hush-hush operations went, but he'd known who would know, and now Lucien was in Washington, D.C., paying a visit to a fed who was in that oh-so-exclusive hush-hush loop.

Von felt a grim satisfaction as he imagined how that meeting might go down.

Basic web searches run by himself, Jack, Silver—hell, even Merri and Thibodaux—hadn't revealed all that much. Or at least hadn't revealed much that would lead them to Heather. Turned out that Strickland was a popular name for funeral homes and Chevrolet dealerships. Who knew?

What they'd needed was a web-runner. Someone who could search deep and fast. Someone they could trust. Or someone who owed them big-time. So he'd figured he'd pay Vincent a little visit while Merri and her partner checked the club for clues to the identity of Dante's abductor or location.

No point to that little visit now.

Von's jaw tightened. Just a night or two ago, he could've put their own web-runner to work on the problem, but Trey's grief had forced him to do the unthinkable both to himself and to Dante, and now Trey was just fucking gone. Transformed into an instrument of revenge for a sister he could never bring back.

Grief could tear a person apart and remake them into someone unrecognizable, someone cold and obsessed, a stranger. As much as Von ached to make Mauvais pay for Simone's death too, he never would've used Dante like Trey had done, never would've risked a friend's heart and sanity.

Of course, in his right mind, Trey never would've either.

Von scrubbed his face with his hands. "Christ."

"So now what?" Merri asked. "You got a plan B in mind?"

Dropping his hands to his sides, Von sighed. "Looks like waiting to hear from Lucien *is* plan B." He didn't like it, but didn't have any other ideas—brilliant or otherwise. And there was still Holly to deal with too.

A moist breeze laced with the smells of fried beignets, whitewashed tombs from St. Louis No. 1, and Mississippi mud momentarily cleared away the rotting vegetation stink from the garbage bags pyramided in the gutter. A brief respite for which Von was grateful.

"Might as well go back inside and—" He stopped, sentence unfinished as the sidewalk tilted beneath him. He grabbed the van's side mirror to steady himself—*what the hell?*—then felt Merri's hard fingers lock around his biceps.

"The stay-awake," she reminded. "Consequences."

The club and the street performed a single swooping pirouette, then settled back down. Von exhaled in relief. "If a little dizziness is all—"

"It isn't," Merri warned, releasing him. "Trust me. It's just getting started. You need to be careful."

Von rubbed a hand over his face. He couldn't afford to be careful. Couldn't afford to Sleep. Not when all he felt from Dante was acid-etched pain. Not when Heather was waiting, uncertain if he'd heard her. Not until he'd found them both.

Von walked into the smoke-reeking club and headed up the stairs to the third floor landing, then his room. It was a smelly mess. Furniture, bedding, curtains, and clothing all stank of smoke and mildew, of dried blood. Sprinkler-soaked throw rugs squished beneath his borrowed sneakers.

Retrieving his double shoulder holster from the back of the chair he'd slung it over before hitting the hay—what? Only forty hours ago or so, but it felt like weeks, a lifetime—he checked the Browning tucked inside each holster and was pleased to see them in fine working order.

Shrugging off the brown leather bomber jacket, Von strapped the rig on. Patting the grip of each gun in turn, he whispered, "Missed you."

The only other belongings Von was able to scavenge from his room were his well-worn leather jacket and his scooter boots—both of which he promptly put on. He was just plain stuck with Jack's gatorfied T-shirt for the time being. He silently renewed his vow to make the drummer eat the T-shirt, one tiny gator at a time.

With Jack's sneakers and bomber jacket tucked under his arm, Von strode from his room and out into the hall—just in time to see Thibodaux heading for the stairs.

"Hey," Von called after him. "Find anything that'll help us?"

Thibodaux stopped on the landing, turned around. He shook his head. "Nothing that y'all didn't already know. Sorry, podna."

Von nodded. "I had a feeling that would be the case. Thanks anyway, man." He glanced down the hall as Thibodaux's foot-steps faded away. Silver stood at the far end, staring at something on the floor in front of Dante and Heather's room, mingled anger and despair chiseled into his pale face.

The scene of the crime—or part of it, anyway.

Von joined him, the odors of copper and cordite—blood and bullets—fading beneath Silver's clean soap-and-cinnamon scent. A dark stain edged out from the bedroom doorway into the waterlogged carpet like a high tide line on a beach. Blood. And lots of it—too much. Von's heart constricted.

"Annie thinks this is her fault," Silver murmured. His body thrummed with tension. "I told her it wasn't, but I don't think she's listening."

"The only one at fault here is her old man," Von said softly. "She'll see that once we bring her sister and Dante home."

Silver grunted, unconvinced.

Von knelt on the wet carpet and touched the maroon high-tide line. *Little brother.* His hand began to shake and, frowning, he clenched it into a fist. More of Merri's consequences?

An urgent sending from Lucien arrowed into his mind, and the stay-awakes and their consequences faded in importance. <*Llygad. The Washington contact was our brass ring. Heather is in Dallas. The Strickland Deprogramming Institute.*>

Excitement surged through Von, driving him up to his feet. Silver looked at him quizzically, dark brows slanting down over his eyes. "What? Is it Lucien?"

Nodding, Von held up a *just-a-minute* hand. <*Holy hell, that's good news.*>

<*I'm on my way there now.*>

Von stiffened. <*Hold your horses or Pegasi or whatever. I'm coming too, damn it. Wait for me. A flight to Dallas is less than two hours.*>

<*My apologies, but I can't wait. The FBI is planning to steal Heather out from under her father's nose and use her against Dante. I intend to reach her first.*>

<*Shit. Okay, yeah, you do that. Keep her safe. I'll contact you as soon as my plane hits the tarmac at Dallas/Fort Worth.*>

<*Until then,*> Lucien agreed, ending the contact.

"Heather's in Dallas," Von said, meeting Silver's impatient

gaze. "I'm joining Lucien, but I need you here to keep an eye on things—like making sure Jack and Annie are safe."

Silver opened his mouth to protest, but shut it again when Von added quietly, "They're mortal, Silver, vulnerable. And Annie needs you. Besides, you're the only one I trust to protect them. Our household can't take another loss."

Silver raked a hand through his purple anime-styled locks, spiking the air with hair-gel perfume. "Fuck," he muttered. "Yeah, okay. But you better keep me in the loop."

"You know I will," Von replied, giving his taut-muscled shoulder a quick squeeze.

"You need a ride to the airport?"

"Nope. My bike's out front. But I *do* need you to take our new SB friends back to Jack's. Keep a close eye on them. And keep me posted."

"Sure. What about your hot friend in the red dress—Holly?"

"Let me worry about her," Von said. "Why don't you start loading up whatever you've salvaged and get everyone back to Jack's?"

Silver nodded. "Will do." He *moved*, blurring down the hall to his room in a cool, cinnamon-scented breeze.

Von turned, then stumbled as the hallway suddenly dipped, then spun. Black spots flecked his vision. Electricity tingled along his spine. Jack's sneakers and jacket thudded to the floor. Grabbing the wall for support, he bowed his head, closed his eyes, and waited for the dizziness to pass.

Shit, not now. Not now. Murphy and his law can sit and spin.

After a moment, Von cautiously opened his eyes. Nothing dipped or spun or twirled. Exhaling in relief, he scooped up the jacket and sneakers, then headed downstairs and into the club proper.

As he headed for the bar where Merri and her partner sat, he felt the mental tickle that was a *llygad*'s warning to stand by, that official information was about to be streamed from the *filidh* into *llygaid* minds. Von righted a stool and sat down at the bar.

"Hear you're headed for the airport," Merri said.

"Hold on." Von tapped a fingertip against the crescent moon beneath his right eye.

Merri uttered a soft and respectful "Oh."

Von didn't have to wait long. As he focused his attention inward, vivid and familiar images streamed into his mind—and simultaneously into the minds of *llygaid* worldwide to be shared with their chosen households—and his belly sank like a fucking anchor.

The *filidh* had finally released Dante's announcement, the one that Von had captured and sent to the master Bards himself almost three nights ago at Dante's request.

Talk about lousy, fucking timing.

When the streaming memory-feed ended, Von closed his eyes and rubbed his forehead wearily with his fingertips. "Christ," he muttered.

<Dante's announcement,> he informed Silver.

<Fuck. Now?>

<Yup. Now. Bets on how long before nightkind start lining up outside hoping to kiss Dante's firm, lily-white ass?>

<Shit.>

Shit indeed.

A sudden, sharp intake of breath dropped Von's hand from his forehead and opened his eyes in time to see Merri's dark gaze unfocus. Von knew that *llygaid* in their individual households were passing along the images now pouring into Merri's mind. Knew the same thing was happening the world over, rippling across timelines, and even into the dreams of Sleeping nightkind—*llygaid*-sent.

Von rose to his feet and walked behind the soot- and water-stained bar, grabbed a bottle of Jack Daniel's off the glass liquor shelf, and cracked the seal. Deciding to forgo the usual tumbler, he drank straight from the bottle.

Fuck Murphy and his stupid goddamned law.

17

BADASS AND
BEAUTIFUL

M ERRI FELT AN URGENT nudge at her shields—a
mental touch she recognized as belonging to her *mère
de sang's llygad*, Juliet. Merri relaxed her shields, then closed
her eyes.

<*Dante Baptiste in an official announcement made at his
Club Hell at approximately eleven p.m. Central Time on March
28th,*> Juliet sent.

Merri frowned, wondering at the announcement's delay.
Then images flooded her mind in detail so vivid it seemed as
though she viewed them through her own eyes, transported in
time and place to Club Hell, to a moment almost three nights
old—a moment taking place right now.

*She stands in front of the Cage, breathing in air thick with
musky pheromones, pungent curls of pot and tobacco smoke,
patchouli, and sweat. At her back, she feels the heated, adrena-
line-soaked press of the club crowd; hears the jackrabbit rush of
mortal pulses mingling with the slow waltz of nightkind hearts.*

And inside the Cage . . .

A lean-muscled form in a shirt of PVC and fishnet and metal straps; low-slung black latex jeans and boots. A metal studded leather collar encircles his milk-white throat. Light glints from the steel ring at its center, from the rings on his fingers and thumbs, but not from the hoops she knows trace the curves of his ears—hidden behind the nightfall of his black hair.

He steps forward, a sinuous and natural panther prowl. Merri's breath catches rough in her throat. She's only seen him frozen in photos or at a distance in grainy or static-freckled video feed, never like this—right in front of her, pulsing heat through her veins with just a simple movement.

Badass and beautiful Dante Baptiste curls one pale hand around the microphone, leaning in just a little, his cupid's-bow lips nearly grazing the mic cover. "This is an official announcement for all you nightkind out there . . ."

Merri had planned to approach Dante—when they finally met—with an open-minded neutrality in order to assess the damage done to him by Bad Seed. She had studied his photos, memorizing every contour of his ivory-pale face, each line of his tight-muscled body, in an effort to inoculate herself against his thought-scorching beauty.

And she believed she had succeeded. Believed herself ready and more than capable of doing what her *mère de sang* had requested of her.

The Conseil du Sang want you to be their emissary to Dante Baptiste. They want you to assess his condition, to determine whether he can be salvaged. As rare and powerful as True Bloods are, no one wants to just throw this boy away. But if he's too damaged, then he's much too dangerous to remain free . . .

Now, watching him in the Cage, Merri knew herself for a fool.

"I'M GONNA SHARE A few things I've learned recently and end the rumors tonight." Dante's kohl-rimmed, deep brown eyes skim the crowd for a moment before he continues. "I'm the Nightbringer's son and I was born nightkind."

Stunned silence from the crowd. Lucien De Noir stands beside the Cage door, his chin lifted, his face nearly luminous with pride.

"Just so there's no confusion," Dante continues into the silence, his Cajun-accented voice shifting into a warning drawl, "no, I won't turn you. No, you ain't getting a taste. No, I ain't interested in claiming power, your fucking household, or your girlfriend."

"Bullshit! You're lying through your fangs!" someone shouts. "You're just trying to win support against Guy!"

"Yeah, that'd be my thought too, in your place," Dante says, unstrapping his latex shirt and peeling it off.

Lusty catcalls scrape into the air at the sight of Dante's bared torso—all lean, defined muscle and ivory skin. A ridged white scar forms an odd blend of pyramids and loops on one pec. "Don't stop there!" someone teasingly pleads. "Keep going!"

Dante turns around, giving the crowd his back. He flexes his shoulder and deltoid muscles, then smooth black wings edged in deepest crimson slide out from beneath his skin in a rush and unfurl, snapping the scent of burning leaves and musk into the air.

Silence swallows the crowd whole, mortal and nightkind alike.

Dante swivels back around with an unconscious and sexy grace and displays the undersides of his wings—streaked in fire patterns of brilliant blue and purple—before folding them shut behind him. He grasps the microphone again, the rings on his fingers and thumb clinking against the metal, yanking it close to the wicked, knowing smile tilting his lips.

"Does that answer the bullshit question? Anyone? Anyone?"

THE IMAGE THAT MERRI was receiving of Dante in the Cage, black dragon wings folded at his back and arching above his head, suddenly wrinkled like the surface of a wind-kissed pond, then smoothed away into nothingness as Juliet withdrew the feed from Merri's mind.

Merri's heart drummed a stuttering cadence against her ribs. Fallen. Not only True Blood, but Fallen. Her racing thoughts hurried back to Damascus and the white stone angels rimming the mysterious cave—where a home had once stood, where a rogue FBI agent and his family had died.

Blue sparks flicker like fireflies over the white stone, skip along the butter-smooth wings. From within the white stone a heart flutters, the sound slowing. Not statues, no. Merri senses power in each stone figure, power that tingles against her gloved fingertips. She remembers tales of Fallen magic, whispers of angelic battles.

Merri couldn't help but wonder how Dante Baptiste— given what she now knew about him—had managed to avoid sharing their fate, especially since he'd been there too, he and Heather Wallace both.

She also couldn't help but wonder why Von, that long cool drink of a nomad, had neglected to mention the fact that Dante was Lucien De Noir's son. *Nightbringer.* A vision of raven-black wings, their edges sharp as a scythe, flaring above bone-white tombs, flashed behind her closed eyes, leaving her both chilled and uneasy.

An aroma of sweet oranges and almonds washed over Merri's senses—Galiana's scent—and then she felt her *mère de sang*'s soothing, mental touch.

<*See, child? What did I tell you?*>

<*'I have a suspicion that events beyond the scope of mortals or even vampires might be unfolding,'*> Merri quoted. <*Do you think Dante's a part of those events?*>

But Galiana ignored her question, asking one of her own instead. <*Did you notice the sigil on Dante Baptiste's chest?*>

<*Sigil? The weird scar?*>

<*The weird scar, sí.*> Amusement buoyed Galiana's sending, an amusement that vanished as quickly as soap bubbles. <*It's the Morningstar's mark. Which tells me that our damaged True Blood plays a very big part in what is to come among the*

Elohim>—finally answering Merri's question—*<I don't know what or how or why. Not yet. But whatever it is, every living being in the mortal world will be touched by it as well.>*

<So what now?> Merri sent. *<Do I still try to assess how damaged he is? With the Fallen involved, does it even matter anymore? I don't think they're going to let us waltz away with him, no matter what I learn. I know his father certainly won't—>*

<Dante's mother was vampire,> Galiana interrupted. *<He belongs to us, child, and we need him. The Bloodline needs him. Without him . . . We'll find a way to negotiate with the Fallen, so stay on course. Have you met him yet?>*

<Not yet,> Merri admitted. For reasons she didn't fully understand, she decided to leave it at that and save the details—Dante's disappearance and the frantic search to find him—for another time. *<But I'll let you know when I do.>*

<This announcement has the Conseil *eager to get him some-where safe>*—a wry note twisted through Galiana's sending—*<meaning, away from the* Cercle de Druide *and that damned Renata Cortini in particular.>*

<Meaning, the Conseil's *collective panties are in a twist.>*

Galiana's amusement poured like sunshine through Merri's mind, warm and full of golden light. *<That they are. Keep safe, Merri-girl.>*

<You too, Galiana.>

As her *mère de sang's* presence withdrew from her mind, Merri became aware of the strained silence surrounding her. She opened her eyes and looked up into eyes as cold and hard as emeralds in a glacier. It hit her then and she uttered a soft groan of disbelief. The announcement, the scene at the club, Dante in the Cage, herself so caught up, so damned rapt. . . .

"You dropped your shields, darlin'," Von said in a low, tight voice. "I think we need to talk."

18

CONSEQUENCES

He'd fucked up. No two ways about it.

Von took another long pull from the bottle of Jack. The bourbon burned smooth all the way down, but did nothing to ease the fury and self-disgust knotting up his guts.

When he'd scanned Merri's mind back at the house, he'd looked for SB conspiracy plots dancing like sugar plums inside her pretty head and when he hadn't found any, he'd thought there hadn't been a need to look deeper.

He'd thought wrong.

The second scan he'd just done verified everything he'd overheard between Merri and her *mère de sang*: the *Conseil du Sang* planned to out-maneuver, outwit, and outflank both the Fallen and the *Cercle de Druide* and lay claim to Dante first.

Motherfuckers. Like Dante was a winning lottery ticket.

And what exactly had Merri's *mère de sang* meant when she'd told Merri that the Bloodline needed Dante? A dark suspicion snaked through Von's mind, one he didn't care to contemplate at the moment.

Ain't got time for this shit. Need to be heading for the airport.

Merri still sat on the opposite side of the counter, a tumbler of brandy in one dark hand. Thibodaux sat beside her, hooded eyes watchful.

"Look," Merri said, "I haven't told anyone that Dante's missing or incommunicado. Doesn't that count for something?"

Von shook his head. "Nope. No brownie points for biding your time."

"I wasn't biding. . . . Jesus, I told you, I was sent on a fact-finding mission—"

"Spying. I'd call it spying," Von interrupted, resting the rapidly emptying bottle of Jack Daniel's on the bar. "And, yeah. I know. To find out how much Dante's been messed up by Bad Seed so that the fucking *Conseil* can decide Dante's future for him. Sound about right?"

"No, *llygad*, it *doesn't* sound about right. Just because that's why I was sent, doesn't mean that's why I'm here."

Placing his hands on the counter, Von leaned in, bringing his face closer to Merri's. "All right. I'm game, darlin'. Entertain me. Why you here, then?"

With a soft, frustrated sigh, Merri shook a cigarette from her pack of Djarum Black, then fired it up with a slim, silver lighter. The aroma of clove-spice tobacco crackled into the reeking air. "It sounds like you've already got your mind made up. So forget it."

"Oh no. You don't get off the hook that easy. Spill, woman. Why you here?"

Merri lifted her chin. "To get to know Dante Baptiste. To find out what *he* wants. And to give back to him what was stolen—his past."

"Amen to that," Thibodaux said. "But he shouldn't watch that flash drive alone, y'hear?" He lifted his gaze to Von's, expression grim. Shadows lurked beneath the surface of his blue eyes. "And not in one sitting. Hell, maybe he shouldn't even watch it at all."

"Maybe," Von agreed. "But that's for Dante to decide." He slid the bottle of Jack across the counter to Thibodaux. The former SB agent flashed him a grateful smile. Lifting the bottle to his lips, he took a long, healthy swallow.

Von straightened and studied Merri for a long, silent moment. She returned his regard with calm, brown eyes. He'd found secrets in her mind, yeah, but no deliberate deception. Still, when it came down to the wire, would she follow her heart and what she knew to be right or obey her *mère de sang*?

"Why didn't you just tell me all this to start with?" Von asked.

Shrugging, Merri blew a plume of clove-scented smoke into the air. "I meant to, but I was a little preoccupied. When were you planning on telling me that De Noir was Dante's father?"

"I meant to, but I was a little preoccupied."

A wry smile twitched at the corners of Merri's mouth. "Touché. But I gotta say—for a *llygad*, you're one smart-ass mofo." She tapped her cigarette against the ashtray, then added, "No offense."

"None taken," Von drawled. "I don't get many compliments like that. Hard to believe, I know. Now, if y'all will excuse me, I need to get to the airport."

"You want backup?" Merri asked, hopping down from her stool. "We—"

Von cut her off with a shake of his head. "Sorry, darlin', can't trust you." He flicked a glance at Thibodaux. "Either one of you. I think your intentions might be good, but your loyalty ain't to Dante. Until that changes . . ." He shrugged.

Frustration rippled across Merri's face, then vanished. "All right," she said. "I can understand that. Is there anything we can do here to help in the meantime? A way to start earning that trust?"

Von opened his mouth to say no, then reconsidered as he took in the club's sorry state. "If you truly want to help, talk to Silver and Jack about how best to get this mess cleaned up and repairs started. They'll know who to call to get the ball rolling."

"Fair enough," Merri said.

Outside, Von locked up the club as best he could, given the

damaged doors, then saw Merri and Thibodaux off in the van with Silver behind the wheel. As he headed down the block for his Harley, keys in hand, he heard the slow, pendulum swing of nightkind hearts behind him. He stopped, suddenly remembering his appointment with Holly.

"I'm sorry, darlin'," Von said, turning around, "but something impor—" His words cut off when he saw who had joined Holly.

Two male nightkind in the formal black kilts, sweaters, and boots of the *filidh* guard, horizontal sword tattoos beneath their right eyes, flanked her. Von didn't see any visible weapons, but then, they didn't need any. Being *llafnau*, they *were* weapons.

"Looks like you're skipping out on me again," Holly said.

"I'm really sorry about that, Miková," Von said, taking a slow step back toward his Harley. "But our meeting needs to wait one night. One night is all I'm asking and then I'll head straight for Memphis—as ordered. You have my word."

"The same word you gave me less than a week ago?" Holly asked, her threadbare Russian accent dropping into a deadly purr. "The same word you gave me not two hours ago? *That* word, Vonushka? You made me look like a fool."

"I'm sorry about that too," Von said, meaning it. "That was never my intention. But all kinds of shit has hit the fan, shit that involves Dante. You saw his announcement. You know what that means." Von took another backward step. The bike was just behind him. "You've got to trust me, Holly. Just one night."

"No. Not this time. You've worn my trust thin."

Von whirled—

—and the street whirled with him. Spinning in a streak of night and orange gaslight, paving bricks and green shutters, stars and pavement. Darkness bled across Von's vision. As the sidewalk rushed up to meet him, one thought pirouetted through his mind before darkness shut the show down.

Aw, crap. Motherfucking pills.

19

LIKE ASHES IN
HER MOUTH

HEATHER HAD JUST TUCKED her fork into the sleeve of her cornflower-blue sweater, the steel cool against her skin, when James Wallace walked back into the dining room—empty now except for her—and slumped into the chair opposite hers, the sharp scent of his Brut aftershave wafting across the table. The line of his clean-shaven jaw was nearly white with anger.

"You were right," he said, light from the overheads reflected in his glasses. "The RN just confirmed it. You *are* being trans-ferred in the morning." He shoved aside the plate containing his half-eaten meal, scattering a few kernels of buttered corn across the tablecloth. "Goddammit. No one contacted me about this."

"I warned you," Heather said, lowering her hand to her lap and folding her fingers over the heel of her sleeve, securing the fork. "Back at the club. The Bureau isn't going to let me just walk away. Not with all the secrets I know."

"That shouldn't matter. You're one of the Bureau's finest—"

"Was," Heather corrected. "*Was* one of their finest. Now I'm a major liability."

"Because of that damned bloodsucker."

"No, dammit, because I learned the *truth*, and Dante happens to be a part of that truth, a truth the Bureau never wanted to come to light. They'll do anything to make sure it stays buried. Anything. Including burying me."

And Dante, but that was a thought she kept to herself.

"I'm beginning to think you're right," James said. "After all, they used me to get to you. Must've put a tail on me or a GPS tracker because I took extreme care in covering my tracks." He raked a furious hand through his gray-flecked blond hair. "I took an official leave of absence to tend to family matters. This is none of their business."

"The secrets I carry are."

"Christ." James pulled off his glasses and pinched the bridge of his nose.

Heather pushed her plate away, the food untouched, her appetite dead, despite the savory fragrance of pork chops baked in rosemary and spicy brown mustard. The strain of being in the presence of the man who'd shot Dante in cold blood and left him to burn, the man who'd drugged and kidnapped her, kept her stomach twisted into hard knots.

Just a little while longer. . . .

Scraping her chair back, Heather rose to her feet. "Dad"— the word tasted like ashes in her mouth—"If I stay here, they'll take me. And if they take me, you'll never see me again."

"I'm not going to let that happen," James slipped his glasses back on, then looked at her. A familiar stubborn light glinted in his hazel eyes. "I checked you in and I paid for your treatment. I can check you out, as well."

Mingled exhilaration and relief flooded Heather's veins, goosed her pulse. Her gamble, based on her father's need for control, was paying off in spades. Clamping her fingers tighter over the heel of her sleeve, she said, "Where will we go?"

"Where they can't find us." James stood, then grabbed his tan trench coat from the back of the chair and shrugged it on. "I brought you here to be healed, restored. And if the powers that be in the Bureau are too ignorant to grasp that, well, then, that's their loss. But they're not getting their hands on you." He swept a glance over Heather, tallying her sweater and jeans, the black Skechers on her feet. "Anything else you need in your room?"

"Nope. This is everything." Everything she'd been wearing, that was, when the self-absorbed, lying bastard had broken into the club, then shot her full of tranks out of so-called fatherly concern. Hardly time to pack a suitcase.

"Good. Let's get you checked out."

ONCE THEY WERE OUTSIDE the building and heading for James's rented Lexus in the parking lot, Heather's relief was so intense, her knees nearly buckled.

It had gone so damned smoothly.

Sue Bieri, the RN in charge of the night shift, had protested of course.

She'd voiced concerns about Heather's treatment and how interruption might affect her progress, had worried about how the FBI would react to her absence, but in the end, she'd had no choice but to print out discharge papers for James to sign.

"Don't worry about the FBI," James had said, offering Sue a grim smile. "I'll call them myself. Thank them for the thought."

Just like that, Heather was free—well, almost. And that almost-freedom smelled like green woods and cooling pavement, car exhaust and sage. She sucked in a deep breath, savored the uncanned air.

James unlocked the Lexus's doors. "In the back seat, pump-kin, passenger side," he murmured, yanking the door open. "Strap yourself in."

Heather arched an eyebrow, but said nothing. The request

didn't surprise her. She got into the car, sliding into the back-seat as requested, knowing that James had put her there to make it more difficult for her to interfere with him while driving.

She was his daughter, yes, but he was no fool.

Once James had slipped behind the steering wheel, he leaned across the seat, his trench coat rustling against the leather, and popped open the glove box. A holstered gun—a Colt .38 like her own—and a pair of tin snips remained inside. But Heather's heart sank at what he removed—flex-cuffs.

"That's not necessary," Heather said, managing to keep her voice even. "I'm not going to cause any trouble. I *want* to get away from the FBI, remember?"

"Oh, I know you do," James replied. "But you also want to go running back to"—the lines creasing his forehead and brack-eting his mouth deepened as his expression corkscrewed into one of utter contempt—"*him*. You aren't free of that bloodsuck-ing bastard yet, so I need to watch out for you. Now, hands up on the back of the seat."

Heather opened her mouth to protest, then closed it again when she saw the set look on his face. She could talk herself blue, she wouldn't change his mind. She considered bolting from the car, but imagined he had more tranks and could put one into her before she made it to the woods.

"The sooner you cooperate, the sooner we're out of here," James said, waving the flex-cuffs.

Heather noticed that the cuffs weren't a single tie, but dou-ble cuffs, which would actually allow her much more mobility than a single tie. Hope surged through her. Maybe she could still put her fork to work like she'd planned, after all. With a sigh of false resignation, she placed her elbows on the seat back and offered her wrists. She felt the fork slide toward her elbow.

"That's my girl," James murmured, looping the cuffs around her wrists, then pulling them tight. A happy, *all's-under-control* smile curled across his lips. "Allrighty, then. Sit back. Fasten your seat belt and let's get this show on the road."

Heather heard a *thunk* as James engaged the car's child-proof door locks.

Christ. You'd think he was transporting Hannibal Lector. Guess I'm lucky he didn't strap a muzzle over my mouth.

Sitting back as requested, Heather strapped her seat belt on and waited, muscles coiled and ready. She glanced out the window into a night scudded with pale streamers of clouds as James started up the Lexus and drove through the parking lot to the guard station at the gate.

Once again, she felt a strong tug to the east, the irresistible siren call that would lead her to Dante. *Soon*, she promised him. *I'll be there soon.*

Heather kept her cuffed wrists discreetly out of sight while the guard on duty at the gate briefly examined the discharge papers, before handing them back to James and waving them on.

"Y'all have a good night," the guard said.

"Thanks," James replied. "You too."

Heather pretended to doze while James steered the Lexus along a night-ribboned highway, headed for the soft glow of lights at the horizon that was Dallas. Keeping her breathing even and her movements as small as possible, she gradually worked the fork down to the heel of her sleeve again, its tines poking and scraping along her skin. Sweat beaded her forehead as she slid the fork into the palm of her right hand. She curled her fingers around the smooth handle.

Risking a quick glance through her lashes, Heather saw James shift his gaze from the windshield to the rearview mirror.

"Are you actually sleeping?" he asked, voice amused. "Or just avoiding conversation?"

"Dozing." Heather opened her eyes and met James's shadowed regard for a moment before he flicked his attention back to the road. "Must be all the drugs that've been pumped into my system since my arrival."

"You gave us no choice, pumpkin. You were pretty hostile."

"Really? Gee. I wonder why."

"Everything I've done, I've done with your best interests in mind."

"You actually believe that, don't you?" Heather said, voice flat.

Now that she was finally free and clear of the institute, she was done pretending, done with the bitter burn of acid at the back of her throat while she played the role of daughter-struggling-to-understand-and-forgive. *Done*.

"Absolutely."

"What about Annie's best interests? Or Kevin's? You have theirs in mind too?"

James's eyes flitted to the rearview, a frown wrinkling his brow. "Of course," he replied, returning his gaze to the road. "Always. But I know it may not look that way. I've had to use tough love on your sister and brother from time to time."

Heather's pulse pounded at her temple. Tough love. Fine words for coldhearted manipulation and emotional abuse. For shoving aside his bipolar daughter, then dangling the carrot of his love and acceptance in front of her just so he could use her; for shutting out his son and belittling him for refusing to follow in James's FBI footsteps.

"Tough love, my ass," Heather said, throat tight. She pressed her fingers against the seat belt latch. She muffled the quiet *snick* with her sleeve, then held the seat belt in place with her arm. "It was never about love, just control."

James shook his head. "You don't have the proper perspective. Being a single parent hasn't been easy. Not by a long shot. But I've always done what was necessary, even if it was hard."

Heather tightened her grip on the fork handle. "What about Mom? Was her murder one of those necessary but hard things too?"

James Wallace went still. He watched her from the rearview, his shadowed eyes unreadable. But mild disappointment underscored his words. "You say that as though I had something to do with it. Good God, Heather, your mother's death—"

"Murder."

"All right—*murder*—was tragic and difficult for us all. But so was the way she lived." The Lexus's interior filled with blue-white light from an approaching car, drawing James's attention back to the highway. The vehicle passed, and darkness returned. "I don't know how many times I came home from work to find you kids alone and hungry because your mother was off drinking or . . . whatever."

"She was bipolar and an addict," Heather said, slowly leaning forward toward the front seats. "She needed help. Just like Annie."

"Your mother didn't want help. Flat-out refused it."

"Again. She was bipolar and an addict." Heather shrugged free of the seat belt. "You should've insisted. Kept her best interests in mind."

Provided you weren't busy blackmailing your partner into murdering her and setting up a local serial killer suspect to take the fall.

Something, even now, Heather desperately didn't want to believe. She hoped with all she had that he would prove her wrong. She shifted her grip on the fork, steadied it. Pressed against the back of his seat.

"I tried, pumpkin, you have no idea," James said softly, his tone low and haunted and utterly false. "As horrible as your mother's *murder* was, in many ways—and I truly hate to say this—it was a blessing. With her gone, you kids finally had stability and a shot at a normal life."

Heather glanced away, a muscle ticking in her jaw. The worst part of that statement? The lying bastard actually believed it. Drawing in a steadying breath, she looked at him again. "I know what you did," she said quietly. "At the club."

"Risk life and limb to rescue you? You're welcome."

"This isn't a thank you, you smug son of a bitch. I know you tried to murder Dante, I know you left him and my friends to burn. I know what you did to Annie too."

"Do you? How is that poss—" A quick glance into the rearview. His jaw tightened. "So Annie was right, you *are* linked mind-to-mind to that bloodsucking bastard. He must still be alive, then."

"No thanks to you," Heather growled, lunging forward and jabbing the fork tines into his neck just above his carotid. "Pull over. Now."

20

RECEDING IN
THE REARVIEW

"WHAT THE *HELL* DO you think you're—"

Heather jabbed the fork harder into James's throat. He winced, his knuckles whitening on the steering wheel. The fork bobbed in time with his rapidly increasing pulse.

"Heather..."

"Now."

Heather applied a little more pressure to the fork as incentive. Beneath the tines, blood stippled James's skin. Sudden sweat glistened on his forehead, at the back of his neck, blotting out the scent of his spicy aftershave. Icy displeasure radiated from him in nearly palpable waves.

Without another word, James Wallace steered the Lexus onto the shoulder of the road. A cold sweat slicked Heather's body, plastered her sweater to her back. She knew, without a doubt, that once James stopped the car, he would stop at nothing to regain control of the situation. To regain control of her.

Even if it meant killing her.

Gravel crunched under the tires as the car slowed to a stop. In the rearview, Heather caught a peripheral flare of red from the brake lights. Adrenaline flooded her veins. She sucked in a breath. Time slowed. Stretched. And everything took on a sharp-edged, crystal clarity.

The muscles in James's neck twitched. His shoulder tensed. But before he could jerk his head away from the fork, Heather threw her upper body over the seat back and slammed the fork deep into his thigh with both hands.

James screamed.

Pulse roaring in her ears, Heather slithered and squirmed her way over the seat, landing on her side. She groped for the glove box with cuffed hands. Slapped the latch. It tumbled open. Beside her, James's cry of shocked pain gave way to a clenched-teeth snarl of rage.

"I don't think so, pumpkin."

A metallic glint, then Heather felt a punch to her lower back, right above her left kidney; felt another. She felt the warm trickle of blood. Bastard was using the fork. She knew it should hurt, knew it *would* hurt, but adrenaline blurred the pain, kept it at bay—for now.

She lashed out with her foot, felt it connect. Heard a pained grunt. And kept kicking. Grabbing the holstered gun with both hands, the worn leather almost slippery beneath her sweat-slick grasp, she fumbled with the holster's snap.

Hands seized her foot, immobilized it. Twisted. Heather felt something give in her ankle and this time, a nauseating twist of pain corkscrewed up into the pit of her belly.

Shaking the holster free of the Colt Super, Heather flipped off the safety and rolled onto her back. Aimed the gun between James Wallace's eyes. Curled her finger around the trigger and began applying pressure.

Her aim was true. Her hands steady. She wouldn't hesitate to shoot.

And in that moment, in the sudden contraction of his

pupils, the thinning of his lips, the emotions chasing across the hard landscape of his face—disbelief to indignation to scorn to ice-cold fury—he knew it too.

Time's slow stretch stopped, snapped back in on itself.

"You don't want to do this," James warned, her foot still held between his hands. "I can only overlook that bloodsucker's influence on you for so long."

Heather ignored the comment, refusing to waste any more time and energy arguing with him or trying to convince him that she was an adult making her own decisions. His opinions had ceased to matter a long time ago.

Breath rasping hot in her throat, she tightened her finger on the trigger, adding more pressure. James released her foot and shoved it away, a muscle bunching in his jaw.

"Leave your cell phone," Heather said, scooting upright on the seat, her aim unwavering. Her ankle was beginning to throb and her back, sticky with blood, stung. "Then get out of the goddamned car."

Pulling his cell phone from one of the trench's inside pockets, James tossed it carelessly onto the floorboards. He held Heather's gaze, his eyes bitter and cold. "I'm not sure I can forgive this, pumpkin. One straw too many and all that."

"Ask me if I care."

"No need. I'm pretty sure I know the answer."

"Great. Now get out."

James studied her for a moment, then nodded—almost as if to himself. Swiveling in his seat, he unlocked the doors, and climbed out of the Lexus. The door shut behind him with a solid *thunk*.

Heather slid into the driver's seat and hit the door-lock button, her pulse still racing. He was outside and she was in, but she still wasn't safe, not by a long shot. Not until he was many miles behind her.

Heather motioned with the Colt for James to move to the side of the road. As he complied, walking around the front of the car, he turned his head and squinted as headlights flared on the road behind them.

Heather shifted and looked out the rear window. The headlights loomed larger and brighter, twin miniature suns illuminating the empty stretch of road and sweeping light and shadows across the brush and trees along its edges. She glanced away, blinking dazzles from her vision. Headlight glow filled the rearview mirror.

The car cruised past without slowing, its passengers probably assuming, given the lack of emergency flashers, that James was heading off into the brush to take a leak. Heather exhaled in relief.

She decided to drive a distance, maybe find a rest stop or gas station, before pulling over to use the tin snips to cut off the flex-cuffs. *Wrestling* with the tin snips would probably be more like it, she reflected ruefully.

Then she would call Annie and ask to speak to Von.

Tucking the Colt into the front of her jeans, Heather fastened her seat belt. She slid the gearshift into drive, then did just that, curling her fingers around the bottom of the steering wheel. She watched James recede in the rearview until he vanished from sight, swallowed by the night.

Deep down, like an ache in her bones, Heather had a feeling that the next time she and James met, it would be the final time—and, for one of them, fatal. Her throat tightened. Even though she never wanted to see or speak to him again, even though a part of her believed he more than deserved to die, nothing in that stark realization offered her any comfort.

With each mile rolling beneath the Lexus's tires, the eastern tug grew stronger, as though hooks had snagged her at heart and mind and were reeling her in. She needed to get off the highway she was on and find one that would take her into Louisiana.

After nearly twenty minutes, she spotted a sign for a gas station five miles ahead. Perfect. She'd pull off, get out of the flex-cuffs, call Von, then get directions and—

Her heart jumped into her throat.

A car was slanted sideways across her lane, lights off, an accident or a barricade, and she was almost on top of it. A figure stepped out from beside the stopped vehicle and aimed something at her.

Jesus Christ, is that a gun?

Ducking down in her seat, Heather jerked the wheel to the left, swerving into the passing lane. She goosed the gas, hoping to arrow past any bullets. The Lexus surged forward, then the soft green dash lights winked out. The headlights vanished. The engine switched off. The sharp odor of ozone and scorched circuits curled through the air.

Heather's heart sank. Not a gun, no. The Lexus had been brought down with a mini-EMP bomb. Headlights flashed on ahead of her and two cars arrowed down the dark road toward her coasting Lexus. Light flared in her rearview as the posed vehicle behind her started up.

A trap. A goddamned trap.

She couldn't help but wonder if someone at Strickland had contacted the FBI to let them know that James Wallace had just checked his daughter out ahead of schedule.

Shit. Shit. Shit.

Heather tried to steer the Lexus off the road to the shoulder, but the damned thing was about as maneuverable as a mountain. She settled for tapping the brakes as she rolled to a stop. Headlight glare filled the car. Unstrapping her seat belt, she leaned over, popped open the glove box, and grabbed the tin snips.

It was easier than she'd expected. A turn with her wrist, an adjustment to the angle, then two quick snips, and her hands were free. Tossing the snips aside, Heather scooped up the cell phone and tucked it into a pocket of her jeans. She pulled the Colt Super and chambered a round.

Two dark sedans pulled to a stop in front of the Lexus. One—the decoy—stopped behind. Doors opened and suited figures sheltered behind them. Air curled in front of the head-lights like blue twists of smoke.

"Heather Wallace," a man's voice called, muffled through the windshield. "Toss out your weapons, then slowly step out of the vehicle."

Guns lifted. Aimed.

Wiping her sweaty palms against her jeans, Heather considered her options. If the Bureau had wanted her dead at this particular moment, they could've arranged for a car accident instead of an EMP guaranteed to stop her without harm. And the guns might actually be trank guns or Tasers.

She'd just escaped from one institution. She'd be damned if she'd just surrender and allow herself to be taken to another—one with top-level security and no visitors allowed. Heather blew out a breath. Okay. She'd started the day with a gamble. No point in stopping now. It was all in or nothing.

Picking up the tin snips, Heather opened the door, and tossed them out as though they were her gun. They hit the pavement with a hard *tunk*. "All right," she called. "I'm coming out."

"Slowly," she was reminded.

She stepped out of the Lexus. Then swung up the Colt and fired several rounds at the lead cars. She whirled, ignoring the twinge in her ankle, and ran for the woods. Startled shouts slashed into the air behind her.

She felt something bite into the backs of her shoulders and, just like the Lexus had, her muscles shut down as an electrical pulse thrummed through her. She flopped to the ground like a dynamite-stunned fish.

Heather heard footsteps in the dry grass, then the rustle of cloth as someone crouched beside her. The Colt was wrenched from her rigid grasp. Polished black shoes moved into her field of vision.

"Here's another taste," a male voice grumbled. Her muscles contracted as another surge of electricity danced through them.

"Shoot at us, will you? Damned fed. I should zap you all the way to Alexandria."

"Knock it the hell off, Roberts. Just cuff her, okay? Let's get moving. We've got a long drive ahead of us."

A grunt of acquiescence, then Heather felt her arms pulled behind her back, felt handcuffs ratchet shut around her wrists. A cold sweat iced her body as she was hauled to her unsteady feet. Her muscles quivered.

Damned fed. Alexandria.

She'd been intercepted by the SB, *not* the FBI.

Heather never dreamed she would wish that James Wallace had reached the Colt before she had. As a steel-fingered hand locked around her biceps and forced her forward, she wished so now. She walked, stumbling, toward one of the dark sedans, knowing she was well and truly screwed.

21

A SIMPLE,
UNAVOIDABLE TRUTH

LUCIEN LANDED BESIDE THE abandoned Lexus, his wings flaring once before folding shut behind him. The car was parked at a slant on the highway's shoulder, the driver's-side door open wide, the interior dark.

A quick glance at the license plate number confirmed that it was James Wallace's rented Lexus, the vehicle Lucien had seen on the Strickland Deprogramming Institute's gate security tapes as Wallace had driven away hours ago with Heather in the backseat instead of the passenger seat—as though he were transporting a prisoner.

Question was, where was he taking her? Or, Lucien reflected grimly as he studied the night-shadowed car, where had he *intended* to take her?

Lucien had arrived at the institute shortly after midnight and, using a bit of power, persuasion, and suggestion—*FBI Special Agent Lucas Black checking on Heather Wallace's progress*—he had learned from the night nurse that Heather had been unexpectedly checked out by her father hours earlier.

He seemed real unhappy that y'all were going to transfer her to a different facility in the morning. I tried to reason with him, but he refused to be reasoned with. Legally, we couldn't stop him. I'm sorry no one contacted you about this yet but, to be honest, we thought it was the responsibility of Strickland's director, not ours . . .

That verified what Lucien had suspected—James Wallace hadn't known the Bureau had used him to get to Heather. Had let him do all the work and face all the danger, just so they could swoop in and seize the prize—his daughter.

And quietly end her life.

Of course, it would be impossible for the Bureau to know that by ending Heather's life, they would most likely trigger the world's end as well when Dante laid waste to it transforming what remained into a funeral pyre for Heather.

Unless I stop him. Lucien's hands knotted into fists at his sides. *Like I stopped Yahweh.* Unbidden and unwelcome, a memory thousands of years old played behind his eyes.

Lucien cradles Yahweh's body against his chest. Light no longer blazes from the creawdwr's face. Tiny drops of scarlet blossom on his skin, blood from Lucien's nose.

Outside, the ground ripples and quakes and it feels as though Gehenna will tear itself apart. With Yahweh dead, it just might.

"What have you DONE?" Lilith screams the last word. She drops to the floor beside Lucien, hands at her temples. She grabs at Yahweh's shoulder.

Lucien smacks her hand away and looks at her. Her hand freezes in midair. She stares at him with stunned purple eyes. "You'll never use him again," he says. He returns his gaze to Yahweh's pale, lifeless face. "He's free . . ."

Headlights shafted through the darkness as a car approached from the opposite lane. It started to slow, a potential

Good Samaritan, until Lucien spared it a single molten glance. Taking in the glowing golden gaze, the dragon-winged silhouette, the driver's eyes widened. The car sped away.

Darkness rolled in once more across the road—and across Lucien's heart.

If it gets that far. If it comes to that. I will find Dante before it does.

A breeze fragrant with the smells of sagebrush and winter-dried scrub fluttered through the length of Lucien's hair, whispered cool against his wings. He walked over to the Lexus's open door, gravel gritting beneath the soles of his shoes.

He knew the car was empty even before he ducked his head inside for a peek. No heartbeats. No faint odor of death. Even so, a keen disappointment knifed through him as he searched the Lexus for any clue as to what had happened to Heather.

An open glove box, an empty gun holster, rental-car paperwork.

A blood-smeared fork on the floorboards.

Severed flex-cuffs.

A few small drops of blood flecking both front seats.

Car keys still in the ignition.

Lucien could read the story easily enough. Heather had used a secreted fork to get the drop on her father, one or both had been slightly injured; she'd managed to get her flex-cuffs off; and someone had grabbed the gun. But nothing—except the flung-open door—hinted at what had happened to Heather or her father after the car had stopped.

They got out, yes, but where did they go?

A chilling possibility occurred to Lucien—maybe it was a mistake to assume that Heather had left the Lexus voluntarily. What if the car had been intercepted, its occupants seized?

No tire marks were scorched black on the highway, no broken bits of red plastic from the taillights or paint scrapes on the bumpers. No flat tires. Nothing to indicate that the Lexus had been forced from the road.

Nothing and more nothing.

Frustration burned through Lucien, strung his muscles wire-tight. He climbed back out of the Lexus and studied the scrub and the woods beyond the road. Closing his eyes, he listened. He heard the small, rapid pulse of animal hearts, of birds, but nothing that indicated a mortal sheltered amongst the trees, hiding in the darkness.

Heather had disappeared. His only link to Dante, gone.

And Lucien no longer knew where to look for her. He felt something deep inside of him crack, then sheer away, like tons of ice sliding from a glacier into the sea.

The truth is never what you hope it will be.

Hearing a metallic double *whomp*, Lucien opened his eyes and watched impassively as both fists slammed again into the Lexus's roof, crumpling it inward. The windshield exploded, spraying shards of glittering glass into the gravel.

Even while a part of himself insisted that this wasn't productive behavior, his fists kept pounding into the car, over and over, until the roof finally merged with the seats. Metal groaned, then shrieked as he wrenched the door off its hinges and tossed it toward the woods. He heard a distant *whomp* as it landed.

Lucien stared at the remains of the shattered, pummeled car, his taloned hands flexing. Aching to destroy something else. Anything else. It was better than admitting he'd been defeated. And with that realization, his savage fury and despair drained away like radioactive water from a broken core, leaving behind a simple, unavoidable truth.

He needed to ask for help.

I'm running out of options, out of time, and I can no longer afford to keep Dante's and Heather's disappearances secret. Not when every world, every life, is at stake.

Especially my son's.

Lucien's wings flared, sweeping through the cool air, and he rose into the night. Closing his eyes, he forced himself to take deep, even breaths. Forced his pulse to slow, his heart to calm.

<Llygad,> he sent, <Heather and her father have vanished. I'm afraid I can't meet you. Have you arrived in Dallas yet?>

Silence.

Frowning, Lucien sent again, a psionic ping to check Von's state of consciousness. He felt the submerged and dreaming rhythm of Sleep—albeit an unusual Sleep given that it wasn't even close to dawn. Yet Von's Sleep seemed to be natural, no drug static blurred his consciousness. How was that possible?

And then he remembered the stay-awake pill Von had taken back at the house while trying to reach Heather. He suspected that the consequences Merri Goodnight had warned about had caught up with the nomad.

"By all that's holy, not now," Lucien muttered.

Contacting Silver, Lucien learned that he'd left Von at the club, preparing to head to Louis Armstrong International to catch a flight to Dallas. Silver hadn't heard from Von since, and when he tried at Lucien's insistence, met with the same result. And came to the same conclusion: stay-awake pill consequences.

<I'll go look for him,> Silver sent. <Make sure he's Snoozing someplace where he won't be crispy-crittered when dawn comes.>

<Good. Thank you.>

<You pick up Heather yet?> Silver asked.

Lucien drew in a deep breath of sage-sharp air and folded up his own fears, quietly putting them away. <Not yet,> he admitted. <Things haven't worked out the way I'd hoped. But I have another plan, one that involves a trip to Gehenna.>

<Gehenna?> Uncertainty shadowed Silver's sending. <Is that smart? If they find out—>

<Don't worry, I don't plan on spreading the word.>

Lucien ended the conversation with a promise to keep Silver informed, now that Von was down for the count.

Abandoning the now-ruined Lexus as a lost cause, Lucien

unfurled his wings and took to the air. As he soared higher and higher in the star-pierced sky, frost iced his hair into translucent tendrils, glittered on his wings, burned cold in his lungs. He flew through the night, arrowing himself toward the gate high above the Gulf of Mexico, the smell of brine and deep water in his nostrils.

He'd briefly considered flying to New Orleans and St. Louis No. 3, to the gate Dante had punched into the wall of a white marble tomb, hammering a hole between worlds with just his flame-swallowed fist and a son's determination to bring his father home again. Lucien's throat tightened.

He went to Gehenna for me, I can do no less for him.

All out of options, yes. Nearly out of time, true. But he would be careful, all the same. If the Elohim in general learned that their *creawdwr* was not only injured but stolen, most likely by ill-intentioned mortals who planned to use him, the Fallen would declare war on the human race.

And if that seat-warming pretender to the throne, Gabriel, or any member of what remained of the Celestial Seven, should learn the truth, they would lead the winged and righteous brigade into mortal skies, setting it ablaze with their wrath.

Once Dante had been found, and the human world reduced to ruin and pockets of trembling survivors, he would be returned to Gehenna and never be allowed to leave again.

And whoever freed Dante during this holy war and kicked the most mortal ass would be bonded to him.

Lucien thought of the lie Astarte had told Dante.

No one can bind you against your will, nor would anyone wish to.

Anyone strong enough *could* bind him against his will, and each would slaughter the other for the chance to do so. Gabriel especially, given his precarious perch upon the black-starred throne because of Dante's violent rejection of him and of his authority. Binding the *creawdwr* would guarantee his continued rule.

Not to mention being a sweet bit of revenge on both father and son.

Lucien absolutely couldn't allow any of them to know what had happened to Dante or Heather. He needed to pretend that everything was fine, that Dante would return to Gehenna as pledged when the time came. As symbolized by the sigil on his chest.

And that very sigil was the only option left. Lucien winged through the night until he caught a glimmer of color in the frozen dark. Where once a golden gate had spun, visible only to Elohim eyes, now there was only an untethered rip in reality. One awaiting Dante's restorative touch.

Voicing his *wybrcathl* as he winged through the rip and past the guards on the other side, Lucien flew into the shimmering colors of the faded aurora borealis undulating across Gehenna's pale night sky. He breathed in the smells of jasmine and smoky myrrh and salt air. The scent of home, yes. For thousands of years. But no longer.

Wings cutting through the air in sure, strong strokes, Lucien aimed himself toward the Royal Aerie. Landing on the marble terrace, he warbled a call to the healer with hyacinth eyes and hair the color of a blue-frosted winter moon—the Morningstar's beautiful daughter.

Hekate's musical response came almost immediately.

22

As Many as It Takes

WALKING INTO THE FIFTH-FLOOR cafeteria for a cup of hopefully fresh coffee, Teodoro wasn't surprised to see only a handful of people scattered amongst its white Formica tables, given that it was nearly midnight.

What *did* surprise him was seeing his supervisor sitting at one, methodically eating what looked like a gravy-slathered turkey sandwich paired with a cherry tomato–topped side salad.

"I thought you'd be home in bed by now," Teodoro commented as he stopped beside Webster's table. "Long gone by the time I got here."

With his salt-and-pepper hair; short, wiry build; and fierce dark eyes, Webster always reminded Teodoro of a banty rooster. At the moment, though, all he saw in the other man's eyes as he met his gaze was a muddied, disgruntled weariness.

"That's what I thought too," Webster grunted, resting his fork on his plate, leaving his sandwich with its savory-smelling brown gravy—roast beef, not turkey—unfinished. "But here I am. And it seems that the interruption to my sleep and your vacation just got a little longer."

Frowning, Teodoro pulled out the chair across from

Webster and sat, resting his briefcase on the floor beside him. "Why is that?"

"We've picked up Heather Wallace," Webster replied. "Stole her right out from under the feds. She's on her way to HQ even as we speak. And the OC wants you to delve into her mind. Could be a while, though. We're moving her by car to avoid any potential difficulties with the airlines."

Excitement pulsed through Teodoro's veins at this unexpected bit of news.

"Which route are they taking and when do we expect them?"

Webster told him, then added, "With food and sleep stops, we're figuring on two days. Sorry about your vacation." He shook his head, expression *almost* sympathetic.

Teodoro left Webster to finish his hot—well, lukewarm perhaps—roast beef sandwich, fetching himself a cup of coffee, before heading for his office on the eighth floor.

He couldn't believe his luck. With Heather Wallace found, there was no longer any need to go back into the searing chaos that comprised the *creawdwr's* mind.

Hey, motherfucker. I don't remember inviting you.

All he needed to do now was intercept Heather and sever the bond she shared with Dante. A bullet fired into her skull would do the trick nicely. And Teodoro knew just the person who could accomplish both.

Caterina Cortini—an assassin for the SB and, quite possibly, their very best wetwork expert, period. The attractive brunette was much more than a killer who neatly wrapped up other people's loose ends. She was also the mortal daughter of Renata Alessa Cortini, a vampire's child of the heart.

And a spy for Dante Baptiste.

Or so she had been, until Teodoro had captured her while she was engaged in a bit of self-assigned and extremely unsanctioned wetwork. Once he'd sunk his mental fingers deep into Caterina's mind, Teodoro had learned—among so many other fascinating things—that the dark-haired assassin had laid her gun at Dante Baptiste's bare feet and sworn complete loyalty to him.

A fact that Teodoro had taken advantage of immediately.

He'd carefully seeded false information into Caterina's mind—information transforming Heather Wallace from Dante's lover into an undercover agent for the Bureau, a coldhearted betrayer of the True Blood prince and *creawdwr* that Caterina had vowed to protect.

Now Caterina was also Teodoro's deadly little puppet.

A puppet he was about to spin into motion.

Striding across the threshold into his office, Teodoro caught a faint but fragrant whiff of frankincense, anise, and paint from the angel trap he'd painted on the floor from the threshold to his desk—just in case Dante Baptiste or even one of the Elohim paid him a visit.

Though the trap with its glyphs and sigils was hidden underneath the carpet, Teodoro still felt an electric prickling along his skin. The protection sigils tattooed centuries before above his heart and solar plexus threaded cool energy throughout his body, insulating him from the spell he'd created and painted on the floor as magical insurance.

Mortals could saunter across without feeling a thing. But if one of the Fallen—or even a Fallen half-breed—should set foot inside the trap, there they would remain, powerless, until Teodoro released them.

The prickling vanished once Teodoro stepped behind his desk and beyond the trap's reach. As he settled into his chair, the leather squeaking comfortably beneath him, he noticed the red message light pulsing on his desk phone.

Someone delivering the news Webster already gave me, no doubt.

After resting his briefcase on the desk's neat cherrywood surface, Teodoro reached over and nabbed the handset. He punched VOICE MAIL, then LISTEN. A woman's voice, smooth, confident and melodic, a voice he recognized as belonging to Seraphina Ivey of the Oversight Committee. A voice he knew well.

"Agent Díon, as soon as you receive this message, please meet me in the tenth-level evidence warehouse. We need to discuss tonight's interrogation agenda."

Teodoro erased the message. He would join Seraphina in the warehouse as soon as he had taken care of one little thing. He had no intention of wasting an opportunity like the one the SB had given him when they'd intercepted Heather Wallace.

Flipping his briefcase open, he pulled an audio jammer and the cell phone he used for his clandestine conversations with Caterina—which comprised nearly all of them—from its interior.

He deftly set up the jammer/iPod look-alike and switched it on. It burbled and chirped, effectively desensitizing all audio recording equipment—including any routine SB office bugs.

Grabbing up the cell phone, he thumbed a brief text to Caterina: *Where are you?*

Less than a minute later, a quiet beep announced her reply: *Germantown, TN. On assignment. Finished. What do you need?*

Have urgent task. Regards D. Call me.

The message had no sooner been sent than Teodoro's cell was ringing. "I'm listening," Caterina said when he answered. Her faint Italian accent was flat, all business.

"*Bueno*. I need you to keep listening."

Teodoro filled Caterina in, but with selective bits of information, changing Heather's kidnapping by her father to a meeting with FBI handlers instead.

"Our people grabbed her when she was on her way back to Baptiste's club. If she's brought into HQ, she'll spill everything to avoid interrogation and then they'll learn who and what Baptiste is—what they've really got on their hands. A Maker. Programmed to obey. To use however they choose."

"Not if I can help it. I'll intercept them and make sure she never says a word. Give me their route and time table."

Teodoro did exactly that, then ended the call. He tossed the cell back into his briefcase; the audio jammer he slipped into a trouser pocket instead. With Heather Wallace's death, the bond she shared with Dante would be severed, giving him that last hard shove into madness.

And stealing all hope from the Fallen.

Teodoro left his office, heading for the elevators.

AS HE WALKED INTO the evidence warehouse on level ten, Teodoro caught the gleam of ivory wings beyond the rows of metal shelves containing plastic evidence tubs and cartons piled with old files. Ivory wings frozen in mid-slash.

He followed the aisle leading to the warehouse's center, breathing in the faint smells of ozone and musty cardboard and things forgotten. Or hidden, he reflected as he strode past the last set of shelves and saw what waited beyond them.

The work of one angry *creawdwr*, Dante Baptiste.

A Fallen Stonehenge.

One carefully reconstructed from photos taken at the Damascus, Oregon, site before the "statues" had been transported across the country to HQ.

Transformed into alabaster statues of exquisite detail and captured motion—standing, crouching, kneeling, flying, fleeing—the fallen angels ringed the concrete floor, capped by those medusaed in mid-flight, wings spread.

Wearing a plum-colored dress belted at the waist and elegant black pumps, Seraphina Ivey waited in front of one the statues. Tall and curvaceous, with dark, golden-blond tresses tumbling to her shoulders in glossy waves, winter-gray eyes, and flawless skin, she looked to be in her early thirties.

She was a good decade older. And, thanks to a nephilim ancestor, one she hadn't even known existed until Teodoro had enlightened her, she would retain her beauty and youthful appearance for many decades more.

Teodoro drew to a stop beside her, but remained silent until he had the audio jammer set up on the concrete floor. Once it was burbling away, he said in a low voice, "Sorry about the delay."

"S has announced that he is True Blood and Fallen," Seraphina said. "Every vampire in the world—including those within the SB—knows by now or soon will, once they awaken and receive the feed from their household *llygad*."

Teodoro stared at her, hoping he hadn't heard right, but the sinking feeling in his belly told him that he had. "How is that even possible? He's stashed away at Doucet-Bainbridge."

"I know," Seraphina replied, worry sharpening the planes of her face. "But apparently S made the announcement several nights ago. It was delayed until the *filidh* had verified his claims."

Teodoro raked a hand through his hair in chagrin. It hadn't occurred to him that Dante would give up his secrets. According to his research, Dante rarely spoke about himself, even in interviews.

Of course, he never knew much about himself until recently, now did he?

"Did he say anything about being a *creawdwr*?"

"No," Seraphina answered. "But he named his father as the Nightbringer. We know him as Lucien De Noir. Do you know anything about him—as the Nightbringer, I mean?"

Teodoro felt a hot and cold shock at that revelation. "No, the Nightbringer's a bit before my time. All I know is that he fled Gehenna after killing the last *creawdwr*."

"And now he's the father of the next," Seraphina murmured. "Talk about karma taking an ironic twist."

"To say the least. ¡Madre de Dios! This is a mess."

"More than you know," Seraphina said grimly. "S's little announcement has the rest of the committee looking at him in a new light and reexamining certain questions."

"Such as?"

"Everything, Teo. Everything. Why is it that wherever S goes, inexplicable events follow? The destruction of St. Louis No. 3 in New Orleans. The bizarre events in Damascus, including"—Seraphina turned and waved a hand at the stone angels—"this. Then there's the matter of S transforming one little girl into another long dead."

"Remind your fellow committee members that there's no proof of that," Teodoro said. "Those who witnessed Violet's so-called transformation might've simply witnessed a bit of True Blood or Fallen illusion, a magical sleight of hand, a—"

Seraphina shook her head. "That's not going to fly. Not now. They want to round S up and bring him in and find out exactly what they have on their hands. They also want Violet's psychological testing ended and for her to be returned."

"Returning Violet won't be a problem," Teodoro said. "I no longer need her."

Which was a relief, truth be told. He liked Violet. Yes, he'd been willing to sacrifice her to a greater cause, but that didn't mean he liked her any less. It would be easy enough to ensure that the girl was brought to him first upon her return to HQ, even easier to alter her memories of the sanitarium and erase those involving her time with Dante.

"And S?" Seraphina stepped closer to Teodoro. She smelled faintly of cherry vanilla perfume. "How damaged is he?"

"Beyond repair. He's already becoming the Great Destroyer."

"Wouldn't it be safer to kill him before he does?"

"Safer—yes. But not nearly as satisfying as forcing the Fallen to kill him instead."

Seraphina cupped a hand to his face, her palm warm against his skin. Sympathy gleamed in her eyes. "I know how much you want this, but how long will the Fallen merely wait and watch? How many mortals will have to die before they put an end to their maddened *creawdwr*?"

"As many as it takes, *querida*."

Seraphina frowned. "But that's wrong. We can't allow it, that's—" Teodoro tenderly brushed his fingers against her temple and her words stopped mid-sentence. Her hand fell away from his face.

Despite the natural shields provided by her nephilim bloodline—diluted as it was by generations of mortal descendants—Teodoro made his way easily into Seraphina's mind, erased her lingering doubts and fears, then withdrew again.

Seraphina blinked, rubbed her forehead, then said, "Um . . . I'll do my best to stall the committee where S is concerned."

"Thank you. That's all I ask," Teodoro said, lowering his hand from her temple. He glanced at the jammer. "Is that everything?"

"Yes." Swiveling around with stiletto grace to face the statues again, Seraphina rested a hand against a Fallen male's stone chest. "I can still feel their hearts. A distant boom like when the ocean surges against a cliff." She cast a winter-gray glance at Teodoro from over her shoulder. "Have you noticed?"

Teodoro nodded. "I've also noticed that the time between beats gets a little longer with each passing day." He smoothed his hand along one cool stone limb, wondering—not for the first time—if the *aingeal* within was aware of his predicament, an immortal trapped in stone. Counting each and every endless second.

Teodoro certainly hoped so.

23

DEADLY LITTLE PUPPET

CATERINA CORTINI STRAPPED ON her shoulder rig, then tucked her SIG Sauer P220 into the holster before pulling on her black blazer. After zipping up her overnight bag, she took one final glance around the motel room with its blue magnolia wallpaper to make sure she hadn't forgotten anything.

Doing this was normally second nature. Done without thought.

But, given the distracting nature of the headaches she'd been enduring off and on over the last week, she made herself look again, more slowly. There. On the nightstand. Her black leather gloves.

Shaking her head in disgust, Caterina grabbed the butter-soft leather gloves and stuffed them into a pocket of her blazer. That never would've happened a week ago. Something was wrong—very wrong. She could *feel* it.

The headaches. Her difficulty sleeping, concentrating.

Her mind felt full of writhing worms.

Could be a brain tumor, a budding aneurysm. I should see a doctor.

She should, yes. And she would. But it would have to wait

until after she'd finished her assignment and Heather Wallace was no longer capable of betraying anyone—let alone Dante Baptiste—ever again.

Díon had said that the intercept team was scheduled to stop in Little Rock, but he hadn't known where they'd be staying with their unwilling guest. Caterina knew from experience that only certain motels were SB authorized and approved—by the accounting department, anyway. And in Little Rock, there wouldn't be more than four or five authorized motels. She would simply check each one.

That would be the easy part. Getting to Heather without killing fellow SB agents would be harder. Of course, if she had no other choice, then she wouldn't hesitate to end their lives as well. But she hoped it wouldn't come to that this time.

Words once given to her by her mentor in black ops—a man recently killed in a vicious home invasion—were words she believed in and lived by.

With each life we end, we alter the future, end possibilities. We become agents of destiny. Severing some, fulfilling others. A hard and honorable duty.

Yet sometimes, it simply felt hard.

Grabbing up her bag, Caterina left her room, checked out of the motel, then went to her rented Nissan Sentra. Unlocking it, she tossed her bag into the backseat, then slid in behind the wheel. She sat there for a moment, motionless, one hand on the steering wheel, the other hand on the door, questions and doubts prickling like thorns at the back of her mind.

I've seen Heather Wallace fight at Dante's side, seen her risk her life for him. Seen him risk life and sanity for her. I truly believed that she loved him, would always stand beside him.

How could she fool all of us—me, the llygad, *Dante himself? It doesn't seem possible.*

(it isn't)

Pain throbbed at Caterina's temples. She stared out the

windshield and into the silent parking lot, troubled in a way she had never been before.

I don't know if I can trust my own thoughts.

(you can't)

Her stomach clenched at the smells wafting into the car—car exhaust from the nearby highway and spicy fried chicken from the Popeye's next door—which seemed to intensify the pain drilling into her skull. She shut the Nissan's door.

Rubbing her forehead, Caterina tried to summon up particulars from the transcripts and photos Díon had shown her of Heather meeting with the FBI in various locations, but her mind blanked and the details eluded her, the images blurred.

"*Dannazione,*" she muttered. She was wasting time.

Unbidden, an image of Renata—slim and small and graceful, dark eyes and pale skin, her chestnut brown hair a cap of Roman ringlets and curls that swept against her white shoulders—popped into her mind and something deep inside of Caterina unknotted in inexplicable relief.

"Sing to me, Mama," she whispered, as though she were once again a child who played at night and slept at dawn, a mortal child adapting to the nocturnal rhythms of a vampire household. "Sing to me."

Still rubbing her forehead, Caterina imagined her mother doing just that, crooning a familiar bedtime lullaby in a voice as comforting as flannel and hot cocoa on a winter night.

Fi la nana, e mi bel fiol / Fi la nana, e mi bel fiol . . .

Pain needled Caterina's temples, behind her eyes. Burned white hot as each imagined and melodic note hooked bits of memory and knitted them together. Wincing, Caterina squeezed her eyes shut. An image took shape.

"*Relax,*" Díon murmurs. "*Submit.*"

Caterina tries to move, but her body refuses to cooperate. Díon's mental fingers are still planted in her brain.

"*You're going to be my sleeper spy, my link to Baptiste and his household . . .*"

"*I won't help you. You might as well just snap my neck now.*"

Díon laughs, the sound low and amused. "*You say that as if you actually have a choice in the matter, mia bella assassina . . .*"

Caterina's eyes flew open. Her heart kicked against her ribs as a stark and furious realization poured through her aching mind. Díon—the bastard had used her, had . . .

Worms wriggled, writhed. And the realization dropped away like a child into an uncapped well. The pain in her head faded, vanished. Caterina blinked. What had she been thinking? Something about Díon . . . something about . . .

Little Rock. Heather Wallace. Backstabbing *puttana*.

But not for much longer.

The redhead's remaining time could be counted in hours. Only two and a half stretched between Germantown and Little Rock. Less, if Caterina goosed the speed limit.

Caterina started the Nissan and drove out of the parking lot.

24

APRIL FOOL'S DAY

HEATHER SCANNED THE MOTEL room, looking for potential weapons or escape routes. One barred window framed by worn gold curtains, two queen-sized beds with matching gold comforters, a nightstand and lamp between them. Bathroom doorway. A TV. Dresser. Closet. Small desk.

Her gaze lingered on the bedside lamp. Potential weapon. Check.

"I need to use the bathroom," she said.

"Nobody's stopping you," Roberts said. "Just leave the door open."

Heather heard a solid click behind her, followed by the *thunk* of the security latch as either Roberts or his partner, De-Agostino, locked the place up. The room smelled like a thrift store—musty, used, and steeped in Pine-Sol and old cigarette smoke—despite the brief infusion of fresh air from outside.

"I need you to take these off so I can," Heather said, turning and lifting her cuffed hands. Arched her eyebrows. "C'mon, guys. Just while I'm in the bathroom. I'm tired, I'm sore, and I have absolutely zero desire to be tased again. Give me a break."

Roberts shook his head. "You can do your business with them on."

"Look, I want to wash up a little too, plus take care of the wounds on my back. I can't do that with these." Heather swiveled her wrists. Light glinted from the steel braceleted around them. "I give you my word—I'm not going anywhere. All I want is to wash up, get something to eat, then crash."

"Food sounds pretty damned good, actually," DeAgostino grunted.

Roberts glanced at his watch. "It's after two. Not much will be open."

"I noticed a Denny's when we hit town. Can always get food to go."

"Works for me," Roberts agreed. "But first . . ." He studied Heather with penetrating blue eyes, his expression dubious. "Let's see these so-called wounds."

"Okay," Heather said, offering him her back. "But you'll have to do the honors."

Cool air brushed her skin as Roberts lifted the hem of her sweater. The puncture wounds had stopped bleeding hours ago, but they still throbbed, as did her ankle.

He whistled low. "What do you think, partner? A tiny vampire with four fangs?"

"Or someone checking to see if she was ready to come out of the oven yet."

Heather rolled her eyes. "Comedians."

Gently lowering her sweater, Roberts asked, "So what happened?"

Heather looked at him from over her shoulder. She knew she walked a thin line. A little bit of resigned cooperation might lower their guard, but too much would make them suspicious. "Does it matter?" she asked, voice flat.

Roberts shrugged. "Not really. Just curious."

Without another word, he strode past her and into the bathroom. Heather heard the plastic rustle of the shower curtain being pushed aside, the porcelain *clunk* of the toilet lid. After a moment, Roberts came back out, carrying an iron. He waggled it at her, a smirk on his lips.

"Aw, damn," Heather murmured. "A shame you found that. I had something I needed to press."

"I can just imagine," he retorted, opening the door and setting the iron outside on the sidewalk. After closing and relocking the door, he walked over to Heather and unlatched the cuff from her right wrist. The other he left untouched. He tucked the key back into a pocket of his dark brown fleece jacket.

"Thanks." Heather rubbed her freed wrist, feeling genuine relief as she limped, ankle throbbing, into the bathroom. Her need hadn't been just an excuse—well, not entirely.

"Leave the door open," Roberts reminded. "And don't worry, no one's going to peek while you tinkle."

Once inside, Heather could see why Roberts had no problem sending her in uncuffed. The window was not only barred, but too small to slither through even if it hadn't been, unless you were, say, three. Plus there was nothing she could use as a weapon, unless—

She studied the small coffeemaker on the counter surrounded by plastic-wrapped mugs, premeasured packets of coffee, tea, and sweeteners. Possibility tingled against her spine. The carafe looked solid—this could work. When the time came. At the moment, a glass coffee carafe and a can-do attitude wasn't enough to face down *two* SB agents armed with guns and Tasers. But one SB agent? Just the right number. She kept her fingers crossed that one of the men would head out in a quest for food.

The sooner the better.

She knew one thing beyond a shadow of a doubt. She couldn't let them take her to Alexandria, Dante beyond her reach. He was south of her now; she felt it in her heart and mind—a magnetic pull directing the compass within.

She wondered if he felt an opposite pull to the north.

I'll bet anything that he does.

Going to the sink, Heather turned on the faucet and waited for the water to warm up. She ached all over. Between the struggle with James and being tased, she felt bruised and sore, exhausted. She'd managed to sleep a couple of hours during the drive over from Dallas, but it hadn't been restful or nearly enough.

She sighed as she looked at the white porcelain bathtub. She'd love nothing more than a long, hot shower to ease her hurts and massage the kinks out of her muscles, but no way would she risk it. Naked and vulnerable with a couple of SB agents in the next room? She snorted. Only in bad movies.

Instead, Heather peeled off her sweater at the sink, draping it over the towel bar. Shivering in her lavender bra, she washed up with warm water and a little cake of perfumed soap, then used a soapy washcloth on her back—rinsing and resoaping until it no longer came back pink.

"Hey, Wallace, I'm heading off on a food run to Denny's," DeAgostino called. "What do you want?"

Heather straightened, relief flooding through her at hearing the words she'd been hoping for, and finished drying off with a rough, white towel. She was famished and deeply regretting the meal she'd ignored at the institute. Everything and anything sounded delicious—even the word *food* had her salivating.

But if all went well, she wouldn't be here to eat it when it arrived.

"Grilled cheese with fries and a side salad," she said. "A vanilla shake would be great too."

"A shake," DeAgostino repeated. "Good idea. Think I'll have one too."

"You about done in there?" Roberts asked.

"Almost." Heather quickly tugged her sweater back on.

"You're not the only one who needs a pit stop," he grumbled. "So hurry up, will ya? Christ. Chicks and bathrooms."

Heather's fingers curled around the sink's cool, wet edge.

He'd cuff her to a chair the moment she stepped from the bath-room. No way he'd leave her able to move around while he was using the john.

A moment later, the front door thunked shut, then Heather heard a car engine roaring to life out in the parking lot. Her pulse kicked into high gear. She and Roberts were alone.

Leaving the faucet running to camouflage any noise, she sidled over to the coffeemaker. She carefully pulled the carafe free. Water would give it more heft, but he would hear her fill-ing it up. And that would put him on alert. Bring him into the doorway, Taser already in hand.

No water. She couldn't risk it.

Heather tightened her grip on the carafe's handle and leaned against the threshold, angling her body to hide the carafe. Roberts sat at the desk, checking his cell phone for messages.

"Okay, it's all yours," she said, pleased that her voice re-mained level despite the tension thrumming through her body. "And in your case? Please feel free to close the door."

"Ha-ha. Another comedian."

"By the way, the faucet won't turn off. At least, *I* can't get it to turn off."

"Christ," Roberts muttered. "Damned cheap motels." He stuffed his cell phone into a jacket pocket, then rose to his feet and headed for the bathroom.

Heart drumming, Heather watched his approach. "Maybe you should just call the manager," she suggested.

"Oh sure, you'd like that, huh?" Roberts said as he reached the doorway. "Give you a chance to claim you'd been kid-napped—"

Heather swung up the carafe and slammed it into the SB agent's temple. His words cut off and he staggered back a step, expression stunned, pained. She immediately clocked him again, then a third time. Roberts stumbled backward, then fell hard on his ass. Blood smeared his temple, dripped down to his jaw. A thick, coppery odor threaded into the air.

Heather lifted the blood-smeared carafe for a fourth blow, but the handle snapped off, sending it rolling across the carpet. Roberts, dazed and blinking, scrabbled for the Taser clipped at his belt. Or for his gun.

Roberts was supposed to bring her in alive, of that much Heather was sure. But given his current pummeled-by-a-coffee-carafe state, she had a suspicion that might be a hard fact for him to hold on to.

A snap-kick to the chin knocked Roberts flat and clacked his teeth together. His head lolled to the side, eyes closed, out cold. Pulse roaring in her ears, Heather bent and fumbled both his Taser and Glock free from their holsters.

A quick search of his jacket produced the handcuffs key. She quickly freed herself, then cuffed Roberts to a leg of the nearest gold comforter-draped bed. Scrambling to her feet, Heather tucked the Glock into her jeans at the small of her back, covering it with her sweater, but kept the Taser in hand.

She hurried over to the desk and picked up Roberts's cell phone. She could call Annie, then speak to Von, but she didn't want to remain here while she did. And taking it with her would be too risky. GPS, sure, but she had no idea what else SB agents might have attached to their phones.

Heather tossed the cell back onto the desk. Nope. Not worth the risk. She'd rather try her luck at borrowing a phone from a friendly stranger. Outside, a diesel engine rumbled, the sound vibrating like a heavy bass note into the room.

Roberts groaned. Stirred.

Time to go.

Heather unlocked the door, then raced out into the chilly night air, teeth gritted against the bolt of pain from her ankle. She slowed to a limping walk when she saw the bus—ALL SAINTS GOSPEL TOUR!—in the parking lot and the presumed saints climbing down from it, trudging wearily to the manager's office. The pungent odors of diesel fuel and exhaust permeated the air.

Suddenly aware of the Taser she held, Heather stuffed it into the front of her jeans, underneath her sweater. She kept walking, edging toward the parking lot's shadows as she wiped cold sweat from her forehead and combed her fingers through her hair in an attempt to look normal. Nonmemorable.

A vehicle turned into the parking lot, its halogen headlights blinding Heather with blue-infused brilliance. The relief she felt when she realized it was a car and not the rented SUV the SB agents were driving died quickly. The car steered past the bus and the little knots of people from the bus and pulled alongside her.

Heather halted, pulse pounding in her throat, and pulled the Glock free from the back of her jeans. She held the gun at her side, ready to swing it up, if necessary.

A window hummed down.

"Wallace," a woman said. Faint Italian accent. A voice Heather recognized.

"Cortini," Heather breathed. "How the hell did you find me?" Not that it mattered, she wasn't about to look a gift assassin in the mouth. This time her relief was so intense, it nearly took her knees out from under her.

Caterina shrugged. "SB agents on an expense account are very predictable. Let's get you out of here before reinforcements arrive."

Hurrying around to the passenger side of the car, Heather slid inside. "Talk about perfect timing," she said with a quick smile. "Thanks."

"No, thank *you*," Caterina countered with a smile of her own as she guided the Nissan out of the parking lot. "You just made things a lot easier for me too."

25

DEEPER INTO HELL

*Y*OU'RE GONNA END UP *hurting everyone around you
because you can't help it.*

*You've done well, S. You failed to protect Chloe, but you
protected yourself. No one can ever be used against you if you're
willing to kill them yourself.*

How does it feel, marmot?

Your nose is bleeding. That's kinda sexy.

Dante's fragmented dreams—little splinters of nightmare
gleefully carving up his subconscious—suddenly whirled together like filaments of razor-edged cotton candy on a thorned
spindle, taking on form, shape, and substance.

A dark and deadly window. Already jimmied. Open and
waiting.

A way out of the shattered depths, maybe.

Or maybe a way deeper into hell.

Dante climbed through without hesitation. Swinging his
legs over the sill, he dropped down and . . .

. . . *finds himself standing on the edge of an empty, weed-
choked parking lot. A car pulls in and glides into one of the slots
marked in faded white paint in front of an unlit building. A faint*

fetid odor hangs in the cool night air—old piss and mildew and neglect. On one side of the building, a sign reads WOMEN, on the other side, MEN. And painted in huge white letters between the two sides: CLOSED DUE TO BUDGET CUTS.

The headlights and taillights wink out and the engine shuts off. Car doors creak open, then thunk shut as two women get out—Heather from the passenger side and from the driver's side, Caterina Cortini, the SB assassin with the nightkind mother.

Dressed in jeans and a blue sweater, Heather stands uneasily beside the car, her gaze scanning the weathered building. She swings her right hand behind her, resting it near the small of her back and the gun that Dante figures she has tucked there into her jeans. Weariness and a fierce determination illuminate her face.

"This is a good spot," she says. She glances up, studying the star-sprinkled sky. "No one around to see De Noir land and get freaked out."

On the opposite side of the car, Caterina nods, her dark coffee-colored hair brushing against the shoulders of her black blazer. "That was the idea."

"When is he supposed to be here?"

"Anytime," Caterina replies. "In the meantime, it wouldn't hurt to check the building and make sure we're actually alone."

"Good idea," Heather agrees, pulling the gun free from the back of her jeans and holding it down alongside her leg. She heads for the shadow-shrouded restrooms, aimed for the side marked MEN.

Caterina pulls a gun from a holster underneath her blazer. She steps up onto the sidewalk. But she doesn't move toward the sign reading WOMEN. Instead, she follows after Heather in quick, silent strides, coming up behind her fast, lifting the gun, her face cold and hard and unforgiving.

Dante tries to move, to blur across the neglected parking lot and rip out Caterina's throat before her finger even finishes pulling the trigger—but his body refuses to obey. His limbs feel like they're encased in cement. Dead weight.

He opens his mouth to shout a warning, but no sound emerges.

Dante keeps fighting, struggling, pouring all of his strength and concentration into moving, dammit, just . . . fucking . . . MOVE as Caterina aims the gun at the back of Heather's skull. The dark-haired assassin's finger curls around the trigger. Then she stops, turns her head, and looks right at him.

And her features shift. She becomes taller. Blonde. Nightkind pale.

Dante goes still. She is no longer Caterina.

Johanna Moore's ice-blue gaze meets his and her generous lips curve into a smile. "What are you waiting for?" she asks, then adds in a commanding near-whisper, "You should do the honors, my sleeping beauty."

Something calm and cold uncoils inside of Dante and slithers into place. Something he can't stop. And he suddenly finds himself in Johanna/Caterina's place, the rubber grip of the gun in his hand, the muzzle aimed at the back of Heather's head, the trigger smooth beneath his finger.

He draws in an easy breath, smells her—lilacs and sage and rain. He hears his own voice, low and husky, saying, "Hey, catin."

Heather starts to turn around.

He pulls the trigger.

Her head rocks forward with the first bullet, then snaps back with the second, tendrils of red hair whipping through the air. She drops like an air-gunned steer. The thick, heady smells of blood and cordite saturate the air. Hunger pulses through him.

Voices buzz around him, annoying houseflies.

You're gonna end up hurting everyone around you because you can't help it.

No one can ever be used against you if you're willing to kill them yourself.

There he is. That's my Bad Seed bro.

How does it feel, *marmot?*

S laughs. "Pretty fucking good, actually."

26

A FAMILIAR AND DANGEROUS VOICE

DANTE JERKED AWAKE, HEART hammering, his body bathed in a cold sweat. Light needled his eyes and he snapped them shut again—too late; the pain in his head intensified. Whatever he'd been dreaming was gone. The last image, tendrils of red hair sinking into a moonlit pool of blood, an image that iced his heart, vanished like smoke in the rain, leaving him with only a disturbing blankness.

Something dark and ugly had happened in the dream. Something that scared him to his core. Something inescapable and unstoppable, a massive boulder rolling straight for a lonely highway, aimed at the single car traveling upon it.

Tendrils of red hair whipping through the air. . . .

Gone.

"Shit," Dante whispered, easing his eyes open again.

And once again fluorescent light from the overheads spiked straight through them and into his aching brain like luminescent ice picks. Squinting, eyes tearing, he lifted a hand to shield his face—or tried to, anyway. But his arms, crossed over his chest, wouldn't move.

Canvas rustled. Leather creaked. His mouth dried.

Dante didn't have to look to know that he was strapped into a fucking straitjacket, but he lifted his head anyway and, blinking away fluorescent dazzles, took a gander and confirmed what he already suspected. Panic settled into his belly and buckled itself in for the ride.

Shit. Fuck. Sonuvabitch.

The straitjacket seemed weathered, flecked with old blood, a patch of fresh blood glistening on the left side, above his heart. And as if that wasn't enough, steel bands restrained him at his chest and thighs, and his ankles were cuffed—no, make that *double*-cuffed—to the table.

Dante strained against the bands holding him to the table, muscles cording in his arms and chest and thighs. The heavy steel biting into his bunched biceps and pecs and thighs refused to budge. He refused to give up. Maybe he couldn't get out of the straitjacket, but he could sure as hell do whatever possible to get his ass off the goddamned table. He fought and battered himself against the steel, not stopping until sweat beaded his forehead and a wet heaviness filled his lungs. He sucked in a breath, the air burning his throat. Pain pulsed deep in his chest.

Shit. Fuck. Sonuvabitch.

What now?

Coughing, Dante closed his eyes and tried to concentrate. At the back of his throat, he tasted blood and the bitter residue of drugs. His head felt full of broken glass and hissing sea-tide whispers, his thoughts punched full of holes.

He was in a room with padded walls, a concrete floor, and a camera snugged into a ceiling corner—and didn't that feel fucking familiar as hell? The door stood open. Beyond, the hall was empty, a teasing temptation out of reach.

Where am I this *time?*

As much as Dante hated that particular question, what he hated even more was knowing that the answer was most likely hidden away inside his own skull.

Ragged pain wheeled through his mind as he struggled to think back to the last thing he remembered, fought to remember *where, when*. He pushed against the blankness. Shoved. Then—

Memory ratcheted into place. Images flickered, running backward—a Halloween strobe light show.

That's Mr. Díon. He's been taking care of my mommy. . . .

A tall, black-suited prick with tawny hair and an immortal's slow pulse.

Tearing into warm, whiskered flesh. Running. The roof.

A hook, slick with light. Handcuffs.

The white padded room. Chloe—no, wait, *Violet*—with her black paper wings.

Blue eyes wide with panic. *C'mon, it's me. Annie. Heather's in trouble.*

Heather, warm and drowsy in his arms, smelling of lilacs and sage, and with a desperate hope, whispering: *Sleep tight, cher.*

Heather. Heather. Heather.

Dante shoved through the pain and drug-woven fuzziness encasing his mind and reached for her—or tried to, anyway. Pain shredded his sending and, for one graying, alarming moment, his consciousness. He blinked black spots from his vision as the pain gradually eased off the pedal.

Shit. Fuck. Sonuvabitch.

Beneath the pain, Dante felt the steady flame of Heather's presence through their bond, a flame currently hidden behind miles of thick, dark glass. Relief flooded through him. Heather was alive. And, as near as he could tell, not here, but somewhere north of him. Maybe hundreds of miles away, maybe just across the street.

But just because Heather wasn't sharing his particular hellhole, didn't mean she wasn't in danger. Didn't mean she wasn't straitjacketed into a hellhole of her own or running for her life. Whatever had happened, whatever had landed him on this table, strapped into a motherfucking straitjacket, could've swallowed up not only Heather, but Von and Silver and Annie, as well.

Shit. Fuck. Sonuvabitch.

Dante hoped to hell he was wrong—that they were all safe, unharmed—as desperation pushed him up against the steel bands again and again. A wet cough tasting of blood bubbled up from his lungs. He finally stopped, slicked in cold sweat, hoping to catch his breath, hoping to breathe, period.

What about Lucien? Searching, he'd be searching. And sending. Over and over and over. Which meant—*I can't fucking receive either. No sending. No receiving. This party keeps getting better and better.*

"Guard your ass, *catin*," Dante whispered, hoping his words would somehow find a way to her. "Do whatever it takes to keep yourself safe. Don't waste energy on me. You and Von watch out for each other. I'll find you again. I won't stop until I do."

Find her again? Yeah? Think that's a good idea?

Fuck you. Absolutely.

An image flashed unbidden behind Dante's eyes, blowing a hole in his certainty like a shotgun blast to the chest.

Her head rocks forward with the first bullet, then snaps back with the second, tendrils of red hair whipping through the air. She drops like an air-gunned steer. The thick, heady smells of blood and cordite saturate the air. Hunger pulses through him.

Dante's breath caught ragged in his throat. The unwavering flame of Heather's presence in his mind reminded him that she was alive, yet he still felt his finger pulling the trigger. Still felt hunger coursing through him as he breathed in the copper and adrenaline scent of her blood.

Still heard his own laughter, silk and 100-proof whiskey, low and satisfied. Now *you'll never hafta worry about her again, yeah? Now she's safe. And so are we.*

We? Fear scraped a hollow in Dante's heart.

Movement in the doorway drew his gaze. A middle-aged

guy wearing an official gray suit and an unofficial smirk stood there studying him, one shoulder resting casually against the threshold.

A steady, hypnotic drumming filled Dante's ears, the succulent sound of the man's heart pumping blood in a high-pressure hiss through his veins. Hunger twisted, a circling shark.

"You don't remember, do you?" the man asked. "Where you are, who I am?"

"But you're gonna tell me, yeah?"

"That I am—again. But, hey, all good things bear repeating. So here it is: Welcome home, S. Welcome back to Doucet-Bainbridge. Welcome to your final destination. And, trust me, it *is* your final destination."

Welcome *home*? Welcome *back*? Memory flickered, then vanished, a finger-pinched flame. Pain pounded at Dante's temples with sledgehammer intensity. He felt the hot trickle of blood from his nose, sniffed it back.

"Name's Purcell, by the way."

His voice. That's fucking familiar as hell too.

It was like a jackhammer drilling against a dam's massive concrete face, gouging a path toward a series of cracks created by the dark, restless waters on the dam's other side—Dante's fucked-up memory.

"Ain't S," Dante replied flatly. "And I ain't staying."

Ain't S? Liar, liar, latex pants on fire. Now who's the big, fat menteur?

Tais-toi. *Shut the* fuck *up. Ain't listening.*

Oh, yeah, you are. Even when you think you ain't, you are.

The impatient sound of snapping fingers drew Dante's gaze back to the doorway and the man lounging against it. Lowering his hand, Purcell questioned softly, "You still with me?"

"Yeah, unfortunately," Dante admitted reluctantly. "Need to change that, though."

Purcell laughed, low and very amused. "You just don't get

it, do you? You're not going anywhere. You're not killing any more of my men. You're done."

Purcell's voice triggered more jackhammer action against the dam. He was an unfamiliar asshole, yeah, but one with an oddly familiar and dangerous voice. The cold smell of deep water and friction-scorched concrete filled Dante's nostrils, a pungent *future* odor that knotted him up with dread.

That jackhammer's gonna break through.

Quiet and level, those words; a stated fact.

Peut-être que oui, peut-être que non. *But before it does, I might still have an ace up my sleeve.*

He hoped.

On the roof, his power had finally flared to life. Sure it had been pale blue and watery, a thin reflection of itself, and had vanished a split second later, but a split second would be all he needed.

Closing his eyes, Dante drew in a wet, shallow breath and summoned his song. Nothing. No electric tingle as flames swallowed his hands. No blue glow, no song, no transforming fire. Nada. He only felt/heard an inner silence, as though some essential thing had been disconnected or blocked or corralled.

Dante opened his eyes in frustration. *Shit. Fuck. Sonuv-abitch.*

"What, nothing? No smart-ass comments?" Purcell said. "No threats to rip out my heart or tear off my head?" He shook his head. "You must still be doped up to the gills."

"Blow me. Given the conversation, I don't think I'm doped up *enough.*"

"There we go. That's more like it. That's the S I know and despise." A cold, contemptuous smile curved Purcell's lips. "And given the multiple times James Wallace shot you before torching your club and disappearing with his wayward daughter, I'd say he must feel the same way about you."

Dante blinked. Heather's *father*? He didn't want to believe it, but if Purcell was telling the truth, and he had a feeling that this time the fucker was—at least mostly, then James Wallace had managed to blindside them all.

"Sonuva*bitch*." Dante stared at the white-tiled ceiling, a muscle jumping in his jaw. "Did the bastard take Annie too?"

"Couldn't say. What do you care, anyway? You've got more pressing concerns."

"*Oui*. Like finding Heather. Like killing you."

"Nice trick for someone who's never leaving that table. Not alive, anyway."

Dante shifted his gaze from the ceiling to Purcell. "We'll see, yeah?"

"That we will," Purcell agreed, his eyes dark green flint. He sauntered into the room, stopping at the foot of the table. "But for now, Violet wants to tell you good-bye before we head out to the airport. And the only way I'm ever going to get her to shut up about it—short of pumping her full of tranks, that is—is to let her."

"She okay?" Dante asked, remembering someone yanking her from his arms—against orders—as the seizure knocked him from the night sky.

"She's fine. Of course, I don't know how long that'll be the case."

"Where are you taking her?" Dante asked warily.

"To HQ," Purcell replied. "Our science and medical geeks are salivating over what you did to her—not to mention the mystery of *how* you did it. They can't wait to get their latex-gloved hands on her and begin their tests and experiments. Kind of like they used to do with you." A mocking grin stretched his lips. "Not that you remember, of course."

"Smug *fi' de garce*," Dante said, his voice low and coiled and full of blood, a venomed promise. "Enjoy it. It ain't gonna last."

Purcell chuckled. "Really? You keep forgetting I'm not the one in a crazy jacket strapped to a table." Touching a finger to the com set curving around his right ear, he murmured, "Bring in the kid."

*   *   *

ANOTHER SUIT ESCORTED VIOLET into the room, box of crayons clutched in her hands. As the little girl walked over to the table, her freckled face somber, her black paper wings rustling behind her, Dante's reality wobbled. The box of crayons shifted into a plushie orca, the paper wings became shadows.

Pain pulsed at Dante's temples, behind his eyes.

Stay here. Stay now. Stay . . .

Reality wheeled.

"Looks like you found Orem, princess," he heard himself saying. "Did one of these bastards give him ba—" His words cut off as a soft voice, one stitched into the very fabric of his heart, whispered from within.

That's not me, Dante-angel. She's not me. I'm where I've always been.

And that would be dead on the floor in a pool of blood, yeah?

Cold shivved Dante's heart, sheeted his soul in black ice. As bad as those words were, the voice speaking them—Cajun-spiced and whiskey smooth—was worse; it was his own.

You won't save her, you know. You'll fail.

"Shut the fuck up," he whispered, the words hoarse, barely audible. *"Tais-toi, tais-toi, tais-toi, tais-toi—"*

"Dante-angel. Who are you talking to?"

He smelled soap and strawberries and coppery blood pulsing beneath freckled skin. Heard the hummingbird patter of a little girl's worried heart. Hunger sat up and took notice. Turning his head, he looked into sky-blue eyes—concerned, curious, trusting. His whispered and furious chant slowed, then trailed away.

Reality wheeled.

Shadows sharpened into paper wings. Plushie fur sloughed away to reveal a bright box of crayons.

"Who are you talking to?" she repeated. "And what does *tay-twah* mean?"

"*Tais-toi* means shut up. And I'm just talking to myself—hence all the *tais-tois*."

"Oh. Okay."

"*Ça va*, Violet? You okay?"

Mingled happiness and relief lit Violet's face. "I'm okay and you remembered!"

"Happens once in a while." A smile tilted Dante's lips, then quickly faded as the girl bent to hug him. "I'm hungry, so it ain't safe to touch me right now, *p'tite*. Okay? I can't move, but I could still bite."

Violet straightened, hugging her box of Crayolas to her chest. "Oh. Even if you didn't want to, huh?" Her gaze zeroed in on the glistening patch of blood on the straitjacket. "Mr. Purcell promised me that he'd take care of you." Her voice took on an accusatory, indignant tone as she swiveled to glare at the man in question. "He *promised*."

Dante shifted his gaze to Purcell. Purcell lifted his eyebrows. "Oh, I'm sure he plans to do just that."

Swiveling back around, Violet studied him for a long moment through ginger-colored lashes, a fierce, desperate light in her eyes. "I don't want to leave you behind. You need someone to remind you what's real and what isn't, cuz you're hurt and you don't always remember stuff."

Dante thought of Heather, of twilight-blue eyes, of cool white silence infused with her scent. He felt a dark-side-of-the-moon tug to the north—or what his aching head told him was north—a tug as true and as inevitable as sunset or moonrise.

"Don't worry about me, *p'tite ange*," Dante said, holding her blue gaze. "Let me do that, yeah?"

"All righty, then, Violet, that's enough chit chat," Purcell said. "Time to get you to the airport and on the way to your mom. Mr. Díon said she misses you very much."

"Can't Dante come with us? Please? *Pretty* please?"

Purcell shook his head, a sympathetic and utterly false

smile on his lips. "He's too sick to travel; his owies, remember? He needs to get better first."

"It's okay, *p'tite*," Dante said, drawing Violet's attention back to him. "I can take care of myself. You just take care of yourself and your mom, yeah?"

"Okay," Violet grumbled.

Dante wished he could plant a *see-you-later* kiss on Violet's forehead, but knew he couldn't risk it. Not with his control cocooned by drugs and his hunger gliding like a shark just beneath the surface, powerful and unpredictable and savage.

Maybe *he* couldn't; Violet had other ideas.

Violet's crayon box thunked to the table as she threw her arms around Dante's neck and pressed her freckled cheek against his, her soft skin like red-glowing embers against his iciness. "I *hate* them," she said in a furious, tear-choked whisper, "for making me go, for hurting you. Mommy says hating is a bad thing, but I don't care. I *don't*."

"It's okay, *chère*, it's all right. I hate them too." Sweat beaded Dante's forehead as he struggled to ignore the *shush-shush* of the blood rushing through Violet's veins.

"I don't wanna go."

"I ain't leaving you there in that place, *ma p'tite ange*," Dante whispered into her hair, throat so tight it ached. "I *will* come for you."

Violet released him reluctantly, then picked up her crayons. "I'll be waiting," she replied, her face solemn.

"Take her to the car," Purcell instructed Violet's escort. "I'll be along soon."

With an acknowledging nod, the suit walked the little girl in her purple Winnie-the-Pooh sweater and tangled red tresses out of the room. Looking at Dante, Violet opened and closed her hand in a resigned farewell as the suit ushered her down the hall and out of sight.

Dante shifted his attention to Purcell. "I'll be coming for you too."

Purcell shook his head. "No, you won't. Because I plan to disregard my orders and put you down permanently. Díon wants you alive so he can smash your sanity to bits. To be honest, I think he's a little nuts. And he has no fucking clue how dangerous you are."

"But you do?"

"Oh, yes," Purcell said. "When I get back, I'm going to kill you. I'm going to take you apart and burn each piece until nothing but ash remains. And then I'll flush those ashes down the goddamned toilet."

"You're gonna *try*, anyway."

"Still a cocky bastard. Good."

Purcell moved up from the foot of the table to stand beside Dante and, reaching inside his suit jacket, withdrew a syringe containing a thick, reddish substance. "Just a little something whipped up by Mother Nature to keep born bloodsuckers in permanent check," he murmured as he bent and jabbed the needle into Dante's neck. "But this is only a half dose. I want you weak, but I don't want you to bleed out. Not yet anyway."

"Ain't you a thoughtful asshole?" Dante said as cold flowed through his veins, chilling him from the inside out. Devouring his strength. He tasted something woody and thick and bitter at the back of his throat. Cold sweat iced his skin.

Purcell dropped the emptied syringe onto the floor. It hit with a hard plastic *tick*. "When it comes to you, yeah. I'm *extremely* thoughtful."

Dante's heartbeat stuttered, paused, then resumed an uneasy rhythm. He coughed, and pain ripped through his lungs. He tasted blood, warm and coppery. Felt its hot trickle from his nose down across his lips. His vision grayed. The world wheeled.

Stay awake. Don't you dare fucking pass out.

Dante bit down, his fangs slicing into his lower lip. The sudden, sharp pain cleared his vision as more blood seeped into his mouth. The wheeling world slowed.

"Y'know, that whole bit of yours with Violet was pretty

damned convincing," Purcell said, folding his arms casually over his chest, just two old drinking buddies shooting the shit. Never mind that one was in a straitjacket. Details.

"Bit?" Dante questioned.

"If I didn't know that you're a sociopath incapable of feeling anything for anyone except yourself, you'd almost have me believing that you actually cared. You're good at pretending. Damned good. Always were. You even managed to fool people who should've known better. But you've never fooled me."

"Think you know me, huh?"

"Better than anyone," Purcell said quietly. "I know what Violet and Heather don't—that you *always* turn on those foolish enough to trust you, the ones who think they're actually safe with you. Just ask Chloe. While you're at it, you could quiz Gina and Jay also. They trusted you too, right? And where did that land them? Oh, yeah, on metal tables in the morgue."

"Go fuck yourself," Dante growled. Pain pulsed through his head, hollowed his heart. From the shattered depths within, voices whispered and droned.

You're gonna end up hurting everyone around you because you can't help it.

She trusted you. Guess she got what she deserved.

No escape for you, sweetie.

That's my Bad Seed bro.

"Go fuck myself, huh?" Purcell questioned, a deep satisfaction crinkling the corners of his eyes. "Sounds like I hit a nerve." He touched the com set curving around his ear. "Graham, Morgan, c'mon in."

Two men in the standard black suits strode into the room, one holding a not-so-standard baseball bat, the other an even-less-standard drill. One was white, the other black, and both were tall and broad-shouldered. They stopped, each taking a place on either side of the table, both eyeing Dante with cold and savage intensity.

"Friends of the men you killed earlier tonight," Purcell said.

"I promised them a little payback. After I see Violet onto her plane, I'm heading to New Orleans to check in with our surveillance team, before returning here tomorrow afternoon. Should give everyone plenty of time to get acquainted."

Shit. Fuck. Sonuvabitch.

Purcell headed for the door, then stopped with a snap of his fingers. Swiveling around, he returned to the table. "Just one thing before I go. I watched you kill Chloe. Watched you tear her throat open. I watched every single thing you did that night."

Dante stared at Purcell, pulse pounding in his temples.

"You never even hesitated. Just sliced and diced and kept on fighting like a good little programmed monster—even at twelve or thirteen or however old you were at the time. Wells and Moore were so goddamned proud of you. Even though she punished you for"—Purcell put air quotes around the next word with his fingers—"'grieving' afterward." He shook his head in disgust. "Fucking little psycho."

Fucking little psycho.

The jackhammer slammed home.

Cracks splintered in every direction across the dam's broken face with breathtaking speed. Dark water began to trickle from a few of the deeper rifts.

Reality took a slow, sideways roll as Dante *remembered* Purcell.

Strapped into a straitjacket, Dante hangs upside down from a gleaming hook. Purcell stands beside the man whose face Dante can't see as anything but a headache-inducing blur. Purcell nudges Chloe's cooling body with the toe of his polished shoe, then glances at Dante. She trusted you. Guess she got what she deserved. . . .

"She was eight years old and you slaughtered her," Purcell now said, stating facts. "Just like you'll slaughter Violet and Heather and anyone else who gets close to you. It's what you do. It's who you are."

"Fuck you," Dante whispered, voice raw, rough.

"No," Purcell replied. "*Fuck* you." Glancing at his men, he said, "Do whatever the hell you want with him. Just make sure he's breathing and aware again by the time I get back from NOLA."

"With pleasure, sir."

Without another word, Purcell strode from the room, pausing long enough to switch off the room's camera. The camera's green power light winked out. The drill whined to life. Dante flexed against the restraints one more time, frustration a cold coil in the middle of his chest. But neither steel nor canvas nor drugs would give an inch.

"This, you bloodsucking son of a bitch, is for the *human being* you turned into a goddamned meal. His name was Josh Bronson."

At that moment—the worst moment possible—an old commercial Dante had once seen on YouTube decided to pop into his head, some candy commercial where sharks on a taste test panel discovered that the guy they'd chosen as the yummiest among the contenders had eaten one of the candy bars before becoming a shark snack.

Steve was delicious, one shark says.

So was Josh—minus candy, but Dante decided to keep that opinion to himself.

Molten pain whirred into Dante's shoulder. He gritted his teeth as warm blood spattered his face, refusing to cry out, refusing to give the bastards the satisfaction. The baseball bat thudded against his ribs, knocking the air from his lungs.

Reality wheeled.

Black water poured in an eager rush from the ever-multiplying fissures in the dam's crumbling face.

Purcell and his men swarm into Dante's water-soaked cell and blast Orem's box-spring funeral pyre with a stream of white foam from the fire extinguisher. Darts from Purcell's trank gun hit Dante in the throat, chest, and hand—but not before Dante snatches the fire extinguisher from the wielder and beats the man to death with it, furious tears gleaming in red-streaked eyes, blood freckling his pale face: Orem's mine, motherfucker. Mine. I ain't letting you touch him.

The dam began to fragment. Water geysered, a roaring waterfall. Concrete tumbled away into star-spinning darkness.

Stepping over Papa's bleeding body, Dante goes to the sideboard and grabs up Mama's leather purse. The other kids watch him in stunned silence, their faces pale, eyes wide and dark. He dumps the purse's contents onto the blood-spattered oak floor—cinnamon Certs, wadded bits of tissue, keys, cell phone, bobby pins, a clutch of crumpled store coupons—and scoops up the wallet with blood-sticky hands.

He divvies up the cash—several hundred that he himself probably earned down in the basement—and credit spikes among the others. Jeannette, the ashy color fading from her dark cheeks, wraps her fingers tightly around her share of the money, and steps forward, gingerly avoiding the bits of blood, bone, and brain smearing the floor.

What about you? *she asks.* You didn't keep nothing for yo'self.

Reality wheeled.

Dante struggled to block the overwhelming flood of memories, fought with savage desperation and every bit of strength the drugs hadn't stripped from him to remain here-and-now. Shielded himself with promises made, promises to be kept.

As lost as I get, I will find you, Heather. Always.

I ain't leaving you there in that place, ma p'tite ange. I will come for you.

Found you, mon cher ami, mon père, and I ain't never losing you again.

You'll always have a clan in me, Von, mon ami, in us. You'll never ride solo.

J'su ici. J'su ici. J'su ici. J'su—

Electricity surged through his skull, arcing along his spine, disintegrating his shields. Dante's vision whited-out. His muscles locked as the seizure battered his convulsing body against the steel restraints. Wrenched loose his stubborn and desperate hold on the here-and-now.

Reality wheeled.

Orem burns on a torn mattress. . . .

Humming happily, Chloe brushes Dante's hair while he practices printing the alphabet. . . .

She trusted you. Guess she got what she deserved.

The dam gave way, collapsing in on itself in an avalanche of concrete and foaming black water. The past swallowed Dante whole, a hungry beast carried in on a dark and unforgiving tide.

I'll make sure you regret every breath you've ever drawn.

No escape for you, sweetie.

How does it feel, marmot?

What's he screaming?

Kill me.

Trapped in the belly of the beast and overwhelmed, his consciousness fading, a savage and desperate fury torched Dante's heart.

Not fucking yet. I have promises to keep.

His song rose, pale and burning, a ghost. His canvas-bound fingers tingled.

Not so fast, dere, p'tit, the past said in the gravelly tones of Papa Prejean as it/he shoved Dante's head under and held it there. *Time for penance, you. Time to take yo' medicine.*

The past carried Dante, drowning in memories, down into the shattered depths. Something stirred in the whispering darkness as he plummeted toward its heart, something shaped of smoldering embers and razored steel. No, some*one* born of straitjackets and meat hooks, of shallow graves and shovels, of endless nights spent handcuffed in a dank basement while pervs played their sweaty little games.

Someone uncoiling from the ashes, pale skin crawling with droning wasps.

Someone Dante knew well.

There's my Bad Seed bro.

S laughs: The truth is never what you hope it will be, yeah?

Yeah. And it usually carries a motherfuckin' shiv.

Beneath his blood-soaked straitjacket, power danced cool and electric along his fingers.

"Fuck penance," S whispered, opening his eyes.

27

No Witnesses

HEATHER WALLACE TALKED A good game. Spun a well-crafted web of lies.

But then, Caterina reflected as she steered the Nissan south at Heather's urging, *so do I.* A skill she'd learned in Renata's household as a mortal girl trying to counter and survive the machinations of bored vampires; a skill honed in the SB.

And a large part of that skill involved listening, so she could then use the liar's own verbal web against them. In this case, knowing the truth definitely helped. Otherwise, Heather's detailed recitation of events at Club Hell—spoken in low, emotional tones—might have been convincing.

The son of a bitch shot Dante with bullets containing sap from a dragon's blood tree, then torched the club, leaving him and Von and Silver to die in the flames.

But then Heather had taken her bit of creative fiction a step too far.

I don't know how it all works, but Dante bonded me, and I feel its pull. I know I can follow that pull straight to him . . .

Caterina couldn't understand why Heather had risked the believability of her story with an outrageous statement like that.

A bond with a mortal would leave Dante ultimately vulnerable. And that wouldn't be allowed.

Maybe Heather had been overconfident. Or maybe an intuitive part of her simply sensed what was coming and was attempting to prevent it. The woman *was* a survivor.

Kill me and harm Dante.

Doubts floated to the surface of Caterina's aching mind like rain-drowned worms.

A bond would mean that Dante had seen into the core of her. She wouldn't be able to hide lies or treachery from him then. And if that were the case, it would mean that I've been the one fooled, not Dante.

No. That was what Heather wanted her to think. Díon had revealed the former fed for who she truly was—a backstabbing undercover spy.

Caterina took one hand from the steering wheel and rubbed her forehead. Her headache hadn't improved since she'd driven from Germantown despite the handful of ibuprofen she'd swallowed. In fact, since Heather Wallace had slid into the Nissan's shotgun seat beside Caterina, her pain had worsened.

"Headache?" Heather asked. "You have anything to take for it?"

"Ibuprofen in the glove box. Snacks too, if you're hungry."

"Great. I'm starving."

A moment later, Caterina had dry-swallowed four more ibuprofen tablets. She heard the crinkle of a wrapper as Heather tore into a package of snack crackers. The smell of peanut butter and fake cheese filled the car's interior.

"The pull's getting stronger," Heather said around a mouthful of cracker. "So south is definitely the right direction. My gut says he's still in Louisiana. We just need to figure out where. If the bastards would stop drugging him, I could reach him."

Caterina cut a quick glance at the FBI agent. Red light from the dashboard glimmered faintly against Heather's face, highlighting the tension in her jaw, her compressed lips, her shadow-hollowed eyes. She held one vivid orange cracker tightly between her fingers.

I could almost believe that she's speaking the truth. She's damned good. Maybe she missed her true calling in Hollywood.

Caterina's fingers twitched against the steering wheel. She itched to reach inside her jacket for her SIG, yank it free of its holster, and fire a bullet point-blank into Heather's temple.

But she had a better plan, one that didn't involve extensive cleanup of the Nissan or torching it; a plan that had been inspired by Heather's kidnapping fairy tale.

"Don't worry," Caterina said, giving her attention back to the white-lined road stretching endlessly beyond her windshield. "We'll find him."

"The sooner, the better," Heather replied. "Can't we go faster?"

Nice touch. Again, she was almost believable.

"Better not," Caterina murmured. "We can't chance getting pulled over. I don't know if anyone's realized you're gone yet or my role in things. Which is why—"

"You dumped your cell after letting Von and De Noir know that you'd found me," Heather finished. "In case you were being tracked. You're right. We can't risk it. Dammit." She sighed. "How much farther to the rendezvous?"

"A few more miles," Caterina replied. "De Noir will probably be able to help you follow that pull to Dante more accurately than I can with a car."

"I hope so," Heather said. Weariness blunted her words, robbed them of force. "We're almost out of time," she added softly, as if to herself.

Well, you are, at least. But Caterina kept that thought to herself. Even though Heather had grabbed a gun from the agent she'd downed back in Little Rock, Caterina had no intention of giving her an opportunity to use it—not like she would have with an opponent she respected.

Spies and traitors only deserve a quick execution.

How did she manage to fool all of us?

(she didn't)

Headlights from cars traveling the opposite way on the other side of the barrier throbbed behind Caterina's eyes, whited out the edges of her vision like a late spring blizzard, ratcheted her headache into high gear. A sick feeling knotted her stomach.

Something's wrong.

But she lost the thread of that thought when she caught a glimpse of the sign she was looking for: REST AREA 2 MILES. A white banner reading: CLOSED had been slapped across it diagonally.

"There it is," Caterina said, nodding at the sign.

Popping the last cheese cracker into her mouth, Heather sat up straight. Relief washed across her face. "Good," she breathed. "And it looks like we won't need to worry about freaking out any civilians."

"No, we'll definitely be alone," Caterina said as she arrowed the car toward the off-ramp. She offered Heather a tight smile. "No witnesses."

28

THE SMELL OF PISS

HEATHER SHUT THE CAR door and looked up, hoping to hear the rush of wings. Bright, cold stars gemmed the otherwise empty night sky. "When is De Noir supposed to be here?" she asked, scanning the black-inked horizon.

"Anytime," Caterina replied. "In the meantime, it wouldn't hurt to check the building and make sure we're actually alone."

"Good idea."

Heather lowered her gaze from the sky and studied the darkened building beyond the sidewalk. On one side, a sign read WOMEN, on the other side, MEN. And painted in huge white letters between the two sides: CLOSED DUE TO BUDGET CUTS.

Pulling her borrowed Glock free from the back of her jeans, she limped across the weed-choked parking lot toward the side marked MEN, pebbles gritting beneath her Skechers. Behind her, she heard Caterina following, the assassin's tread soft, sure, and quick.

"I'll take the other side," Caterina said.

Heather stepped up onto the sidewalk. Dizziness spun her thoughts. For a split second, she thought she smelled Dante— frost and fire and fallen leaves—thought she felt his heated presence, thought she heard his husky voice.

"Dante?" she whispered, halting.

Again, she thought she heard his voice, but not in her mind through their bond. Instead his voice haunted the chilly air like an autumn ghost, like a faraway echo.

Catin, *look out. Run!*

The skin prickled on the back of Heather's neck, triggering her inner alarms. Adrenaline surging through her veins, she ducked and swiveled smoothly to her left, while swinging the Glock up in both hands.

A muted *thwip* burned through the air where her head had just been.

Heather felt a cold shock to find herself practically nose to nose with Caterina instead of the unknown SB or FBI assailant she'd expected. Her finger flexed against the Glock's trigger.

Time slowed, stretched out like a loaded slingshot—then snapped back. Three things happened simultaneously and with breath-stealing swiftness.

A gun barrel was jammed against Heather's left temple in a heated, cordite-scented kiss.

She fired the Glock as her hands were knocked aside, the gunshot cracking like winter ice through the night.

Electric pain jolted from Heather's wrist to her shoulder as Caterina seized the Glock and twisted it. The gun dropped from Heather's pain-numbed fingers to clatter against the sidewalk.

Caterina kicked away the gun. She regarded Heather with hazel eyes devoid of emotion. Perspiration glistened on her forehead. Strain etched stark lines around her mouth. "How did you fool us?" she demanded. "All of us—Dante, the *llygad*, me. It's important I know how you did it."

Heather's muscles ratcheted another turn tighter. *This isn't just betrayal. Something's wrong with her. Very wrong. But whatever it is, I'm not going to stand here and let her kill me. I'm not going to die in a rest area parking lot surrounded by weeds and silence and the stink of piss.*

"I don't know what you're talking about," Heather replied,

inching her hand toward the hem of her sweater and the Taser hidden underneath it. "And I could ask the same thing of you. You gave your word to Dante. I watched you put your gun at his feet and promise to guard and defend him."

The gun barrel jammed harder into Heather's temple. Leather creaked as Caterina's finger tightened on the trigger.

"That's exactly what I'm doing," Caterina said, her voice cold enough to hang icicles from the eaves of the restrooms.

As Caterina squeezed the trigger a second time, Heather dropped to her knees. She felt something blaze past the top of her head, almost skimming her scalp. A split second later the SIG's muted *thwip* reached her ears.

Heather yanked the Taser out from beneath her sweater and fired. The prongs hit the assassin in the throat. Caterina stiffened, muscles rigid. She toppled over, hitting the pavement hard, and knocking the gun from her grip.

Heather jumped to her feet and delivered a solid kick to the assassin's temple. She didn't stop the current running through Caterina's body until after she'd scooped up the SIG and aimed it.

But once Heather stopped the current, Caterina's eyes closed and her body went limp. She was out cold.

Or pretending to be.

Panting, pulse pounding through her veins, Heather crouched and shoved the gun's muzzle against Caterina's chest, right above her heart. Several long minutes slipped past. Nothing. Not a twitch or flutter. Not faking, then. Keeping the gun muzzle firmly in place, she searched Caterina. She found the car keys in a blazer pocket, along with a smartphone.

Well, well, well. What do you know? Heather pulled the phone free, relief flooding through her. *Guess the meeting with De Noir wasn't the only thing she lied about.*

One quick call, then she'd hit the road.

Heather punched in Annie's number.

29

It's Now or Never

Brows angled down into a deep, frowning V, SB agent Bryan Graham glanced at his partner, then back at the vamp strapped to the table. "What'd he just say?"

"Dunno and don't care." Morgan hefted his blood-spattered drill in one beefy hand. "At least the seizure's over. About fucking time too. I was getting worried that we'd have to quit before we even got really started."

S blinked, dazed, his attention focused on the ceiling. Tendrils of black hair clung to his sweat-slicked face. Blood smeared his lips, trickled from one nostril, oozed a deep red snail's path from his ears down along his pale neck to disappear beneath the collar of his straitjacket.

Graham nodded. "Yeah, no point in beating the crap out of a guy when he can't appreciate the effort you're putting into it." He'd only managed to wallop the bloodsucker a couple of times—good, solid bone-breaking blows (well, or would've been if the wallopee had been human)—before the seizure had struck, bringing the fun to a screeching halt.

Graham had never witnessed an actual, honest-to-God seizure before and, even though he felt pretty damned certain that human seizures lacked the speed and violence of vamp fits, he'd pass on witnessing another—human or vamp—thank you very much.

S's body throws itself with mouth-drying speed against the restraining bars in violent, muscle-twisting convulsions. His head is a thrashing black-and-white blur, flinging warm droplets of blood from his bitten lower lip into the air.

"Break time's over, you murdering bastard," Morgan informed S cheerfully. His drill whined back to life. "Hope you enjoyed it."

S coughed, then turned his head and spat blood onto the floor. "I'm a little disappointed by the lack of an in-flight snack," he said hoarsely, "but you'll do. Hell, you're a big boy. More of a seven-course banquet than a snack, yeah?"

The cheerfulness vanished from Morgan's hazel eyes as his expression darkened. "Asshole," he gritted, bringing the drill down, its whirling bit aimed for the bloodsucker's canvas-covered belly.

Graham narrowed his eyes. Was that *light* shimmering on the table from underneath S? Maybe a reflected glare from the overheads? "Wait," he called. "What the hell's that?"

His partner paused, the drill poised a breath above S's straitjacket and the taut flesh beneath it. He regarded Graham from beneath his blond brows, snapped, "What's what?"

"*That*," Graham said, nodding at S's prone form. Faint bluish light rippled along the straitjacket's arms, spreading into its midsection. "See it?"

A frown furrowed Morgan's forehead as his gaze shifted back to his drill and S. His frown deepened. "Dunno," he said, taking a wary step back. "Never seen anything like that before. You?"

"No. Maybe it's a born vamp thing."

"Maybe." Uncertainty shadowed Morgan's eyes.

S turned his blood-smeared face toward Graham and studied him from beneath coal black lashes with eyes gone golden.

Pulse picking up speed, Graham tightened his grip on the bat's blood-slick aluminum handle. Freaky gold eyes. Mysterious blue glow. WTF? Purcell hadn't mentioned anything unusual about S. Only the obvious—make sure the prick doesn't get loose.

"I hear your heart," S said, his straitjacket awash in blue light, his voice soft and low and hungry. "I'm gonna drink it dry. Savor every drop."

Graham managed a derisive chuckle despite the chill touching the base of his spine. He stepped closer and swung his bat up—*c'mon, batter-batter-batter*—winding up for a blow that would knock the bloodsucker's ass into the future faster than a 1.21-gigawatt-fueled DeLorean. "How about you drink *this* instead?"

At the apex of Graham's swing, S's straitjacket dissolved into hundreds of small, blue-scaled fish and spilled away. Graham froze, heart vaulting into his throat, his mind unable to process what he was seeing. In fact, his mind was pretty damned busy screaming: *What! The! Fuck!* Which was soon followed by (but not quickly enough): *Run!*

The tiny sapphire fish tumbled to the floor, slapping moistly against the concrete before swimming into the air with strokes of jeweled fins.

"Dear God," Morgan breathed.

A heavy metallic *thunk* behind him told Graham that his partner had just lost his grip on his drill. Graham felt that he was about to lose his grip on a whole lot more.

Sweat beading his forehead, S rested his palms against the table. Thin blue flames licked across its gleaming, *wavering* surface. Table and restraints splashed to the floor, a sudden blue waterfall, delighting the fish who hadn't yet taken to the air.

And S . . .

S stood barefoot in a puddle of burning water, a dark, tilted smile on his bloodied lips, blue flames flickering unsteadily around his pale hands. Blood and bruises streaked his white torso from bondage collar to the top of his leather pants. Semi-healed bullet wounds. Drill insults. Bat injuries.

Not possible. Not possible. Not possible, Graham's mind insisted. But Graham was unable to move his gaze from those burning hands.

S flexed his shoulders. Graham heard the soft whisper of velvet against skin, then smooth, black wings unfolded behind S, arching above his head and snapping the smoky scent of burning leaves into the air.

Graham's heart tried to kick its way free of his chest. His brain had already left the building—but not before babbling, *Wings like a dragon. Or a demon. Yes! A demon. A beautiful and deadly bloodsucking prince of darkness.*

Graham crossed himself automatically, a habit that required no thought, despite the decades that had passed since he'd last stepped inside a church.

S snorted. "You kidding me?"

Graham caught a sudden, sharp whiff of piss. *I just peed myself,* he mourned. But a corresponding lack of wetness told him otherwise. Relief swirled through him as he realized the guilty party had to be Morgan.

S sucked in a pained breath, wincing. He stumbled, the flames vanishing from his hands. "*Merde,*" he whispered.

Hope launched Graham's pulse and mind into hyperdrive. Demon or bloodsucker or Prince of Fucking Darkness, S was still in bad shape, thanks to the drugs.

It's now or never. Make your move.

Graham considered the Glock holstered beneath his jacket, doubting he could be fast enough or steady enough to get a bullet into S's head or heart before the bloodsucking bastard took him down. But the unlocked door—no need to lock it when a securely restrained bloodsucker was never getting off the table alive (Graham felt an urge to giggle here, an urge he quickly throttled)—was another matter.

Glancing at the thick, steel door, Graham measured the

distance. Run. Grab handle. Yank. Bolt through. His muscles bunched, thrumming with adrenaline, the desperate need for flight. But what about Morgan? Could they both make it?

Shifting his attention to his partner, Graham nearly jumped out of his skin when he realized that the bloodsucker had moved without a sound and in the blink of an eye and now stood right in front of him. And his eyes were no longer gold, but red-streaked brown.

S's smile deepened, revealing his fangs. "Run," he said.

Graham tossed the bat and whirled.

S TOSSED THE MORTAL's emptied heart aside, then rose to his feet, wiping his mouth with the back of his hand. He'd feasted on both men, and the intoxicating taste of their blood—copper and wild berries and adrenaline—lingered on his tongue.

"Black Steve and White Steve were both delicious."

Pushing his hair back from his face, he stepped over Black Steve's cooling body and went to the door. Renewed, blood-fed energy thrummed through his veins, slowing his own blood loss, but doing little as far as healing his wounds.

S touched a hand to the half-healed wound above his heart. Winced. At least the wet heaviness had lifted from his lungs and he could breathe a little easier.

Grasping the door handle, S listened. He heard the faint sound of distant heartbeats, the low murmur of voices, the steady *beep-beep-beep* of medical monitors and, fainter still, someone screaming with the regularity and rhythm of a metronome.

Someone ain't happy. Can't say as I blame 'em.

S pulled the door open, then slipped out into the hallway, easing the door shut behind him. He paused for a moment, wondering which way led out, right or left? Right looked to be a dead end, the corridor ending in a concrete wall, while from the left he heard soft voices as two people—a man and a woman—discussed modifying med levels for a couple of difficult patients.

Right it was.

Tucking his wings away, S *moved*, blurring down the hall, past the medic station and the source of those soft voices, leaving startled gasps and a trail of bloody footprints behind him. Ahead were stairs leading up, a possible exit. Just as he reached them, bits of his conversation—Dante's conversation, whatever—with Purcell replayed through his mind.

When I get back, I'm going to kill you. I'm going to take you apart and burn each piece until nothing but ash remains. And then I'll flush those ashes down the goddamned toilet.

S slowed to a stop at the base of the stairs. He heard footsteps above. Laughter.

We'll see, yeah?

That we will.

"For fucking true," S whispered, swiveling around.

He *moved* again, heading back the way he'd come, aimed for the medic station, a runaway train, a missile arcing down from the sky, good old-fashioned death on the hoof or, in his case, death on socked feet.

A smile iced his lips. Purcell was in for one helluva surprise.

S unleashed his hunger.

30

CARNIVAL

SILVER THANKED THE COUNTERMAN, then walked out of the pepperoni-and-garlic-fragrant DaVinci's Pizza, fisting his hand shut around the key ring he'd fished earlier from a puddle in the gutter out front. He'd recognized it as Von's the instant he'd seen the winged Harley logo stamped into its water-soaked leather fob.

The keys bit into his palm and the undersides of his fingers with dull metal teeth, speaking a truth Silver didn't like. Not one damned bit.

Von wasn't just Sleeping, he was missing. Like Dante. Like Heather. And, thanks to his pill-induced Sleep-coma, just as unreachable. As was Lucien, gone to Gehenna on some mysterious mission and beyond the range of Silver's sendings.

Silver wove through the ever-growing crowd of nightkind and mortals gathering in front of the closed club. The air prickled with a carnival atmosphere of mystery, spine-tingling anticipation, and dark possibilities. Voices buzzed into the night like sugar-drunk flies.

"It's almost two. I don't think the club is going to open. That's late, even for us. I heard rumors that someone tried to

burn it to the ground and, frankly, it smells like they almost succeeded."

"I was there that night, y'know. Saints of Ruin played—so fucking awesome, then Dante got into the Cage and oh my God . . ."

"Fathered by one of the Fallen. A True Blood. Right under our noses. I hear the clock ticking away on Mauvais's rule and influence . . ."

"DanteDanteDanteDante . . ."

His name, a prayer murmured by nightkind and in-the-know mortals alike, a chant of lust and greed and want. Silver shook his head.

They don't even know him, not really. They only know what he is, not who. And they could care less, the shitheads.

Soon every power-hungry nightkind yearning for a new BFF with Fallen ties and a yummy, endless supply of super-charged blood would be arriving in fanged hordes and camping on the club's scorched doorstep. Hell, some already were.

Dante had known that would happen, of course. Had been expecting it. And, according to Von, planning to kick ass.

But that had been *before.* Before James Wallace. Before Heather had been kidnapped. Before Dante had vanished like a sheet-draped volunteer in a magic act.

Now you see him. Now you don't.

Hoping no one recognized or spotted him—and thus tried to stop him—Silver made his way over to where Annie was busy pacing out a short, tight figure eight along the curb in front of Von's Harley, puffing away on another Camel.

A quick glance up the busy sidewalk confirmed no Merri. Looked like the former SB tagalong was still busy with her own Von-whereabouts reconnaissance.

If the stay-awakes knocked the man down, then I want to be there to help him back up again. And I definitely want to say, 'told ya,' when I do.

Stubborn-ass nomad.

Silver had the feeling that Merri Goodnight planned to give Von more than just an earful—a *lot* more. But, given what he'd just learned, Silver seriously doubted she'd have the opportunity any time soon.

Dammit, Von. What the hell have you done?

Annie looked like a Bourbon Street regular in jeans that Jack claimed one of his sisters had left behind, a too-big Cajun Anarchy T-shirt, and fuzzy purple slippers. All she was missing were the Mardi Gras beads, the big-ass plastic cup full of booze, and the drunken WHOO-HOOs.

But Annie's body language dispelled the drunken partier illusion as she smoked cigarette after cigarette, her free hand flexing at her side—fisted, open, fisted, open. Restless. Driven. Prickling with fury and grief and guilt. Thin white scars ran vertically along the inside of each wrist, mute testimony to the depths she had plumbed in the past.

Depths Silver understood well.

Annie slanted him a sidelong look as he drew up alongside her and handed her a fresh pack of smokes. Even though shadows smudged the skin beneath her eyes, the blue depths of her irises glittered with feverish light. A light Silver recognized— she was manic as hell. Swept up in a bipolar tsunami, rising and rising and rising.

The fall, when it came, was going to be a motherfucker. And she wouldn't fall alone. She'd take everyone who cared about her along for the ride.

Something else he understood well.

And that was the main reason he'd brought her along with him while he searched for Von's Snoozing nomad ass instead of leaving her at the house with Jack and Emmett. They wouldn't know how to deal with her. He did.

Silver understood what Annie was going through better than most. Life on the streets as a mortal teen had taught him that much. A life, in the long run, that he hadn't survived. Or wouldn't have, if not for the vampire who'd slapped the knife from his hand and yanked him off that Portland bridge before he could toss himself into the river's cold, dark embrace ten years ago.

And who had become Silver's *père de sang*.

Silver's gaze rested on Von's Harley. Street light gleamed on the Fat Boy's handlebars and glinted darkly from the matte black gas tank. He could use Cian's advice right about now. But he had a feeling reaching out to his *père de sang* at the moment would be heavily frowned upon by Lucien.

Secrets. So many goddamned secrets.

"So," Annie said, ending her latest figure eight and fuzzy-slippering to a halt beside him. "Didja learn anything?"

"You mean, aside from the fact that I'll never get the stink of garlic out of these clothes?" Silver plucked at his T-shirt, nose wrinkling. "Yeah, I did. But I don't want to repeat myself, so let's wait until Merri gets back."

Annie nodded, cigarette smoke streaming from both nostrils. "Good thing the clothes belong to Jack, huh? Looks like garlic is just another fucking myth as far as keeping nightkind away goes."

"Pretty much—aside from the smell."

"Hah. I knew there had to be a drawback to those super-senses."

She eyed the twenty-four-hour tavern on the other side of St. Peter—Aunt Sally's Tavern & Heavenly BBQ—her expression that of a bear who'd just stumbled across a salmon-stuffed ice chest. Exuberant zydeco music bounced from the tavern's outside speakers in a nonstop, move-your-ass-and-come-on-in, blazing accordion rhythm.

"If you're still hungry, we could grab a bite when Merri gets back," Silver said.

"I ate less than an hour ago. I don't know why I'm so freaking hungry."

"Yeah, you do. Annie, you don't hafta pretend with me. I know you're pregnant."

Annie stared at him. "Fuck."

"Lucien found out when he peeked inside your head to see what had happened."

"Fuck," Annie groaned. "Mind-raping bastard."

"More of a mental B and E."

"Whatever. I know *why* he did it. I get that. But it doesn't mean I have to fucking *like* it."

"No," Silver agreed softly. "It doesn't."

Annie puffed away on her cigarette in silence, expression guarded. Pale blue smoke jetted from her nostrils. Silver had no idea how far along Annie was, but he figured she couldn't be too far gone. During the times they'd been together over the last couple of weeks, her belly had remained flat and firm beneath his skimming fingers.

When did chicks start to show, anyway? Three months? Five?

"Do you know who the baby-daddy is?"

"No clue. I hooked up with a couple of guys after I skipped out of the treatment center and got wasted—as usual. Who knows? Maybe I got knocked up *at* the treatment center." At Silver's arched eyebrow, she added, "Hey, I was bored. And I wasn't the only one. Fucking seemed like a good way to pass the time."

"Hey, no argument here. So what do you think you're gonna do?"

"I don't know. I don't want to think about it right now."

"Does Heather know?"

Annie sighed, nodded. "I told her that morning, the same morning that my asshole father stormed the place." She spat into the gutter. "Prick."

"My old man was a prick too. A boozed-up bullying loser who used his family for punching bags."

"I hope you made the bastard pay."

Silver shrugged. "I had more important things on my mind—like surviving. The Portland streets made my old man look like Mary Poppins."

"How about after you were turned? Did you make him pay then?"

"Nah. I forgave him then."

Annie stared at him. "The fuck? *Forgave* him? Why the hell would you do that?"

"I dunno. Maybe so I could live again. Maybe so I could leave the past and my old, unhappy life behind. Maybe because I had a new father—one who actually wanted me."

"Huh," Annie said, nonplussed. "Sounds like you missed one hell of an opportunity to me. I don't think my dad deserves forgiveness for what he's done. And he's sure as hell not going to get it."

"Hey, again, no argument here. I'm with you on this one. Some things you can't forgive."

"Exactly." Annie sparked up a fresh cigarette from the butt of the old.

Watching her, Silver shook his head. "Smokes and booze ain't exactly good for baby, y'know."

"Neither's having a bipolar fuckup of a mom," Annie retorted. Old pain flared in her eyes, vanished. "I should know. I had one. And who says I'm even keeping it?"

"No one," Silver replied. "That's your decision, and I'm not trying to influence you one way or another on that point. But until you decide, maybe you should keep the booze and nicotine to a minimum. Just saying."

"What's it to you, anyway? It's not like it's yours. Dante told me that turned-nightkind shoot blanks."

Silver rolled his eyes. "I know it isn't mine. That's not what this is about." He dropped his gaze to the weathered sidewalk underneath his sneakers as he gathered his thoughts. Whenever he looked at Annie, he saw himself again on the Portland streets, desperate and alone, stubbornly shoving away what few friends he had because being alone was all he thought he deserved.

"What *is* it about, then?"

"Being your friend."

Annie snorted. "Oh, don't worry. My getting knocked up hasn't changed your 'with benefits' status."

Silver raked an exasperated hand through his hair. "Fuck, Annie, stop being a dick. Just for five minutes, okay?" He closed the distance between them. "I'm just saying you can talk to me. I'm here. You're not alone. That's all. Christ."

Annie studied him from beneath her lashes, her hands knotting into fists, then unknotting again, then she stretched up on her slippered toes and planted a warm kiss tasting of nicotine smoke and ashes on his lips; a kiss that he returned and deepened.

"So garlic doesn't work, huh?" Annie said, ending the kiss.

Silver frowned at her abrupt change of topic, then realized it wasn't a change but a self-protective gas-pedal stomp into reverse. He glanced at his—Jack's—garlic-redolent T-shirt. "Oh. Right. Nope. It might make us gasp for air, but that's about it."

"So what *does* work against vampires? I mean, given that just a couple of weeks ago I didn't even know you guys existed outside of paranormal romance novels and the CW Network, I wanna weed truth from fiction."

Silver shook his head. "Can't tell ya. Trade secret. When we're turned, we each take a solemn vow *not* to spill the details of how best to ice our asses. Sorry."

Annie nodded. "Smart. Especially during a breakup." She tilted her head, studying him. "Y'know with your hair like that, you remind me of that Zero character in those manga books of yours—except your hair is purple, not silver-white, and your eyes are silver, where his are violet, and not to mention that you're flesh and he's not—but other than that . . ."

Silver blinked, surprised by the comment, then felt a pleased smile stretch across his lips. "Zero Kiryu, huh? Didn't know you liked *Vampire Knight*."

"Gorgeous nightkind, sex, and betrayal, what's not to like?"

Another voice chimed in. "Mmm-mmm. I hear you, girl. And he *does* look like Zero."

Catching a whiff of spice and smoky cloves, Silver turned to face Merri. She stood on the curb, her weight on one hip, arms crossed over her suede-jacketed chest. Frustration and a deepening concern glimmered in the dark depths of her eyes, despite the amused smile curving her lips. And that told Silver all he needed to know. Nothing new on Von.

Aside from what he'd learned.

"Merri's here, so spill, dude. Anybody see our missing nomad?"

"Pizza dude said he saw Von," Silver said, tucking Von's keys into a front jeans pocket. "But he wasn't alone. Three others were with him, a blond chick and two guys in kilts—all nightkind."

Merri straightened, dropping her arms to her sides. "Kilts. That sounds like the *llafnau*," she said, voice grim. "And no one else would dare lay hands on anyone marked with a crescent moon. No one with brains, anyway. You can bet your sweet ass that if *llafnau* were in the French Quarter, they weren't here to drink Hurricanes and traipse about on vampire tours."

Silver nodded, jaw tight. That was his thought too. Dammit. The only question was: "Why would they come after Von?"

"You know why," Merri said softly. "Think about it. Von kept silent about Dante until that announcement. Kept silent. Lost his impartiality. He broke his oath to the order."

"Shit." Silver drew in a deep breath, then exhaled slowly. "If Von broke his oath, then it was to protect Dante. And I know there's nothing Dante wouldn't do to help Von—if he was here. Same goes for me. There's gotta be something I can do."

"Maybe there is," Merri said. "I think I've heard from my *mère de sang* that the *llygaid* compound is in Memphis. If that's true, we could be there in seven hours. I'll contact Galiana for the address."

"Aside from the fact that you're hot for Von's tattooed nomad ass, why would you do that? What's it to you? Von ain't your friend, ain't your *llygad*. Hell, he doesn't even trust you."

Merri held his gaze, chin lifted. "I know. And I can't think of a better way to start earning it than by taking a rescue run to Memphis. Unless you'd rather sit on your ass at Jack's house and twiddle your thumbs?"

"Fuck, no."

Silver raked a hand through his gel-spiked hair as he pondered Merri's suggestion. Her words resonated deep within him, a pealing bell. She hoped to gain Von's trust and he hoped to regain Dante's. He remembered a nearly week-old conversation with the nomad about just that.

He doesn't trust me.

Nope. Not anymore. But he does *care about you, man. You still have a chance to earn his trust again.*

Silver had no doubt Dante would be all for a rescue run to Memphis. And, until Lucien returned, sitting on his ass at Jack's house, twiddling his thumbs would be *exactly* what he'd be doing.

No thanks.

"Yeah," Silver said finally. "I like the idea. Jack and Emmett could take turns driving the van during the day while we Sleep in back. I don't want to leave anyone behind."

Merri nodded. "Smart. That works. The *llygaid* will be Sleeping too. Whatever they plan to do with Von won't happen until after sunset. We'll be there in plenty of time."

"Look, I'll drive, okay? But on one condition." Annie's gaze skipped over to the zydeco-bopping tavern. Lingered. "Can we eat now?"

Silver laughed. "Food it is. And a beer sounds good."

"Maybe even two," Merri agreed.

As Merri and Annie started across the narrow street for Aunt Sally's, Silver paused to take another look at the buzzing crowd of nightkind and mortals milling restlessly in front of the club. Excitement pulsed through him when he saw a towering figure strolling through the crowd, moving with an orca's powerful grace through a school of sardines, thinking Lucien had returned—until the figure stepped out of the shadows, revealing short red hair. And a pair of nightkind companions.

One was a stranger with short, stylishly cut burgundy hair, wearing jeans, a short-sleeved black shirt, and an expression of knitted-brow concern on his *Esquire*-handsome face. Mediterranean *Esquire*, Silver amended, given the guy's hawk nose. But the other Silver knew all too well—Guy Mauvais. The aristocratic shithead was dressed in an ash-gray frock coat, slacks, and fancy white shirt with lace cuffs and neckpiece, his wheat-colored hair loose about his shoulders.

"Hey," Annie called. "You coming?"

"Yeah," he replied, his gaze never wavering from Mauvais's pale face. "Go grab a table and order me an Abita. I'll be there in a minute. Just remembered something."

"You sure?" Merri questioned, really asking, *You need backup?*

"Yeah. I'm sure. Just give me a minute."

"Okay," Merri said. "You got it, then."

A knot of grief and cold fury and frustration tangled itself around Silver's heart as a conversation with Von, this one about Simone's death just five nights ago—a fiery death Silver himself had barely escaped—sounded through his mind.

We all need time.

People always say that, like time is fucking OxyContin. Like I could just down a handful of time and not worry about it hurting any more. Instant fix. But I can't. And time takes fucking forever to heal. How's that for ironic? Fuck time. And fuck Mauvais for taking her from us.

I hear you, bro. And trust me, Mauvais is fucked—he just don't know it yet.

Renewed grief tightened Silver's throat, burned behind his eyes.

He fucking will now.

Silver *moved.*

31

GOLD INTO DIAMONDS

THE SMELL OF SMOKE, of scorched wood and rubber and plastic, of fire-dousing chemicals clung to Club Hell's shutter-style green doors like a whore's cheap perfume. Mauvais's gaze shifted from the thick chain looped through the door handles to the hand-scrawled CLOSED UNTIL FURTHER NOTICE sign nailed to the doors.

Mauvais drew a lavender-scented handkerchief from the sleeve of his shirt and breathed in its soothing scent. "Well, it seems we've wasted our time," he sighed. "The place is closed and"—he paused, leaning in toward the door and listening for heartbeats, before straightening again and swiveling around— "empty."

"So I see," Loki murmured.

"Apparently those rumors about a fire and shootout were true, after all," Giovanni said, his smooth Italian purr full of a regret that Mauvais suspected was every bit as false as his own. "Makes sense, then, that Dante, his household, and his father would go underground for the time being, *si?*"

"Perfect sense," Mauvais agreed, taking a final sniff of lavender before tucking the handkerchief back into his sleeve.

"Perhaps we should give it a week or two or three and then return."

Giovanni nodded. "At the very least."

Loki laughed, a low, amused chiming, his gleaming gaze flicking from Mauvais to Giovanni and back again. "You're doing it again. Both of you."

Mauvais arched one eyebrow. "*Oui?* And what would that be?"

"Playing your little vampire games. Trying to misdirect me with half-truths and outright lies. Tap-dancing madly. But all you've managed to do is fuel my curiosity."

"We only wish to protect what belongs to us," Giovanni said, his voice heated steel. "Your grudge is against this Lucien De Noir, not his son. What the Fallen do to one another is none of our business, but Dante is a True Blood—"

"And Fallen," Loki said quietly. "Which makes him Fallen business."

Not for the first time, Mauvais regretted the timing of the release of Dante's announcement. He regretted even more the inadequate shields of the younger vampires aboard the *Winter Rose* while in the presence of a fallen angel.

A very curious fallen angel, and one adept at plucking thoughts and emotions from fledgling minds.

"No." Giovanni shook his head. "He is vampire first. Our bloodlines are determined by the mother. Dante's mother was *vampire*, not Fallen. Therefore he is *ours*."

Laughing once more, Loki shook his freshly-barbered head—*Time for a change. Do you happen to have a barber on board, as well?*—his red locks cupping his skull and curving against his temples in a rakish cut that reminded Mauvais of long-ago highwaymen and Romantic poets.

Now there's *a dangerous combination*, he mused.

"Vampire bloodlines mean nothing," Loki said, once his musical laughter had ended. "Less than nothing. Only Dante's Fallen bloodline matters."

Giovanni stiffened. His sea scent, deep and stormy, intensified. When he opened his mouth for what would no doubt be a scathing—and disastrous—rebuttal, Mauvais gave the Italian's shoulder a warning squeeze.

<Calm yourself,> Mauvais chastised, <and keep quiet. I shall handle this.>

Giovanni snapped his mouth shut. He glanced away, jaw tight, hazel irises slashed with red. <Then do so. But quickly. Before he actually finds Dante Baptiste.>

Offering Loki an apologetic smile, Mauvais said, "No one is playing games. Not now, anyway," he amended smoothly. "I truly believe waiting a few weeks for things to cool down, to give Dante time to return, would be wisest."

Loki regarded Mauvais with shrewd, golden eyes. "And once Dante does, what glib lie will slip from your tongue then, hmm? That by the time you realized Dante had returned, he'd already departed for a tour of Europe? Or will I need to snatch the truth from *another* member of your household?"

"That *was* unfortunate," Mauvais admitted ruefully.

But it *had* allowed him the opportunity to slip a tracking chip onto the back of Loki's torc while he'd been distracted questioning Rafe. If the immortal should catch wind of Dante's whereabouts first, Mauvais intended to follow.

Although stunned by Dante's little coming out announcement, Mauvais had also been pleased to realize that his suspicions about the defiant *marmot* had been correct.

True Blood and Fallen. And utterly invaluable to the vampire race.

And with that realization, Mauvais's long-held desire to have one of the Fallen standing at his side transmuted into a desire to have Dante standing at his side instead, an alchemical bit of magic—not lead into gold, but gold into diamonds—crafted by equal parts ambition, practicality, and a deep-rooted instinct for survival.

We are stagnating. Our Bloodline diluted, tainted. Dante's blood will renew us. Inject much-needed chaos into our ordered existence.

Convincing the young True Blood to overlook the fact that Mauvais had ordered his home burned to the ground, resulting in the death of a household member, could prove to be a bit of a challenge, however.

A challenge, oui. But not impossible. Not with the future of our race hanging in the balance.

"It would ease our minds if we knew what you intended for the Nightbringer's son," Mauvais said. "True Bloods have become increasingly rare, and we're quite loath to lose one because his father is involved in some kind of blood feud with you. Surely you can understand our concern."

A slow smile curved Loki's lips. "I mean this Dante no harm. In fact, I hope to become indispensable to him. The most intimate of friends."

Mauvais found himself oddly unsettled by the fallen angel's reassuring words. The tension radiating from Giovanni's tightly strung body suggested he'd also found the words less than comforting.

Giovanni confirmed this by sending: *<He's lying.>*

Mauvais sighed. *<Of course he's lying.>*

"A noble gesture, given your animosity toward his father," Mauvais said to Loki, with an acknowledging nod.

"Indeed," Loki murmured, his attention now fixed on the crowd. "Interesting mix of individuals. What manner of *creaw . . .* creature is this Dante?"

Wondering what word Loki had intended to use before changing it to *creature*, Mauvais followed the fallen angel's line of sight. The swelling crowd was mostly composed of vampires—the majority of them out of town strangers; they glided like pale sharks amongst the mortals. Usually it was the other way around, Dante's and Inferno's mortal fans choking the sidewalk in leather and velvet and fishnet and musk.

"He's a rare beauty," Mauvais mused. "Riveting. But he's

also a defiant prick and a true pain in the ass. Disrespectful, sarcastic, a catalyst for chaos."

Loki chuckled. "I like him already."

"Well, since he's not here and no one knows where he is . . ." Mauvais began, his words stopping as he caught a peripheral flash of movement from the street, movement aimed straight for him. He deftly sidestepped the onrusher, grabbing a handful of purple hair as he did, and slammed his would-be attacker face-first into the club's stone façade.

Breathing in the clean, sharp smells of soap and cinnamon along with the scorched and bitter reek of rage—and *garlic?*— Mauvais spun the vampire around and pinned him to the wall with a hand to his pale throat.

Purple hair, red-streaked silver eyes, a snarling and cornered panther dressed in jeans and a black Voodoo Fest T-shirt, the smooth-cheeked youth looked no older than sixteen. But Mauvais knew better. This vampire was young, *oui*, but he was no longer a teenager. He *did* look familiar, however.

Perhaps he was a member of that traitorous Vincent's household?

"Motherfucker," the youth spat, struggling to twist free of Mauvais's implacable hold. "You killed her. You took her from us. And for what?"

Mauvais tilted his head, considering the accusation. "*Oui*. Most likely I did—whoever she was."

"Simone. Her name was Simone, you jackass. She died because of you."

"And no doubt you intend to make me pay, rue the day I was born, and/or tear out my heart and feed it me. How very tedious and melodramatic of you. And, to be honest, I don't know which is the worse crime."

"Tedious," Loki said. "Without a doubt. Melodramatic is entertaining at least."

The youth's gaze shifted to Loki, nostrils flaring. Panic fired in his eyes; extraordinary eyes, Mauvais reflected, eyes the color of moon-kissed silver.

"Fallen," the young vampire breathed.

Mauvais tensed, a dark suspicion creeping into his mind. Most vampires wouldn't know Fallen by scent alone since most had never encountered one of the immortals. Except for those, of course, in Dante's household. A chill iced the base of Mauvais's spine. *Mon Dieu*. Could his luck really be this bad?

"You've been around Elohim before," Loki stated in a chiming purr, coming to the same conclusion as Mauvais. "Do you know the Nightbringer? Or his son?"

"I've seen them at the club," the youth replied, his fury banked, but not gone, "but I don't know them."

"Ah, a shame. What's your name, boy?"

"Silver."

"He's just angry about some girl," Giovanni dismissed. "Simone. This is tedious, Guy. Send him on his way so we can hunt."

Mauvais nodded, relaxing his hold on the boy's neck. "*Oui*. Excellent idea. We've wasted enough—"

"You and Giovanni can go hunt," Loki interrupted, one large hand locking around the boy's shoulder. The boy winced as black talons sank into his flesh through the T-shirt. "Or do whatever you wish. Silver and I have a few things to discuss, including how to tell when one is lying."

Mauvais shared a dark, despairing look with Giovanni as the fallen angel forced Silver into the narrow alley between Club Hell and DaVinci's Pizza.

<*He's a member of Dante's household,*> Mauvais sent.

Giovanni bowed his head and buried his face in his hands.

32

SHAPE-SHIFTER

SILVER STARED AT THE fallen angel, cold fingers closing around his heart. For the first time since Dante had disappeared, he was grateful he didn't know where to find him. The angel studied him with eyes as cold as winter stars, his scent crackling with ice and cold stone, the fallow earth of ancient graveyards.

"I have no desire to harm you," the fallen angel said, pulling his talons free of Silver's shoulder, but not releasing him. "Or Dante. But my patience has been worn thin. So I will ask you one more time, and if you lie to me again, I will be forced to gather my information in a more direct manner."

"Ain't lying," Silver replied, pleased at the steadiness of his voice. "I don't know Dante or the Nightbringer. I came to the club to see him tonight, after his announcement, y'know? But, as I'm sure you noticed, the place is fucking closed."

Silver felt two anxious presences hovering in the alley's narrow mouth. He had a feeling it was Mauvais and his burgundy-haired buddy, but didn't risk a look. He kept his attention fixed on his captor's cold and handsome face.

The angel's lips twisted into an eager smile. "A more direct manner it is, then."

Silver's heart leapt up into his throat as the fallen's tall form rippled, a shadow undulating behind a thundering waterfall, dark and primal and as terrifying as the thing lying in wait beneath every three-year-old's bed. Before Silver could shut his eyes or look away from the disturbing sight, the rippling stopped.

Dante stood in front of him dressed in the black latex jeans and fishnet-PVC-metal-strapped shirt he'd been wearing that night in the Cage when he'd done his coming out gig.

Fear iced Silver's heart.

Shape-shifter.

Dante was pressing against him, his heated lips brushing against Silver's. Energy electrified the air, tingled along Silver's skin, raced along his spine, into his skull. The smell of ozone filled his nostrils. Dante's gleaming hair lifted in a blue-black corona around his head. He touched a long, taloned finger to Silver's forehead.

Lightning strike.

Standing under a tree in a downpour.

Finishing that final lap in the pool while thunder rolled overhead.

White light exploded through Silver's skull. His body stiffened, muscles locked and thrumming as electric energy sizzled through him.

A soft voice sounded through his thoughts, a pealing bell that he couldn't ignore, a lover's seductive command. <*Lower your shields*, cher. *Let me in.*>

A cold sweat beaded Silver's forehead. Not Dante. *Not* Dante.

<*Let me in*, p'tit. *Let me in. Let me in. I need to be inside you*, mon ami.>

The pealing bell reverberated through his consciousness, ringing and echoing and vibrating, crumbling to dust all other thoughts. Shattering his focus.

Silver's shields fell.

And a dark, complicated, and powerful presence poured in. Silver felt no pain as his memories were—not ransacked, not precisely, but clicked open like folders on a computer. Each folder held hundreds of interconnected memories, images, sensation.

No pain, but he felt despair in spades.

As the search continued, Silver thought he heard/felt a song—wild and searing, hungry. A song that left him breathless and dizzied. A song that filled his mind with Dante's image, his autumn scent. Then it was gone.

"*Anhrefncathl*," the fallen angel whispered in Dante's voice.

The dark presence withdrew from Silver's mind and the electric thrumming pinning him like a moth against the alley wall vanished. Boneless, his legs dumped him onto the alley's rain-puddled floor.

Silver sucked in air, head throbbing, oddly soothed by the zydeco bouncing from the tavern speakers across the street. The world hadn't ended after all. Not yet, anyway. He glanced up in time to see the fallen angel's form ripple, shifting back to himself. Black wings unfolded from wing-slits cleverly tailored into his suit jacket.

With a single strong stroke, he took to the air, a triumphant smile on his lips. Silver's despair deepened. He had a feeling that somehow, some way, the fallen angel had managed to lock onto Dante.

That song . . .

Silver drew his legs up, wrapped his arms around them, then rested his forehead against his denim-clad knees. "Jesus," he whispered, his voice sounding as shaky as he felt inside.

"Are you all right?"

Silver lifted his head and looked up. Burgundy hair, concerned hazel eyes. Mauvais's buddy—Mr. *Esquire* Euro Edition. A quick glance down the alleyway confirmed the Creole bastard's absence.

"No, I'm pretty fucking far from all right. Where did Mauvais go?"

"He left for his riverboat some time ago," the stranger said in a low voice flowing with European grace. He crouched down beside Silver. "Said he needed to check on something, hoped that it still worked." He spat on the alley floor. "*Bastardo.*"

"Who the hell are you, anyway?" Silver asked. "And what are you doing here?"

"My name is Giovanni Toscanini. And I know yours, as well—Silver. Along with the fact that you're a member of Dante Baptiste's household."

"You ain't said what you're doing here." Silver rose to his feet. He walked from the alley to the sidewalk, knowing Giovanni Tosca-whatever was following, then turned to face him.

"I'm here to help Dante Baptiste."

Silver snorted. "Yeah, right. Help him how?"

Giovanni glanced to his left, face wary. Silver followed his gaze to the club. The crowd had grown even larger.

"Ass-kissers and idiots," Silver muttered. He returned his attention to Giovanni. "What makes you any different?"

Giovanni considered him for a long moment, illumination from the gaslight dancing reflected in his eyes, ghost flames. When he finally spoke, he pitched his voice low. "I believe it best we speak elsewhere. Too many potential eavesdroppers—including the SB agents who keep eyes and ears on the club at all times."

Silver straightened, startled. "How do you know that?"

Closing the distance between them with one quick step, Giovanni whispered into Silver's ear, "The same way I know what all those ass-kissers and idiots over there don't—that Dante Baptiste is a *creawdwr.*"

Silver's heart gave his ribs one hard kick. *Creawdwr.* Giovanni *knew.*

Giovanni stepped back and answered the question that Silver knew had to be burning in his own eyes, the same question knuckling his hands into fists, and pumping adrenaline into his blood. A *fatal* question for Giovanni if he didn't answer it right: *How, motherfucker? How do you know?*

"An inside source—one who is working for Dante Baptiste."

Silver gave the buzzing, restless crowd a long look, then returned his attention to Giovanni. Was he ally or smooth-talking foe? Should he trust him or stake his ass? There was no one Silver could ask. Von was out of commission and missing and Lucien was silent in Gehenna. This time, he was on his own.

"C'mon, then," Silver said. He started across the street for Aunt Sally's Tavern & Heavenly BBQ without waiting for an answer.

He knew Giovanni would follow.

33

NIGHTKIND AND CATS

THE TANGY AROMA OF honey-and-whiskey-barbecued pork ribs permeated the air inside Aunt Sally's Tavern & Heavenly BBQ, thick enough to taste, alongside the buttery smells of skillet-fried corn bread and dark, foamy beer.

Annie and Merri had grabbed a booth near the rear of the tavern, probably the only one available, given the surprising late night crowd. Sliding in beside Annie, Silver made introductions as Giovanni sat beside Merri with a murmured, *"Bella."*

Merri gave him a cool, professional once-over, her dark eyes drinking in details Silver suspected he would've—and probably had—missed. "Look like you could use a drink," she said, handing him her half empty bottle of Dixie Crimson Voodoo Ale. "Rough night?"

Giovanni slanted a wry glance at Silver before returning his attention to Merri. *"Sì.* But it's starting to improve," he said, raising the moisture-beaded bottle to his lips and taking a long, grateful swallow.

"Go on and finish it," Merri said. She pulled a pack of Djarum Black from her jacket pocket. "I'm going outside for a smoke."

Giovanni scooted out of the booth, denim squeaking against vinyl, and stood so Merri could slide out and leave. Once she had, he sat back down again.

"Okay. So spill—" Silver began, only to be interrupted by a cheery female voice.

"Here's your pork special, sugar," the waitress said, resting a heaping platter of sauce-slathered ribs, collard greens, and corn bread in front of Annie. The aroma—spicy and sweet and savory—filled the booth. "Anyone else need anything? More beer? You fellas need menus?"

"No menus, thanks," Silver said, "Just a round of Abita Amber."

"You got it, sugar." With a wink, the caramel-skinned waitress sashayed away. Once their beer had been delivered in frosted mugs, Silver looked at Giovanni. "One more time," he said. "Your inside source—the one working for Dante. Spill."

"She's an SB agent," Giovanni replied, voice low. "And my sister. Caterina Cortini."

"Shit, you're that assassin chick's brother?" Annie said, eyes wide with surprise. "She mentioned that her mother was night-kind, but I didn't realize that her entire family was too. She never said a fucking word about that."

Giovanni shrugged. "Why would she? She was adopted into a vampire household as a toddler. For her, it is the norm and not worth mentioning."

Silver glanced at Annie. "The chick you told me about, right? The one in Oregon, at the motel?"

"That's the one," Annie confirmed. She tucked her napkin into the front of her tee, grabbed a sauced-up rib and tore into it with her teeth, making happy little humming sounds as she chewed.

"So who sent you to offer Dante help?" Silver lifted his mug to his mouth and took a long swallow of the smooth, malty brew. Hunger nudged him like an elbow to the gut, reminding him that he needed to feed.

"The high priestess of the Cercle de Druide," Giovanni replied. "Renata Alessa Cortini—my *mère de sang*. I'm to offer

Dante support and guidance and protection from those who would use him."

Silver snorted. "Yeah, and that'd be everyone—from those ass kissers gathering across the street, to the Fallen, to the average mortal Joe—once they find out what you already know, that Dante's a Maker."

Giovanni flashed a pointed glance at Silver from beneath his dark lashes, before his gaze flickered over to Annie. His tone was light, despite the warning seeded within his words. "I don't believe this is information a mortal should be privy to."

"Too late, asshole, this little mortal's been all privvied up," Annie said, her voice even despite the irritation scorching the sweetness from her scent of vanilla, lavender soap, and nicotine. "My sister's Dante's girlfriend, so, yeah, I know what he is. And he scares the holy living shit out of me. You should be scared too. I've seen him knock fallen angels from the fucking sky and turn them to fucking stone."

"Where is your sister, *bella*? And Dante?" Giovanni said, leaning across the table, his pale face lit with a predatory curiosity. "We thought perhaps that Dante and his household had gone underground following the rumored shootout and the very real club fire. But why would your sister leave you behind?" He flicked a look at Silver. "Or Dante, you?"

"Heather and Gorgeous-but-Deadly are out and about," Annie returned, not even blinking. "No one's been left behind. And as for street rumors or rumors of any kind, dude, never listen."

Silver had to admit she was good, damned good. She had *him* convinced and he *knew* she was lying. Yet all Giovanni had to do was slip inside her mind and ferret out the truth for himself—just like Lucien had done.

Just like that shape-shifting fallen angel did to you, kissing you with lips like Dante's, peeling back your defenses.

"She's right," Silver said, the hard edge in his voice shifting Giovanni's penetrating gaze away from Annie and to himself.

"You ain't gonna score points by accusing us of lying. And if you ever hope to meet Dante, you need to be talking to *me*, not grilling Annie."

Giovanni blinked, raked a hand through his hair. "*Ma naturalmente. Ti prego di perdonarmi.* I meant no disrespect"—his expression soured—"I'm afraid my dealings with Guy Mauvais have left a bad taste in my mouth. My apologies."

Silver shrugged. "There's your problem right there—*dealing* with Mauvais."

"I was supposed to bring Dante Baptiste a gift," Giovanni said with a sigh. "But Loki's presence aboard the riverboat made that rather impossible."

"What gift was that?"

"The head of Guy Mauvais."

"Forget it, man. Find something different. That bastard belongs to us."

"Seriously?" Annie asked, staring at Giovanni. "A motherfucking head as a motherfucking gift? Nightkind are just plain weird. Or maybe they're cats. How is that different from a tabby magnanimously dropping a mouse butt at your feet? Well, okay, yeah, a person's head is way different from a mouse butt, but still . . ."

"No, not so different, *bella*," Giovanni murmured. "Perhaps we *are* cats."

Silver sipped at his beer, wondering what he should or shouldn't tell Giovanni, wondering if he could risk trusting him, when he saw two men in jeans and light jackets walk into the tavern, paper to-go coffee cups from Café du Monde in hand. Authoritative strides and posture. Clean-cut. Com sets disguised as Blue Tooth units curving around an ear on both men.

Undercover agents.

Those Shadow Branch eyes and ears that Giovanni had mentioned earlier.

And they've been right across the goddamned street this entire time. Watching. Listening. Recording. Maybe even eating chips and drinking and taking notes while Heather's father did his thing.

Maybe they even knew who'd grabbed Dante. It couldn't have been an SB snatch, otherwise Giovanni's sister—SB assassin and Dante's spy—would've passed the word along to her brother. Or to Von or Lucien or *someone*.

Unless she'd been dropped from the info loop. Or been made.

Silver stared, blood pounding through his veins, as one of the men, tall and dark-haired, pulled open a door marked TENANTS ONLY near the restrooms. Both men stepped inside. Before the door swung shut, Silver caught a glimpse of a shadowy staircase leading to the apartments above. Footsteps thudded against wood risers, the sound a faint and temporary zydeco back beat.

The tavern's front door opened, then Silver smelled nicotine and cloves as Merri walked inside. She stopped beside the booth, her gaze also on the door marked TENANTS ONLY.

"You see them?" she asked, voice tight.

"Sure did."

"What is it?" Giovanni asked, his words followed by a knowing, "Ah."

Gaze still fixed on the door, Silver said in a low, flat voice, "You knew, right? Because your sister told you the fuckers had rented a room upstairs."

"Sì. It was information I'd hoped to hand over to Dante. But," Giovanni added after a thoughtful pause, "perhaps ending this particular little problem will make an even better gift than Mauvais's head."

Feeling a gentle nudge against his shields, Silver thinned them enough to admit the Italian's sending.

<Shall we hunt, fratello? Spill blood together?>

Hunger, sharp as a straight razor, gleamed in Giovanni's hooded hazel eyes. Silver's own hunger awakened and, judging by the knowing smirk on his lips, the Italian saw the same straight-razor gleam in Silver's eyes.

"Bad idea," Merri said, scooting into the booth beside Giovanni, effectively blocking him in. "You take these guys out, the SB will know that their surveillance op has been blown. I can guarantee you they won't shut it down. They'll simply move it to a different location. *And* amp up their security. You won't solve anything. Right now, you know *exactly* where your enemies are. Better to keep it that way."

Giovanni sighed, the hunter's fire in his eyes dimming. "She's right, *bello.*"

"Those bastards upstairs might know where Dante is," Silver said, holding Merri's gaze. "Hell, maybe they watched the whole thing unfold. I can go up there and rip it right out of their minds."

Giovanni went still. "Watched *what* unfold?" He looked from Silver to Merri to Annie, his expression darkening. "Has something happened to the *creawdwr*?"

Silver groaned in disbelief, slumping against the booth's cushioned back. "Fuck. Fuck. *Fuck.* I can't believe I just did that—spilled the beans. No torture involved. Lucien is gonna kill me."

Annie, slab of corn bread poised near her lips, regarded Silver with smug blue eyes. "And you thought I'd be the one to blab, didn'tcha?"

Merri raised her hand. "I know I did. Glad I didn't bet on it."

"Fuck. Fuck. *Fuck,*" Silver repeated, raking both hands in frustration through his hair. Once Giovanni learned the truth and passed it on to his *mère de sang*, Silver had no doubt that the entire Cercle de Druide would know as well.

The secret was unraveling.

"Tell me what's happened," Giovanni urged, leaning against the table. "I give my word that I will do anything and everything possible to help. But if you keep silent, I can do nothing."

Silver saw honest concern in Giovanni's hazel eyes, heard it in his voice. Time to roll the dice. Trust him or stake him. But first, a little insurance. Silver tapped at Merri's shields and the former SB agent thinned them immediately.

<If I don't get the answer I want,> Silver sent, <snap his neck. By the time he heals and is back on his feet, we'll be long gone.>

<Will do. What answer do you want?>

<You'll know it when you hear it.>

Shifting his attention to Giovanni, Silver said, "Okay. But I need your word that it goes no farther than you until we get Dante back."

Giovanni drew in a breath, considering. The fact that he didn't immediately agree to the terms suggested sincerity to Silver, that Giovanni actually valued his word. Sitting beside the Italian, Merri sipped at her beer, her casual demeanor deceptive. She was a coiled cobra.

Giovanni slanted a sideways look at the petite former SB agent, before returning his gaze to Silver. A knowing smile brushed his lips. He nodded. "You have my word. I will keep to myself anything and everything you confide in me—until Dante is safe. Besides," he added in a low voice, "I'd hate to be so rude as to force *bella* Merri to abandon her beer in order to stake me. Or would she shoot me?"

"Who says I can't do both?" Merri murmured.

Giovanni held both hands up in mock surrender. "Not me."

Tension uncoiled from Silver's muscles. Picking up his mug, he drained it, then leaned forward against the table and started talking. He skipped over most details—like Dante's slipping between the past and the present and his lack of control over his power—and sketched events in broad terms, finishing with, "Something went wrong with Lucien's search for Heather, so now we're just waiting for him to haul his winged ass from Gehenna with a new and improved plan B."

Fire burning in his eyes, Giovanni opened his mouth, then snapped it shut when a sudden buzzing noise—like the world's largest bumblebee—vibrated into the air. Annie twitched, startled. Reaching into her jeans pocket, she yanked out her cell phone. She frowned as she read the caller ID.

Leaning in for a look, Silver saw: C Cortini. *Wait. As in Caterina Cortini? Why would she be calling?* His heart skipped a beat. *Holy shit. Maybe she has news about Dante.* He nudged Annie's knee with his own. *Answer it.*

"Want me to put it on speaker?" Annie asked, wiping her barbecue-sauced fingers on a napkin before picking up the cell again.

Silver shook his head. "Don't want any eavesdroppers. Besides, we'll"—he nodded at Giovanni and Merri—"be able to hear just fine."

"Nightkind supersenses," Annie grumbled. "Must be nice." Thumbing the Talk button, she said, "I hope you have some good fucking news for us."

"Annie, thank God. Listen to me, okay? I need to speak to De Noir or Von."

"Holy shit. Heather," Silver said, sitting bolt upright, pulse racing, as relief swept across Annie's face, lit her blue eyes. He snatched the phone from her hand.

Some good news at fucking last.

34

THE CLOCK RUNS OUT

I'M NOT GOING TO *wait for you or De Noir, not for anyone.
I can't—there's no time. But as soon as I find Dante, I promise
I'll let you know exactly where we are. You go after Von. You find
our nomad and bring him home. And, Silver?*

Yeah?

Thanks for watching over Annie. I owe you.

*Ain't doing it for you. Doing it because I want to. Hey, you
felt anything through the bond from Dante?*

*No. Nothing new, anyway. But don't worry—I'll call as soon
as I find him.*

Heather goosed the speedometer to 85 mph, mulling over
everything she'd just learned, including her brief, tense conversation with the assassin's nightkind brother after she and Silver
had respectively filled each other in—Von missing, De Noir
silent and most likely still in Gehenna, Mauvais and his new
Fallen friend, her escape from SB agents and Cortini.

She tried to kill you?

*Yes, but something was very wrong with her. I've seen Dante
when his programming was triggered and, well, her behavior kind
of reminded me of that. Like someone else was pulling the strings.*

Molte grazie for not killing her. Where can I find her?

At an abandoned rest stop on I-530 South, near Pine Bluff.

The night blurred past in a streamer of oncoming

headlights and red taillights, of soft light glittering from windows in faraway homes, of white lines disappearing beneath the bulleting Nissan. Heather's hands white-knuckled against the steering wheel.

I feel like I'm running out of time, catin.

No, cher, no. I refuse to lose you.

Too late. Too late. Too late. The clock has run out.

Heather shoved aside the despairing and traitorous thought, refused to examine yet again what she had felt through the bond nearly an hour ago—a shattering desperation, a crumbling resolve, an overwhelming sense of loss.

She hadn't lied to Silver just to protect him from bad news; she'd lied because she hadn't been able to say the words, hadn't been able to force them from her throat.

I think what we've all feared, what we all fought to prevent, has happened—

. . . I think he's had all he can take, doll. Heart and mind . . .

—and Dante has finally broken.

Eyes burning, Heather pressed harder on the gas pedal, following the bond, following her heart, to Baton Rouge.

I feel like I'm running out of time, catin.

No, cher, no. I refuse to lose you.

That was a promise she intended to keep.

ANNIE TUCKED HER CELL phone back into her jeans pocket, watching as Silver rubbed his face in frustration. The relief—*hell, be honest, the fucking* joy—she'd felt at hearing her sister's voice, a voice she'd feared she'd never hear again, dimmed a little at Silver's expression. "Since I seem to be lacking nightkind eavesdropping power, what did she say?"

Silver sighed. He looked at Annie from beneath his dark lashes. "She's okay, she's going after Dante and ain't about to wait for us to catch up."

Merri scooted out of the booth so that tall, dark, and snobby

Giovanni with his sexy Italian purr of a voice could slide out. He pulled a handful of twenties from the pocket of his designer jeans and tossed them on the table. "My treat," he said with a sexy half-shrug. Looking at Silver, he added, "And thanks for taking me into your confidence."

"Remember, you gave me your word."

Giovanni nodded. "I won't say anything, not even to Renata until *after* Dante is safe." He headed for the tavern's entrance. "I'll be in touch after I've taken care of Caterina," he called over his shoulder as he pulled the door open. "*Ciao, belli.*"

Silver shook his head. "Hope I didn't make a mistake there."

"If it's any comfort, I don't think you did," Merri said. "But if his *mère de sang* suspects he is hiding something from her, believe me, she'll pry it out of him."

"Then let's hope he's good at hiding shit. Ready to quit sitting on your ass and twiddling your thumbs?"

"What do *you* think, Zero-boy?" Merri snorted, rising to her feet. "But we should feed before we go. Looks like there's any number of willing volunteers across the street."

Silver looked up at the ceiling, regret on his face. Annie figured he was thinking about the tasty SB agents upstairs. "Okay," he said, lowering his gaze to look at Annie. "Wait here, all right? We won't be long."

"I'll order another beer, so take your time." Annie lifted her mug and polished off her Abita, ignoring Silver's frown.

Silver and Merri *moved* across the room in double streaks of pale skin and black clothing, of purple and black hair.

Neither Aunt Sally's red-checker-aproned staff or the scattered handful of people chowing down on late night/early morning platters of pork ribs and grilled shrimp noticed their passage across the room and out the door—except maybe as a cool breeze or ghostly chill.

Still, Silver and Merri's nightkind speed had nothing on Dante's. And if he'd been truly awake the day her coldhearted bastard of a father appeared in the hall, James Wallace would never have stood a chance.

But Dante *hadn't* been truly awake, he'd been fighting Sleep, struggling to keep from nodding off again, to keep his eyes open, but aware enough to shove her out of harm's way at the last moment.

His blood, spattering hot upon her cheek, her lips.

Glistening so dark on his white skin.

Annie's belly squeezed tight, killing her appetite. The yummy, comforting taste of beer and tangy barbecue sauce soured on her tongue. She pushed the plate away without even looking at it, her restless thoughts roiling, bubbling up and down, up and down, up and fucking down.

Steeping her in guilt.

Dante. Heather. Blood. Trank guns. The sharp smell of gasoline. *You've reached the voice mail of James William Wallace, please leave a message.* Dante. Heather falling, the gun skittering from her hand. The sound of a gunshot shattering the air—

Stop! Slow the fuck down and concentrate on what's happening right now.

Sucking in a harsh breath, Annie tried to do just that, but her thoughts immediately slipped back to Heather and Dante and James Wallace. The coldhearted prick rat-bastard could be a fucking double agent working for the FBI *and* the SB for all Annie knew.

And he just dumped me on the sidewalk.

Something wheeled open inside of Annie, something as cold and empty and black as the belly of a plundered coal mine. Something endless.

She'd called the rat-bastard over and over in hopes of finding out where he'd taken Heather, in hopes of luring him back to New Orleans as she played the tearful, contrite, *don't-leave-me-all-alone-with-the-bloodsuckers-daddy-please* daughter, but his phone had gone straight to voice mail each and every time.

He's written you off. He's got the daughter he cares about. Nothing new, right?

Right, and look where that got her—tranked, cuffed, and dragged away.

Maybe I'm the lucky one.

Percolating, her thoughts, bubbling hot and cold, up and down, loud enough to hear the *perk-perk-perk* echoing from the inside of her skull.

Needing another beer, a drink to drown out the goddamned bubbling noise, Annie waved at the waitress, then pointed at her empty mug once she'd captured the caramel-skinned woman's attention. With a nod, the waitress beelined for the bar, returning a moment later with a freshly filled mug.

Annie swiveled around in the booth so she could rest her back against the wall and keep an easy eye on the tavern's door. She rested a hand against her T-shirted belly and as she did, Silver's words blossomed in her memory as bright and shining as his silver eyes.

I know it isn't mine, that's not what this is about . . .

Look, I can't say I know what you're going through—I don't. But I do know that you don't hafta face this alone.

She rubbed her belly reflectively. Maybe, just maybe, that would be enough. With Silver's help and Heather's, maybe she *could* do this, could be a good mom.

The only question was: did she *want* to do this?

Maybe it was time to find out. Silver stepped back into the tavern. His silver eyes seemed luminescent, brimming with moonlight. He curled a *let's go* finger at her.

My very own vampire knight.

Annie rose to her feet, leaving her beer untouched.

35

ANGRY LOA

"WELL? IS THE DAMNED device working?" Mauvais demanded as he strode into the dimly lit wheelhouse. "Do you have Loki's location?"

Phaedra looked up from her instruments, her beautiful and ageless café au lait face awash in the pale green light emanating from the navigation instruments, her lambent eyes glowing in the gloom.

Before she could reply, Mauvais observed with more than a little relief as he drew to a stop beside her, "The power is working again."

Phaedra nodded. "For now." She rapped her knuckles for luck against the cedar-planked wall before returning her attention to the GPS screen. "Looks like your Fallen guest is headed north. Maybe Baton Rouge. Maybe not. Too early to know."

"North," Mauvais mused, studying the moving blip on the green-lit GPS and the ever-shifting topography surrounding it. So many mysteries contained in one simple action—a fallen angel's sudden and swift flight through the waning night.

So many mysteries.

Loki and his deadly feud with the Nightbringer.

Dante's disappearance on the heels of his stunning revelation.

The shootout and fire at Club Hell.

Someone who didn't know Dante would think he'd simply gone into hiding following the violence at the club, but Mauvais had never known the irritating and stubborn *marmot* to run from a fight.

No. And he would never leave members of his small household behind if—for whatever unimaginable reason—he had decided to hightail it from New Orleans.

Silver had played it smart by playing dumb. And it might've worked too, but for his reaction to Loki's presence.

Mauvais had no doubt that Loki had plucked Dante's location from Silver's mind, along with anything else he desired to know. The young, purple-maned vampire's defenses would've amounted to no more than an apple's easily peeled skin beneath the sharp blade of the fallen angel's power.

No, Silver had never stood a chance.

Not once Loki had *shifted*, his body shimmering, rippling, transforming, into Dante's pale and lean-muscled form. Silver had been lost the moment Loki-as-Dante's white hands had cupped his face and brushed heated lips against his mouth.

Let me in, mon ami. *Let me in.*

Shape-shifter.

Mauvais was more than a little grateful that he'd witnessed that seductive bit of metamorphosis; he'd had no idea Loki possessed that particular talent. *Forewarned is forearmed.* Such clichés, though trite, were nonetheless true and worth more than a tanker load of hot, fresh blood.

"Are we to follow, my lord?" Phaedra asked.

Just as Mauvais opened his mouth to reply in the affirmative, blue light danced from one navigation screen to the next in a shower of sparks, leaving each screen dark in its wake. The sharp scent of ozone filled the air as the dim overheads winked out.

"Here we go again, goddammit," Phaedra muttered,

scowling, and slapping cut-off switches. "Looks like we ain't following shit tonight. Almost enough to make me think there really is an angry *loa* on board."

"If by angry *loa* you mean ancient wiring, then yes," Mauvais said, voice level despite the frustration curdling his belly, "I believe you might be right. In which case, an electrician should be able to ameliorate it."

"True that, my lord. I'll make it happen—if Edmond hasn't already done so. In the meantime, you can track Loki from your car with this." Phaedra handed Mauvais a small smartphone-size tracker. "Just plug it in, synch it, and go."

"Ah, *très bien*," Mauvais said, offering his navigator a genuine smile, relieved that he wouldn't be delayed after all. Slipping the portable receiver into a pocket of his frock coat, he turned and exited the wheelhouse.

The pungent odor of kerosene mingled with the cool, fishy aroma of the Mississippi as Edmond and a young male *apprenti* relit the lanterns along the deck, moving with smooth and silent efficiency from one to the next.

Standing in a pool of light spilling out across the deck from one of the hissing lanterns, Mauvais tugged at the lacy cuffs of his sleeves, saying, "Edmond, have the driver bring my car around at once. I'll wait on the wharf."

"*Oui*, my lord."

"Oh, and Edmond?"

"My lord?"

"Rafe and Nikolai will be accompanying me."

"Very good, my lord. I shall so inform them."

Edmond motioned for the *apprenti* to continue with the lanterns, then swiveled around with a smooth, precise, almost military grace and headed for the stairs leading belowdecks.

As Mauvais started for the gangplank leading down to the wharf, he remembered the guest he'd abandoned in the French Quarter in his eagerness to return to the *Winter Rose* to see if his James Bond efforts had paid off or not.

A high-ranking and hot-tempered guest.

Mauvais came to an abrupt halt. "*Merde*," he said with a soft groan. Half turning, he called to his majordomo once more.

The soft sound of Edmond's descending footsteps stopped. "*Oui*, my lord?"

"If *Signor* Toscanini should return, please offer him every courtesy, including the finest from my wine cellar and the choicest mortals from my personal menagerie. Inform him that I have gone to rescue that defiant prick Dante Baptiste from the Fallen and shall return shortly."

The slightest pause, then, "Of course, my lord. I shall so inform *Signor* Toscanini."

Mauvais frowned, considering. "Perhaps we should leave out 'defiant prick,' *oui*?"

"*Oui*. Wise decision, my lord." Edmond's quiet footfalls resumed.

Mauvais's heart slammed into his throat as he swiveled around to find himself facing an inexplicable figure, a flickering, shifting male shape composed of blue neon ones and zeroes.

"You ain't going nowhere, you." The figure's voice sounded utterly human, dancing with Cajun rhythm. Waist-length dreads of gleaming and twisted bundles of wire undulated in the air, electric snakes curling around a neon Medusa.

Mauvais sucked in a shocked breath. The hoodoo conjurer had been right, after all.

You got an angry loa *on dis here boat . . .*

And exactly how does one placate an angry *loa*? Mauvais wondered, mouth dry. Had it been sent, a nasty trick set into motion by a rival or enemy? Or had it chosen him because of something he'd inadvertently done—or not done?

Mauvais lifted his hands slowly, palms out. Took one prudent step back. "If I have offended you, it was unintentional, and I apologize. What would you have me do to free myself and my boat?"

The figure stared at Mauvais with eyes like endless black ice. "I want you to burn like she did, motherfucker. She screamed in agony until the flames she breathed in burned away her larynx and ashed her lungs. My sister, my *mère de sang*, my Simone."

Mauvais froze, remembering words Silver had spat at him in the Quarter not even an hour ago: *Simone. Her name was Simone, you jackass. She died because of you.*

Not a curse, no. Revenge.

Mauvais caught a blur of flickering blue-edged movement, then felt something shatter against him. He smelled kerosene — and much worse. Flames swept over him eagerly, devouring his clothing, the flesh beneath. The stench of burning hair filled his nostrils.

"Burn, you motherfucking *fi' de garce*."

A high-pitched wailing pierced the night, a siren of agony vibrating from his own throat. Choking on the acrid reek of his own roasting flesh, Mauvais raced, flailing, across the deck to the railing and hurtled overboard

He plummeted, blazing, an April bonfire, into the cold, night-black waters of the Mississippi.

36

A MOTHER'S GRIEF

A MOIST, BRINE-SCENTED WIND whipped through Lucien's hair, pushed at his folded wings. He studied the night-darkened sea crashing around the weathered rocks far below, ghostly spume spraying into the air. Beneath his feet, he felt the booming vibration as the sea crashed into a cave hollowed below into the cliff face.

"How much longer?" he asked.

"He'll be here soon," Hekate's soft voice answered from beside him.

Lucien said nothing, a muscle ticking in his jaw. Leave it to the Morningstar to take his own sweet time even while the trumpets blew and the stars fell from the skies.

Enough time had already been wasted presenting himself to Gabriel and assuring the royal pretender that everything was fine with Dante, that his visit to Gehenna had been prompted merely by a desire to see, once more, a certain silver-haired enchantress.

But engrossed in directing the cleaning of the *creawdwr's* receiving chamber, a room unused since Yahweh's death more than two thousand years, Gabriel had barely paid any attention to Lucien's presence, let alone the reason for his visit.

Finally waving Lucien away like an annoying summer fly, Gabriel had said only, "Why should I care? She's no longer my hostage. She may do as she pleases. And if that includes becoming entangled with her mother's former lover, the murderer of our previous *creawdwr*, then so be it. I have better things to worry about."

Hekate's silver bell of a voice pulled Lucien away from his thoughts. He looked at her, certain she'd asked him a question, one he hadn't heard. Pale moonlight rippled along her looped and coiled—and now salt-spray-beaded—tresses. Night hollowed her cheeks, pooled deep in her hyacinth eyes. Drew him in.

"Forgive me," he murmured. "I'm afraid I didn't—"

Hekate shook her head. "Nothing to forgive. I know you have a lot on your mind—including whether you can trust my father to do the right thing."

"There is that. But I believe he will. It's in his own best interests."

"For now."

"What did you ask me while I was woolgathering?"

Hekate hesitated, then turned her gaze to the restless sea. "If you knew why Dante refused to restore my mother. She was helping you, after all. Trying to protect him from the others. It makes no sense."

Lucien shook his head regretfully. "I don't know the answer to that. I haven't had time or opportunity to discuss the matter with Dante. But I will, I promise, once he's home and safe."

"Thank you." Hekate flashed Lucien a quick, grateful smile before giving her attention back to the sea. "So restless," she murmured. "When I was a child, my mother told me that Yahweh's mother, Leviathan, lived in the ocean and that when it stormed and the sea was wild and restless, it was just Leviathan grieving her only child."

Leviathan. A chill touched the base of Lucien's spine. "Do you still believe that?"

"When I was young, yes. But now, of course not. For the longest time though, storms like this made me think of death and loss and a mother's tears."

Watching the white-capped waves, Lucien nodded. "I can understand that."

"I've only heard stories about her—Yahweh's mother. She left Gehenna for the mortal world centuries before I was born."

"To hunt her son's killer."

"You." Hekate's voice was soft, absent of accusation, simply stating a fact.

"Me," Lucien agreed. He drew in a deep breath of chilled, briny air. Underneath, he caught Hekate's sweet scent—apple blossoms and cool, shaded water.

"How have you managed to elude Leviathan all this time?"

"I haven't," Lucien replied, shifting his attention from the sea back to Hekate's lovely face. "She found me once, nearly ten years ago. After I summoned her."

"By all that's holy, why would you do such a thing?"

"Desperation. Fifteen years imprisoned within an *aingeal* trap will do that to you."

Hekate stared at him. "Imprisoned? Where? How?"

Lucien shook his head and shifted his gaze back to the heaving dark waters below. "How? My own foolishness. Where? A tattoo shop on the Oregon coast. As to the question you *didn't* ask—why—as Nightbringer, I often forced mortals to face the consequences of their own selfish actions and greed."

"I take it that *you* were those consequences?"

"That I was." A wry smile pulled at the corners of Lucien's mouth. "Your mother used to accuse me of being judgmental and arrogant. She wasn't wrong. Once I left Gehenna, I continued my work as Nightbringer. I continued *very* diligently, forcing the mortal world to face what I would not—God was dead. I left entire cities in ruin, the air choked with the ashes of the dead."

"All to forget Yahweh," Hekate said slowly. "To forget what you had done. What you *had* to do."

"To escape," Lucien corrected, old sorrow tightening his throat. "There *was* no forgetting."

Not the whispered sound of Yahweh's weary voice: *Let them have me, my calon-cyfaill. Let them bind me, chain me to their will. Let it be done before it's too late. Let it finally be over.*

Nor the weight of Yahweh's lifeless body in his arms.

"And did it work?" Hekate asked softly.

"It did. For centuries. Until I hunted down a woman who enjoyed scamming the bereaved out of their pensions and savings. She was to be the last before I began my new life in New Orleans."

"New life?" Hekate's voice dropped into a husky, knowing murmur. "Ah. Dante's mother. So that's who reawakened your heart."

Lucien nodded. "Genevieve." He studied the foam-tipped waves below. "My scammer turned out to be nephilim and not mortal. She'd also laid a trap for me—one I walked right into—and forced me to recount my own sins in detail for fifteen very long years."

Fifteen years—unaware that Genevieve was pregnant, unaware that she had been murdered after their son's birth, leaving the newborn in the hands of monsters. A son Lucien had no idea even existed.

"So you summoned Leviathan to free yourself." Hekate's voice was stunned. "Or was it atonement you sought, not freedom?"

"Both, perhaps," Lucien replied. In truth, he was no longer certain. Behind his eyes, memory stirred.

Leviathan answers in a violent storm that shakes the cliff. She rises from the deep, a valley of endless folds and marine darkness and cascading water that never touches the sea or ground. Her wybrcathl, a furious subsonic bellow, shatters the tattoo shop's windows and fractures the building itself.

As sea spray washes away the sigils and angelic script encircling him, Lucien is freed. He battles Paloma and both are injured, but before he can finish the fight, Leviathan envelops them both in an undulating dark tide that slides over them like a bowl.

Lucien realizes that he owes Leviathan the story that Paloma had demanded; the story of his murder of her only child—Yahweh. Standing in an oceanic night lit only by the phosphorescent flashes from bizarre creatures swimming within Leviathan, Lucien gives the transformed and fallen angel the last moments of her son's life. And the reasons for his death.

At the end of it, she asks, <Do you have any children?>

<No.>

<Best you keep it that way. For I shall claim your firstborn as my own—to kill or to love, as I deem fit.>

Leviathan pulls away, recedes, and returns to the seething sea, leaving Lucien untouched. Physically, at least.

After he'd discovered Dante's existence, Lucien had often wondered at Leviathan's silence, eventually coming to believe that, with her long search for her son's killer finally over, Leviathan slept in lightless ocean depths, hibernating beneath tons of watery pressure, and beyond the reach—so far—of Dante's *anhrefncathl*. Or so Lucien hoped with each beat of his heart.

A wind-chilled hand touched his shoulder, the fingers nearly cold as ice against his skin. He shivered.

"Lucien, tell me the story from the beginning."

Turning his head to look at her, Lucien wrapped Hekate's icy fingers in his, then lifted them to his lips. Kissed them. "It's a long story, one for another time."

"I like long stories," she murmured, stepping closer. The wind molded her moss-green gown against her curves, coaxed rosy color from her cheeks.

"So do I," a voice said from above them. "And I hear you have a good one."

Lucien looked up to see the Morningstar kiting down from the night sky, moonlight gleaming along his alabaster wings as they slashed through the brine-laden air. Giving Hekate's fingers one more kiss, Lucien released her hand. He swiveled to face her father.

"Good isn't the word I'd use," Lucien said. "Bad, with the potential for worse."

The Morningstar landed with ease, despite the wind. He folded his wings behind him with a graceful flutter. He was dressed for the sea weather in black plaid trousers over sturdy black boots. Regarding Lucien with golden eyes, he said, "Let's hear it, then."

In a voice prickly with his own swallowed pride, Lucien obliged him.

37

No Longer the Ancient World

Finished with his grim recitation, Lucien watched as the Morningstar paced along the cliff's rocky edge in long, furious strides, pebbles gritting beneath his boots. The wind—heavy with the smell of impending rain—whipped through his short white hair and plucked at his trousers. Anger radiated from him in dry ice waves, scorching his bitter orange scent.

"I *knew* Dante should've remained here," the Morningstar growled.

"He didn't want to," Lucien reminded. "And no one could've forced him without suddenly needing to adapt to additional or perhaps fewer body parts."

"Will you help or not?" Hekate asked. "You sealed the blood pledge, therefore you can use it to track Dante."

"Yes, I can," the Morningstar agreed. He ceased his pacing and turned around to face them both, winter frost in his eyes. "But once I do, what shape will his sanity be in?"

"What makes you question his sanity?" Hekate asked.

The Morningstar waved a negligent hand. "We've all witnessed his seizures, his odd tumbles into a past he doesn't seem to remember. He was already standing at the crumbling edge of the abyss. He might've already fallen."

Lucien shook his head. "You have no idea what Dante's endured."

"I know more than you think. *Much* more. Mortal minds are so easy to read."

Lucien stared at the Morningstar, chilled to the bone.

Mortal minds.

Heather. Annie.

If the Elohim should learn about Dante's past, about Bad Seed, about what had been done to him—the programming implanted within their *creawdwr*, they would kill him before allowing a mortal agency to control him.

"Dante's stronger than you think," Lucien said.

"Dante may be strong, but he's also exhausted. Even I could see that."

"So, are you saying it's too late?" Hekate asked her father. "That you won't even try? We can't just give up, we need—" Her words trailed away, her gaze turning inward as she received a sending. She blinked, frowning.

Lucien glanced at the Morningstar and saw that he shared his daughter's introspective expression and was most likely the source of the sending.

Hekate blew out an exasperated breath. "Fine. I'll give you ten minutes."

"For what?" Lucien asked.

"A bit of privacy," the Morningstar answered. "So we can discuss arrangements."

"Ah. Arrangements," Lucien murmured. "Of course."

Lucien watched as Hekate stepped away to unfurl her creamy white wings. They glimmered ghost-pale in the darkness, their undersides the iridescent lavender of seashells. She rose into the night, then quickly flew out of sight.

"Wise," Lucien said. "Can't have your daughter seeing you for who you really are."

The Morningstar laughed, genuine amusement in his voice. "The child is five centuries old. Trust me, she has no illusions on that score."

"No. I suppose not," Lucien agreed, turning to face the Morningstar. "Let's have it, then. How much is your help going to cost me?"

"Now, now," the Morningstar chided, his lips curving into a mocking smile. "My *help* is freely given." He stepped forward until he'd narrowed the distance between them to a mere handspan. "It's your *failure*—as a guardian, as a father—that will cost you."

Lucien's hands knotted into fists. He barely felt the bite of his talons against his palms. Holding the Morningstar's now gold-flecked gaze, he growled, "Name your price. But know this before you do—I'll never agree to anything that negates Dante's free will."

"Such as putting a mortal—like Annie—ahead of his well-being? That's exactly what you did when you rescued her while your son was being stolen from inside the club."

Angelic power crackled electric along Lucien's fingers, snapping the sharp smell of ozone into the briny air. "Consider your next words carefully," he warned.

An answering thrum of power vibrated from the Morningstar and into Lucien. Elohim challenge. The ozone scent thickened. Then the Morningstar's expression shifted from anticipation to regret as he took a reluctant step back.

"Before we play any Elohim games, we have a *creawdwr* to find."

Lucien exhaled, releasing his power. "We do."

"But we also need to discuss what we plan to do if his sanity has been broken. I know all about Bad Seed and what was done to Dante. And no," the Morningstar added, giving Lucien a knowing look from beneath pale lashes, "I haven't told anyone else."

"And you won't," Lucien stressed, holding the Morningstar's wintery blue gaze.

"Of all the many things I am, fool is not among them."

"Yet."

"Your faith in me is quite touching, brother," the Morningstar said in a voice as dry as a desert wind. "Now, Dante—his sanity?"

"Dante's bond with Heather has kept him balanced. Once we've located him, we can keep him sedated and safe until we find her."

"And if we *don't* find her?"

"We will," Lucien replied. Stepping to the cliff's edge, he studied the whitecapped waves crashing against the rocks below. "We must."

"While I applaud your optimism, I don't share it," the Morningstar said. "Do you remember the device created by that nephilim scientist? The one designed to preserve what was left of Yahweh's sanity, maybe even restore it?"

"*An Banna Cruach,*" Lucien said slowly, as a memory awakened, one buried long centuries before. "The Steel Bond."

"The bond that cannot be severed, yes," the Morningstar mused. "That's it."

"It was an invention of pure desperation," Lucien said, turning to look at the Morningstar, "a last ditch effort. An effort finished too late, at that."

"It was meant to be implanted within Yahweh, am I right?" the Morningstar asked. "To rechannel the *creu tân* in some fashion in order to safeguard his sanity?"

"Yes, but it was never tested, so we'll never know if it would've worked. It might not have," Lucien replied, impatience sharpening his tone. "In any case, it was built with a full-blooded Elohim *creawdwr* in mind, not a mixed-blood Maker."

"If Dante's sanity has broken and Heather isn't found, we may have no other choice—aside from killing him, that is."

Lucien laughed. "You talk as if the damned thing still existed. Loki destroyed—"

"No, he didn't," the Morningstar cut in. "He killed the

nephilim who invented it, oh yes. Loki wanted Yahweh to become the Great Destroyer. He thought that would be fun beyond measure. But he never had a chance to destroy the Bond. Someone stole it from him before he could."

"And who was that?"

A smile brushed the Morningstar's lips. "Michael."

Hope sparked. If the Steel Bond still existed, it might save Dante when nothing else could. "And where is it now?"

"Keeping Michael company inside his tomb—in theory, anyway. Besides, as you said, it may not even work on a True Blood–Fallen *creawdwr* at all. A *creawdwr* we still need to find."

"That we do," Lucien agreed. "So name your damned price."

"Let's think of it as a penalty, not a price. A penalty in two parts."

"You can call it whatever you want, just name it."

"First, I want Lilith back, restored once more to flesh."

Lucien nodded, surprised, but not unpleasantly so. For a deal with the devil, that particular request/penalty was more difficult than morally challenging. "I'll do my best to convince Dante. But no guarantees. He's stubborn under the best of circumstances."

"I've noticed," the Morningstar said dryly.

"And the second part?"

"To ensure a lasting alliance between our houses, I want a hostage."

And there it was, the moral compromise, the true deal with the devil.

Lucien regarded the Morningstar for a long, silent moment. He caught a flash of white in his peripheral vision, heard the rush of wings beneath the wind. Hekate.

"Dante will never give up Heather," Lucien warned.

"Of course not," the Morningstar said. "She's bondmate and *cydymaith* both. I had no intention of asking for her."

"Who, then?"

"Her sister, Annie. The mortal you were so busy rescuing."

"No. Impossible. She's pregnant. Choose another. Choose me."

"Pregnant?" The Morningstar's eyes shone with a speculative light. "Truly? Well, that changes everything. Annie no longer interests me as a hostage."

Relief flooded through Lucien. He was just about to offer himself again as hostage, when the Morningstar's next words stole the air from his lungs.

"I want the child in her womb, once born."

"Are you mad?" Lucien asked, voice flat, disbelieving. "This is no longer the ancient world. You can't lay claim to newborns. No."

The Morningstar shrugged. "As you wish. I shall find and free Dante without you, then. And I will do whatever I deem necessary to stabilize his sanity." His alabaster wings unfurled, sweeping through the air. He lifted into the brine- and storm-scented night.

"Damn you, wait!"

The Morningstar paused, hovering, his wings beating through the air. He tilted his head, regarding Lucien with shadowed eyes. "I'm waiting, but not for long. I have a *creawdwr* to salvage. And please keep in mind that any promise you make will be sealed in blood—unbreakable."

Lucien tasted something dark and bitter at the back of his throat. He knew Dante would never forgive him for the vow he was about to make. Suspected he would never forgive himself.

I would lay the world to waste for my son. What is one mortal infant?

Lucien realized in that moment that he and Leviathan weren't so very different.

For I shall claim your firstborn as my own—to kill or to love, as I deem fit.

Eyes burning, Lucien slashed a talon across his palm. Blood welled up, dark and fragrant, binding him to the words he now spoke in a low voice. "The child shall be yours. Now take me to my son."

The Morningstar revealed his sharp teeth in a dark and wolfish grin. "With plea—"

"Father!"

Hekate landed on the cliff in a frantic flurry of wings. As she swiveled to face them, Lucien's gut knotted at the panic and uncertainty he saw darkening her eyes and leaching color from her face. From above and all around, cries sounded through the rain-lashed night like frightened sea gulls. As Lucien listened, he closed his eyes, pulse pounding at his temples.

"They're gone," the Morningstar said, voice stunned, a man learning his cancer is terminal. "The skygates have unraveled."

38

WELCOME TO THE HORROR SHOW

THE AIR REEKED OF blood and pissed-pants death.

Blood glistened on the walls.

Slicked the tile floor in long, dark smears.

And on the alarm panel ripped from the wall beside the security desk—a bloody left handprint that Dante studied like a stark and mysterious paleolithic cave painting from where he lay sprawled on the floor. He lifted his bloodstained left hand. Compared.

Probably mine.

Lowering his hand, Dante wearily closed his eyes. His head pulsed with pain, a never-relenting, white-hot pressure as though his head was caught between tons of shifting rock. Trapped beneath the rubble of a cataclysmic internal earthquake, despite having escaped the shattered depths—for now, anyway—when a seizure had knocked S's ass to the blood-smeared floor.

Just taking a time-out. Catching my breath.

Got a full schedule of killing ahead.

A chill touched Dante soul-deep. He no longer knew if his thoughts were his alone or belonged to S. Figured it no longer mattered at this point. Words Lucien had said to him in the back of the Perv's van popped into his aching head.

S doesn't exist. Only Dante. S is a part of you, child. The rage you deny, the pain you ignore. You are Dante Baptiste, son of Lucien and Genevieve. Not S. Not the child of monsters.

Dante had a feeling the fucking FBI and SB—not to mention everyone cooling on the floor—would heartily disagree.

Opening his eyes and wishing for a pair of shades, Dante squinted as light from the overheads needled into them. He rolled up onto his hands and knees. He needed to haul ass. Needed to find an exit, then Heather.

Sure about that?

Memory coughed up an ugly image.

His finger squeezes the trigger. Her head rocks forward with the first bullet, then snaps back with the second, tendrils of red hair whipping through the air.

Dante shivered, suddenly cold, the nightmare image refusing to fade. Sweat beaded his forehead, dampened the hair at the nape of his neck. White light strobed furiously at the edges of his vision. He needed to warn Heather away. He couldn't trust himself—and neither should she. Until he had himself—including the part of him that was S—under control, she wouldn't be safe.

No one would be.

Hoping the blood he'd gulped down (Nah, make that S. Credit where credit's due, yeah?) during the sanitarium slaughter had diluted the drugs in his system enough to keep his sending from bouncing around the inside of his skull like a rubber bullet, Dante reached for Heather through their bond.

Catin, keep away. Run from me. Run as far—

The floor tilted beneath his knees, interrupting his sending, and scattering black flecks across his graying field of vision. An intense spinning sensation pureed his thoughts. Blanked his mind. Pain needled his temples, blowback from the sending.

"Boy, you need to get your ass down to the basement and now," Papa said, his voice bayou bred and two-packs-of-Winstons-a-day gravelly. "Enough with dat school nonsense. Someone coming to see you. And trust me, he ain't interested in whether or not you know yo' ABCs." The *fi' de garce*'s raspy laughter ended in a cough. "Waste o' time, anyway. Chloe should be doing her homework insteada teaching you dat bullshit."

Hands curling automatically into fists at the sound of Papa's voice, Dante blinked until his vision cleared. For a moment, he thought he saw a gore-splashed corridor graffitied with a primitive and bloody handprint—then it was gone.

A dream, maybe. A really fucked up dream. But no more fucked up than Papa Prejean and his motherfucking basement-prison bordello.

"Fuck you," Dante said. "I'll be there in a minute."

He was kneeling beside Chloe's bed, facing Papa who stood in the doorway in jeans and a fresh, white wifebeater bracketed by suspenders. Despite a liberal dosing of Florida Water, Dante still smelled Papa's sweat underneath the cologne's sweet orange, cloves, and lavender fragrance.

Papa frowned, deep lines furrowing his forehead. "Dere you go, running dat foul mouth o' yours again. Sounds like I should rinse it out with somet'ing stronger dan soap. Mebbe dat gasoline out in the garage'll do the trick."

"Leave him alone," Chloe said from behind Dante. He heard her heart beating hard and fast, speaking up despite her fear, and with each frantic, hummingbird beat, Dante heard the rhythm of her courage.

Papa slanted a sour look at her over the top of Dante's head. "Hush, you. Or I'll put my hand upside your head."

Reaching back, Dante squeezed Chloe's knee, then rose

to his feet. The room wobbled, became a corridor dotted with crumpled bodies, a trail of bloodied bread crumbs underscored by a steady and muffled *whomp-whomp-whomp* and leading to—

Chloe's room. Papa in the doorway, a Winston smoldering between his fingers and curling pale smoke into the air to battle it out with sweat and Florida Water.

Dante swayed on his feet, pain a sledgehammer pounding against the inside of his skull. "You're gonna need more than handcuffs—"

Whomp! Whomp! Whomp!

The sound reverberated through Dante's aching head. The booming heartbeat of a giant or the smack of furious fists into a punching bag or—

The room wobbled again and Dante stumbled, thumping shoulder-first into the wall.

—or the thud of feet kicking in desperation against a thick, steel door.

Dante blinked. Chloe's room vanished. A corridor replaced it, one full of bodies and blood and the stink of death and cordite. A paleolithic handprint. The SB sanitarium. He sucked in a breath, concentrated on remaining in the here-and-now.

Guns were scattered across the tile. Medical staff in white-and mint-green scrubs lay entangled among the bodies of black-suited agents. Whether S's work or his own, and pretty sure it didn't fucking matter in the long run, Dante felt no regret. Not when he thought of little girls in Winnie-the-Pooh sweaters deliberately locked into rooms with wounded and starving nightkind.

I've got promises to keep.

Wiping blood from his nose with the back of his hand, Dante pushed himself away from the wall.

From within their locked rooms, inmates pounded against the steel doors with fists and feet and anything not bolted to the concrete, their violent and desperate drumming an aural gauntlet that Dante passed as he staggered unsteadily down the corridor, looking for an exit sign and hoping against hope he found one before the past played python and swallowed him down its dark gullet again.

I could unlock the doors.

I could let them all go.

I could play with them.

Until Purcell returns.

"No," Dante whispered. "Ain't stopping. I'm getting the hell out of here." Pain pounded and drummed in his head, keeping time with all the thumping fists and feet.

Wantitneeditkillitburnitburnburnburn . . .

Darkness nibbling at his vision like a hungry mouse, Dante stumbled to a stop. He leaned against the wall and rubbed his temples with trembling fingers. He struggled to shut out the fucking noise, to dampen the pain. To think.

Send it below or fucking use it.

Problem was, *below* was full to the brim and hands crawling with wasps were locked around his ankles, fingers digging in to yank him down again.

Underneath the kicking and hammering and muffled yells, he heard someone singing—*hey, that's one of my songs*—voice husky and low and simmering with a barely contained rage. A voice he recognized.

"I am what you made me / no matter where you hide / where you run / I will find you / I am what you made me / nothing can stop me / I have nothing left to lose / I'm coming for you . . ."

Purcell.

The SB and the FBI.

The psychotic assholes locked behind those doors.

The motherfucking world.

They have it coming in fucking spades, yeah?

Letting the song trail away, unfinished, Dante whispered, "*Oui*, for true."

Then let's give it to them.

Dante opened his eyes and his heart jumped into his throat. He was no longer leaning against the wall. Instead, he stood in the wide-open doorway of an inmate's room, his blood-grimed fingertips resting on the door's keypad. He hadn't realized that he'd even moved, let alone keyed open the door.

"Shit," he breathed, jerking his hand away from the keypad.

Light from the corridor spilled into the room, revealing someone curled on the stark and narrow bed in the white-padded room's center. Someone with golden curls spiraling to her straitjacketed waist. The mattress creaked as she struggled to sit up. She looked at Dante, blinking in the light, her pale face uncertain, her brown eyes drug-dilated.

Dante's breath caught in his throat, his stunned heart pulsing hard and fast.

Fire scorches her lungs. Blackens her skin. Devours her with relentless teeth.

"Simone?" he whispered.

"What did you say? Who . . . who are you?" she asked in a tremulous voice, a voice deeper than her own had ever been. Somehow masculine. But that was okay. She was alive. And that was all that mattered.

Wrong. This is all wrong. She burned. You felt her die. Wake the fuck up.

Maybe she didn't. Maybe someone stole her before it was too late.

You fucking felt her die.

But Von's words, spoken in the graveyard hush of St. Louis No. 3, filled Dante's mind: *A spoken thing or wished-hard thing takes a shape within the heart.*

"Takes shape," Dante continued aloud. "Becomes real."

"Who are you?" Maybe-Simone asked again. "What was going on out there?"

Feeling light-headed, like the floor was dropping away from beneath his feet, Dante stepped into the room. A high-pitched buzzing filled his ears. The room wheeled, spinning like a merry-go-round caught in a Category 5 blow-down.

Dante snapped his eyes shut. Steadied himself with a hand to the padded wall and waited for the gut-wrenching dizziness to pass. Once it had and once the floor was motionless beneath his socked feet again, he opened his eyes.

And found himself standing in front of a tomb in the silent heart of St. Louis No. 3. But this St. Louis was whole and intact, not the shattered ruin he still needed to set right.

How did I get here?

Like stove-warmed taffy, reality and dreams stretched beyond their normal shapes and boundaries and merged. Took a new shape within his heart.

Shadows clung to the tomb's moon-washed marble like black-leafed ivy. Beneath the sweet perfume of graveyard flowers and cherry blossoms, Dante caught a whiff of bones moldering behind old marble, of ice and cold stone and fallow hearts.

From within the tomb's dank depths, something stirred. He heard the dusty grit of time, of ashes and bone, beneath sandal soles. Then: "I've missed you, *cher*."

Dante's breath caught rough at the sound of that voice— Cajun-musical and wistful, it pierced his heart like a knife.

Simone appeared in the tomb's open mouth, darkness sluicing away from her like black water. She knelt upon the threshold in fire-crisped tank top and cut-offs, hair tumbling over her shoulders in long, golden spirals that framed her pale, soot-streaked face in luminous curls. Her magnolia scent was scorched and blackened, all sweetness seared away.

Dante took another step forward, then dropped to his knees on the stone walk in front of her. "Miss you too." He started to reach for her hair, but before his fingers could so much as graze a silken strand, he stopped, then knotted his hands into fists atop his leather-clad thighs. He couldn't trust himself.

Didn't dare.

Down in the wasp-droning shattered depths, someone laughed.

A cold finger pressed against his lips, hushing the words he'd been about to say—*My fault,* chère. *I failed you and Trey both. You died because of my fucking mistakes.*

"I don't want you taking blame or refusing comfort. I only want you to make them pay. Make them burn for me, Dante."

Shadows crept from the tomb's arched mouth and slithered over Simone, stealing the light from her golden curls and veiling her face in inky darkness. Only her voice remained, a fierce but fading whisper.

"Make every single bastard burn, make the world burn, *mon cher ami, mon ange,* and set me free."

Dante grabbed for Simone, his desperation—to keep her from the tomb's icy darkness, to hold her safe—outweighing his self-distrust. His fingers closed tight around her arm. He yanked her free from the fetid shadows, free from fiery death, from the unalterable past.

And back onto a bed in the sanitarium, once again buckled into a straitjacket.

"How about getting me out of this thing, buddy?" she asked in a deep voice mysteriously empty of Cajun rhythm.

But that was okay. She was alive. She'd never burned, never—

Pain scraped across Dante's thoughts. He sucked in a breath as a warning floated up from the droning, whispering depths.

Ain't Simone. That's Papa in a Simone-suit playing possum.

Dante's heart kicked hard against his chest. He narrowed his eyes. *Oui.* Made sense. The masculine voice. The questions, all innocent and confused. He could see it now. Papa playing him for a motherfucking fool, just waiting to snap the cuffs around his wrists and trap him once more in the basement's moldering darkness.

Fucker won't stay dead. How many times do I need to tear out his goddamned throat?

Dante shook his head, laughing low, the padded walls soaking up the smoked whiskey and velvet music of his voice, exposing the cold, knowing tone underneath. "You must really think I'm an idiot."

"What? I don't—"

Dante laughed again. "Sure you do. 'Boy needs a lesson,' right? Ain't those your words? 'Boy *always* needs a lesson.'"

Papa's voice turned desperate, but Dante heard the slyness crouched beneath the words. "I don't know who you're looking for, but you've got the wrong—"

Thick shadows drifted like dark smoke across the padded walls, transforming them into cold and dank concrete blocks. In the basement's corner, the furnace rumbled to life, a comforting sound despite the furnace's predatory, shadow-twisted posture.

Welcome home, S. Welcome back, petit.

"Yeah? I don't think so." Dante pinched Papa's doughy chin between his fingers. Fury knotted the muscles in his chest. "And you know what? Fuck you."

Deep within the basement's dark and water-stained heart, Dante set to work. And Papa screamed and screamed and screamed.

THE PUNGENT SMELL OF blood, thick and wet and fresh, filled Dante's nostrils. Blinking, he stared at the body sprawled upon the blood-soaked mattress—a man buckled into a straitjacket. A man he didn't recognize. Blond hair lay across his openmouthed face in lank strands. Fear looped icy coils around Dante's belly. He couldn't remember who he thought he'd been killing.

Something about playing possum in a Simone suit. Holy fucking Christ.

A bloody hole cratered the dead-dead-dead inmate's chest right at heart level. Pulse drumming at his temples, Dante looked down at his hand. At what he held tight between his blood-sticky fingers.

Not the stuff of valentines, maybe, but kinda cool all the same, yeah?

Tais-toi, *you.*

The pale heart spilled from Dante's hand, hitting the concrete floor with a soft, fleshy *splat.* The high-pitched buzzing returned, erasing the silence. He rose to his feet slowly, wiped his hands against his leather pants.

Plucking a heart from some deserving motherfucker's chest was one thing—

—*and who says that cooling corpse on the bed wasn't deserving? He was locked in here, after all. Might've been an SB experiment just like you. Me. Us.*

—but ripping it from some straitjacketed *fi' de garce?* What if it had truly been Simone? Or Heather? How about Violet or Von?

No one can ever be used against you if you're willing to kill them yourself.

Fuck you.

The truth is never what you hope it will be.

"Ain't listening," Dante muttered, even though he was—he couldn't help it. He stumbled back out into the corridor, into air thick with the reek of death, of coppery blood and pungent piss. The silence soothed the ache in his head.

Silence.

He paused, taking in the flung-open doors on either side of the corridor, doors that had been closed and locked the last time he'd stood in the corridor, feeling cold to his soul—and listened.

No thumping, no pounding, no steel-muffled shouts.

No heartbeats but his own.

Bloody footprints trailed from one flung-open door to the next. Remembering the heart he'd held in his hand, Dante didn't need to look inside the rooms to know what he'd find.

Had to be done. They were locked up just like you, yeah? For the same reasons.

Little fucking psycho.

Dante swallowed hard. He had to haul ass out of this fucking place, and he had to make sure he kept away from Heather and everyone else that he cared about.

Smart move. But first we need to wait for that asshole Purcell.

Dante shook his head. "No. I'll deal with him some other time. Ain't staying." But he noticed his socked feet remained motionless. Noticed that his blood-grimed hands flexed restlessly at his sides. Noticed with a deepening sense of frustration and despair that his body seemed to have no intention whatsoever of searching for an exit.

Welcome back, S. Welcome home.

Ain't finished here. Not by a long shot.

For true, that. Maybe waiting wasn't such a bad idea, after all. Give the drugs time to wear off. And once they had, he'd be able to reach Heather, Von, Lucien—everyone. But that realization snaked cold and uneasy around his heart.

Keep away. Run from me—

"I am what you made me / no matter where you hide, where you run," Dante heard himself singing, "I will find you . . ."

"Dante?"

Dante whirled at the sound of his name, song dying in his throat. A tall figure stood motionless in the shadows at the corridor's far end. A tall figure with wings arching above his head and eyes burning like stars.

Lucien.

Relief flooded through Dante. Lucien would keep Heather safe. Keep her far from S and his-ours-no-*his* itching trigger finger. Keep her—

Electricity arced through his mind, short-circuiting his thoughts, locking his muscles, and dropping him to the floor as the seizure blossomed full flower. He felt himself gathered into strong arms, caught a glimpse of long, black hair, golden eyes, but Lucien's scent of deep earth and green leaves eluded him. All he smelled was blood and ozone and crackling lightning. Pain seared his joints, wrung his muscles like wet rags.

Warm fingers brushed at his temples. <*Child, let me in. Let me help you.*>

There was no need to ask, his shields were already falling. But this Lucien's psionic touch was different. Unfamiliar. Wrong.

The fallen angel holding him wasn't his father.

Deep inside, someone laughed and laughed.

Pain pierced Dante's mind, stuttered his heart as someone searched through the mountainous debris of his fractured memories, creating a kaleidoscope of ugly images whirling into one another, each set of foster parents blurring into the next, an infinite looping montage of casual cruelty and heart-hollowing loss.

—Papa and Mama Prejean.

—Chloe and her plushie BFF Orem.

—Gina and Jay.

—The Perv (another Bad Seed bro, yeah?) and his van of horrors.

—Ronin's fingernail slicing across Jay's throat.

—Johanna Moore and the white-coated man with the blurred face.

—Simone and Trey.

—The sanitarium.

—Heather. Heather. Heather.

The fallen angel breathed blue fire into Dante and he felt his thrashing body go limp, but the storm crackling through his mind raged unabated.

<*So beautiful, little* creawdwr, *and so damaged. I like that. We shall do wondrous and terrible things together, you and I. Awful things.*>

Dante's vision narrowed onto the blood-freckled ceiling, then whited out as entire constellations were born behind his rolled-back eyes in explosions of icy light.

39

PLANTING SEEDS

So easy. Far easier than he'd ever imagined.

Loki withdrew from the blood-drenched *creawdwr*'s oh-so-broken mind and laughed, the sound of it floating down the corridor like a cheerful birthday balloon.

All that fretting for nothing.

He'd flown from New Orleans following the faint and dying echoes of a song he'd barely heard, pondering the best ways to manipulate Dante's trust and fretting over how to get the Nightbringer's son to drop his shields. To let him in.

Just to take a peek at a *creawdwr*'s inner workings.

Or those of the Great Destroyer.

Loki had a fertile imagination, one he employed constantly, but he never could've imagined arriving at a better moment—just as a seizure dropped Dante right into his arms, his shields already crumbling thanks to a near-lethal mix of vampire tranquilizers, True Blood poison, and pure, simple exhaustion—mental, emotional, and physical.

Fate had finally landed on Loki's side.

And no wonder Dante—or S, as he sometimes thought of himself—was exhausted. Loki grinned in approval as he drank in Dante's handiwork.

He's been a very busy boy.

Crumpled into dark pools of their own thickening blood,

bodies clad in either black suits or medical scrubs littered the blood and gore-festooned corridor. Then there were the doors flung open on either side of the corridor and leading into rooms full of silence and the rich reek of coppery blood and musky fear.

Nothing like a little slaughter to perk up a place. Child has talent.

Loki looked at Dante, still held within his arms, with genuine fondness. The first mixed-blood *creawdwr* in history—a pale-skinned reality in leather pants and blood-smeared flesh that no one had ever thought possible—if they'd given it any thought at all.

Mine to guide. Mine to wind-up and turn loose. Mine alone.

Well, perhaps not completely, Loki reflected sourly as he regarded the intricate and raised white scar high on the left side of Dante's chest. The Morningstar's mark. And—as gleaned from Dante's unprotected mind—a blood pledge to return to Gehenna to restore the fading land.

A pledge the narcissistic Morningstar would live long enough to regret. Deeply.

Loki pushed Dante's blood- and sweat-dampened hair back from his face. Drew in an appreciative breath. Wild and fey, Dante's beauty, burning with a dark and mesmerizing heat and all the deadlier for it. Helen's beauty launched only a thousand ships; Dante's would ignite worlds.

The Great Destroyer.

How long have I waited for this? How many eons?

More than he cared to count. But no longer. The waiting was finally done.

Lifting his gaze, Loki studied Dante's first dark miracle—a secret, government-run sanitarium/brainwashing facility transformed into a silent abattoir. And all while drugs and poison had been busy short-circuiting his power, not to mention his sanity.

"Bravo," Loki whispered.

I can't wait to see what he does next. And I've got a ringside seat.

Once the drugs wore off, once Dante had healed, and once he had full use of the *creu tân* again, Loki had a feeling that a certain quote from the dusty Old Testament would once more ring true—a promise like a searing white nuclear light, one that left nothing but shadows in its wake: *And there shall be great wailing and gnashing of teeth.*

And when the Elohim finally heard Dante's song and came winging down from the heavens into the sanitarium's parking lot—*excuse me, apologies, abattoir*—and discovered themselves blocked from entering the building due to the spell Loki had carefully cast in his own blood before going inside?

Furious would only be the start.

Loki laughed, a happy sound brimming with anticipation. Lowering his head, he pressed his lips against Dante's in a gentle kiss. Tasted copper and salt. Breathed in the scent of burning leaves, November frost, and bone-deep grief.

He yearns to turn back the hands of time, to save those he's lost, to protect the mortal woman, the red-haired lovely, who is drawing ever nearer. He yearns for what he can never have. Ah, but he is young and still foolish and doesn't know better. Yet.

Beyond the sanitarium's thick walls, Loki felt the increase in Louisiana's vibration as the night waned, giving way to the approaching dawn. But before Sleep claimed Dante, Loki needed to plant a few seeds.

Thanks to Dante's fallen shields, he knew just how to do it.

Closing his eyes, Loki exhaled, then *shifted*. Energy prickled over his skin, a hundred million bee stings all at once, a familiar and much loved sensation. Once his new form had settled into place, he opened his eyes, adjusted his transformed clothing, then lowered his head and breathed a stream of energy between Dante's slightly parted lips. The *creawdwr's* long-lashed eyelids fluttered but remained closed.

Loki patted Dante's cheek, then said in a low, concerned drawl. "Dante, hey. C'mon, man. Hey. Can you hear me? Wake up, little brother."

40

NORTH STAR

A S THE NIGHT BLED away, fading to gray as predawn stretched rosy fingers along the horizon, Heather slowed the Nissan to a stop, parking on the quiet, somewhat secluded street in front of a tall building—a quick count tallied eight stories—glowering with institutional grimness. The inward North Star pull she'd been feeling and following since Dallas now pulsed with an urgent, feverish intensity.

Herehereherehereherehere . . .

Locking her fingers around the steering wheel in order to keep herself from just bolting from the car and dashing into God-knows-what, Heather forced herself to sit still and study the building and its surroundings. She knew her bond with Dante had guided her true when she read the sign posted in the modest green swath of lawn between the front doors.

Doucet-Bainbridge Sanitarium
Medical Research & Treatment
PRIVATE

Heather's knuckles blanched white against the steering wheel. She had no doubt this was another FBI/SB run facility like the one in D.C., another circle of hell masquerading as psychological research for the public good.

And Dante was here.

Again, something deep inside her whispered and cold fingers closed around her heart. Heather tucked Cortini's confiscated SIG Sauer into her jeans at the small of her back, then regarded her borrowed Glock and Taser.

Seems I have a regular arsenal, she mused. *An arsenal I'm definitely going to need against a building full of security and who the hell knows how many random SB, maybe even FBI, agents, research techs, and medical staff.*

Heather's pulse drummed a little faster. Sweat dampened her palms. Despite the odds, she knew she wouldn't wait. She would go inside and she would stop at nothing to bring Dante back out again. The trick would be managing to do so without triggering every alarm in the building or winding up as another involuntary resident in a padded room.

At least Dante's Sleeping now—or soon will be. The bastards can't hurt him while he's Sleeping.

Can they?

She hoped the answer was no, but the cold knot in her belly suggested otherwise.

How the hell do you plan to carry him if you do find him? Into the morning light? Wrapped in what? You need to wait for nightfall.

Sighing, Heather trailed her fingers wearily through her hair. Exhaustion was nibbling away at the adrenaline that was keeping her on her feet. Siphoning her clarity of mind.

Herehereherehere . . .

The internal tether linking Heather to Dante continued to pull and tug and pulse. Dante's presence burned at the back of her mind, blazed in her heart, a blue-white star.

She'd thought the bond-GPS would switch off once she'd found him, but maybe she needed to touch him before that could happen. Maybe she needed to make her way past the thorns and kiss his lips, a reversal of roles, the Princess breaking the spell enchanting the pale, black-haired Sleeping Beauty.

No waiting. She was going inside.

But first, I need to let the others know where I ended up.

When Annie answered her phone, Heather filled her in, wishing her sister was safe in New Orleans, not driving a van of Sleeping nightkind (and a pair of awake mortal males) to Memphis, but short of requesting that Jack and Thibodaux stuff her kicking and screaming onto a NOLA-bound Greyhound, Annie was in for the long haul.

But the alternative, Annie alone with her grief and her guilt, wasn't an option either. Maybe finding Von and hauling his tattooed bacon out of the fire might help Annie focus, channel her frantic energy.

A pang cut Heather heart-deep. Von. Small comfort that Silver and Merri believed the nomad wasn't in danger of losing his life, just his status as *llygad*.

They might kick him out. Maybe even wipe out his memory. I don't think they'd execute him for being an oath breaker, but I don't know that for sure. Llygaid are real fucking secretive, Red. Wish I knew more.

Red, huh? That's new.

Yeah, well, obvious nicknames are better than none, right?

I suppose. Which reminds me, Silver-boy, what's your real name, anyway?

What was that? Couldn't hear you. You're breaking up . . .

"Do you know if Silver has heard anything from De Noir yet?"

"Nothing so far," Annie replied. "We figure he's still at Fallen Central. But don't worry, as soon as the big guy makes contact, we'll make sure he knows right where you are."

"Thanks," Heather said. "Keep safe, okay? I'll call as soon as I can."

"I wish you'd fucking wait for De Noir, but I know you won't," Annie said. "So you keep fucking safe too, hear me?"

"Loud and clear," Heather replied, her throat suddenly tight. Ending the call, she switched off the cell and slid it into her pocket.

Don't need it going off at an inopportune moment.

Tucking the Taser into the front of her jeans beneath her sweater, she grabbed the Glock, then got out of the car. Pain stabbed up from her ankle, a white-hot blade. She bit her lower lip, waiting it out. She felt pretty sure that it wasn't broken but badly sprained and in desperate need of ibuprofen, elevation, and an ice pack.

Heather sighed. *Yeah, in a perfect world—which this definitely isn't.*

Once the pain had returned to a dull throb, she closed the Nissan's door quietly and studied the sanitarium parking lot and entrance.

Wait. Was that graffiti painted on the doors and windows?

Heather frowned. How had the taggers even managed to shake their cans of paint before security swarmed over them and shoved said cans up their artistic urban asses, let alone practically tag the entire building? And something about the graffiti seemed familiar, something itching at the back of her weary mind.

Her gaze skipped from the dark paint to the eerily silent parking lot. Beneath the pinkish glow of the lot's lights, condensation misted the windshields.

These cars have been here all night.

Heather didn't see a single car in the lot that looked like it had been driven in recently. Maybe the night shift hadn't handed the reins over to the morning crew yet. Maybe, for all she knew, they worked in forty-eight-hour shifts.

Maybe, but she didn't think so. Something felt off, wrong.

With the Glock held down at her side, Heather walked down the street toward the parking lot in a deliberately casual stride—or as casual as a limp could be, anyway, breathing in cool air smelling of dew and distant roses, just a local out walking her insomnia in the predawn.

Stopping at the parking lot's mouth, Heather got her first good look at the symbols painted on the front doors and windows and her heart gave one hard, startled kick before resuming its regular rhythm—but at a much faster pace.

Now she knew why the symbols seemed familiar; they reminded her of the mark the Morningstar had seared into the pale skin of Dante's chest, his promise to return to Gehenna.

Not graffiti. Fallen sigils. Elohim glyphs—and etched in blood, not paint.

Fear burned cold along Heather's spine. She didn't know what the sigils were for or why they'd been placed, but she knew what they meant.

She wasn't the first to find Dante.

While Dante was injured and doped and lost to an ever-shifting past and present, one of the Fallen (and she desperately hoped it was only one) was with him right at this very moment.

"Shit," Heather breathed. "Shit, shit, shit."

She had no idea how the Fallen had found Dante, let alone learned of his disappearance, but the thing that truly troubled her—even more than the *how*, was the *why*. Why were the Fallen keeping him here? Why hadn't they taken him back to Gehenna the moment they'd found him?

A dark possibility unfolded within her mind. Maybe Dante was being kept here, because whoever ran this sanitarium—FBI, SB, a combination of both—whoever had grabbed Dante in the first place, had simply been following directions.

Fallen directions.

Maybe someone had been incapable of accepting Dante's refusal to be a good little *creawdwr* and kiss Celestial ass and thought a few well-taught lessons would improve his attitude.

Maybe.

And where were the mortals who worked inside the sanitarium? Enchanted and sleeping on the floor? Dead? Vanished in a puff of angelic smoke?

Only one way to find out.

Ignoring her ankle's protest, Heather hurried over to the first parked car and crouched down beside it. She scanned the building, looking for movement, any indication that she had been noticed, but nothing disturbed the lot's thick blanket of silence, a silence like the first deep snowfall of winter.

Nothing moved. Nothing slow enough for her to see, anyway.

Heather straightened from her crouch, moved to the next car, then waited again. Still nothing. Just as she was about to make her limping run to the next vehicle, a car pulled into the parking lot, a forest-green Lexus.

Crouching down, Heather kept an eye on the newcomer, a man wearing what looked like scrubs, as he parked the Lexus in an empty slot.

Looks like I was wrong about that shift change.

The man climbed out of the Lexus and Heather saw that she was right about the scrubs—his were mint-green, the short sleeves revealing forearms thick with black hair. He locked the car with a tap of his smart key, then started across the parking lot. He stopped abruptly, frowning, his gaze on the sanitarium. He stared, his expression shifting from a puzzled frown to a blank slate. All expression vanished from his face. Swiveling around, he returned to his car in quick strides, unlocked it, slid inside, and drove off.

The hair prickled on the back of Heather's neck. What the hell was *that*?

Heather watched as another car glided into the lot—a standard black government-issue SUV this time, driven by a man in a black suit—and the same exact events unfolded. Park, head across parking lot, freeze, go blank, then turn and leave.

Another car, then another, as staff members and agents pulled into the lot, then left again after gazing at the Fallen-marked building.

Why not me? Heather rose from her crouch. She regarded the building for a long moment, knowing a Fallen spell had to be the reason for the day shift's about-face, but why hadn't it affected her too?

Whatever the reason, maybe the caster wouldn't be expecting anyone to saunter past the spell, and had his or her guard down. Heather could only hope.

Adrenaline flooding her system, she finished her slow-motion race across the parking lot and trotted up the long concrete steps to the entrance.

41

UNCOILING FROM
THE ASHES

THE VOICE, LOW AND urgent and as familiar as his own, encircled Dante's awareness like a fisherman's net and hoisted him up from the whispering depths and his haunted dreams, a gathering of the lost—Simone, Gina, Jay. Their bodies like ice, their hearts dead and empty.

He looked back as he ascended and saw their upturned faces, moon pale and expressionless, disappear one by one into the darkness like stones beneath black water. Grief coiled around his heart.

I'm so cold, sugar, Gina called, her words like knives, each one piercing deeper than the one before. *I need you to make it right. Make them pay so I can be warm again. Torch the goddamned world, sugar. Make it burn for me.*

Simone nodded as her face winked from Dante's sight. *Make the world burn,* mon cher ami, mon ange, *and set me free.*

Set things to rights, cher, Jay urged, sinking into those black waters still clad in his blood-soaked straitjacket. *Make them pay in blood and fire.*

"They'll burn," Dante promised in a rough whisper.

"What was that, little brother?"

Dante opened his eyes to a red-lit gloom. The overheads were out and emergency lights had winked on, giving the silent corridor an apocalyptic feel. He blinked. Someone leaned over him, someone with nut-brown hair tied back in a ponytail, someone who smelled of leather and gun oil and frost.

Someone whose voice *hadn't* been a dream.

"Von . . ."

Or Papa in a Von-suit. Fucker won't stay dead, remember?

"Right here, man."

Dante forced himself up onto his elbows—or tried to, anyway. The seizure had left him drained, every muscle wrung dry despite all the blood—gallons and gallons, fucking buckets—he and/or S had sucked down. He felt hollowed out, like he had nothing left. He fell back onto the tiled floor, bathed in a cold sweat. Black pinpricks poked holes in his vision. He swallowed hard.

"Shit," he muttered, voice hoarse. "More fucking awesomeness."

"Here. Hold on." Leather creaked as an arm slipped around Dante's shoulders and gently helped ease him into a sitting position. "Better?"

"Yeah. *Merci, beaucoup.*" Blinking away more black pinpricks, Dante found himself looking into Von's gleaming green eyes and felt an intense surge of relief. Something flickered at the back of his memory—a tall, winged figure. "Is Lucien here too? I thought . . ."

"Nah, just me, man."

Dante reached up and cupped Von's face between hands that seemed a little less than steady, dammit—be honest, a *lot* less—and pulled him in for a quick, grateful kiss. "Fuck, am I happy to see you, *mon ami*," he said, releasing him. "Did you find Heather too? How the hell did you find—"

Boy needs a lesson. Boy always needs a lesson.

Reality began to wheel. The corridor started to drop away.

Dante squeezed his eyes shut and concentrated with everything he had on remaining in the here-and-now, fought to grab onto it with both hands. But the here-and-now was fucking slippery as hell.

Dante-angel, run, run, run!

No escape for you, sweetie.

Welcome home, S. Welcome back.

Set things to rights, cher. *Make them pay in blood and—*

A hand grasped Dante's shoulder, the palm hot against his skin, and shook him gently. "Wherever you think you are, little brother, you ain't there. Hear me? You. Ain't. There."

Dante seized that urgent voice and held on for all he was worth. He opened his eyes. He was still in the corridor, Von kneeling beside him.

"You okay?" Von asked, dark brows slanted down in a worried V.

Dante nodded. "For right now, yeah. What were we talking about?"

"About how I stumbled across your ass." Von grinned. "I found a suit in the know and yanked the info—along with pretty much everything else—out of his mind. Probably needing a diaper change right about now. But"—his grin vanished as he looked Dante over, fire igniting in the green depths of his eyes—"I think the motherfucker got off easy. Looks like you've been through hell and then some. I'm betting you gave back as good as you got."

"Not even close. The fucker won't stay dead."

"Which fucker?" Von asked, throwing a puzzled glance down the corridor. "They all look pretty damned dead to me."

Pain pulsed at Dante's temples. His memory blanked. "Fuck. *Je sais pas,*" he admitted. "Don't remember."

Von returned his attention to Dante. "Then I was right," he said. His expression of grim resignation left Dante uneasy.

"Right? About?"

"Sending Lucien to intercept Heather, to keep her away from you. Away from what you still need to do."

Nightmarish images swirled behind Dante's eyes, crimson and violent.

His finger squeezes the trigger. Her head rocks forward with the first bullet, then snaps back with the second, tendrils of red hair whipping through the air. . . .

"Then he'd better hurry," Dante said through a throat gone tight. Deep within his mind, his heart, he felt a *hereherehere* tug, one that felt stronger with each passing second. "Cuz she's real fucking close. And that means—"

Run from me, catin. Je t'en prie.

"She's in danger," Von finished. "I know, little brother. *If* she finds you. But Lucien will stop her, don't worry. He'll keep her safe. Right now, Sleep is on the way and we've got a few things to discuss before we go under."

Dante nodded. "That bit about what I still need to do, yeah?"

"Yup." With a sigh, Von rose to his feet.. "You can't let any of these fuckers—FBI, SB, nightkind, Fallen—get away with this shit. I know I told you in no uncertain terms that you needed to learn how to control your gifts and your past before taking action against anyone, but that was before."

Dante stood, steadying himself with a hand against the wall when the corridor did a slow twirl. "Before what?" he asked, the sinking feeling in the pit of his stomach suggesting he might not want or like the answer.

"Before you started to go nutso, little brother," Von replied, voice husky. "Take a look around. Time's almost up. Do you even remember doing any of this?"

Dante did as Von suggested and looked, *really* looked. Men and women in medical scrubs were included amongst the black-suited bodies sprawled and fetal-ball-curled on the floor. And the bloody footprints leading from one room to the next told him everything he needed to know. Whatever this building might've been once, it was now a morgue. The air alone, reeking of blood and of flesh just beginning to decompose, told him that.

Although Dante knew he was responsible for each body on the fucking floor, he didn't remember killing a single one.

"No," he admitted reluctantly. "I don't."

Trust me, bro. We had fucking fun.

Tais-toi, *you sonuvabitch.*

Laughter. *Faites-moi.*

"Soon you won't know any of us, not even Heather," Von said, the words low and level. "Time's almost up, man."

Dante slumped against the wall, feeling gut-punched and breathless. He heard only truth in his friend's words. Trailing both hands through his hair, he whispered, "Fuck."

"You need to set things right while you still have some sanity left. Make these motherfuckers pay—for Simone, for Gina and Jay, for Chloe, hell, for you too—before it's too late. All you need is the courage to walk the path you were born to walk. With a friend at your side."

Make them pay so I can be warm again.

Make the world burn, mon cher ami, mon ange, and set me free.

Set things to rights, cher.

Dante rubbed his temples with the tips of his fingers, trying to focus past the noise and the never-ending ache. Trying to resist Sleep's narcotic embrace.

Promises he'd made to the living whispered against the demands of the lost.

As lost as I get, I will find you, Heather. Always.

I ain't leaving you there in that place, ma p'tite ange. I will come for you.

Found you, mon cher ami, mon père, and I ain't losing you again.

You'll always have a clan in me, Von, mon ami, in us. You'll never ride solo.

"I can buy you some time, sanity-wise." Von said in quiet, earnest tones. "But you're gonna need to close off your bond with Heather first, especially if you want to keep her safe. Once you've done that, then you learn to ride that madness of yours like a bucking bronco. Make it do what *you* want. Use it to set things right."

"No. Heather—"

"Will be safe," Von cut in, "*if* you close the bond. You can't risk cutting it, not with the shape you're in, but if you seal it at your end, you'll keep her free from mental harm—plus she won't be able to home in on you anymore. Then Lucien won't have a problem keeping her away."

Heather's voice whispered through Dante's memory, a conversation held in the honeysuckle- and rose-perfumed courtyard as he'd struggled with Trey's loss at his own blue-flamed hands and what that meant for everyone he loved.

I'm not leaving you. You can't make me. You don't have the right.

Too dangerous, catin. *Ain't risking you.*

That's my decision, not yours. I choose you, Baptiste, and everything that comes with you.

Dante felt a smile flicker across his lips. "Then you don't know my pigheaded woman. Lucien will hafta tie her down. She won't stop."

"Maybe not. But with the bond sealed, she won't be able to find you."

Dante wasn't so sure about that. Not only was Heather a damned good detective, something beyond their bond linked them—and always had—something intrinsic and soul deep. One way or another, she would *find* him.

Just as he would find her.

His finger squeezes the trigger. Heather falls and falls and falls.

Icy fingers closed around Dante's heart.

"I know your concentration is a little fucked right now, so let me help you close the bond."

It might not stop Heather in the end, but if he could slow her down . . .

Run from me, catin. Je t'en prie.

Dante nodded. "*Oui*. Yeah. Let's do it."

The nomad wasted no time in crossing the corridor. He stopped in front of Dante and brushed the backs of his fingers against Dante's temples. A smile ghosted across his lips, a smile Dante returned in kind. Von started speaking, but a high-pitched humming filled Dante's ears, drowning out Von's words.

Dante sensed the past opening up beneath him, a bottomless lake he treaded, fighting to keep his head above its dark waters. He wanted desperately to remain in this moment, to *believe* in it.

This is Von, goddammit . . .

You sure about that?

A determined frown furrowed Von's brow and, for a split second, it seemed like his form rippled. A warped reflection in a funhouse mirror.

See? I told you. Fi' de garce is doing it again. Fucker won't stay dead.

Yeah? Well, then we'll kill him as many times as it takes.

Dante stabbed his fingers into Von's chest—*ain't Von. Just motherfucking Papa in a Von-suit*—his fingers tearing through leather and black pearl-buttoned shirt, ribs and heated flesh. Wrapped around the pulsing heart.

Papa/Von's mouth opened in a soundless gasp. He looked down. "Little brother—"

"No, *fuck* you, you don't get to say that to me. Only Von can. And you fucking ain't Von." Dante yanked Papa's heart from the bloodied hole in his chest and tossed it down the corridor.

Papa dropped to the floor with a heavy, boneless thud, his Von-suit rippling away to reveal not Papa but a big dude with short red hair and empty eyes.

Dante tilted his head, studied the newest body on the tiles. "Huh."

Another suit. Papa's like those fucking Russian nesting dolls. One skin suit after another, but I don't know this one.

Sleep washed over Dante in a numbing, narcotic tide and he stumbled back a step, shaking it off—or trying to, anyway—like a dog from a leash. He had one crucial thing to do yet before Sleep claimed him, one crucial thing to protect his woman of heart and steel.

Before he forgot who she was.

Papa in his now heartless skin suit had been both right and wrong. Closing the bond wouldn't stop Heather, but *severing* it would.

Don't chase her away. Lure her in. We'll play. It'll be fun, je te promets.

Before he forgot why it mattered.

A cold sweat beaded Dante's forehead. Knotting his hands into fists, he fought Sleep's relentless surge with everything he had—scared to his fucking bones it wouldn't be enough. Darkness pinpricked his vision. He sent to Heather, not knowing if it would reach her or not. Then he imagined slicing through the bond tethering them together with a red-hot knife. Both ends whipped away like fallen power lines.

The northward tug vanished. And the blue-white star of Heather's presence, anchor and beacon both, and still buried beneath miles of dark glass, went with it. Pain pierced Dante's heart. His breath caught rough and raw in his throat. Fiery sparks snapped in the darkness behind his eyes. His mind sizzled, a bonfire of agony. Electricity thrummed down his spine as the severed bond jump-started another seizure. His muscles locked.

Now she's safe.

Dante closed his stinging eyes in relief, lashes wet against his skin, as the seizure continued to kick his ass. He felt himself hit the floor beside Papa's body. Felt his skull bounce off the tile. The sparks became a super nova.

Sleep wrapped Dante up in thick, narcotic chains, shoved

42

THIS IS THE BEGINNING
OF THE END

ANNIE STEERED THE VAN down I-10, the tires humming along the blacktop, C.C. Adcock's sexy swamp-rock/bluesy voice curling from the iPod Jack had docked into the van's system, singing about a woman who just doesn't know how to be good to her hard-working man.

Maybe that hard-working man needed to learn how to load a dishwasher or cook a three-course meal or fold up a basketful of clean laundry if he wanted his woman to remain thrilled about *being* his woman.

Just saying, y'know. A word to the wise—don't be a self-entitled douchebag.

Beyond the windshield, dawn stretched fingers of rose, peach, and orange into the brightening sky, a color combination that made Annie think of raspberry sorbet and orange sherbet—a thought she quickly regretted as her stomach knotted. Nausea rolled through her in a throat-burning acid wave. Cold sweat beaded on her forehead.

One minute I'm devouring anything that doesn't fucking scurry away fast enough, the next I never want to hear, see, smell, or think about food again. Ever.

"Pregnancy sucks," Annie muttered through clenched teeth.

"Sorry to hear that, sugar. Peach?" Jack asked, offering her a juicy slice from the tip of his pocket knife.

Annie shook her head, swallowed hard, then fumbled at the window control button. Cool air smelling faintly of exhaust and wild grass wet with dew poured inside as the window hummed down.

The nausea gradually subsided and Annie breathed a little easier. She glanced at Jack. The drummer sat slouched in the passenger seat, one booted foot up on the dash, contentedly thumbing peach slices into his mouth. The aroma, sweet and sunny, did nothing to improve her mood or her nausea.

"If I puke, I plan to puke on you," Annie announced darkly. "Repeatedly."

"Hey, now. No need for vomiting, targeted or otherwise."

"Says you," Annie muttered.

"Hey, podna," Emmett called from the back, "I'll take more of that jerky, if you have any left."

As Jack handed what remained of the bag of jerky back to Emmett, Annie found herself wishing Silver and Merri had left both men behind at Jack's sister's house when they'd dropped off Eerie along with a bag of tuna-flavored kibble, wishing that she was driving in non-food scented, blissful, silence.

They're mortal, Annie. And Jack is a part of our family. He's my responsibility, just like Thibodaux is Merri's. We need to keep our family safe.

But who was keeping her sister safe? She was mortal too. And alone.

I wish you would wait . . .

I can't.

Tension thrummed through Annie's body, whitened her knuckles against the steering wheel. She wanted to get to

Memphis as quickly as possible, find Von, grab him, then haul ass to join Heather in Baton Rouge, even though in her heart of hearts, she knew that whatever was going to happen would have happened and been long done by the time she arrived. Hell, probably before she even hit Memphis.

A quick glance at the speedometer hovering at 80 mph had Annie easing her foot just slightly off the gas pedal.

Christ! Slow down. The last thing you need is a fucking ticket.

Another thing she didn't need was having to explain why the people in the back refused to wake up and fetch their identification. And she sure as shit didn't want to screw up her chance to make things right.

Annie's foot dropped down on the accelerator again, her lips compressed into a thin white line. The van surged ahead, a stallion under spurs.

PINE BLUFF, ARKANSAS

CATERINA'S HEAD WAS TURNED to one side on the pillow, eyes closed, her hair a spill of dark coffee across the white satin case. Giovanni studied her as Sleep crept into his veins, deeply troubled by her unhealthy pallor, by the shadows bruising the skin beneath her dark lashes, by the far from peaceful expression on her face.

"Keep her sedated until I awake," Giovanni instructed. "I think the dose we gave her should keep her under until twilight, but"—he shrugged one shoulder—"she's strong-willed."

"Of course, *signor*," Sondra murmured. A mortal friend of the Cercle de Druide, she kept a day-house, a vampire bed-and-dinner, for members traveling in the area.

Giovanni double-checked Caterina's restraints, making sure she was safe and secure and couldn't escape while he Slept. Finally satisfied that she wouldn't be able to work her way free, despite her training and deadly skills, he sighed and raked a hand through his hair, leaving it in disarray.

Caterina's mind had been tampered with, of that Giovanni had no doubt. Detecting the alterations within her unshielded mind had been easy enough.

From the moment Renata had first carried Caterina into their home, the toddler's chubby arms wrapped around her graceful neck—*Look, Vanni mio, we have been given a gift*— he'd quickly grown to understand Caterina's mind, comprehending how she thought and dreamed and schemed, this little mortal, *our* little mortal, dancing among vampires.

She'd been an annoying nuisance, at first, *sì*, one he'd resented—no denying it. But over time, and almost without his knowing when or how, Caterina had transformed from nuisance to family, his *soeur de coeur*—a true sister of the heart.

And whoever had tampered with her had damaged her, perhaps permanently.

Giovanni's jaw tightened, his gaze never wavering from his sister's pale, vulnerable face.

"*Qualcuno pagherà*, Caterina *mia*," he vowed. "*Qualcuno pagherà a cara prezzo*."

Someone would most definitely pay.

Questions remained: Who? Why? Could the damage be healed, the tampering undone? He wished he could contact Renata, but given that it was early afternoon in Rome, his *mère de sang* still Slept, safe and secure behind cool marble walls.

Sleep surged through his veins, narcotic and inescapable. His eyelids drooped. A hand lightly touched his arm.

"This way, *signor*," Sondra urged, slacks whispering as she stepped into the doorway.

Giovanni allowed the redhead with a matronly shelf of bosom to lead him to the room next to Caterina's, then thanked her for her hospitality. Once she'd left the room, shutting the door behind her, he stripped down to his boxer briefs before collapsing drunkenly onto the pale rose silk sheets.

He sank into the fathomless waters of Sleep like an iceberg-gouged ship, chased into the dark by a single, chilling thought: Where had Loki flown off to in such a rush?

The French Quarter

IN A SMALL POWER boat on the Mississippi, Edmond gently swaddled his master's burned body in fresh water-soaked blankets, covering him from now-bald head to blackened and curled toes.

Swallowing hard against the meaty stench of seared flesh, Edmond sat down beside Mauvais, then uttered one terse word: "Go."

Phaedra opened the throttle and steered the boat away from the flame-engulfed *Winter Rose*. With a hollow heart, Edmond watched as the fire department geysered water on the blazing riverboat from several high-powered hoses.

With a sharp, splintering crack that boomed into the night like ancient cannon fire, the *Winter Rose* snapped in half. One half, still burning, slipped—foot by foot—into the inky waters. Distant voices shouted. Blue and red and white lights strobed through the graying night.

The majordomo blinked stinging eyes. The smoke, of course. The gritty ashes.

He didn't know how the fire had started—not for certain, but given its swiftness, the reek of kerosene, and the death of the *apprenti* he'd left in charge of refueling and relighting the lanterns, he believed an accident with one of the lanterns must've occurred.

But hadn't he also caught a faint whiff of ozone as he'd pelted up from belowdecks at his master's agonized screams?

You got an angry loa *on dis here boat . . .*

Edmond had no idea how long it would take his master to heal from his devastating injuries or how much blood would be required during the process, but Mauvais would have all he needed and more.

The Winter Rose *may be gone, but the majority of my master's household has survived the fire. At least I can give him that good news.*

Pale tendrils of peach and hyacinth curled across the brightening horizon. Gaze still on the burning, foundering *Winter Rose*, Edmond said, "Faster."

"No shit," Phaedra muttered, pushing the speedboat as hard as it could go.

Racing the dawn.

DALLAS, TEXAS

JAMES WALLACE WATCHED AS the big rig and its friendly driver pulled away from the curb with a deep, concrete-vibrating rumble, exhaust belching black smoke stinking of scorched oil into the air.

The driver had talked nonstop all the way into Dallas, but James had thought the one-sided conversation a very small price to pay, considering he could still be standing on the highway with his thumb out.

Once the truck had merged—more like bulldozed—into traffic, disappearing from sight, James turned around and studied the building across the sidewalk from him, his requested stop.

VISION CONSULTING
International Accounting & Financial Planning

James had no doubt that talented accountants did indeed work at Vision Consulting. An effective front needed to be a functioning one. But, thanks to interagency contacts carefully cultivated throughout his long career with the FBI, he knew

Vision Consulting for what it truly was—a hidden division of the Shadow Branch.

And he also knew that the moment he walked through those black-tinted glass doors, there would be no turning back.

James brushed road dust from his slacks, noting the four tiny bloodstained punctures marring the fabric. The wound beneath throbbed.

A fork. A goddamned fork. Clever girl, his daughter.

But a daughter now lost to him forever.

The image of Heather aiming his own damned gun at his forehead was burned into his brain. He hadn't seen one iota of bluff in her blue eyes, only grim determination.

She would've pulled the trigger without blinking.

James's anger was a glacier encasing his heart. Deep down, he suspected he was grieving. Heather, *his* Heather, had died the moment she'd met Dante Prejean-Baptiste. Yes, the godforsaken bloodsucker had saved her life when she'd been shot in D.C., but at what price?

Heather had returned to Seattle a different woman and had chosen a vampire over her own father, throwing away everything she'd ever worked for—including her humanity.

James remembered a twelve-year-old Heather throwing her arms around him and hugging him after she'd learned of her mother's death. She'd held on with a quiet desperation, her face buried against his chest. Given her lack of tears at the time, he'd had the strangest feeling that this was a loss she could live with. Her words had proved him right.

It's just us now, pumpkin, he'd said. *You, me, Kevin, and Annie.*

Daddy, that's all it's ever been.

James felt a pang of sorrow, of regret. He blinked burning eyes.

She's gone. My Heather. Gone.

And the FBI, the Bureau he'd devoted his life to, had played a hand in that heart-hollowing loss. They had betrayed him also. His SAC had promised he would be allowed to get Heather the treatment she so desperately needed to free her of Baptiste's deadly influence, so she could be restored to them all—a daughter to James, a skilled and talented agent to the Bureau.

They'd lied.

The Bureau had used him to track Heather. Without their plan to move her, he never would've signed her out of the facility. Never would've lost her on a dark and lonely Texas highway. Never would've watched her aim a gun at his face.

The Bureau had stolen Heather's single chance at redemption. They were as responsible for her death—for he had buried her in his heart—as Baptiste was.

Straightening his jacket, James drew himself erect, crossed the sidewalk to those black-tinted doors, pushed them open, and strode inside.

One good betrayal deserved another.

"I need to see your superior," James said to the young man in the black-framed hipster glasses sitting behind the front desk. "Tell them that James William Wallace is here."

He would give the SB everything. Including the woman who had once been his daughter.

GEHENNA

WITH THE MORNINGSTAR AND Hekate on either side of him, Lucien strode down the Royal Aerie's main corridor, past the line of blue-bladed shovels branching from the marble walls on other side, mute evidence of Dante's inability to control his power.

Mute evidence of his brutal, but hidden, childhood, as well.

A bitter truth burrowed into Lucien's heart. Until Dante was whole, his past exhumed, examined, and integrated, he would never be able to control the *creu tân*.

I had hoped to spare him those memories. A desperate hope, and impossible.

In New Orleans, the sun was rising. Dante, wherever he was, would be Sleeping now. A fact for which Lucien was grateful. Once the Morningstar led him to Dante, he planned to take his son back to Jack's house, where Hekate could heal Dante of any lingering damage from James Wallace's special rounds.

As for Dante's mind . . .

Lucien looked over at Hekate. She walked at his left with chin held high, lamplight gilding her moon-silver tresses. What she had told him as they'd flown from the cliff side circled through his mind, each word a bead on a rosary, a prayer of hope.

It's possible I might be able to shore up your son's mind. Wall up his past, hide it from him, until he can stabilize.

For how long?

Not long, it'll be only temporary. But it'll give you the time to help him learn about his past, to accept it.

And if he doesn't?

Then his psyche won't survive when the wall comes down again.

Grim hope, but hope, nonetheless.

An unwelcome entourage in the form of Gabriel and the remainder of the Celestial Seven followed Lucien and his companions in tense silence down the Aerie's main corridor to Dante's gate, the fast-paced clatter of sandals and boot soles loud against marble.

From within the Aerie's depths, cries and wails and anxious *chalkydri* flutings filled the sandalwood-and-hyacinth-scented air, a Greek chorus of despair. The skygates had vanished. What part of their world would unravel next? Where was the *creawdwr*?

Good question, Lucien thought grimly. *One I hope to answer very soon.*

"Tell your son that his human bondmate is welcome also," Astarte said as they reached the gate Dante had created, literally punched his way in from one world to the next. "I have servants preparing chambers for them both."

"I'll let him know," Lucien replied, pausing in front of the smooth-edged hole marring the corridor's south wall.

"Perhaps an honor guard—"

The Morningstar laughed. "By all means—if you want Dante to refuse. Have you forgotten his disdain for authority?" His gaze settled on Gabriel. "I imagine you haven't—*brother*."

Gabriel folded his arms over his bare chest and leveled a cool, green gaze on the Morningstar. Lamp light glinted from the braided silver torc curled around his throat. "No, I haven't, indeed."

"We don't wish to antagonize the boy," Uriel said to Lucien. "All we ask is that you impress the urgency of the situation upon him."

"Of course," Lucien said, promising nothing.

Dante's well-being came first, as far as he was concerned. Even at the expense of Gehenna's existence.

Gabriel stepped forward, his unbound hair—a rich, warm caramel—brushing against his narrow hips and the scarlet kilt belted over them. "How can we trust you?" he asked. His gaze skipped from Lucien, to Hekate, to the Morningstar. "Any of you?"

Lucien met and held his gaze. "What choice do you have?"

Without waiting for an answer, Lucien ducked through the gate, folded wing tips scraping the top rim, and stepped into the *creawdwr*-shattered cemetery. St. Louis No. 3 should've smelled of dewed grass and young cherry blossoms, of the dawn. Should've, yes. *If* it were dawn.

But it wasn't.

Instead the sun was hanging over the western horizon and the warm, late afternoon air vibrated with the rush of heavy traffic on the street beyond the cemetery's broken walls. The faint, sun-warmed fragrance of cherry blossoms wasn't enough to mask the odor of decay and old death released from tombs that Dante had unintentionally cracked open like eggs with his power.

Fear spiked through Lucien.

Time was stalling in Gehenna, unraveling like its skygates.

The Morningstar's grim voice echoed Lucien's realization, "It's worse than we thought."

"It is," Lucien agreed, turning to see Hekate and her father standing beside him amongst the crumbled crypts and broken cypress and oak trees that gave mute testimony to a *creawdwr*'s power and a son's desperate determination.

Found you, mon cher ami, mon père, and I ain't losing you again.

Unfurling his white wings, the Morningstar took to the sky. The lowering sun chiseled radiant diamond dazzles from his wings as he soared ever upward. Lucien followed, Hekate at his left wing.

Now I will find you, mon cher fils. And no one will ever take you again.

Not even if it meant the end of Gehenna.

ROME, ITALY

RENATA ALESSA CORTINI STIRRED on her bed, suddenly restless beneath her cool linen sheets. Even locked in Sleep's iron grip, she knew she was no longer dreaming; she was Witnessing, her inner vision unfurling images that chilled her to the bone, quick flashes of nightmare, glimpses into that-which-may-be.

In a hallway gleaming with faint red light, a fallen angel with black wings and short, ginger locks lounges upon a throne composed of dead and stiffening bodies . . .

The night burns, the sky on fire from horizon to horizon . . .

Dante Baptiste uncoils from a bloodied tile floor, his pale, breathtaking face smeared with blood, his eyes dark wells of madness, loss, and simmering rage . . .

A tattoo of a running black wolf inked beneath a desperate green eye . . .

Pale blue flames explode out from around the Great Destroyer's lean body in transforming tongues of cool fire. His kohl-rimmed eyes open as his song rakes the burning night . . .

A sign emblazoned with the words: Doucet-Bainbridge Sanitarium; *Fallen sigils painted in blood upon glass . . .*

A woman's voice: I'm here, I'm here. Stay with me, cher. *She is all that stands between the* creawdwr *and the end of the world, all that stands between the Great Destroyer and the never-ending Road . . .*

A hand wreathed in sapphire flames, blue light glinting from the rings encircling thumbs and fingers, touches the rough surface of a parking lot. A frost-rimmed hole opens beneath that burning hand, an emptiness, a void that devours the parking lot, then spreads . . .

I have promises to keep, Dante whispers, *blood trickling from one nostril. Then he puts out the world's light.*

Darkness and screams filled Renata's mind, followed by utter silence. Her pulse thundered in her ears, keeping time with her frantic heart.

She had never felt so cold.

Something had befallen Dante Baptiste, of that she had no doubt. She was less sure if he'd been seized by mortals or the Elohim or both. And, whether on purpose or accidentally, whoever had Dante would twist him into the Great Destroyer.

He is ours, not theirs. They cannot have him. This beautiful and deadly young creawdwr *belongs to the vampire race; he is ours to train and guide and love.*

But what frightened Renata even more than the very real possibility of Dante becoming the Great Destroyer was the fact that Dante's mortal bondmate might hold the key to the world's continued existence, along with everything and everyone it contained.

A fragile mortal with a butterfly's lifespan.

Heather Wallace needs to be safeguarded at all costs. If she dies, so do we all.

Renata needed to get to New Orleans. She needed to contact Giovanni and Caterina, find out what they knew. Much needed to be set into motion and immediately. Yet no matter how aware she was, Sleep still held her body a prisoner until dusk.

But *only* her body.

By feeding small amounts of her blood every night to her personal *domestica*, she could awaken the girl with a touch of her mind through their temporary blood bond and issue orders to be carried out.

Renata did so now.

She sent to the girl curled sleeping in a cot at the foot of her bed, brushing her dreams aside like cobwebs and touching her drowsing consciousness.

<*Flavia, awaken.*>

Through her inner eye, Renata saw the girl stir, her dark brown eyes opening wide, all trace of sleepiness gone. Flavia raised up on her elbows, ebony locks tumbling past her slim shoulders, and gave her attention to her mistress's Slumbering form.

"*Signora?*"

Renata began telling her of all the things that needed to be done or set into motion before she rose with the twilight. When she finished, Flavia threw back her quilt and rose quickly from her cot. And set about her mistress's work.

43

A Child's Whisper

DESPITE HEATHER WALLACE'S ESCAPE from custody in Little Rock, using a coffee carafe and a field agent's own Taser, embarrassing facts which that particular agent wouldn't be living down anytime soon, Teodoro's vacation remained on hold.

Only temporarily, the SB brass had reassured him. The red-haired FBI agent had vanished into the night, true. But they expected her to be quickly reapprehended once she popped up on their grid again.

And she would pop up again, but not alive.

Teodoro's deadly little puppet would make sure of that.

Teodoro glanced at his cell phone again as he rode the elevator down to the eighth floor and frowned. Soft Muzak floated from the elevator audio panels, bland and cheerful, a neutered version of a popular rock song.

It'd been hours since he'd received a text from Caterina, a single-word message—*acquired*—telling him that the assassin had found Wallace. He'd received nothing from her since.

Caterina's silence, her lack of response to his texts, left him uneasy.

He couldn't imagine Heather Wallace escaping Caterina, but he *could* imagine Caterina deciding to spend some quality time with her captive, teaching Wallace the painful cost of her "betrayal" of Dante Baptiste before executing her.

Even so, the delay still troubled him.

Teodoro continued to frown at his cell, his thumbs poised above the touchscreen, as the elevator slowed to a stop. The doors glided open, revealing a brightly lit corridor leading into the medical unit.

He let out his breath in a low, frustrated exhalation. No point in sending another text. He would simply have to wait for Caterina to make contact. Slipping his cell phone back into his trouser pocket, Teodoro stepped from the elevator and headed down the corridor, the sharp smell of antiseptic prickling his nostrils.

Aside from Caterina's extended silence, things had been going very well. Seraphina had convinced the rest of the Oversight Committee not to bring Dante Baptiste in until the majority of the attention generated by his unexpected and unprecedented announcement had faded. The young True Blood was too hot to grab.

A smile flickered across Teodoro's lips.

By the time they realized Dante was no longer at his club in New Orleans, Heather Wallace would be dead, their bond severed, and Dante's sanity shattered. At that point, it wouldn't be Dante Baptiste they needed to deal with, but the Great Destroyer.

"Back so soon?"

The cheerful voice startled Teodoro from his dark reflections.

A nurse in lavender scrubs, her shining chestnut hair tied back in a ponytail, was standing on the threshold of room 416, a clipboard in her hand and a smile on her lips. Her name tag declared her to be *Robin Graham* LPN.

Slowing to a stop, Teodoro returned Robin's courteous

smile. "I just wanted to look in on Violet before I clocked out for a nap."

Robin stepped out of the doorway and into the corridor. "She's finally asleep and"—she arched one warning eyebrow— "I hope to keep her that way. She's been shuttled back and forth like a suitcase, poor little thing."

"I'll whisper my wishes for sweet dreams."

"See that you do," Robin said, softening her words with a quick smile. She walked away, headed for the nurses' station, her shoes squeaking against the floor.

Once she was gone, Teodoro took her place in the doorway and rested one shoulder against it. Violet slept on her side in the darkened room, her freckled face peaceful. Her black paper wings, crumpled and crinkled and a bit tattered after the flight from Baton Rouge and the drive from Dulles, poked up from the back of her nightie.

Looks like she talked the nurses into letting her wear them, Teodoro mused, folding his arms over his chest.

Intercepting Violet once she'd arrived at HQ had been easy and wiping her memory clean of the time she'd spent with Dante at the sanitarium, along with any memory of Dante—not to mention himself—being at Doucet-Bainbridge, had been even easier.

You're still hoping to see your angel. It's been a long time.

It has an' I miss him. When will I see my mommy?

Tomorrow. I promise. She's asleep right now, honey.

Okay. Thanks, Mr. Dion.

Whether or not Violet's sedated mother would ever accept her transformed daughter was another matter. For Violet's sake, Teodoro hoped so.

"Sleep well, sweetie," Teodoro whispered. "Keep safe."

As he turned to go, he heard a sleep-thick voice whisper, "He'll come for me, you know. He promised."

The hair on the back of Teodoro's neck prickled. Slowly, he turned around. Violet watched him drowsily, her eyelids weighted by thick, brown lashes.

"What did you say?" he asked slowly.

But Violet's eyes shuttered closed again and her breathing slid back into the easy rhythm of sleep.

Teodoro stood there a moment, staring at the sleeping child. He knew he hadn't imagined what she'd said, but also knew what she'd said was impossible.

He'll come for me, you know. He promised.

Teodoro had erased anything Dante might've said to Violet at Doucet-Bainbridge from her memory. She *couldn't* remember. Not even in her dreams. He backed away from the doorway, uncertain and chilled to the bone.

Maybe it's a promise Dante made back in Oregon when she'd been hit by a bullet intended for someone else; a promise given after he'd remade her in Chloe's image. Those memories are still intact, after all.

A wave of relief swept over Teodoro. *Yes. Of course.*

Turning, he headed for the elevator in brisk strides, his confidence restored. He shook his head, chagrined. Spooked by a dreaming child's utterances like a peasant quivering in an oracle's dank cave.

He needed sleep. He hadn't rested in days. And while his Fallen half didn't need sleep, his human half had its limits—and he was near the end of those limits now. He would allow himself a short nap only. Anything longer would have to wait until after he'd witnessed the Elohim forced to kill the *creawdwr* they'd awaited for eons.

Then he'd sleep the sleep of the righteous, long and deep and untroubled.

AN ANGRY BUMBLEBEE BUZZ drew Teodoro up from dreamless sleep. It seemed as though he'd just shut his eyes, but he received a shock when he glanced at the sleepbay's bedside clock and realized hours had passed—*long* hours. It was almost 6 p.m.

So much for a short nap.

"*Mierda,*" Teodoro muttered, sitting up and scooping the buzzing cell from the end table. *Must be Caterina—at last.* His frown deepened when he looked at the screen. The number displayed belonged to Richard Purcell, not his little wind-up assassin.

"We've got problems," Purcell said without preamble once Teodoro answered the call. "I can't get into the building."

"You're calling me to tell me that you're locked out?"

"I wouldn't call if I was just locked out of the fucking building. I'd phone someone inside. But, you know what? No one inside is fucking answering. I'm calling because every time I drive into the parking lot or walk in—I've tried both ways—I find myself back at the motel a short time later, thinking about my wonderful day at work. Something goddamned weird is going on down here. There's graffiti on the sanitarium doors and windows, more like some kind of symbols, actually."

The chill Teodoro had felt earlier in Violet's room returned in full force. What Purcell was describing, his inability to enter the sanitarium's parking lot for more than a few moments before finding himself at home again, stank of Elohim magic. A blood spell designed to keep mortals away.

"What kind of symbols? Describe them," Teodoro ordered, standing. He grabbed his neatly draped trousers from the chair back, tucked his phone between chin and shoulder, and pulled them on.

"I'll do you one better. I'm sending over a picture of one."

By the time Purcell's photo had finished loading on his phone, Teodoro's heart was pounding hard and fast and his chill had deepened into glacial ice. He stared at the image of the blood sigil—a No Trespassing, No Admittance sign—and realized that the Fallen had found Dante Baptiste.

If they force-bonded their unstable, young *creawdwr* before Heather Wallace died, then all of Teodoro's hard work would be for nothing. He frowned, studying the image. If the Fallen had found Dante, why would they put up sigils to keep out other Fallen?

Maybe it was vampires who had stumbled across Dante, not Fallen. Or maybe the Fallen had split into warring factions. Again.

"You still there?" Purcell's voice rose from the phone, a fly's irritating buzz.

"Of course." Teodoro mentally thumbed through his options, gradually realizing that if the Fallen were indeed on the scene, he had next to none.

"Oh, there's one other little thing you should know."

"And that is?"

"Heather Wallace. I think she's inside."

"Impossible," Teodoro said flatly. "You're mistaken."

"I don't think so. I checked out a car parked down the street. It was unlocked and the rental agreement in the glove box was signed by Caterina Cortini, of all people. And judging by the cracker crumbs on the passenger seat, Cortini wasn't alone. Now what would she be doing in Baton Rouge, let alone Doucet-Bainbridge?"

Teodoro went still. A very good question. Had Heather somehow managed to override Caterina's conditioning and convince his assassin that Dante was missing and in need of their assistance?

"I wouldn't know," Teodoro lied smoothly. "I'm not her handler. But how does Heather Wallace figure into this? All you have is a car rented by Cortini. An *empty* car."

"I pulled fingerprints from the steering wheel, Díon. Used my laptop to scan and upload them to the SB database. They matched what we have on file for Caterina Cortini and Heather Wallace."

"Are you saying Cortini is helping Wallace?"

"Who the hell knows? All I *do* know is that I found a Little Rock gas receipt in the car. Cortini knows the SB travel routes and she *does* have bloodsucker relatives—some pretty damned powerful ones. Or maybe *you* sent her to intercept Wallace."

"Why would I do that?"

"To break S. You keep yapping about that, right? So maybe when you learned that our people had found Wallace, you decided to use a little of that Jedi mind-trick bullshit of yours to convince one of our own wetwork specialists to kill Wallace or maybe you just bribed Cortini or whatever, but, yeah, I'm pretty damned sure you're behind this."

Teodoro didn't like how close Purcell had come to the truth. *He suspects too much. I need to remedy that.*

"So where are they, then? Both are mortal, they wouldn't be able to go inside anymore than—" Teodoro stopped speaking abruptly, as a memory gleaned from his sojourn inside Dante's firestorm of a mind popped into his thoughts; a memory of Dante healing Heather when she had been mortally wounded in D.C., making her whole with song and blue flames.

Heather Wallace was no longer entirely mortal, then. But Caterina was—so she should've returned to her car and driven away—perhaps repeatedly. Since the car was still parked where Purcell had found it, Teodoro believed Heather had traveled to Baton Rouge alone. Meaning she had somehow escaped Caterina, perhaps killed her. No wonder his texts had gone unanswered.

It seemed his imagination was sorely lacking, he reflected ruefully.

"Mortal? Instead of human?" Purcell questioned in low tones. "Interesting choice of words."

"I think you know, or at least suspect, more than you claim to, Richard."

"Richard now, is it?" Purcell said after a long pause. "Like we're buddies or something?" then adding without waiting for a response, "So *do* you know what those symbols represent?"

"I do. Something I would have to wipe from your memory if I told you."

"Ah. That shit again. Christ. Look, just tell me what to do so I can get back inside. Wallace managed it, so can I—*if* I know what I'm dealing with."

"Where are you?"

"Outside the parking lot, but out of view. Tell me how to avoid the parking lot hypnotic trance hoodoo bullshit."

Raking his fingers through his hair, Teodoro considered his options again. He could never make it to Baton Rouge in time to keep whoever had found Dante—Fallen or vampire—from leaving with him and his mortal bondmate. And, even if he did make it in time, killing Wallace might prove difficult, if not impossible, if she was with Fallen and/or vampires and in the company of Dante Baptiste.

But Dante could kill her. Unmake her.

With just the right word. Words Purcell knew.

Teodoro's lips relaxed into a relieved smile. "I can get you back inside, but you need to listen closely to my instructions and follow them to the letter."

"I'm listening."

SLOUCHED IN THE PASSENGER seat of his Chevrolet Suburban, Purcell was making yet another visual sweep of the sanitarium with his binoculars before settling down to follow Díon's bizarre instructions, when a figure—a *winged* figure—landed in the parking lot.

White wings, gleaming ivory hair, tall. A man wearing what appeared to be black plaid trousers and boots.

A man with *wings*. Purcell lowered the binoculars and blinked. Before he had time to process the information his eyes had delivered to his brain, two more figures kited down from the cloud-flecked early evening sky to land gracefully beside the first figure.

The male was also tall with black, waist-length hair and black wings, but wearing regular slacks instead of plaid; the silver-haired female, curves draped in what looked like a Grecian-style gown, fluttered her wings in a blur of white and lavender before folding them at her back.

Slowly, heart pounding against his ribs, Purcell raised the binoculars back to his eyes. And received yet another shock: he recognized one of the winged creatures, the black-winged male.

Lucien De Noir. S's sugar daddy.

Sweat popped up on Purcell's forehead as he pondered the implications of what he was seeing. Not angels, their wings weren't feathered, but smooth. If not angels, then what— demons? Aliens? Gods from fucking Mount Olympus?

He wasn't sure and at the moment it didn't matter, really. They were here and he had no doubt whatsoever they were here to fetch S. He also had no doubt this was the reason that prick Díon had kept threatening to wipe his memory.

Drawing in a deep breath, Purcell studied De Noir and his winged companions. They were observing the sanitarium and looking very unhappy. And Purcell chuckled in relief as the reason why became clear.

The symbols seemed to be keeping them from entering the building.

He watched as De Noir vaulted into the sky, ink-black wings spread wide as he flew away. Looking surprised, his companions sped after him. Interesting. Maybe S's sugar daddy wasn't immune to the goddamned parking lot spell either or maybe he was off for a spell-busting crowbar. In any case, it was time for Purcell to get to work.

Lowering the binoculars, Purcell tossed them onto the passenger seat. He yanked open the SUV's glove box, then pulled his pocketknife free from its cluttered depths. He flipped the blade open. Hesitated.

Díon's instructions had been more than a little nuts, but if they got him inside the sanitarium again, then—nuts or not— okay. He'd roll with it. What other choice did he have?

All we need is a bit of blood magic to protect you from the parking lot spell.

Blood magic. Christ. Whose blood?

Your own, of course.

Shit. I had a feeling. What about the damned symbols on the building?

Not meant for you. Forget those. Concentrate on my instructions.

And Purcell had. Even now Dion's voice ran through his mind like an irritating commercial jingle that made him groan every time he caught himself humming it.

No more stalling, he thought, drawing the blade gingerly across his palm. Blood welled. *Time to man up.*

Purcell cupped his stinging palm, creating a tiny well, and dipped a fingertip into its flesh-cradled ruby depths. Looking into the rearview mirror, he painted the first symbol on his forehead between his eyes.

Once symboled up and once the sun had set, he would continue to follow Dion's instructions and strap on a small helmet-cam and make sure it fed into the mind reading prick's cell phone so he could monitor the action as it all went down.

Motherfucker wanted to watch. No problem. Watch he would.

Purcell planned only one itty-bitty change to Dion's S sanity-bashing plan. He'd forgo the part where Heather Wallace died at S's programming-triggered hands and just kill the fucking little psycho instead.

Okay, sure, that was more than an *itty-bitty* change—it was an entirely different plan, but so fucking what? S was too dangerous to play games with, an all-important fact that Dion seemed incapable of grasping. So Purcell, good guy that he was, would help him the fuck out.

As for Heather Wallace, she could stay and die or she could walk away. Purcell didn't really give a rat's ass. The choice was hers. She'd never been anything more than a pawn, anyway.

And Díon—along with his mind-wiping threats—could go screw himself. The next time they met it would be with the muzzle of his Glock against the back of Díon's skull. Purcell suspected he'd be doing the SB a favor when he pulled the trigger. He felt a dark and mocking smile tug at his lips.

Hell, they might even give him a promotion.

44

AS LOST AS I GET

WITH A SOFT, PAINED groan, Heather opened her eyes. She was on the floor in a corridor filled with soft red light. *Emergency lighting,* a more alert part of brain pointed out helpfully. With another groan, she shut her eyes again. Her head throbbed. She tasted blood at the back of her throat.

Where am I? And why the hell am I on the floor?

She rolled her thoughts backward. Texas. The man who used to be her father. The SB and Little Rock. Caterina Cortini. The rest stop. The Fallen-marked sanitarium—

Catin. Pardonne-moi.

Heather's eyes snapped open again. "Dante," she whispered, remembering exactly why she was on the floor, why her head felt like a coconut being pounded non-stop against a rock, why she no longer felt the *hereherehere* tug of the bond.

Dante had severed it.

And she hoped, prayed, wished with all she had, that he'd done so deliberately. Otherwise, it meant—

"No," Heather growled, pushing herself into a sitting position. Pain pulsed at her temples, then faded. "No. No. No."

The fact that she was still alive gave her hope that Dante

was, as well. She was a novice where bonds were concerned—how they were made or what happened when they were un-made, but she suspected that, as a mortal, she might not survive his actual death.

Yet her traitorous mind offered a possible scenario: What if Dante severed the bond *prior* to death—a death he knew was coming—in order to keep her alive?

Catin. Pardonne-moi.

Heather closed her stinging eyes, refusing the tears, refusing the hard knot of grief in her chest, refusing to believe he could be gone. "Not giving up on you, Baptiste," she rasped through a throat gone so tight, it ached. "I know you're alive. You *have* to be. So you hang on. Hear me? Hang on."

I refuse to be too late.

Opening her eyes, Heather wiped at them with angry swipes from the heel of her hand, before picking her Glock up from the floor. She rose to her feet, one hand to the wall to steady herself, wincing as a bolt of hot pain shot up from her twisted ankle. Her headache returned with her increase in altitude.

Neither would stop her. Nothing could.

Heather limped down the silent, red-lit corridor, the hair prickling on the back of her neck, her sense of horror deepening with each step she took.

Dear God. What the hell happened?

Or maybe the correct question was: *Who* the hell happened.

She found her answer on the third floor, in air thick with the coppery reek of blood and the ever-thickening stink of death.

Even in the dim lighting, there was no mistaking the dark smears and spatters and Rorschach splashes on the walls and floor for anything other than blood. No mistaking the forms—black-suited agents and medical staff in green scrubs, male and female—sprawled and curled like pill bugs on the polished tile. And Heather didn't need to crouch beside the bodies for a closer look to see how they had been killed.

Each had died beneath sharp, sharp nails or fangs or merciless, pale hands.

Oh, Dante, oh, cher. Looks like you made sure no one had time or voice enough to stop you through your programming— whether they knew how or not.

A few of the agents had died with fingers locked around the grips of their guns, and judging by the faint and fading scent of cordite beneath the thick smell of blood, more than one had gotten off a few shots.

She hoped none had hit their target.

They brought him here. They had to know what could happen if he slipped their leash of drugs and pain and mental torture. They brought him here against his will. They got what they deserved.

As Heather's gaze skipped from the black-suited bodies to the crumpled and bloodied forms in green scrubs, she realized she might be wrong, that not all had deserved what they'd received. Then she spotted syringes filled with a dark reddish substance, clutched between the stiffening fingers of two of the slaughtered medical team, and her sympathy drained away.

What do you want to bet that's the dragon's blood tree resin Von told me about? The True Blood poison that's keeping Dante from healing at best and slowly killing him at worst. So much for do not harm.

Doors stood open at either side of the corridor, some lying flush against the wall as though flung or ripped open. Noticing a trail of bloody footprints leading from the nearest cell to the one across from it, then to the next, the dark prints disappearing into shadows stained red by the emergency lights, Heather felt the cold tingle of fear against her spine.

I think he's had all he can take, doll . . .

Dante's voice, low and husky, raw with emotion he kept

shoving aside, whispered through her memory, words from another time, another place of slaughter.

Run from me. Run as far as you can.

Heather's throat tightened. *Oh,* cher. *What have you done?*

But she already knew the answer to that: whatever he'd needed to survive. Just as she'd wished and prayed he would.

Hang on, Baptiste. Please.

Stepping past and around the bodies, Heather moved with caution, Glock held in both hands, her finger resting on the trigger. In the eerie silence, the quiet tread of her shoe soles against the tiled floor sounded as loud—to her, anyway—as those of a weekend hiker lumbering through crackling, summer-dried underbrush.

Heather winced, wishing she could move nightkind-silent, but doubted it would make any difference even if she could. Whichever one of the Fallen was keeping Dante company had probably heard the rapid beat of her heart the moment she'd crawled into the sigil-etched building.

And knew precisely where she was.

So what were they waiting for—applause? What Fallen game had she stumbled into?

Which brought up even more troubling questions: Why was Dante still here in this place of nightmare and blood and torture? Why hadn't he been scooped up by his winged "rescuer" and flown back to Gehenna already?

One possibility stopped her cold, rooted her feet to the floor.

Maybe they had. Maybe Dante was in Gehenna right now. Without the bond, she wouldn't know. She could be searching for someone who was no longer here.

Or worse, no longer breathing.

Heather closed her eyes, pulse pounding at her temples. Despite the cold fingers closed around her heart, she knew Dante was alive. And something deep inside of her, maybe an intuitive knowing, maybe some fundamental change Dante had unintentionally made when healing her in D.C., whispered over and over: *He's here*.

Heather choose to believe that whisper. Opening her eyes, she resumed her search.

When she reached the first open cell door, she saw Dante slumped on the floor at the far end of the hall, his pale skin gleaming like moonlight in the gloom. Faint red light glinted from the ring in his collar. He rested on his side, one arm half curled beneath his head.

Her breath caught in her throat, a near sob.

The next thing Heather knew, she was dropping to her knees beside him, the Glock once again tucked into her jeans beneath her sweater, her trembling hands smoothing his bloodsticky and sweat-damp hair back from his face. She had no memory of crossing the corridor, no memory of moving at all. But that didn't matter.

She'd found Dante—her North Star, her nightkind of fire and twilight, her man.

"Baptiste," she whispered, bending to kiss his lips, his forehead. The icy feel of his skin shocked her. "I'm here, *cher*. I'm here."

She placed her hand over his chest and didn't release her breath until she felt the slow, reassuring thump of his heart beneath her palm. His fevered heat was gone and Heather knew that couldn't be good. Blood oozed from his nose. Spattered his pale, beautiful face. Stained his lips. His expression was worlds—*galaxies*—away from peaceful.

Blood grimed his fingers, smeared his hands, and streaked his forearms. Heather thought of the bodies littering the floor, thought of the footprints marking a wet, dark path from door to door, and she blinked furiously, eyes burning.

I feel like I'm running out of time, catin.

No and no and no.

Heather's jaw clenched when she saw the bullet wound right above his heart, half healed and trickling blood, and thought of the man who'd put it there.

May the bastard rot in hell.

Remembering her dream/vision of Dante running up flights of stairs with a red-haired girl wearing a Winnie-the-Pooh sweater and black paper wings in his arms, Heather stiffened. She scanned the corridor anxiously.

Violet. Where was Violet?

Heather refused to believe that history had repeated itself and that Violet now lay in a pool of blood, blue eyes wide open and empty like those of the little girl he'd killed and who haunted his heart, his long-lost Chloe.

He'd been only a boy then, little more than a child, abused and manipulated by adults—both mortal and nightkind—driven by instincts and a hunger he didn't understand and had no idea how to control.

Dante was no longer a boy, no longer a shattered child. He was a man of quiet strength and fierce loyalty. *He* would *never* hurt Violet. No matter how lost he got, no matter how far he fell. She returned her gaze to Dante, brushed the backs of her fingers against his smooth, icy cheek.

As lost as I get, I will find you, Heather. Always.

"You'd better," Heather said, each word scraping free from a too-tight throat. "I'm holding you to that, Baptiste. Come back, damn you. Come back to me."

Eyes burning, Heather dug her borrowed cell phone out of her jeans pocket. Disappointment curled through her. No calls had come in while she'd been passed out on the floor. Meaning no one had heard from Lucien yet. But given the time displayed on the screen, it was nearly sunset. Dante would be waking soon.

The question was: would *soon* be soon enough?

So far, Heather had seen no sign of the fallen angel responsible for the parking lot spell and sigils. For all she knew, he or she could be watching her right now. Could she afford to wait until Dante awakened? Her gaze returned to the wound above his heart. Her fingers curled against her palms, nails biting into the skin. And if his injuries prevented him from waking up?

I don't think I can afford to wait. The dragon's blood tree sap isn't the only thing poisoning him. This place and all the twisted memories it holds is twice as toxic.

She'd find blankets in one of the cells and use them to shield Dante from the sun. If she worked it right, she should be able to lift Dante in a fireman's carry. Getting to her feet with his weight draped across her shoulders would be another problem altogether. Not for the first time, she was grateful that he was five-nine and not six-two. She would just have to hope that determination, desperation, and adrenaline would be enough.

It'll have to be.

And if it wasn't? If her injured ankle refused to hold?

Then, when Dante awakened at twilight, he would find her beside him. Now that she'd found him again, she wouldn't leave him. Not even to save her own ass. Which would piss Dante off if he knew.

So let him get pissed off. We're in this together. Side by side and back to back.

Tucking the cell phone back into her pocket, Heather was preparing to rise to her feet to begin her search for blankets when a familiar and totally unexpected voice drawled, "I go to fetch my heart and put it back where it belongs—an action only necessary due to my regretful underestimation of the *creawdwr*'s paranoia—and lo and behold, who do I find waiting upon my return but the lovely Heather Wallace."

Hair prickling at the back of her neck, Heather looked up. Von stood across the corridor, arms folded over his chest, a grin parting his mustache-framed lips. But Von's green gaze had never been that darkly gleeful, never that calculating, his words never so formal.

"I don't know who you are," she stated quietly, "but I *do* know you're not Von."

The grin widened. "Well, shit. So far this shape has fooled no one." The imposter rubbed his chest, a rueful expression on his face as he glanced at Dante. "Call me Loki. Yes"—he sighed, clearly anticipating the question—"*that* Loki."

Heather swung one knee over Dante's body, protectively straddling his Sleeping form, as she pulled the Glock from beneath her sweater and lifted it in one smooth motion. She knew that bullets of any caliber were practically worthless against the Fallen, even as a distraction, but still wanted the reassuring grip of the gun in her hand, no matter how illusory that reassurance might be.

Loki grinned, approval gleaming in his eyes. "What a fierce little guard dog. Loyal. Protective. A one-woman rescue team. No wonder the *creawdwr* bonded you."

Heather kept her face still. *He doesn't know what Dante's done. And I think I just discovered one of the reasons he found it necessary.*

"You have no business wearing Von's face. Afraid to show your own?"

Loki laughed, as delighted as though she were a dancing hamster in a pink tutu.

She took that as a *no.*

I know from my Norse mythology classes in college that Loki was a shape-shifter, but can all Fallen change shapes?

"No," came the drawled reply. A disquieting reply in Von's familiar voice. "Only a special few of us possess that particular talent . . . darlin'."

Heather tightened her shields. Her lips compressed into a grim line. Bastard had read her thoughts. She needed to make sure that she kept her shields up and reinforced at all times. Her life—and Dante's—might depend on it.

"And speaking of special talents"—Loki tilted his head and studied her with Von's green eyes, now crow-bright—"how did you get past my spells?"

"Without a bit of difficulty," she retorted, keeping the

Glock aimed at the heart beating beneath Loki's idly rubbing fingertips. "Others are on their way," she lied—well, a partial lie. She had no idea when or if Lucien would show up, but fervently wished it would be sooner rather than later—"An entire army of nightkind, Fallen, and mortals. You still have time to escape. Just leave Dante and go."

The green eyes flicked down at Dante. Mingled fear and excitement danced there for a split second, bright embers, there and gone so quickly Heather wasn't even sure she'd seen anything at all.

"You think I want to *escape*?" he whispered, lifting his gaze to hers. No fear, no excitement, no bright embers.

"If you're smart, yes."

Loki chuckled, a sound lacking warmth or humor. "And what would one little mortal know of 'smart'? Or of Elohim desires?" He offered her a mock sympathetic smile. "No doubt you even think you *understand* Dante."

Heather's chin lifted as she held his gaze. But she kept silent, deciding to save her breath. Nothing she said would make any difference to this shape-shifting, egotistical bastard anyway.

Despite the slaughter surrounding her, she knew who Dante was, knew his heart.

But even the strongest heart can break.

Heather's throat constricted. *Yes. Oh, yes.* And that was why she needed to get him out of here and somewhere safe before that happened.

And if it already has?

Heather shoved the disquieting thought aside. *Not now.*

"I'm betting you think that when Dante awakens, he's going to be the vampire—excuse me, apologies—*nightkind* he was when he went to Sleep, broken and haunted and full of suppressed rage, am I right?" Loki asked, a slow grin parting his lips. He continued without waiting for Heather's reply; his knowing, arrogant words had her tightening her grip on the Glock. "If so, you'd be wrong. Very, *very* wrong."

"I don't think so, you son of a bitch," Heather replied, her voice Arctic ice. "I *know* Dante."

"And that will be the death of you," Loki said, voice flat, his grin gone. His form rippled, like wind-stirred water, became fluid. When he spoke, his voice flowed from masculine tones to feminine and all registers in between. "It won't be your Dante who awakens—not at all."

I feel like I'm running out of time, catin.

I think he's had all he can take, doll.

"Bullshit," Heather declared, her voice rough and low, unsure who she was trying to convince—Loki or herself.

Liquid, musical laughter filled the corridor, followed by words Heather suspected had been stolen from Dante's mind. "Keep telling yourself that."

"Bastard." She glanced down, unsettled by the sudden fluidity of Loki's shape. After a moment, she risked a look up and her heart lodged in her throat at *who* Loki had become. Dark brown eyes full of mischief, milk-white face framed by silken black hair, cupid's-bow lips curved into a wicked and knowing grin. His frost and burning leaves scent perfumed the air.

Dante—but minus his heart, his warmth.

"Hey, *catin*."

"You need to work on your Cajun accent. You sound *nothing* like him," Heather lied, chilled by just how much he *did* sound like Dante.

The grin widened, revealed fangs. "I believe he would say 'bullshit' to that."

"*I* believe he'd tear your heart out again, play a little kick-ball with it."

"Not quite twilight, *chérie*. Looks like we have a little time. Whaddaya say we get to know each other a little better?"

Heather's hands tightened around the Glock, desperation and despair pouring through her in equal measure. *How the hell do I keep a fallen angel away?* "You're not going to win any points with Dante—"

Heather's words died in her throat as Loki dissolved into a blur of motion that ended with him bending over her, his face—Dante's face—three inches from her own.

"I think he's going to be too busy unraveling the world to worry about me," he whispered. A golden fire lit his eyes. "Besides, I'm not exactly interested in winning points."

Heather squeezed the Glock's trigger and kept squeezing, emptying the magazine of its ten remaining rounds. The gunshots boomed and roared in the close confines, echoing like cannon fire down the corridor, and leaving her ears ringing. Dark blood bloomed in a tightly spaced circle of wounds just beneath Loki-as-Dante's pale sternum. Wounds already healing.

The dark brows slanted down. "Ow," he growled, wrenching the Glock from Heather's grip and tossing it down the corridor to clatter against the floor tiles. "That actually hurt."

"Good. It'll hurt even more when Dante—"

Loki-as-Dante pressed taloned fingertips against Heather's temples. The lightning storm scent of ozone crackled into the air. The hair lifted on her arms, the back of her neck. Her skin tingled beneath his talons. Fear iced her spine, stole her breath. A smile tilted the oh-so familiar lips.

"I like a good fight, *catin*. So keep it going," Loki murmured in Dante's voice. "I hope you're telling the truth about others being on their way—especially the Elohim. I feel in a mood for a little chat with my brethren. But first, let's learn all about you."

Let me in, chère. *Let me in.*

Electricity surged through Heather's mind, a mushroom cloud of devastating white light. Her shields blew apart, Tinkertoys caught in a nuclear wind, and darkness—eager and gleeful—rushed inside. She felt her body convulse, no longer under her control. She couldn't even scream.

But she tried. Again and again.

45

FALLEN MAGIC

"WHERE ARE YOU GOING?" the Morningstar called from behind Lucien. "Dante is *behind* us."

The spell's repelling force—like hands shoving at his chest, like a frantic voice endlessly yelling, *Darkness comes and death, flee-flee-flee!*—vanished as soon as Lucien had flown beyond its range.

"Lucien, wait!" Hekate's concerned voice. "Your son is in that sanitarium."

Wings slashing the air like knife blades, Lucien wheeled around to face Hekate and the Morningstar. "Don't you think I know that?" he answered, his voice harsh even to his own ears. "Dante is Sleeping inside a sanitarium sealed with Elohim blood sigils, alone with whoever put them there. And I couldn't *think*, let alone *act*, because of that damned spell. I had to pull free of its influence."

"How very odd," the Morningstar murmured. Late afternoon sunlight transformed the ice melting from the edges of his alabaster wings into hundreds of tiny, fiery prisms. He tilted his head, curious, cataloguing potential weaknesses for future use. "We need to figure out why you were affected and we weren't."

Lucien already knew why. The answer burned like bitter acid at the back of his throat. "My protection sigils are gone. Have been for nearly twenty-four years."

Comprehension blossomed in Hekate's hyacinth eyes. "The story you told me earlier while we waited for my father."

Swallowing back the questions she no doubt yearned to ask, she touched the small leather bag looped through the belt around her waist and said, "We must remedy that, then."

"THERE. ALL PROTECTED," HEKATE said, wiping silver ink from her opalescent talons with a napkin. The ink's wild mint aroma scented the air, cutting through the smell of spicy fried chicken.

"Thank you." Lucien studied Hekate's handiwork. The protection sigils inked into his chest, above his heart and solar plexus, glimmered like moonlit winter ice and tingled cool against his skin like camphor, a sensation already fading.

They sat at a small table inside a Popeye's restaurant, hidden behind an illusion woven by the Morningstar that showed a table occupied by plump fast-food aficionados instead of a trio of fallen angels engaged in a tattoo session.

"It was because you couldn't return to Gehenna," the Morningstar mumbled around a mouthful of red beans and rice. "At least, you couldn't until just recently."

Lucien glanced at him, frowning. "What was?" he asked, ignoring the Morningstar's aggrieved *why-aren't-you-keeping-up-with-my-train-of-thought* expression.

"Why you've remained without protective sigils for the last twenty-four years," he sighed, pushing back from the table, his meal of red beans and rice, plus biscuits finished. "No mortal possesses the secret of our protective spells."

"True enough," Lucien admitted.

"How *did* you lose your original sigils?" Hekate asked. "I thought they were permanent, to protect us from mortal and vampire summoning spells."

Lucien's thoughts traveled back to Lincoln City and the tiny tattoo shop perched above the cliff-lashing Pacific, back to the woman he'd hunted, only to end up as prey himself.

With one twist of her hand, Paloma summons the ink out of Lucien's skin, siphoning it through his pores, and unraveling his protection sigils. The silvery ink spatters to the floor, tiny beads of mercury. A heartbeat later, he finds himself trapped inside a magicked circle in a windowless room etched with powerful sigils and angelic script from wall to wall and floor to ceiling.

"They are," Lucien finally answered, rising to his feet. "But it's a long story and we don't have the time. We need to get back to Dante."

As the three of them walked out into the Popeye's parking lot, the Morningstar commented, "Not really much need for the protection sigils anymore. Very little summoning going on these days—unlike the thirteenth and fourteenth centuries. Not with the Internet gods holding mortal attention."

"True," Lucien agreed. "And I, for one, don't miss it." Unfurling his wings, he leaped into the sky.

LANDING ONCE MORE IN the sanitarium's car-dotted parking lot, Lucien folded his wings behind him, flicking beads of moisture into air smelling of distant wood smoke and dew. For a moment, he thought he caught a faint whiff of Heather's scent, but dismissed it. Even if she had escaped and made her way to Baton Rouge, the spell would've turned her around and sent her home.

No, just wishful thinking.

He studied the silent and sigil-painted building, feeling an electric tingle as his protective glyphs shielded his mind from the repelling spell's *flee-flee-flee* command.

All Fallen magic, whether offensive or defensive, was dark, but—he felt a fierce smile curve his lips—not half as dark or deadly or determined as a father seeking his stolen child.

Lucien arrowed a thought into Dante's Sleeping mind: <*I'm here and I'm not leaving without you.*> The sending vanished like a coin into the black depths of a wishing well, yet still he hoped it had buried itself deep into his son's dreaming subconscious.

As for whoever held him—Lucien strode straight for the sigil-tattooed doors, voicing a *wybrcathl* of challenge, of sharp-taloned promise, into the evening air as he approached the sanitarium.

Wings snapped and fluttered as Hekate and the Morningstar descended behind him.

"Wait," Hekate called. "Something doesn't look right." But her warning came too late.

Five feet from the doors, pain exploded within Lucien, an internal pipe bomb that sucked the air from his lungs and knocked him to his knees. He bent over, forehead pressed to the sidewalk, teeth gritted, body knotted, as pain raked and clawed and burned.

He felt as though he'd walked straight into a high-voltage barbed-wire fence and swallowed broken glass—not to mention that pipe bomb full of nails. His one regret was his newfound inability to pass out.

"You need to move!" Someone shouted. Hekate, he thought, but the humming in his ears made it hard to know for certain. "Roll! Crawl! *MOVE!*"

Lucien wanted to snarl that *she* should try rolling or crawling or moving while *her* insides were being pureed and see how reasonable she found that particular suggestion—yet he knew she was right. He *had* to move.

Forcing his spasming muscles into motion, Lucien managed a one-shouldered roll toward Hekate and her father and away from the building. As he did, the pain vanished. "By all that's holy," he panted, staggering up to his feet. Aside from a few twinges along his spine, he felt fine. "What was *that*?"

"A new kind of spell," Hekate said, frowning as she studied the sanitarium. A light breeze, smelling of distant lightning and impending rain, swept a silver ringlet across her forehead. "Our protection is working against the repulsion spell, but not this one. This isn't a typical banishing spell. It's unlike anything I've seen before," she admitted reluctantly, shifting her violet gaze to Lucien. "I didn't notice the difference until now."

"Neither did I," Lucien replied, shaking his head.

Hekate touched his cheek, her fingers soft against his skin. "Are you all right?"

Lucien offered her a smile. "Aside from feeling foolish, yes."

A melodic *wybrcathl* shivered into the air in response to his earlier one, a defiant manifesto that both shocked and chilled Lucien—especially given its source.

"Loki," Lucien breathed, stunned. "Here and flesh again. How? He should still be stone and guarding a tomb in St. Louis No. 3."

"So that's what happened to the sly bastard," the Morningstar mused. "I'd wondered."

Lucien gave him a sidelong glance. "No doubt. Given that he was here doing your bidding."

The Morningstar sighed. "So he must've claimed. And everyone knows each word Loki utters is purest truth. But whose bidding Loki was or wasn't doing doesn't matter at the moment. If you didn't free him, then who?"

Lucien remembered standing in St. Louis No. 3 several weeks ago and watching his son disappear into the night on the back of Von's Harley. Remembered the fading feel of Dante's power skipping along Loki's stone shape, remembered the faint smell of his unique blood. Remembered the paper prayer folded at Loki's stone feet.

Keep her safe, ma mère. *Even from me.* S'il te plâit.

Lucien rubbed his face with his hands, exasperated. In seeking truth, Dante had somehow managed to unravel the spell binding Loki.

Ah, child, what have you done?

He lowered his hands as the *wybrcathl* continued, each information-drenched trill deepening the chill he felt inside. Loki held not only Dante, but Heather as well. Detecting her scent in the parking lot hadn't been wishful thinking, after all. Lucien stared at the bespelled building, wondering how Heather had managed to get past whatever spell Loki had spun into motion to keep mortals out and realizing she might not be completely mortal anymore. And as for Loki—

"He plans to help Dante become the Great Destroyer," Hekate whispered in shocked tones, "then guide him in the world's destruction."

"If Loki succeeds, then your son must die," the Morningstar said, his grim gaze piercing Lucien to his very core. "Even if it means Gehenna dies along with him."

"Then we need to make certain Loki doesn't succeed," Lucien growled.

"What would you suggest we do?" Hekate asked, frustration shadowing her face.

"That you both get out of the way."

Lucien wheeled around to face the blood-glyphed building. He took a deep breath, centering himself, gathering power, then closed his eyes. He smelled ozone, pungent and thick, felt his hair lift into the air, like midnight lengths of seaweed carried on the electric tide of his power. His hands knotted into fists at his sides. He sensed the Morningstar and Hekate backing away from him, heading for the parking lot's gates.

Lucien opened his eyes. And voiced his *wybrcathl*, unleashing his pooled power through his vocal cords in a sledgehammer of sound. Car windows exploded in each vehicle, one after another, a shower of glass tinkling against the pavement while car alarms blared and beeped in cacophonous accompaniment.

The sanitarium's windows blew out simultaneously, shards of glass raining to the well-manicured grounds and parking lot in a gleaming, deadly shower. As though rapped by a giant fist, the front door buckled inward at the same time.

Lucien ended his song, hushed his power. He bolted for the nearest shattered window, but when he grabbed hold of the windowsill to haul himself inside, he was hit by another pipe bomb of devastating pain. Releasing his hold, Lucien fell to the ground, glass crunching beneath his knees.

Hekate rushed over to join him. "What happened?"

Something very close to despair tightened Lucien's throat.

"The bastard didn't just paint the blood sigils on the windows and doors." He looked up into Hekate's concerned eyes. "He painted them on the windowsills as well."

Hekate offered him a hand and Lucien accepted it. Her grasp was cool and strong as she pulled him up to his feet. "Then we shall look for another way in," she said.

But as the minutes melted away and the sun began to sink into the horizon in a blaze of furious color, Lucien's heart sank as well.

Time had just run out.

"Since we've failed to get inside," the Morningstar said, "we need to convince Dante to come out to us. Lure him away from Loki's influence."

But a dark suspicion had rooted itself in Lucien's heart, a suspicion he now voiced. "He's my son and half Fallen. The sigils will keep him inside, just as they keep us out."

As Loki had intended.

Lucien reached for several Sleeping minds, but found only one rising from dreams—Silver's—and filled it with the day's grim and frustrating revelations. As he did so, he saw a car pull into the parking lot, then screech to a halt. A man in a black suit climbed out, gun in hand, his expression a blend of disbelief, determination, and shock as he stared in Lucien's direction.

"Would blood wash away the sigils?" Lucien asked Hekate, eyeing the mortal. "Or act as a bridge across?"

"Not Elohim blood, no. It would be repelled by the spell. But *mortal* blood . . ."

The man's face blanked as Loki's spell kicked in and he started to get back into his car.

A dark smile tugged at Lucien's lips. "Good."

He *moved*.

FACE PAINTED WITH BLOOD symbols like some goddamned primitive hunter, helmet cam strapped into place, and gun in hand, Purcell made his move as the first stars appeared in the darkening sky. The shards of glass strewn on the lawn—thanks to De Noir and his pulverizing vocals—echoed the glittering starlight above.

And speaking of De Noir, he and his pals stood in the parking lot's heart, engaged in some kind of winged confab. An unhappy one, too, judging by all the scowls.

And no wonder. They were still outside. Standing amidst all that twinkling glass.

And it was that very glass that had made Purcell abandon his original plan to slip into the parking lot, sidle over to the far edge, and use the parked cars for cover as he made his way to the sanitarium's side entrance.

After De Noir's little opera of destruction, Purcell had realized that he'd never make across without giving himself away as bits of ex-car windows crunched beneath his shoes. But thanks to De Noir, Purcell no longer needed a door to gain access to the building.

Skirting the parking lot altogether, Purcell stealthed his way through the overgrown field on the other side of the sanitarium's fence to the back of the building and the truck delivery bay.

Purcell walked in careful and deliberate steps to the empty window beside the now-dented back door. A few shards of glass jutted up from the sill like broken teeth. Hands gloved for just this very reason, Purcell pulled the last bits of glass free and placed them on the pavement.

Tiny bits of pulverized glass crunched beneath Purcell's gloves as he grabbed the windowsill and hoisted himself up and over.

He was inside.

46

FALLING APART WITH BREATHTAKING SPEED

"HOLY HELL," VON GROANED.

Taiko drummers had somehow taken up residence inside his skull and were now busy pounding the living daylights out of his brain. Slitting open one eye, he did a quick survey of his surroundings from the cold rock floor he was sprawled upon.

Moonlight trickled in through chinks in the timber and rock walls, revealing a stone-encircled well in the small, unlit building's center. Weathered buckets and cobwebbed tools hung from nails hammered into the walls.

The cool air smelled of old wood pocked with decay and insect husks, of rust and moss and dank rock, of deep, still water—and not at all familiar.

Don't know where I am, but at least it ain't a jail cell. I think.

Von opened both eyes reluctantly and eased himself up into a sitting position, pulse thundering at his temples. "Crap."

Hunching forward, he closed his eyes again and rubbed his aching forehead with his fingertips.

Ain't had a hangover in decades, what the—

He never finished the thought.

Memory poured into his mind in a nightmarish flood of images—Dante missing, Heather stolen, Merri's stay-awake pills, Holly with her angry baby blues and her black-kilted *llafnau*.

Looks like you're skipping out on me again.

One night is all I'm asking and then I'll head straight for Memphis—as ordered. You have my word.

The same word you gave less than a week ago? The same word you gave me not two hours ago? That word, Vonushka? You made me look like a fool.

"Shanghaied," Von muttered, thumping the back of his head against the rough-hewn wall in disgust, instantly regretting it as the taiko drummers inside his skull launched into a double-time rhythm. "Shit. Shit. Shit."

Holly and her *llafnau* had carted his pill-Snoozing ass back to the plantation and tucked him inside the *llygaid* academy's well house for safekeeping until he awakened. He'd bet his left rim that the door wasn't even locked. Who needed locks when you had the nightkind version of SEAL Team Six on hand?

With a disgusted sigh, Von opened his eyes. His headache intensified, the nearly translucent slivers of moonlight creating and stuffing another enthusiastic taiko drummer into his already crowded skull.

Von winced and resumed rubbing his forehead. He remembered his conversation—decades ago, it felt like—about the pill and its consequences with pretty little *Conseil du Sang* spy Merri Goodnight.

No wonder she'd given him that amused smile. She'd known exactly what he was in for and knew he wouldn't need anyone to remind him of his *consequences-we-don't-need-no-stinking-consequences* bravado or to say "I told you so." Nope. Not when she knew he'd be kicking his own ass repeatedly and hard.

Besides, his own personal drummers were oh so busy, busy, busy pounding those consequences into his skull. Literally. Motherfuckers.

Taking the damned stay-awakes had been worth it since they'd allowed him to contact Heather before their temporary link dissolved, but he had no intention of ever downing another.

Von shut his eyes again and waited for the pain to dial down a notch or five. How the fuck did Dante do it? Deal with, live with, his monster migraines?

A quicksilver thought flowed into his mind and Von's eyes opened in surprise. <Von, your ride is here. Wake your tattooed nomad ass up.>

<My tattooed nomad ass is wide awake, along with the rest of me, and regretting the fact, big-time. And what the hell do you mean by 'my ride is here'? You saying you're in Memphis?>

<Wow. Sharp as ever. Seriously. No one would ever suspect that you took a bullet to the head. Yes, we're in Memphis. Just a few blocks west of the compound. And we've got a plan to spring you.>

Von frowned. <How the hell did you find the compound and who's we?>

<Me and Annie, Jack, Merri, and her partner. And as for how, Merri's mère de sang gave us the location.>

<And what about Heather? Dante? Did Lucien . . . >

<Heather found Dante, and Lucien's there now too, but—>

<But? Christ, I hate that damned word. Go ahead, give me the bad news.>

And Silver did just that, filling Von's mind with images as he brought him up to speed on everything that had happened since the stay-awakes had dropped him on the sidewalk at Holly's booted feet.

Mauvais and his companions outside the club.

The shape-shifting fallen angel.

Giovanni and his offer of help from the High Priestess of the Cercle de Druide.

Heather's escape; her call.

The decision to drive to Memphis on nomad rescue detail.

Lucien's return with the Morningstar and his daughter in tow.

The magic-grafittied sanitarium.

Heather inside with Dante. Lucien outside and unable to get in.

One image in particular chilled Von.

Dante's heated hands cup Silver's face and he leans in close, a dark and wicked light glittering in his kohl-rimmed eyes. He brushes fevered lips against Silver's. "Let me in," he whispers. "Let me in, mon ami."

Chilled, yes. But not for long. Fury surged molten through Von's veins. The pain in his head lessened. Shape-shifting motherfucker. But at least they now knew what they were up against. The whole forewarned, yada, yada thing.

<*Wasn't your fault, Silver,*> Von sent. <*Remember that. Coulda—woulda—happened to any of us. Now, you mentioned something about a plan?*>

<*Yeah, man.*>

It was a good plan, simple, and just might work because of those two facts.

Von knew he had to face the music where the *filidh* were concerned, and under normal circumstances, would do just that. Under normal circumstances he would simply thank Silver but remind him that this was *llygaid* business and *llygaid* business *only*. He would stand and take his lumps.

He *was* guilty of breaking his oath, after all.

But circumstances were just about as far from fucking normal as you could get and remain in the real world. He had no idea how long it would take the master bards to hear his case, strip him of his rank, and send him packing, but he couldn't afford the time it would take to find out.

Not with Dante a good six or seven hours away.

Not with Dante and Heather trapped with a shape-shifting fallen angel inside an Elohim-magicked building.

It wasn't enough to hope that Heather had managed to stabilize Dante, not as bad as Dante had been slipping; it was asking too much of one mortal woman.

She needed help.

And she'd fucking get it.

<Let's do it. But if things go south, split. Don't try to take on the llafnau. You'll fail and might even end up with an actual stake in your heart.>

<As Thibodaux would say: Roger that.>

<Y'know, that phrase has a totally different meaning for the British.>

<Shut up. Do you want to be rescued or not?>

Von grinned. *<Yes, please.>*

Promising to see him in a few minutes, Silver ended the conversation.

Von slipped a hand into a jacket pocket, felt the glide of paper beneath his fingers—the charcoal sketch of Dante he'd picked up from the street in front of the club. At least he hadn't lost that.

<Little brother,> he sent. *<You there?>*

But this sending didn't snag or rebound from barriers created by drugs and pain and madness. Instead it went through, unhindered even by Dante's personal shields. Hell, he was still *Sleeping.*

<Von?>

Chaos and pain swirled through Dante's sending—and more than a little madness. The buoyant relief Von felt turned to lead and plummeted into his belly. *<Here. Just hang tight, okay? We're gonna get you out of there.>*

<Oh, I'll bet. I ain't playing your game, Papa. I saw through your Von-suit and I ain't falling for this either. Fuck you.>

Von-suit? Holy hell, the shape-shifting fallen angel.

Panic burned cold through Von's veins. *<Ain't no trick or game, Dante. It's me. Whoever is there with you—besides Heather, that is—is a shape-shifter. He's the one playing games with you, little brother.>*

<I told you once already, motherfucker, you ain't got the right to call me that.>

Out of nowhere, a comet slammed into Von head-on, hammering him deep into the earth in an explosion of white light and furious song—music unlike any he'd ever heard before. Blinking away the black spots stitching across his vision, he realized he was facedown on the cool stone. His headache pulsed with renewed life and he tasted blood at the back of his throat.

With a low groan, Von pushed himself up onto his hands and knees. He wiped away the blood trickling from his nose. "Holy hell."

With no effort at all, Dante had eighty-sixed him from his mind with a savage, mouth-drying power. Silver's trickster fallen angel hadn't wasted any time in messing with Dante's fragmented sense of reality. He no longer knew who was true and who was pretending. Was even Heather safe? Had to be. Von refused to think otherwise. Even out of his head, Dante would never ever hurt Heather.

But if he believed she was Papa wearing a Heather-suit? What then?

Fear ice-picked his heart.

My best friend, my companion, my little brother, is losing his mind and he has the power to take us and the world with him.

Hold on, you stubborn sonuvabitch. Hold the fuck on.

But Von had a sinking feeling that, no matter how stubborn he was, Dante couldn't hold on much longer; that things were falling apart with breathtaking speed and it might already be too late.

47

To Hell in an Express Lane Handbasket

His eyes protected by the smoke-lensed matte black goggles he'd picked up in the Quarter before they'd hit the road, Silver pressed up against the compound's thick river rock wall and watched as rapidly approaching headlights starred the night.

Silver's muscles coiled. His heart picked up speed. This *had* to work.

"Get ready," he whispered.

"Shit, they're moving fast," Merri murmured. "I hope to hell they're wearing their seat belts."

Silver nodded in silent agreement. He'd tried to talk Annie out of participating and, for a moment, when she had rested a hand against her still-flat abdomen, her night-shadowed eyes thoughtful, he thought he'd succeeded. Then she'd shaken her head.

Why should everyone else take all the risks?

Everyone else ain't knocked up.

Annie had surprised Silver by laughing.

True enough. But I'm no good at being on the sidelines, Zero mine. I always end up getting into trouble.

And that had been that. Annie had jumped into the back of the van, an active participant in what Silver hoped would be a daring and successful nomad rescue.

As the van barreled through the compound's black iron gates in an explosion of screeching metal, Silver and Merri scaled the wall.

VON ROSE TO HIS feet when the well house door opened suddenly, ushering in evening-cooled air sweet with the scents of magnolias, pear blossoms, and fresh-mown grass from the plantation's massive yard and myriad gardens. Moonlight outlined the curves of the figure standing in the doorway—Holly Miková.

Her hair framed her pale face in silken waves. She'd changed her rose-red miniskirt for a pair of curve-hugging jeans and her black sweater for a lacy, cobalt-blue blouse. She regarded Von with shadowed eyes, all trace of smiles—smug, chiding, or otherwise—absent from her garnet-red lips.

<*Better hustle your ass, kiddo,*> Von sent to Silver. <*They're moving me.*>

"Put this on," Holly said. She extended what looked like a black silicone bracelet—if silicone bracelets hummed with electricity.

But Von knew what it was, had expected it. A telepathy blocker. No sending could go out or be received as long as it was worn.

Hoping Silver had set his plan into motion, Von took the slim bracelet from Holly and slipped it on his right wrist. His skin prickled beneath the protected current. He reached out a hand to balance himself as mild vertigo spun through him, then vanished.

"I hope this means we're only going steady," Von drawled, dropping his hand from the wall. "Cuz I'm *much* too young to be getting engaged. My mama would never say yes."

Holly rolled her eyes. "Next time I'll just hit you with a Taser."

Grinning, Von followed Holly outside onto the flagstone walkway leading through lush lawns to the moonlight-silvered plantation house. Holly said nothing, the silence thick between them, a silence Von decided not to break—not yet, anyway. Instead, he listened to the soft sound of their boots against the stones and the lonely songs of night birds in the trees.

No guards trailed after them—at least, none that he could see, hear, or sense. Which didn't mean they weren't there, but he had a feeling he and Holly were alone. And when it came right down to it, there was no place for him to run and no point in doing so. He'd never get past the currently unseen *llafnau*.

Not unless something distracted them.

Von mentally crossed his fingers for luck. *C'mon, Silver-boy.*

As Von walked the meandering stone path, he felt a pang of nostalgia as memories decades old stirred and dusted themselves off, reminding him that once this had been home, his instructors and fellow students a family that he had loved as a newborn nightkind as much as he'd loved his mortal nomad clan.

Soft light gleamed in the windows of the three-story house, spilling across the porch with its graceful Grecian columns and onto the immaculately trimmed lawn. He and Holly walked past the garden maze and the training field, now occupied by a handful of students in navy blue sweats blurring through the obstacle course under the careful scrutiny of their instructor—a tall, ginger-haired woman dressed in forest green.

Von grunted in sympathy, remembering his own time on that same grueling course. "Some things never change." He paused to watch, stalling for time. Listening for Silver's distraction.

"Some things, *da*," Holly agreed, halting beside him.

From the street beyond the compound's walls, Von heard the roar of an engine hauling ass. He turned just in time to see a black van—Lucien's van—batter through the gates with a squeal of ripping metal. Headlight glass flew through the air. Brakes screeched, filled the night with the scorched smell of burning rubber.

As if Scotty had just beamed them down from the fricking *Enterprise*, figures in black leather kilts and boots blurred across the lawns and down the driveway to the now-stopped van.

Von froze when Holly jammed the muzzle of her gun against his temple.

"Don't move," she said. "Not a muscle."

"Ain't moving, darlin'."

Von watched, heart hammering, as Annie popped out of the back of the van, shrieking, claiming that the men inside had kidnapped her, were going to force her to marry one of them since she was pregnant, but wouldn't name the baby-daddy.

Jack and Thibodaux exited the van with their hands up, surrounded by stone-faced *llafnau*, both alternating between apologies for the gate and berating the hysterical Annie for grabbing at the wheel and causing the accident in the first place.

"I've seen that van before," Holly said softly. "Friends of yours, Vonushka?"

"If they are, they deserve a reality TV show of their own—*Redneck Shotgun Weddings*, maybe. Could be a hit."

"That's not an answ—" A blur of cinnamon-scented movement, then Holly's head twisted sharply to the right. The gun slid away from Von's temple as she collapsed, neck broken, to the ground. Merri scooped up Holly's gun and tucked it into a pocket of her suede jacket.

"Cutting it close," Von growled, peeling off the blocker from his wrist.

Silver flashed him a quick, fanged grin just as Von caught another streak of motion, then another. His stomach dropped to his socks. Too late. Too fucking late.

"Run," he yelled, hoping the *llafnau* would be content with just him.

But they weren't.

Before Silver could even turn or before Merri could swing up her gun, both of them crumpled to the dewed grass beside Holly, necks equally broken.

One strong, cool, implacable hand braced against the back of Von's skull while the other grasped his chin. He heard, "Looks like now we get to carry you, asshole." The hands twisted his head to the right.

One sharp pain.

Then nothing.

48

BECOMING

HEATHER BLINKED UNTIL THE ceiling came into focus again. She felt like she'd taken a shotgun blast to the head, her brain full of holes, her memory Swiss-cheesed. She wiped blood away from beneath her nose with a shaking hand. Tasted it bright and coppery on her tongue.

Let me in, chère.

Her stomach clenched. No, make that she *wished*—desperately and hard—that her memory *had* been Swiss-cheesed. She remembered Loki's mental assault all too well.

Where is your bond? What has that beautiful, insane little half-breed done? I told him to close it, not sever it. If he's damaged himself—

Heather knew what Dante would've said to that and repeated it now in a barely audible whisper: "Blow me."

Pain pounded a red-hot spike through the center of her forehead when she tried to turn her head to see Dante. She swallowed back a groan and held utterly still until the pain eased. She could feel Dante on the floor beside her, felt her arm against his, the iciness of his skin chilling her own.

How much poison have the sons of bitches pumped into him?

Carefully and oh-so-slowly, Heather turned her head. Dante still Slept even though she was pretty sure the sun had set. His pale, blood-streaked face seemed troubled, uneasy. The skin beneath his eyes was smudged blue with exhaustion. He was Sleeping, yes, but he sure as hell wasn't resting. Her heart kicked hard against her ribs when she noticed the blood pooled inside his ear.

He'd knocked her on her ass when he'd severed the bond. Maybe he'd knocked himself on his ass too—and when he could least afford it. As much as she hated to admit it, maybe Loki had been right to be concerned.

The fallen bastard.

"Baptiste," she said, gingerly sitting up. "Hey, *cher*." Her vision grayed and she lowered her head until she no longer felt faint. She watched as little blood flowers blossomed on her jeans. *Nose is still bleeding, dammit.*

Something small and hard, like a pebble, pinged off Heather's shoulder.

"Hey there, pumpkin."

Not possible. Maybe I'm not awake.

But she was.

Heather followed the voice to her right, hand automatically sliding to the small of her back and the backup she hoped was still there, tucked into her jeans; then froze, heart in her throat, when her gaze locked onto the trench-coated speaker. Gray-threaded blond hair, hazel eyes hidden behind glasses, a fatherly smile, the sharp scent of Brut.

James Wallace.

But what was he sitting on? A chair—no, a goddamned *throne*—made out of . . . Heather's mouth dried, unable to believe what she was seeing. James Wallace lounged upon a throne composed of the contorted and broken bodies of the dead, colorful scrubs alternating with black suits. She swallowed back her nausea.

Dear God.

James Wallace lifted a hand and tossed another pebble at her. It landed near her hip, skittering away on the tile and her stomach clenched again as she realized it wasn't a pebble, but a small piece of bone. "Oh, I hope I didn't awaken you," he said.

"I was stunned, not unconscious—as you well know," Heather replied. Her nausea melted away beneath a surge of surprised relief when she felt the comforting weight of the SIG still tucked into her jeans at the small of her back.

Either Loki missed it or the arrogant SOB simply doesn't care because, for him, a bullet is only an annoyance at worst. I unloaded ten goddamned rounds in his chest and all he said was "ow."

"I believe the traditional greeting is hello."

"Nice try, Loki," Heather said. "But I know you're not my father."

"Loki?" Her father tsked chidingly, shook his head. "Is it so hard to believe that I had a tracking device implanted when you were first admitted to Strickland? That I had help waiting in the wings when you so unceremoniously dumped me on that highway?"

"No, I can believe all that," Heather replied. "It's the part about getting past a Fallen spell and cooperating with a fallen angel that I have a hard time believing."

The fatherly smile stretched into a feral grin. "Maybe you don't know me the way you think you do, pumpkin. Maybe you don't know *any* of us the way you think you do—or the things we've had to do."

Most likely true.

And that realization hollowed Heather's heart. "I know you're a coldhearted lying bastard—no matter who you are. I don't need to know anything else."

Sliding his glasses off, James Wallace retrieved a handkerchief from a pocket of his trench. "What about your mother?" he asked, using the handkerchief to wipe smudges from his glasses. "I know you think I either had her killed or did the deed myself, but no matter whether I'm a cold-blooded killer or a devoted father or both, you can't deny the relief you felt or how much better your life became the moment you learned she was dead."

Heather stared at him, her certainty slipping away. Words spoken twenty years ago returned to haunt her.

It's just us now, pumpkin. You, me, Kevin, and Annie.

Daddy, that's all it's ever been.

Not relief, no. Just the sad and simple truth. Isolated by her bipolar disorder, Shannon Wallace had never been a part of the family—her mother had always been alone, even when her children held her hands; a fate Heather wished with all her heart to spare Annie.

"Nothing to say, pumpkin?"

Heather shook her head, throat too tight for speech. Doubt chiseled away at her certainty. Maybe she'd been wrong. Maybe her father *had* not only tracked her to Doucet-Bainbridge, but was about to make a confession that she badly wanted—needed—to hear.

Maybe. But not likely. James Wallace would've killed Dante the moment he spotted him Sleeping in the blood-splattered corridor. He never would've left him alive.

Loki had other plans.

"You're not my father. So drop it."

James Wallace slid his glasses back onto his nose and re-pocketed the handkerchief. "Ah. Looks like the proverbial jig is up. You're a hard woman to fool." He grinned. "But I so enjoy trying."

"That makes one of us," Heather muttered, pushing her hands through her hair. Her injured ankle throbbed and ached even though she was sitting; she doubted she'd be able to put much, if any, weight on it.

Some rescue this turned out to be.

Swiveling to face Dante, she leaned over and gently patted his cold cheek. She cast an anxious glance at his chest to make sure he was still breathing, before saying, "C'mon, Baptiste. Time to rise and shine."

"He's *becoming*," Loki said in her father's voice, his tone hushed, expectant. Excited. "He needs to keep Sleeping until his transformation is complete. His throne"—he patted one hand against the hideous flesh-chair he sat upon—"awaits him."

Loki's brass-knuckled words seemed to knock the air out of Heather's lungs, left her struggling for breath.

The night burns, the sky on fire from horizon to horizon.

The never-ending Road.

The Great Destroyer.

One or both or neither.

"He'll never sit there," Heather scoffed, a quiet denial. As she looked at Dante's pale face, the blood staining his lips, an idea presented itself. One she quickly buried. She glanced over her shoulder. A smug smile twisted Loki-as-James's lips. "And you're wrong. He'll never be what *you* want him to be."

Loki opened his mouth to reply, then closed it again, his head tilting to one side. "Seems like we have a guest—a mortal one. How lovely. A gift for the *creawdwr*. He'll be wanting to bathe in blood by the time he awakens."

Heather felt a moment's panic until she realized that there was no way it could be Annie, that she would've reached Memphis only a short time ago and couldn't possibly be in Baton Rouge.

Loki rose to his feet, his form and voice rippling, shifting. "Given your condition and his"—he indicated Dante with a nod—"I expect you'll stay right here while I'm gone. So be a good little guard dog and keep our *creawdwr* safe."

Then he was gone, leaving the fading scent of Brut in his wake.

"Christ," Heather muttered. "What an arrogant prick."

Not knowing when he'd be back, she didn't waste any time. She scanned the floor around her for anything sharp. She picked up the bone-pebble Loki had tossed at her, then dropped it in disappointment.

Shit. Shit. Shit.

Then her gaze landed on Dante's hands with their black-painted nails. His sharp, sharp nails. The fact that they were caked in dried blood spoke volumes about their effectiveness. A muscle flexed in Heather's jaw. No other choice. No time.

"Sorry, *cher*," she whispered as she sliced a small cut into Dante's wrist with a finger from his opposite hand. Crimson blood welled up on his white skin. Healing blood. A temporary link. Heather lowered her face to the wound and drank.

PURCELL CLIMBED THE STAIRS, his furious heart a drum guiding each careful step. They were all dead, near as he could tell. At least they were downstairs—agents, medics, patients—the air thick with the reek of thickening blood. Who knew what blood-drenched horrors awaited on the upper floors?

How many times did I fucking warn them? How many times did I urge them to kill the little fuck? How many goddamned times?

Question is: why the hell is he still here? What's he waiting for?

But Purcell knew the answer to that question. S's threat—no, a promise—spoken in a low, coiled voice sounded through his memory.

I'll be coming for you too.

Looked like he'd simply decided to wait instead.

Another school of tiny blue fish, their jeweled scales glittering in the light from his helmet-cam, swam past him, also on their way up and just as happy as fucking punch.

And again, all Purcell could think was: *Sure. Why not? The world's clearly turned itself upside down. So why not have motherfucking air fish?*

Reaching the second floor landing, Purcell revised Díon's plan one more time—more of a reversion to the original, actually. Not to bash S's sanity to bits, but to make him suffer—just on the off chance the son of a bitch felt something, *anything* for Heather Wallace.

He'd make sure S took his time killing her.

Then, when that was done, S would join her.

"We'll see, yeah?" Low and amused, Cajun-spiced.

S was on Purcell before he could even swing his Glock up for a shot. His breath *whoof*ed from his lungs as he was slammed up against the wall. The light from his helmet-cam hit the ceiling at a skewed angle. S pressed against him, all heated skin and taut muscle. Adrenaline raged through Purcell. His heart rate kicked into high, fight-or-flight gear. The words he needed to say to keep himself alive poured out of his mouth without conscious effort.

"Wake up, Rip Van Winkle. It's time to quit sleeping and go to work. The Brothers Grimm have a job for you. Once it's done, you can dream again."

S pulled back, although his hands remained locked around Purcell's biceps. He tilted his head, a curious light in his now-golden eyes. "Now, why did you think that would stop me from killing you?"

Fear iced Purcell's spine. S's programming should've been triggered. He should be standing still, an empty vessel awaiting instructions, not asking questions.

And his eyes—gold like S's winged sugar daddy outside.

"Maybe you should drop the *sugar* and just make that *daddy*."

Purcell stared at him feeling like he'd just taken a punch to the gut. Might be true, probably was, but that didn't concern him at the moment. What did was the fact that S's programming hadn't responded to the words coded to awaken it.

"Rip Van Winkle," he began through a mouth gone dry. "Wake up—"

S laughed. "Oh, I'm awake. But I can't wait to find out why you thought fairy tale references would make me as docile as Mary's little lamb." Purcell broke into a cold sweat when S touched a taloned finger to his forehead, then said, "Little pig, little pig, let me in."

Lightning strike.

Purcell screamed.

49

RACING THEIR FATES

"C'MON, BAPTISTE. ON . . . YOUR . . . *feet!*"
With his arm looped over her shoulders, Heather surged to her feet, grunting with effort, despite her blood-renewed strength, as she supported his Sleeping weight. She felt a slight twinge from her nearly healed ankle, but that was all.

She froze as a scream cut through the air—a primal, high-pitched shriek of utter terror. And she had no idea if it'd been torn from a male or female throat. Her belly clenched.

Loki had found his mortal gift for Dante.

The scream stopped abruptly.

No time to waste. If she had to drag Dante to an exit, she goddamned would.

Shifting Dante's weight against her, Heather tightened her hold on him, fingers locking around his wrist, his waist. Sweat popped up on her forehead. "C'mon," she urged, before deciding to test the blood link.

<Cher, *please. Wake the hell up.*>

He stirred against her. "*Quitte-moi tranquille,*" he muttered, sleepy voice thick with irritation.

Elation soared through Heather. "That's it. That's right. Wake up. We've got to get out of here before he gets back."

Dante's eyes snapped open. "Papa," he growled, all sleepiness gone. He straightened and the weight against Heather disappeared, but his arm remained around her shoulders. "Is Chloe okay? Is—" His words died in his throat as he took in his surroundings. His dark eyes locked on Loki's flesh-and-bone throne. Panic and confusion rippled across his face. "The fuck is that?"

"One of the things we're running from."

His face blanked. "Is it for me?" he asked, voice hollow. "Is that my next fucking test?"

Heather's throat constricted as she thought of the boy Dante had been—and currently was—and what he must've endured at the hands of Wells and Moore. "No," she promised, releasing him and turning to cup his face between her hands—his cold, cold face. "No more tests. Not now. Not ever again. You're free, Dante. We just need to get you out of here."

<Come back to me, Baptiste. Come back to the here-and-now.>

He searched her eyes as she held his gaze, his hands rising to rest upon hers. Blood trickled from his nose and she read pain in his dilated pupils, but also an earnest and desperate desire to connect, to remember.

<I should know you, huh?>

"It's almost there," he said. "Your name. But . . ." He dropped his hands and shook his head. "Gone." He coughed, and the thick, liquid sound of it scared her.

"Let's worry about that later, okay?" Heather said, lowering her hands from his face. "For now, let's get out of here. We don't have much time," she added, throwing a glance over her shoulder. Nothing moved in the corridor. Yet.

"Okay," Dante agreed, pushing his hair back from his face. "Save ass now and ask questions later, yeah?"

Heather grinned in genuine amusement. "Most definitely yeah."

She started down the corridor, pausing to slip a steadying arm around Dante's waist when he stumbled. She waited until his dizziness passed and he gave her a thumbs-up, then they resumed walking. She kept her arm around his waist and he didn't argue—which told her volumes about his injuries, about how badly he was hurt.

"Almost there," she encouraged as they hurried down the stairs to the first floor landing and the emergency exit at the bottom.

Dante nodded, flashing her a tilted and bloodied smile, saving his breath.

Heather shoved on the push bar and grinned in relief when the door swung open, admitting the cool night beyond along with the smells of wet grass and cooling concrete. She stepped outside, holding the door open. "Hurry," she whispered.

Dante took a step forward, then doubled-over, arms hugging his chest, teeth gritted in pain. He fell to his knees, then curled up on his side, every muscle knotted and taut.

Panic burned through Heather. She grabbed Dante by the shoulders and tried to haul his ass over the threshold and outside, but it was like trying to pull a two-ton bull or Mount Rushmore—a groaning, agonized Mount Rushmore. He had become impossibly, inexplicably heavy. Her muscles strained. Sweat trickled between her breasts.

Then, exhausted, she reversed course and dragged him back inside. The door swung shut behind her. Dante went still and fear knifed her heart. She dropped on her knees beside him. "Baptiste?"

"It stopped," he said, wonder and relief in his hoarse voice. "Like a motherfucking switch had been flipped. It just stopped." Dante uncurled from the floor and sat up, leaning his back against the wall. He scowled at the door. "What the fuck was that?"

Heather sighed, sat down beside him. His earthy, autumn scent filled the landing. "The sigils. I think it was the goddamned sigils. They must work both ways. Shit."

"Look, they don't affect you, so go. Get out. Don't worry about me. I'll find another way. What's your name, anyway?"

Heather felt a smile flicker across her lips. <*Heather.*> Her smile faded as she watched Dante's face blank. She wondered if her name or the blood link had just pinwheeled his memory open, spun him back to the here-and-now.

He looked at her and Heather saw recognition ignite in his eyes. "*Catin*," he breathed. "I knew severing the bond wouldn't stop you. You found me—like I knew you would, cuz I woulda done the same. I just don't know if that's a good or a bad thing."

Heather laughed. "It's a good thing, you stubborn sonuvabitch."

But Dante's face blanked again. His hands knotted into fists. Pounded knuckled blows to his leather-clad thighs. As though he were fighting against himself.

"Dante, what is it? Talk to me, *cher*."

<*Stay here with me.*>

"*T'es sûr de ça, catin?*" Dante licked blood from his lips. A dark light burned in his eyes. "Yours, yeah? Yum. Wouldn't mind some more."

Heather's mouth dried as she realized she wasn't looking at Dante, but S or maybe even the Great Destroyer.

He is becoming . . .

No and no and no.

Fear coursed through Heather, bright and cold. Dante wasn't just shifting between the past and the here-and-now, but between the man she knew and one he'd been programmed to be.

"Fun, yeah?" His head tilted. His gaze fixed on the pulse in her throat.

"You with me, Baptiste?" she said through a mouth that felt full of ashes.

"Run," S said.

Heather didn't hesitate. She jumped to her feet and slammed out through the door, grateful he couldn't follow. She had no doubt Dante was the source of the "run." She also had no doubt that he'd just saved her life.

* * *

REALITY WHEELED. DANTE GRABBED ahold with both hands. But the here-and-now was damned slippery and he didn't know how long he could hang on.

Stubborn-ass woman. All heart and steel, ma chérie.

Gotta get her the fuck out of here. Gotta see her safe.

Images of sapphire flames, of plucked hearts, unmade hearts, of his finger curling around the trigger of a gun filled his aching mind.

J'su ici, catin.

Run from me. Run as far as you can.

Nothing like a good chase, yeah?

Dante drew in a ragged breath. He shivered, so cold that he expected his breath to plume the air white. He had to end this.

You ain't gonna save her, y'know. Shit, you can't even save yourself.

Watch me.

Planning on it, bro. Laughter. Low and amused. Happy.

Fi' de garce.

You should know, yeah?

Voices whispered. Wasps droned and burrowed. Dante squeezed his eyes shut, struggling to silence the internal aural storm. Stomping everything down below and kicking the door shut was no longer an option.

There was no more below. No more door to kick shut.

As the din gradually quieted, Dante realized one faint whisper didn't come from within. He opened his eyes, gaze following the sound to the ceiling. Upstairs. Someone was upstairs still alive, still breathing and talking in a low, steady murmur. A brief silence, followed by the raspy cough of a longtime smoker.

Like maybe two packs of Winstons a day, yeah?

Time to take yo' medicine, p'tit.

A dark smile tilted Dante's lips. He opened his eyes.

Gotcha, Papa. Time to take your own damned medicine.

Staggering up to his feet, he *moved*. When he hit the third floor landing and breezed through the door, he spotted something lying on the floor, a dull metallic gleam.

A gun.

Dante stared at it, winter descending upon his heart. Unaware that he'd even moved, he found himself picking it up. His fingers curled around the rubber grip as naturally as if he'd always held a gun, been born with one in his hand. He felt the cold trickle of sweat along his temples.

Put it down. Or go back and toss it out to Heather. She's gonna—

Low murmurs from above snagged Dante's attention. He tilted his head, tucking the gun into the back of his leather pants, then he headed back to the landing. As he raced up the stairs, he felt a little girl's weight in his arms, heard her black paper wings rustling, caught a glimpse of red hair. Then he was blurring through a crowded club, a woman smelling of lilac and sage, of evening rain, a woman of heart and steel, hugged tight against his side, a woman who disappeared as another little girl, red-haired and freckled, took her place as they ran through a park in the rain, trying to outrace their fates.

Laughter. *You kidding me? You are their fates.*

Reality wheeled, reminding him of promises made.

Make them pay so I can be warm again.

Make the world burn, mon cher ami, mon ange, and set me free.

Set things to rights, cher. Make them pay in blood and fire.

Reality wheeled yet again.

His finger squeezes the trigger. Her head rocks forward with the first bullet, then snaps back with the second, tendrils of red hair whipping through the air.

That's my boy, a woman's voice, Johanna Moore's voice, whispered in the unlit, broken alleys of his mind. *No one can ever be used against you if you are willing to kill them first.*

Don't listen to her, Dante-angel.

Blurring past landing after landing as he raced up the stairs following Papa's distant voice, he whispered, "I ain't. Don't worry."

But deep down, he wasn't so sure.

And that scared him to his core.

HEATHER LEANED AGAINST THE metal exit door, afraid if she didn't her trembling legs would dump her onto the sidewalk. She sucked in cool, moist air until her hammering heart slowed its frantic pace.

"Shit," she breathed, closing her eyes and thumping the back of her head lightly against the door. "Shit, shit, shit."

She'd never been frightened of Dante before—*for* him, yes. But never *of* him. That had just changed.

What have those bastards done to you, cher?

He's had as much as he can take, doll . . .

Von, she despaired. *Wish you were here.*

No way she was leaving Dante alone with Loki. No way she was leaving him, period. Maybe she could find some tranks inside or a heavy dose of morphine, something that would knock him out. Maybe the sigils wouldn't affect him if he were unconscious. Maybe—

"Heather?" A deep, incredulous rumble. A familiar and oh-so welcome voice.

Heather opened her eyes and confirmed the information her ears had just given her. Relief almost dropped her on the sidewalk despite the door's support. "Lucien!"

Two other Fallen stood with him—the Morningstar and his daughter.

Heather frowned. Was Lucien holding a bucket? Filled with dark paint or—

A thick, coppery odor curled into her nostrils. Her throat constricted.

—blood.

"Do you have a plan," Heather asked, nodding at the bucket in Lucien's hand. "Or are you making it up as you go?"

A wry smile tugged at the corners of Lucien's mouth. "I believe it's the latter."

Heather pushed away from the sigil-marked door. "That's good," she said, voice rough. "And here's why: Dante has severed our bond and he's falling hard and fast. We don't have time for plans."

50

WATER INTO GASOLINE

DANTE WALKED DOWN THE fifth-floor corridor in his stocking feet, idly trailing the fingers of his left hand along the wall as he followed the whispers to their source: last door on the left.

Yanking it open, he stepped into the padded room's red-lit interior, attention fixed on the figure kneeling in one corner, facing in, hands clasped at chest level. Incense curled sweet and smoky into the air, but didn't mask the smell of piss. Another figure, tall and winged, stood in one corner. Dante ignored him.

"Hey, Papa," Dante said. "*Comment ça va*, you sonuvabitch?"

The soft, monotonous whispers stopped. The praying man swiveled around on his knees to face Dante, blood symbols flaking from his face. Dante grinned. Motherfucking Purcell—but he wore a priest's purple satin stole over his charcoal gray suit. Something dangled from his hand, something Dante recognized from another time, another place—a rosary. He met Dante's gaze with frightened olive green eyes.

"Don't forget your lines," the fallen angel in the corner admonished with a snap of his fingers. "Really. After all the drilling we did."

Swallowing hard, Purcell said, "It's time to bring forth your light."

Dante stumbled back against the doorway as reality wheeled yet again. His vision splintered as a memory sheared up from below, a memory born here, in this place.

Facedown on a bare mattress, the smell of his own blood thick in his nostrils. The air's cool breath paints searing pain across Dante's back. His heart thunders in his ears.

"No one lights a lamp to cover it with a bowl or to put it under the bed," a man's low voice says, his words both instruction and prayer. "No, he puts it on a lampstand so that people may see the light when they come in."

"Ain't hiding an angel inside me, asshole," Dante whispers for the millionth time. But Father Michael Moses—former Jesuit, current psycho—ain't listening.

Another cut and fresh blood spills hot down Dante's side, soaking into the mattress beneath him. He bites into his constantly healing lower lip. Black flecks whirl through his vision. He twists his wrists again and again, hoping that the cuffs have somehow weakened.

But they haven't. And his strength is draining away along with his blood.

"For nothing is hidden but will be made clear, nothing secret but that it will be known and brought to light." Warm breath touches the cup of Dante's ear. "I see your light within. I shall bring it forth," Moses promises. "As God commands."

His fingers grasp the edges of Dante's cut skin and yank, peeling it back to reveal the wings that aren't there.

Dante screams . . .

REALITY WHEELED.

My turn.

S stood in the doorway, one pale, blood-smeared hand braced at either side. A thin trickle of blood trailed from one nostril. Pain pulsed behind his eyes. But it had nothing on the rage pulsing inside his heart. He studied the figure kneeling inside, stinking of fear and piss.

Michael Moses. Former Jesuit priest. Current penitent monster.

No, that's Purcell. SB agent. Current maybe-penitent monster.

Who gives a fuck?

S stepped inside. Blue flames crackled to life around his hands, filling the room with an eldritch light. "I know you, motherfucker," he said, his voice holding just a dash of dark wonder. "You ain't Papa. But I know you."

I know you. *I remember.*

"My gift to you," the fallen angel said.

"And who the hell are you?"

"Loki, little *creawdwr*. And your gift is Moses and Purcell, Wells and Moore, Papa and Mama Prejean—anyone you wish him to be. He's ground zero for your night of reckoning." Loki stepped from the corner his tall, lean-muscled body clad in a suit tailored for the black wings folded behind him.

Tall as the Nightbringer. Short, red hair. Familiar.

Like one of those Russian nesting dolls.

Gotcha, Papa.

"And what do you get out of it?" S asked.

"The right to stand at your side," Loki replied. "Not to bring forth light, but the darkness hidden within. I shall guide you on your path. I shall be a pillar of fire by night and a column of smoke by day."

S felt a cynical smile tilt his lips. "As God commands, yeah?"

The fallen angel lifted nearly incandescent eyes to S's. "The only God here is you. A dark and bloody God. An Old Testament God. A God for whom an eye for an eye should never be enough."

S laughed, the sound dark and coiled and amused. He

slanted a look at Purcell-Moses-Who-the-fuck-ever. "Guess that means I'm gonna need to see what's under *your* skin."

"I WAS AFRAID OF that," Lucien said after Heather described what had happened when she'd tried to get Dante out of the sanitarium. He hefted the bucket—beheaded gas can, really, stolen from his donor's car—of blood. "If this works, it'll get us in and Dante out."

"If it doesn't work," Heather said, "I'm going in, regardless. I won't leave him alone." *With Loki. With himself. With his past.* Cold fingers closed around her heart. *With his madness.*

Run.

I refuse to lose you, cher. If you fall, you won't fall alone.

She watched as Lucien splashed the sigil on the outside of the door with half of the bucket's contents, then moved to open the door and hold it when he gave her the nod. He tossed the remainder of the blood clotting in the bucket across the threshold, then threw the empty bucket aside to clatter against the sidewalk.

Slanting a quick glance at Hekate, Lucien stepped past the door and across the threshold in one long-legged stride. No convulsions. No sudden jack-knifing to the floor. No dead spider imitation. Excitement curled through Heather.

"It worked," she said, knowing she was stating the obvious, but it was *worth* stating.

A smile brushed Lucien's lips. "Indeed."

"They are coming," the Morningstar said, his gaze on the cloud-scudded sky. "I knew they wouldn't wait. Not when we've been gone for so many hours."

Heather heard a rush of wings—dozens, maybe hundreds—the sound filled the night. She joined Lucien inside the building. "How did they find us?" she asked.

Lucien's expression iced over. "Gabriel most likely had us followed."

"We'll hold them," Hekate said. "Go. Hurry."

Closing the door, Heather raced up the stairs, Lucien right behind her.

"KILL ME FOR MY own actions, not for the actions of a sick priest bastard I was against from the get-go," Purcell blurted—and S was pretty sure he *was* Purcell. So someone inside kept claiming. "Fight me man to man."

"Like you did me? Trussed to a table?" S crouched down in front of Purcell. Drank in the adrenalized scent of his fear. "I think you said something about taking me apart and burning each piece until nothing but ash remained, then flushing those ashes down the goddamned toilet. Does that sound about right?"

Purcell gave a low groan. "Just kill me, you motherfucker. Get it over with."

"Over *that*?" S laughed. "Hey, boys will be boys, yeah? We can take it. But little girls? That's another fucking story."

"You should know," Purcell said, his tone the resigned register of a man on his way to visit the death chamber. But no lethal injection here. No. Nothing so clean. Welcome to Ol' Sparky, motherfucker. "Right? You have first hand experience."

She was eight years old and you slaughtered her. Just like you'll slaughter Violet and Heather and anyone else who gets close to you. It's what you do. It's who you are.

"C'est vrai," S said in a monotone. He reached up in a blur of movement and snapped Purcell's neck. The SB agent toppled bonelessly to the floor. S rose to his feet, his heart a wasteland.

Loki applauded politely. "Beautifully done. Perhaps a bit too quickly, but with practice—"

"Practice makes perfect, yeah?" S asked, closing the distance between them.

"Definitely. And I'm the perfect tutor." Loki grinned. "I will teach you everything you need to know and I'll show you how to walk your true and proper path."

"No need, Papa. I already am."

Power crackled along S's fingers. Reflected blue in Papa's ever-widening eyes. The stormy scent of ozone filled the room. S felt his hair lifting into the air.

Papa dropped to his knees. "The Great Destroyer," he breathed, eyes bright.

Kneeling in front of Papa, S cupped his child-pimping foster father's false face between his flame-wreathed hands and kissed him hard on the lips. "For Chloe," he whispered. Releasing him, S stood. And watched.

Blue flames spread throughout Papa's body, glowing beneath the skin like sapphire embers. His Loki skin-suit dissolved, revealing the structures beneath—muscles, tendons, ligaments.

"Let's see you hide now, you *fi' de garce*. No more Russian nesting dolls."

Papa screamed.

But not for long.

"BY ALL THAT'S HOLY," Lucien whispered, staring at the flesh-and-bone throne situated in the middle of the third floor corridor. "Tell me that Dante didn't—"

"No," Heather assured him. "That's Loki's work, but he made it for Dante. For the Great Destroyer."

"Then Loki's gone mad."

"I think stark raving mad would be more accurate."

The fetid smell of decaying flesh, of spilled guts, festered in the air. A stench Heather could barely stomach even with her human sense of smell. She couldn't imagine what it must be like for Lucien or Dante.

Heather headed for the stairs, freezing in place when a wailing scream from several floors above sirened briefly into the air, then died. Her skin goose bumped.

I feel like I'm running out of time, catin.

No, cher. I refuse to lose you.

I fought my way here, coffee pot, Taser, and gun, and I refuse to be too late.

Lucien stared up at the shadowed ceiling, his face troubled. "Maybe you should stay here."

Ignoring his suggestion, Heather raced up the stairs, following her heart and her blood link to the fifth floor—and to Dante. She knew Lucien followed, knew neither one of them might be safe. As she ran, she chambered a round in the SIG. She hoped she wouldn't need to use it, but if she did, she knew she'd only have one chance and one chance only. She trusted Dante not to hurt her.

She couldn't say the same of S.

HEATHER PADDED DOWN THE corridor, making sure to keep to the right-hand wall because inside the opposite wall, beneath the now-vibrating plaster, wasps droned. Four rifts marred the wall's surface in long, lazy lines and in those black depths, wasps crawled, their metallic bodies glittering like moonstruck mica in the dim red emergency lighting.

Four rifts. As though left by trailing fingers.

Heather found it hard to breathe, fear was an anvil on her chest. Looking up at Lucien, she saw the same fear shadowing his face.

<Hold on, Baptiste. Hold on, damn you.>

They found Dante in the last room on the left, tossing the contents of a mop bucket onto a cot holding what looked like a larger-than-life-size anatomy dummy and onto a gray-suited body crumpled on the floor. The pungent aroma of gasoline soaked the air.

"Mop water into gasoline," Lucien said quietly. "That's a new one. And I think we've found Loki—or what remains of him."

And that was when Heather realized that the thing lying on the cot *wasn't* an anatomy dummy, that given the body's size and the golden eyes—still aware, still watching—it had to be Loki.

You think I want to escape?

Heather guessed that question was now moot. And after what the bastard had done to her, ransacking her mind, rifling through her memories, let alone what he had most likely done to Dante as well, she almost wished she could light him up herself. Almost. And it saddened her to realize that not even two months ago, she never would've considered doing such a thing.

"Will it kill him?" she asked Lucien.

"No, he's Elohim. But I'm sure he'll wish it would."

Heather shook her head. "I can't let Dante do this."

"Leave it alone. Loki brought this upon himself. He more than deserves it."

She started forward, intending to stop Dante anyway, but Lucien stopped her instead with a steel-fingered and taloned grip to her shoulder.

"Leave it alone."

"I don't think that's a good—"

Heather heard the slide of velvet across skin, then saw Dante's wings arch up over his head. Gold light glimmered in his eyes as he turned to look at her with a stranger's gaze. Blue flames flared to life around his hands.

A song blazed into the air unlike anything Heather had ever heard before. It set her blood on fire, angelic symbols burning behind her eyes. A savage and furious song.

A beautiful song.

A song of chaos.

Dante turned away and tossed a lighter onto the cot. WHOOMF! Fast-burning flames engulfed the cot and the golden-eyed figure upon it, then swept across the floor to swallow the gray-suited body. The nauseating stench of roasting flesh rose into the air.

"*Now* the fucker will stay dead," Dante said, something close to bliss on his pale face as he watched the roaring flames devour the room's padded walls.

Freed from Lucien's hold, Heather backed into the corridor, away from the heat and the smoke, gun in hand. A streak of motion, pale flesh and black leather, the heady scent of burning leaves and November frost, then Dante was standing in front of her, close enough that she could feel his heat. Or lack of it. A dark smile tilted his lips.

<*Baptiste, wake up. Haul your ass out of the abyss,* cher. *Wake up!*>

"Hey, *catin*," Dante—no, Heather corrected, not Dante, S—said, his voice smooth silk and bourbon. Black and blue flames snapped along his fingers. With one quick motion, he yanked the SIG from her hand, tossed it down the corridor, then shoved the muzzle of his own gun against her temple, his finger tight against the trigger. Her heart leapt into her throat.

"I've been dreaming about this," he whispered.

Then Dante finally answered her in the only way he could.

REALITY WHEELED.

The corridor vanished in an explosion of white, icy light. S's finger spasmed against the gun's trigger, but all he heard was the distant click of an empty chamber. He fell, convulsing, as the seizure had its way with him.

Pretty damned funny, really.

He'd tossed away a loaded gun in favor of the empty one Dante had picked up earlier in the corridor.

Reality wheeled.

The night whirls around Dante, a streak of pale clouds and glimmering stars and skeletal branches. He no longer feels Chloe's hand. He tries to shove her away, tries to tell her to run, but his voice and lips don't work either—numb and far away. He falls, the rain-beaded grass rushing up to meet him.

No escape for you, sweetie.

Reality wheeled.

Fire scorches her lungs. Blackens her skin. Devours her with relentless teeth.

Welcome home, S. Welcome back.

Set things to rights, cher. Make them pay in blood and fire.

You won't save her, you know.

The truth is never what you hope it will be.

Yeah, and it usually carries a motherfucking shiv.

Reality wheeled. And wheeled. And wheeled again.

Dante's song raged unabated into the night. Set it ablaze.

51

ANHREFNCATHL

D ANTE'S SONG SLASHED INTO the night. An aurora borealis of blue flame undulated across the sky. The ground shook and shuddered, a restless beast answering its master's call. Hekate watched from the sanitarium's glass-sprinkled parking lot as the sanitarium burned, fierce yellow-white flames snapping from windows and roof. Chunks of masonry fell from the building to shatter in the parking lot.

"Why haven't they come out?" she asked, struggling for balance as the earth shuddered beneath her feet. "Something must be wrong."

"That's an understatement," the Morningstar said, "given that Dante has apparently lost his fight." He looked up and Hekate followed her father's gaze to the Elohim silhouetted against the flaming skies as they circled above the burning building.

Wybrcathl trilled and warbled songs of despair and lost hope, of another *creawdwr* lost to madness. A young *creawdwr* who needed to be killed before he wrenched mortal and Elohim worlds apart.

"Is there any way to stop him, short of killing him?" she asked.

The Morningstar nodded. "Perhaps. *An Banna Cruach.*" He met his daughter's gaze. "We need to find Michael's tomb and then we need to hope that the bond—if it truly exists—will work on a mixed-blood Maker."

* * *

At Louis Armstrong International Airport, Renata Alessa Cortini and her well-dressed entourage had just disembarked from her private jet when the earthquake struck. She looked up into the sky and her heart turned to ice. An aurora borealis of blue fire danced and undulated across the sky; a sky filled with Elohim.

Images from the vision that had brought her from Rome—a vision coming true at this very moment—flashed behind her eyes.

In a hallway gleaming with faint red light, a fallen angel with black wings and short, ginger locks lounges upon a throne composed of dead and stiffening bodies . . .

The night burns, the sky on fire from horizon to horizon . . .

Dante Baptiste uncoils from a bloodied tile floor, his pale, breathtaking face smeared with blood, his eyes dark wells of madness, loss, and simmering rage . . .

A tattoo of a running black wolf inked beneath a desperate green eye . . .

Pale blue flames explode out from around the Great Destroyer's lean body in transforming tongues of cool fire. His kohl-rimmed eyes open as his song rakes the burning night . . .

A sign emblazoned with the words: Doucet-Bainbridge Sanitarium; *Fallen sigils painted in blood upon glass . . .*

I have promises to keep, Dante whispers, *blood trickling from one nostril. Then puts out the world's light.*

Not knowing if the ground would ever stop shaking, Renata ordered her driver to take the youngest members of her household to Doucet-Bainbridge. As for herself and her older children—she rose into the humid air, spiraling upward.

Anhrefncathl and thousands of *wybrcathl* summoned Leviathan from her decade long sleep. The sea boiled and bubbled with warbled information. But one piece she held close, a priceless pearl: the *creawdwr* was the Nightbringer's son.

Leviathan rose like a mountain from the deepest chasm of the Atlantic, an ocean of endless folds rippling across the sky.

Do you have any children?

No.

Best you keep it that way. For I shall claim your firstborn as my own—to kill or to love, as I deem fit.

She had a promise to keep.

HEATHER DROPPED TO HER knees beside Dante's convulsing body, coughing as smoke and flames crept into the corridor. Her skin tightened in the heat, felt fevered. Ever widening wheels of blue and black light spun out from around Dante, sinking through the floor and cycling through the ceiling, transforming everything they touched. Black ivy beaded with tiny sapphire blue eyes blinking in the acrid smoke draped the walls.

Ceiling tiles fell as the earthquake continued its violent, apparently endless motion—and Heather suspected that the earthquake would end when Dante's seizure did. The floor shuddered, tiles rippling as though suddenly fluid. Cracks zigzagged through the walls, the ceiling, and the floor. Gleaming wasps flitted out of the cracks. The air vibrated with their droning.

My kingdom for a syringe full of morphine to ease my prince into Sleep.

"Time to go," Lucien said. "I'll carry Dante—but not you or we run the risk of him changing you as well."

Coughing, Heather shook her head. Smoke stung her eyes. "You don't need to risk it either. Not yet. Let me try to reach him through the blood link."

Lucien studied the buckling ceiling. "Hurry."

Heather nodded and closed her eyes.

*   *   *

PAIN AND WHITE LIGHT pinwheeled through Dante's mind as reality wheeled and circled and wheeled again. Electricity spasmed through every muscle. Splintered memories shifted together, forming pictures that broke his heart. Voices whispered and demanded, wasps droned and burrowed and he's fucking had enough, enough, *ENOUGH.*

<*Baptiste. I'm here.*>

The pinwheels slowed as the image of a beautiful red-haired woman flared behind his eyes, an image that smelled of sage and lilacs in the rain, a fragrant midnight garden.

It's quiet when I'm with you.

I'll help you stop it forever.

We're in this together, face-to-face and back-to-back.

I trust you.

Don't.

<*Baptiste.*>

As lost as I get, I will find you, Heather. Always.

Dante reached back, pouring himself through the blood link and forging a new bond as he did. The blue-white star of Heather's presence suddenly appeared, burning bright and unobstructed at the bruised center of his mind, radiating a cool, white light. Silence poured in, hushing the noise, quieting the internal storm.

His convulsions stopped.

Dante opened his eyes.

Grasping his hand, Heather helped him up to his feet. He touched his forehead to hers, his hands on her hips, trying hard not to think of what he'd almost done to her, the gun against her temple, his finger on the trigger. "*J'su ici, catin,*" he whispered, throat tight. "*J'su ici.*"

"And you found me," she whispered back. "Like you promised."

"Always."

"We need to go," Lucien said. "And we need someplace safe from—"

A subsonic bellow blasted through the air, hitting the sanitarium like a fertilizer bomb. Dante wrapped himself and his wings around Heather as the building collapsed in a roar of stone and screeching metal. Waves of midnight water doused the fire.

Leviathan descended.

52

A DARK PATH

VON DECIDED THAT HE preferred getting his neck broken to being interrogated. Worse, he wasn't even being questioned by the *filidh*.

"I suggest you start talking," Galiana said. She sat in one of the Bards's great chairs, the tops of each carved into stag horns. "Otherwise it will be one of the mortals who will pay the price."

On his knees, hands cuffed behind his back, Von slid a sidelong glance at Merri. Her stiff posture and frozen expression spoke volumes. She had no idea her *mère de sang* had been using her. Silver was beside Merri, also on his knees, also cuffed.

Jack, Thibodaux, and Annie had been stashed elsewhere. But Von had been assured all three were safe and unharmed. He didn't know if he believed that.

Dammit. They'd all be safe if I'da nixed the rescue plan.

Von drew in a deep breath of smoky air fragrant with myrrh. He remembered the feel of the charcoal sketch beneath his fingers, remembered the image it bore and the penciled-in title—*Secrets*. Felt precious time slipping away.

Remembering the rage, loss, and madness simmering in

Dante's sending—*I ain't playing your game, Papa*—Von realized that the time for secrets was over. Too much was at stake.

Forgive me, little brother.

In a low voice, he started speaking, holding nothing back.

"*CREAWDWR,*" GALIANA BREATHED, BOTH wonder and worry chiseling her dark face. "A vampire Maker. But a damaged one."

"He just needs time to heal," Von said. "And I need to get to him, move him somewhere safe. Somewhere quiet. And I need to go now. We all do."

"I have a private jet," Galiana mused. "We could be in Baton Rouge in a little over an hour."

The floor started shaking. A chair toppled over. Light fixtures swayed.

"Outside!" someone yelled.

Von jumped to his feet and ran, dodging falling furniture and broken lightbulbs on his way out the front door. He raced down the steps and onto the lawn, then looked up. His mouth dried. His vision—if that's what it was—was coming true.

An aurora borealis of fire danced across the southern sky. The ground shuddered, then quieted once more. The Great Destroyer had awakened. Von's heart sank. Dante had chosen a path. A dark one.

Galiana stared at the sky in horror. "What does it mean?" she whispered.

"We're going to need that plane," Von said. "Now."

Hold on, little brother. Hold on.